Praise for
Dangerous Boys

"Gifune is among the finest dark suspense writers of our time."
—Ed Gorman, Edgar Award nominated author

"Extremely well written and quite compelling, *Dangerous Boys* hits all the right marks. It's a novel you'll enjoy reading and regret when the last page is turned. Reminded me a bit of Dennis Lehane, a bit of Martin Scorsese, and a bit of S.E. Hinton."
—Grant Jerkins, author of Abnormal Man

"*Dangerous Boys* may well be the best thing Greg F. Gifune has written. Stunning, breathtaking, and a bloody nightmare of a ride, this crime novel will reverberate through every inch of your heart and soul."
—Trey R. Barker, author of the Jace Salome novels

"*Dangerous Boys* is *Vision Quest* meets *The Outsiders* with a dash of *Less Than Zero* thrown in. If none of those references make any sense to you, then you have some reading to do... AFTER you devour *Dangerous Boys*! Whether you want nostalgia, pain, darkness, sex, violence, or struggle, you'll find it here."
—Frank Zafiro, author of *Blood on Blood*

"Gifune continues to astound, able to perfectly balance the darkest parts of humanity with its most tender moments. *Dangerous Boys* is Gifune at his best."
—Ronald Malfi, author of *Bone White*

"Fast, brutal, vivid action—and dialogue as sharp as a broken pool stick. These boys are gonna kick your ass!"
—Steven ⁙⁙⁙⁙⁙ ⁙⁙⁙⁙⁙⁙ ⁙⁙ ⁙⁙⁙⁙ ⁙⁙⁙⁙ *he Tomb*

DANGEROUS BOYS

ALSO BY GREG F. GIFUNE

Novels

A View from the Lake

A Winter Sleep

Babylon Terminal

Blood in Electric Blue

Children of Chaos

Deep Night

Devil's Breath

Dominion

Gardens of Night

Judas Goat

Long After Dark

Midnight Solitaire

Night Work

Orphans of Wonderland

Rogue

Savages

Saying Uncle

The Bleeding Season

The Living and the Dead

Novellas

Apartment Seven

Catching Hell

Drago Descending

Dreams the Ragman

House of Rain

Kingdom of Shadows

Lords of Twilight

Oasis of the Damned

Sorcerer

The Rain Dancers

Collections

Down to Sleep

Heretics

GREG F. GIFUNE

DANGEROUS BOYS

DOWN&OUT
BOOKS

Down & Out Books
3959 Van Dyke Rd, Ste. 265
Lutz, FL 33558
www.DownAndOutBooks.com

The characters and events in this book are fictitious. Any similarity to real persons, living or dead, is coincidental and not intended by the author.

Cover design by JT Lindroos

ISBN: 1-946502-52-9
ISBN-13: 978-1-946502-52-0

For the great Ed Gorman,
with respect and thanks.
Rest well, my friend.

CHAPTER ONE

We rolled through the city, stealth and confident, predators in a sea of night. Always loved the dark. Made me feel alive and powerful, like a restless spirit set free once the sun went down. Always liked the heat, too, but that summer of '84 was hot. Really hot. A series of heatwaves slammed Massachusetts one right after the next, like ducks in a row. Ducks straight out of Hell's furnace. And no one in the commonwealth was spared, not even those of us on the southeast coast, an area known for cool ocean breezes during even the worst summer months.

Dusk had settled quickly, and the night was getting stronger. Once darkness took hold, the city turned even more dangerous than in daylight hours, but the neighborhood we found ourselves in was quiet and seemingly deserted. On a lonely side street, less than a full block from the waterfront, a breeze rolled in off the nearby Atlantic Ocean, but it was hot and thick and did nothing but move the stagnant air around a little and fill it with the smell of saltwater and the pungent aroma of dead fish from the nearby seafood plants. From a dive bar halfway up the block, a lone figure emerged, stopping at the curb long enough to light a cigarette. The guy cupped the flame, drew a deep drag, then exhaled through his nose as the dark sedan we'd stolen slowly rounded the corner at the top of the block and pulled into a space across the street. In the car, four guys—me among them—watched as the man stepped off the curb and started down the street, his long, dirty-blond hair dancing in the hot breeze.

"*That's* him?" Aldo asked, scratching at his nose with a gloved hand while resting the other over the steering wheel. "*This* fuckin' guy?"

"Yeah," Petie said, clearing his throat awkwardly and fidgeting about in the backseat like a kid with bedbugs. "That's him."

"You're sure."

"Yeah."

"You got to be sure, Petie."

"I'm sure. That's the guy."

"Then everybody get on the clock." He turned to Petie and Fritz in the backseat. "Here we go."

We stepped from the car in unison, moving like separate parts of a single organism. Aldo and I headed straight for the guy while Fritz and Petie crossed the street so they could close on him from the opposite direction. Dressed in black, we blended into the growing darkness, as was our intention, there then gone then back again, hallucinations in a bad trip.

The man stopped. His cigarette glowed bright orange then died as it fell to pavement and was crushed beneath the toe of his sandal. If he'd noticed us, he gave no indication. I could hear the blood in my veins pulsing in my ears and the beat of my heart in my chest. He looked maybe four or five years older than us, but we already knew he wouldn't be any trouble. Focusing on the task at hand, I cracked my knuckles and shook my hands a little, loosening them up for what was about to come.

By the time the man saw Aldo and me walking toward him, it was too late to run. And he knew it. Instead, he stopped and nervously looked around. When he realized Fritz and Petie were coming up behind him, he held his hands in the air like the victim of a robbery, which he likely figured he was at that point.

"Hey, man, what—okay, what—what's this all about? Can I help you guys, I—what's up, dude, hi, I—what's up?"

Aldo hit him first. He kept the bat down by his leg until the last moment then swung it viciously and without warning. Following through with a fluid motion, the bat slammed into the man's side with a horrible thud and buckled him immediately. With an incredulous look, the man cried out, stumbled off the curb and into the street, clutching his shattered ribs and gasping for breath. He tried to run, but we all knew he'd never make it. He wasn't going anywhere.

Fritz and Petie followed him into the street.

The guy screamed for help but didn't have the wind to make much noise with his ribs in that condition. "What are you guys doing, I—who are you, what do you want, man? Ain't got much bread on me but you can have what I—"

Fritz hit him with a solid combination to the kidneys. The blows dropped the guy to his knees.

As he knelt there, coughing and gasping and babbling through tears, I stepped forward and kicked him in the side with everything I had.

Grunting, the man flopped over onto his back. Chest heaving, he coughed again, spraying spittle as he held his side.

I grabbed him by his Grateful Dead T-shirt, lifted him off the pavement enough so that his head wouldn't bounce against it, then punched him twice in the face. The man cried out as his nose exploded blood and snot, sending ribbons of both into the steamy night air. I dropped him back to the street and moved away, shaking my hand. It stung. Fucker had a face like granite.

Aldo looked up the street, then down. "Still clear," he said flatly.

Petie moved in. "Look at me," he said. "You know who I am? You recognize me now?"

It took a few seconds, but through the blood and tears and darkness, the guy gave a slow nod.

"Good. I got something for you." Petie unzipped his fly, pulled his cock free and urinated on the guy, spattering his face, neck, and chest with a strong and steady stream. "Drink up, asshole."

The man tried to squirm away but couldn't. Finally resigned to what was taking place, he shielded himself as best he could with his hands.

Aldo, stunned by what was happening, let a quick burst of *what-the-fuck* laughter slip free. "Holy shit, Petie, that's fucked up, bro."

"Fuck this guy," he said, shaking out the last drops. "He's lucky I ain't got to shit or I'd be droppin' a steamer on his head, too."

Guess we'd all gotten lucky on that count.

Once finished, Petie put himself away, zipped up, then reared back and kicked the guy in the crotch. As he prepared to deliver another, Fritz grabbed him and hurried him back to the car.

Aldo and I stayed behind.

Gagging and weeping, the man curled into a ball.

Using the tip of my boot, I rolled him over onto his back and pinned him there, flat on the pavement. "Stay."

He did.

"Good boy."

Aldo crouched next to the man, careful to avoid the puddle of urine. "This is what happens when you put your dirty little hippie prick into pussies where it don't belong. Like Tammy's. You see what I'm sayin' to you?"

The man gagged, then vomited onto the pavement.

"Christ." I waved at the air. "Like this fuck didn't smell bad enough already."

Unfazed, Aldo wagged a finger at him like a parent reprimanding a child. "Don't you ever do nothin' to make us come lookin' for you again, you piece of shit. You do, we'll finish the job, understand?"

"I—I'm sorry, man, I—she said she and her boyfriend broke up, I'm sorry!"

"I don't give a shit if you're sorry."

The man looked at him helplessly, crippled with pain and terror.

"Tell me you understand," Aldo said.

"I understand. I do, I—I understand, please—"

"What?" Aldo held the bat close to his ear, as if it were speaking to him. "Uh-oh."

"What? What's wrong?"

"I don't believe you."

"Why, I—"

"My bat. He thinks you're lying, too."

"Your bat? Hell you talking about, man?"

"I get very upset when I think someone's lying to me."

"No, I—I swear, man, I—I'm not, I—please, no more, all right? Please." The guy put his hands up in front of him and winced. "This shit hurts so bad, and—and that dude, he—he fucking *pissed* on me, man!"

"Did you just raise your fuckin' voice to me?"

"No. No, I did not."

Aldo looked at me. "Did he just raise his voice to me?"

"Little bit, maybe. Kind of sounded like he did."

"I'm sorry," the guy gasped. He began to weep. A grown man lying in the street covered in another man's piss. "I get your message loud and clear, okay? I got it. No more. Please, I—I'm a pacifist, man."

"You're a what?"

"A pacifist."

"Fuck's that?"

"Huh?"

"You're a *what*?"

"P-Pacifist, man, a pacifist."

Aldo looked at me. "Hell's he talkin' about?"

"Means he don't fight. Doesn't believe in violence."

He turned back to the man. "Well, whatever you call someone who *does* believe in violence, that's what I am, what we are, so don't make us come back."

"I won't. I promise. I *won't*."

Aldo casually laid the bat over this shoulder and strolled back to the car. I followed, hesitating near the passenger side door. I could hear the man sobbing and muttering, but I didn't look back. With a heavy sigh, I slipped into the car.

The sky to the north was black as coal, streaked with strange smears of orange clouds peppered with what looked like ash. Like the whole world was burning. Maybe it was. Wouldn't have mattered to us either way.

Night kept falling, bringing everything deeper and deeper into darkness, but nothing could hide what we'd done.

None of us cared.

We weren't in the hiding business.

No one said anything for a while. Except for the sound of our breath, everything was eerily quiet, so I watched the city lights and the night sky glide past the windows and pushed the memory of that poor, bloody, piss-drenched bastard as far from my mind as I could.

I'd just turned twenty, and the city, the suburbs—all of it— were mine. All I had to do was step up and take it. Problem was, I didn't want any of it. All I wanted was out. Not a lot scared me, especially in those days, but the unknown always seemed to get it done. Like the man said, the devil you know. Back then, everything was still out in front of me, waiting just up ahead. Only I didn't know it. Didn't believe it anyway. Not then. All I knew for sure was I didn't want to end up like everyone else around me. I wanted better. But who the hell was I?

We eventually stopped at an abandoned old factory down by the projects in the south end and gave the car to a guy Aldo knew who ran a chop shop just over the state line in East Providence. Once we'd unloaded the sled and Aldo got paid, Dino Abruzzo picked us up, and we all piled into his brand new metallic blue Z-28 IROC. Aldo took the passenger seat, which meant I had to jam myself into the small backseat with Fritz and Petie.

"What's up, pussies?" Dino screamed over the Ozzy tune

blaring from his car stereo. "You take care of that problem?"

"Yeah." Aldo grinned like a shark. "Won't be seein' him no more."

"Cool. Anybody else hungry? I'm fuckin' starving. Let's get some eats."

Dino Abruzzo. We called him Ma, which was a nickname that stood for *Mental Abruzzo*. He'd acquired it in sixth grade, long before being expelled from high school junior year. At six-five and two hundred and sixty pounds of muscle and bad attitude, Dino was that kid in junior high who looked thirty, a monster by the time he was thirteen, and the toughest guy I'd ever known. He had a heavy rep he backed up whenever he got the chance, and much as we all loved him, we knew how crazy and dangerous he was, so unless it was absolutely necessary, we usually left him out of the kinds of things we'd handled earlier because we didn't want them to get out of hand. Unlike the rest of us, Dino had little to no control over his violent tendencies, and once his hair-trigger temper was tripped, there was no stopping it or him. This was a guy who'd gotten out of his car on the way to his junior prom and pulled a man out of his truck at a red light, just so he could beat his ass nearly to death because he'd cut him off. Then he showed up to prom a few minutes later with his horrified date on his arm and blood all over his tuxedo and fancy ruffle shirt. Dino thought it was hilarious, even later, when the police showed up and took him out in cuffs. Took seven cops to hold him down and get those cuffs on, but when it was all said and done, three of them wound up in the hospital and he went to lockup. Since he was only seventeen at the time, he did a year in juvie. He'd been in and out since the age of nine, so for Dino it wasn't exactly a big deal. Not much was, really. I'd known him since elementary school and had always been a little afraid of him. In high school, we'd once had a dispute over a girl, and before I knew what was happening he'd knocked me out with a single punch. Felt like someone had hit me with a fucking sledgehammer. He apologized for days, following me around like a guilt-ridden little kid, helping me out and doing whatever I needed to make up for it, all the while promising he'd never do anything like that again. And he never did. But still, when it came to Dino, it was like hanging out with a tiger. All fine and good until the tiger went tiger on your ass. Couldn't blame the tiger, it was just being a tiger. Only one left to blame was yourself. Just the same, tough as Aldo and the other guys were, there was nobody better in a pinch than Dino. You felt invincible with him by your side. And most of the time, you were.

"Wanna get a slice over at the Greek's?" Petie suggested.

"Fuck that Greek cocksucker," Dino growled.

"Aw, he's all right, Ma. He's a nice old dude, and the food there's good."

"You want pizza we'll go to Dominic's and get it made right, by an Italian. Greek assholes, fuck they know about pizza? Cheap imitation Italians is all they is. Butt-fuckers."

"I could go for a slice," I said. I hadn't eaten since that morning, when I'd wolfed down a bowl of Fruit Loops on my way out the door to meet the guys.

"What about that new place over by the mall?" Aldo said.

"The Italian place?" Dino asked. "It just opened."

"So?"

"So when a new place opens, you should wait a while until they work all the bullshit out. If they don't, they close. If they do and people are still going after a few weeks, you know it's probably good."

"I don't know if I got the cash for that kinda place anyways," Petie said.

"Broke-ass motherfucker." Fritz sighed quietly. He rarely spoke, but when he did, it was usually memorable.

"Oh, and you're rolling in the dough, Rockefeller?"

"Fuck it, we can go try it," Dino said. "Just get somethin' cheap, Petie."

"Think they got pizza, though?"

"It's an Italian place, ain't it?"

"Yeah, but not all them sit-down joints got pizza, Ma."

"So get somethin' else."

"It ain't that fancy or nothing, just a family place," Aldo said. "I don't know nobody that went yet, but maybe it's good. I could go for a decent meal."

I kept quiet and watched the night. I didn't give a shit where we went, long as they had food there.

"Maybe you should just drop me off," Petie said. "I should probably go smooth shit out with Tammy, you know?"

"Yeah, you wouldn't want her to be mad at you for kickin' the Christ out of the guy she was cheatin' on you with." Aldo turned and threw him a look. "You need to wrap shit up with that bitch, Petie. Ain't you had enough of this crap?"

Petie laughed a little, but it was mostly nerves and embarrassment. "Hey, you know how it is, man."

"No, I don't. I don't know how it is. Here's what I know. Tammy's a no good cheatin' twat. What's this, four or five times now?"

I came up with six right off the top of my head but didn't say anything. Last time had been about two months before. We'd left Ma out of it and Fritz had something else going on and couldn't make it, so Aldo and I had been the ones to pull her and some guy out of the backseat of a car on The Avenue, the bustling, main, several-mile drag in the city where everyone cruised and congregated once the sun went down and the streetlights kicked in. Petie hustled her away while we threw the guy a beating and scared him enough to never go near her again. Not even two years out of high school, and Tammy, who worked the counter at Dairy Queen and wasn't exactly destined for greatness anyway, had already become something of a legendary skank. But Petie had a thing for her since sophomore year, and he'd been taking her shit like some love-starved puppy for almost five years. Every time she cheated she'd apologize, throw him some lame excuses, cry, and then fuck the shit out of him. And he forgave her. Every time. I didn't care who Petie was with—none of us did—but I knew where Aldo was coming from. None of us minded violence when it was necessary, a few of us even liked it, but we were all getting tired of having to go knock guys around because his slut girlfriend couldn't keep her legs closed for ten minutes.

"When you gonna learn?" Aldo pressed. "She's no good."

"Take it easy. Come on, man, you're talkin' about the woman I love."

"She cheats on you all the time, you fuckin' retarded bastard."

"Hey, not for nothin', Ally, but you cheat on Candy all the time, too."

Aldo peeled his leather gloves off and threw them at him. "That's different. I'm a guy. It's not the same thing when a guy does it. Especially one as sexy as me. What can I do? I don't wanna cheat, but they just keep throwin' all that fine pussy at me. Who am I to say no? It's a public service I'm performin' over here."

"Christ on the cross, Ally," Dino moaned, "you got more bullshit than a fertilizer franchise."

"Yeah," Petie laughed, throwing the gloves back at him. "What Ma said."

"Whatever." Aldo rolled his eyes and faced front. "Don't matter how you slice it. Tammy's a punchboard. And you're a moron."

"Aw, give him a break," Dino laughed. "Petie's just so happy he found a chick that'll fuck his ugly ass he don't want to lose her. Dude with a thimble dick like his can't be all choosy and shit, right, Petie?"

"Do me a favor, Ma. Don't help me out on this one, okay?"

"*Ohhh Petie-pie!*" he said in a cartoonish falsetto. "*I love your teeny weeny peeny!*"

"Well," Fritz said evenly, "I *was* hungry."

"Seriously, though, thanks for helping me out, you guys,"

Petie said with his usual awkwardness, squirming around uncomfortably between Fritz and me. "I appreciate it, fellas."

Aldo reached back, palm open. Petie slapped it.

Nothing more needed to be said.

"Wait a minute, wait a minute." Dino held everyone up at the curb, just outside the restaurant. "You *pissed* on him?"

"All over the prick."

"God*damn*, Petie, that's fuckin' sick as shit. Good job."

Petie puffed his chest up, proud of himself and loving the acceptance Ma was showing him. "Drank water all day. Tons of it. Had to go like a racehorse, too, but I held it. Saved it up for the bastard. Didn't want to whip it out and have nothin' but my dick in my hand, you know?"

"Yeah," Fritz said, slinking by and heading for the door. "Nothin' worse than comin' up dry when you've been waitin' all day to piss on a guy."

Everyone laughed then hesitated at the door. Aldo looked up at the lighted sign, which featured a fat cartoon caricature of an Italian chef with a bushy mustache holding a plate of spaghetti and meatballs. Behind him were the flags of Italy and America, the words *Family Restaurant* beneath them. "Uncle Tony's," he mumbled. "Original."

"Hey, you're the one wanted to come here," Dino reminded him.

"Come on," I said, slapping him on the back. "It's an Italian restaurant in a fuckin' strip mall. Probably sucks, but I'm starvin'."

Inside, we found a sea of tables beneath bright fluorescent lights. From the tacky stock photographs of Italy in cheap frames to the paper red-checkered tablecloths, it looked like someone had converted a convenience store into a restaurant when no one was looking.

But for an older couple in the far corner, we were the only people there.

A young waitress about our age who looked vaguely familiar hurried past with a tray holding a couple salads. "Welcome to Uncle Tony's. Feel free to sit wherever you'd like, guys."

"How about in another restaurant?" Dino chuckled.

"Nobody here," I said. "That can't be a good sign."

"Just means we'll get our food faster, that's all." Petie led the way and we all followed him to a large table in the center of the dining area. The chairs were black metal jobs with cheap padding.

We sat there a few minutes, taking the place in.

I lit a cigarette. Fritz bummed one, and the other guys, none of whom were smokers, just sat there, waiting on what appeared to be the only waitress working to get to us.

She arrived a few minutes later, looking harried but with a smile on her otherwise pretty face. A skinny but athletic-looking brunette with big blue eyes and hair piled high on her head, her makeup was heavy, especially around her eyes, and her perfume showed up a good ten to fifteen seconds before she did. "Hi, I'm Ashley," she said pleasantly. "I'll be your waitress tonight."

"Your last name Witherspoon?" Dino asked.

"Yeah."

"You got a brother Todd?"

"Yeah, I do, actually."

"Little older than you, right? Cock-eyed motherfucker, wears big thick glasses. Real good at math. Huge fuckin' nerd."

She blushed and nodded.

"I know that guy," Dino said. "Used to do my Algebra homework for me."

Fritz cleared his throat. "Voluntarily I bet."

Ashley feigned laughter. "Anyway, can I get you guys something?"

"Menus would be nice," Aldo said.

"Oh my God!" She hurried away and came back quickly with

a stack of enormous laminated menus. "Here you go. Sorry about that."

Nobody said anything so I told her it was all right and to give us a minute. When she moved away, I flipped through the menu, which seemed to have an endless number of pages. "Quite the selection, huh?"

"Cheap enough," Petie grunted. "No pizza, though. Figures."

"I'll tell you what," Dino said, "that lasagna don't look half bad."

"Don't go by the pictures," I told him.

"Motherfucker can't read," Aldo said with a straight face, "how you expect him to pick something out if he don't go by the pictures?"

Everyone laughed, Dino harder than anyone, and Ashley returned with glasses of water for everyone. Once she'd put them down she pulled a pen and pad from the apron of her uniform.

"I'm gonna get that lasagna," Dino told her. "And a Coke."

"Okay." She scribbled on the pad then turned to Petie. "And you?"

"Wait a minute," Dino said. "That's it?"

She cocked her head. "I'm sorry?"

"Nothing comes with it? No soup or salad or nothin'?"

"No, just the lasagna. We have soup and salad, but it's extra."

Dino made a face and looked away.

"Don't worry about him," Petie said with a smile. "I'm having the cheese ravioli, and let me get some iced tea with it."

"Manicotti and a Dr Pepper," Fritz said evenly.

I ordered spaghetti carbonara and a Coke.

"Okay, thanks, guys. It'll be out in a few minutes."

"Hey," I said, stopping her, "could we get some bread, too?"

"Bread?"

"Yeah, some bread, maybe a little butter."

Ashley seemed thoroughly confused. "You mean like garlic sticks?"

"What the hell's a garlic stick?"

"It's a breadstick with garlic on it."

"No thanks, just some bread's good."

"I don't think we have bread."

"You don't have bread?"

"I don't think so."

"What the hell kind of Italian restaurant don't have bread?"

She shrugged.

"Well, could you go find out for me?"

"Yeah but...like...what do you want exactly?"

I looked to the others, all of whom looked as perplexed as I was. "Bread."

"No, I know you want bread, but like, you mean a slice of it?"

"A slice?"

"Is that what you want? Like a slice of bread with butter on it?"

"Are you serious?"

"Sorry, I'm trying my best, I—I'm new, we just opened."

I sipped my water. "Okay, no problem. I'm just asking if we could get some bread for the table. It's what happens in Italian restaurants, they give you bread. On the table. Sometimes it's even hot."

"Hot?"

Fritz puffed his cigarette, a huge smile on his face. "This is the best conversation of *all* fuckin' time right here."

"Richie, I don't think they do bread," Aldo said.

"What are you talkin' about? All Italian restaurants do bread."

"From the sounds, this one don't."

"We're Italians. In an Italian restaurant. Bread's part of the meal."

"Yeah, you and me know that, I'm just sayin', she obviously

14

don't know what the hell you're talkin' about, so they probably don't have it."

"What kind of Italian restaurant don't have bread, though?"

"It sound to you like they got bread, Richie?"

I turned back to Ashley. "Just, if we could get a loaf a bread, that'd be good, okay?"

"You want a whole loaf of bread?"

I stared at her, dumbfounded.

"I'm going to have to go ask, okay? I'll be right back."

As Ashley hurried away, I took a hard drag on what was left of my cigarette and crushed it in the plastic ashtray in the center of the table. "You believe this shit? She looked at me like I asked for cotton candy or somethin'."

"When she comes back," Fritz said, "if you ask her for cotton candy, I'll buy you dinner."

"Hilarious. Bread's not that important to you, wiseass."

"No, Richie, it's not." Fritz butted his cigarette, leaned his head back, and exhaled a stream of smoke at the ceiling. Dressed entirely in black like the rest of us, he wore black wayfarer sunglasses all the time, too. Indoors, outdoors, sunny, when it rained, night and day. The only blond in our group, he wore his hair in a buzzed flattop and sported inverted dangle cross earrings in both ears because he knew it got a rise out of people.

"He's a kraut," Aldo said, giving him a playful push. "What do you expect? You got to talk to him about sauerkraut and bratwursts and shit or he don't care."

We were still hassling each other when a thirtysomething guy showed up at our table. In slacks and a silky shirt that looked inspired by something a cavalry officer might've worn in one of those old westerns the cable channels showed in the middle of the night, he looked like some yuppie real estate salesman from Connecticut. "Hiya, fellas!" he said with a blindingly white smile. "I'm Randy, the owner and general manager here at Uncle Tony's. Ashley said you had some questions about the menu, so I thought I'd stop by and see if I can be of some assistance, help answer any questions or concerns you might have."

"I just wanted some bread," I told him. "That's all."

"Okay, well we do have garlic sticks and—"

"Jesus Christ," I said, my patience gone at this point. "I don't want fuckin' breadsticks."

Aldo held a hand up. "Richie, let it go, huh?"

"I want to help make your dining experience here as pleasant as possible," Randy said, "but I really need you to do me a favor and watch your language. Think you can you do that for me?"

"Do you know what Italian bread is?" I asked him.

"Of course."

"Do you have any?"

"We have a two-slice garlic bread option that's available with entrees, but there is an additional cost. It's listed on the menu under *Extras*."

"Okay, well I want a loaf of the bread you make the garlic bread with. On the table. With some butter. Think *you* can do *that* for *me*?"

"We don't offer free bread. I'm sorry."

"Fine. I'll pay for it. I just want some bread with my meal. Not garlic bread, not garlic sticks, just a plain sliced loaf of Italian bread and some butter."

"I'm afraid we don't offer that option."

"In an Italian restaurant."

Randy smiled, but it was as forced as his customer service.

"Is your chef Italian?" Dino asked suddenly. "What's his name?"

"I really don't see how that's relevant."

"Reason I ask is, the only Italians I see in here are me and my friends."

"Don't forget the fat fuck on the sign," Petie said.

"Look, fellas, I don't want any trouble here, okay? Why don't we all—"

Dino stood up. Hard and fast, nearly knocking the table

over as he did so. "I asked you a question. You fuckin' deaf?"

"Dino," I said, "it's cool, forget about it. It's just some bread."

"Nah, fuck this guy, Richie. Answer the question, pussy."

"All right, you all need to leave. Right now. Or I'll call the cops, got it?"

"You won't make it to the phone."

"Look what you done now, with your bread bullshit," Aldo said, shooting me an annoyed look as he gently took hold of Dino's arm. "Ma, it's cool. Sit down."

"No. I asked this piece of shit a question and he's gonna answer it or I'll beat it out of his ass."

Randy's cheeks flushed and his hands began to shake. "What is it," he said, clearing his throat nervously. "What is it you'd like to know?"

"What's your chef's name?"

"Albert."

"What's his last name?"

"Costa."

Dino shook his head and let out a small laugh, but there wasn't anything funny about it. "So let me get this straight, *Randy*, you got a *Portagee* cookin' in an Italian restaurant owned by a...a..."

"If he calls this guy white bread," Fritz said softly, "I swear to God I'll be on the floor laughin'."

"...a whatever the hell you are."

Randy stared at him, saying nothing.

"No wonder they don't got any bread." Dino motioned to me. "You want me to smash this snooty fuck, Richie?"

"I want you punks out of here," Randy snapped, his voice shaking worse than his hands. "I'm warning you, you need to leave right now!"

"You're warnin' *me*?" Dino started around the table.

"No, he's not, that's not what he meant." Aldo caught his arm. "We're leavin', let's go."

"Get out!"

"Hey!" Aldo said, slamming a hand down on the table so hard two glasses of water fell to the floor. "Shut your mouth. Go in the back and play with your napkins or whatever the hell you do, all right? Before he gets so mad I can't stop him from doin' all kinds of fucked up shit to you. We're leavin', all right? Just fuck off, before you get hurt."

Randy backed away but remained in the dining room, trembling while glaring at us from behind a nearby empty table.

Aldo and Petie got Ma out of the place and back into the night, leaving Fritz and me behind. I stared down Randy a minute, pissed at him, pissed at myself, pissed at Dino for taking it to places it didn't need to go.

What else was new?

As I turned and walked out, I heard Fritz say, "On second thought, Randy, looks like we're gonna need that loaf of Italian bread to go."

Ten minutes later, we were downtown and parked outside a supermarket. Aldo ran in without explaining what he was doing, then emerged a minute or so later, walked up to the car and fired a loaf of Italian bread into the backseat directly at me. "There's your goddamn Italian bread."

I sighed and shook my head. "What, no butter?"

Everyone laughed, but I still felt bad about what had happened.

"Come on, let's go," Aldo said to Dino as he slid into the passenger seat.

"What's the rush?"

"It's possible I forgot to pay for the bread."

We ended up having dinner a few blocks over at The Hot Dog Cave, the best little dog shack in the city. It was still early, the streets weren't hopping yet, and unlike most nights, there was no line. We all got dogs, fries, and frappes, and then sat on some nearby benches and ate our dinner.

"Sorry I blew our dinner," I said.

"Fuck that place," Dino said around a huge chunk of chili-cheese dog, "can't beat a good dog."

"The Hot Dog Cave to the rescue, baby!" Petie slurped what was left of his coffee frappe and flashed me a smile. He had mustard on his teeth.

"Yeah," Aldo chimed in, "definitely. Who needs that dump? Besides, we want good Italian food we can get that at home, am I right?"

They knew I felt like shit for letting things escalate to the point where Ma got upset, and I was grateful, but end of the day, no matter how good, we were still eating hot dogs.

"Except for Fritz," Petie said. "Fritz thinks Ragu in a jar's good eatin'!"

"Come on, man," Fritz replied in his usual deadpan tone, "everybody knows the best Italian eatery's between your grandma's legs."

"You fuckin' asshole!" Petie threw the empty frappe cup at him.

Fritz dodged it easily and continued eating.

"My grandmother's a goddamn saint! You hear me? A *saint*!"

"What is she the patron saint of exactly?" Fritz said.

"Fritz," Aldo said, laughing, "don't."

"Pussy juice?"

"Sonofabitch!"

Dino laughed so hard he choked a little on his hot dog. "You gonna let him talk to you like that, Petie? About Grammy?"

"Ma, come on," Aldo said, "don't make the shit worse."

"You know I'm only jokin', Petie," Fritz said.

Petie settled down, nodded, and regained control of himself. "Yeah. Okay. I know. Sure, man."

"I wouldn't lick that skunk pussy with your tongue."

Dino and Aldo fell over, howling with laughter as Petie jumped on Fritz, wrestling with him playfully and calling him every name in the book. Me, I just sat on the back of the bench and ate my hot dogs.

They were a mess, all of them. But they were my friends, my brothers.

They were all I had.

Making as little noise as possible, I slipped into the dark apartment then closed and locked the door behind me. I moved through the small kitchen and into the adjacent bathroom, plugged a small nightlight into the socket so I could see what I was doing, and ran water in the sink. I peeled off my black leather driving gloves and held them beneath the trickle of warm water. Blood ran into the basin, turning the silver stopper crimson. As it escaped down the drain, I watched the blood swirl, and my mind drifted back to that poor hippie.

"What are you doing?"

The sudden intrusion of my mother's voice startled me.

I looked up from the sink, saw her standing in the bathroom doorway in a lightweight cotton nightgown, one with kittens on it. I'd gotten it for her last Christmas. I rinsed out the last of the blood and put my gloves on the counter. "Sorry, didn't mean to wake you."

"Is that *blood*?"

"Go back to bed, Mom."

"Don't dismiss me, Richie. I'm your mother. Who do you think you're talking to?"

"Sorry."

"No, you're not."

I turned the water off and dried my hands with the towel hanging on a rod next to the counter. "You should get some sleep."

"Where you been, Richie?"

"Just out with the guys is all."

"Twenty years old and still running around with that trash."

We'd had this conversation a few thousand times already, so I let it go. "I'm going to bed, Mom."

"Hold on a minute," she said, her words slurred like always. "Stay up and talk to me for a little while."

"It's late."

"Just a little after midnight."

"I'm tired."

"What were you doing tonight?"

"I told you, hangin' out with my friends."

"Hanging out with your friends. Did you call Mr. Montero?"

"Not yet."

"What are you waiting for, Richie? He's not gonna be hiring forever."

I looked at her and forced a smile. My mother was forty-five years old and looked at least ten years older than that. Her once beautiful skin was pale and creased, her raven hair streaked with gray and her body weak and hunched over. "Yeah, okay. I'll call him tomorrow."

"That's what you said yesterday."

"You gonna let me out of the bathroom or what?"

She stepped aside, and I moved into the kitchen. She followed, her bare feet padding across the tile floor.

"Hotter than Hell in here," I said.

"I got the fans going in my bedroom, but they're not helping."

"I'll get us an air conditioner tomorrow."

"How you gonna afford an air conditioner, Richie?"

"They're not that much." I opened the fridge, found several bottles of beer, which meant she'd had company while I was out. Whenever my mother bought beer, she got cans. I popped the cap and took a long pull. It felt good going down, so cold.

"Help yourself."

"I'll replace it."

"Sure."

"I'll talk to Aldo tomorrow about an air conditioner. He

knows a guy."

"Aldo Genaro's a lowlife criminal, just like the rest of his no-good family."

"He's not a criminal."

"Every one of them in that family is, going back two generations."

"He's my best friend."

"You need to get better friends."

I held the bottle up as if in evidence. "So do you."

Her face turned to stone. "I won't have stolen goods in this house."

"Yeah, okay."

"Don't *yeah*, *okay* me, Richie. I mean it."

"Just sayin', we need an air conditioner, I'll take care of it. Okay?"

"Take care of it how?" She crossed her arms over her chest and glared at me. "By stealing it?"

"I'll pay for it, all right? Top dollar, you feel better?"

"You don't have a job, but you always have money. How's that work?"

I pushed off the counter, leaned in close and gave her a kiss on the cheek. Her skin was clammy, and she smelled like booze and cigarettes. "Why you givin' me such a hard time tonight?"

"I'm worried about you."

"Don't worry about me. I'm fine."

"You're not fine. You've got no job, you run around with those idiots you call friends and act like you're still in high school, doing God only knows what. Dino Abruzzo should be in a hospital for the criminally insane, that German kid's a creep, and Petie Trezza? *Really*, Richie? I'm pretty sure he's at least partly retarded."

"That don't make him a bad guy."

"Oh, it *don't*? Listen to the way you talk. I taught you better than that. You sound just like that street trash you run around with."

"It's just words, Mom." I moved by her, into the living room, where there was at least a window with an old box fan going. "Don't make a federal case about it, okay?"

My mother followed me. "Promise me you'll call Mr. Montero tomorrow."

"I promise I'll try, all right?"

"You don't want to work, is that it?"

"Down the fish houses? No, I don't."

"You too good for that, Richie?"

"Maybe."

"Your father, God rest his soul, worked his fingers to the bone at—"

"My father's been dead since I was four." I took another pull on the beer bottle. "And I'm not him."

"No," she said softly, her eyes red and glassy, "you're not."

I looked away. She wasn't wrong. When my father died, he took pieces of us both with him. Pieces we needed. "Yeah, well, I'm sorry about that, too."

"Don't you think it's time to grow up and do something with your life? You're not a teenager anymore, Richie. Running around getting into fistfights, are you kidding me?"

"I didn't get into a fight."

"Then how'd you get blood all over your gloves?"

"Everything's all right." I gulped more beer and thought about making a break for the hallway and the sanctuary of my room. "Just let it go."

"Tell me what happened."

"Nothing happened. It's no big deal."

"There's someone's blood all over your gloves, and it's *no big deal*?"

"The guy's fine. He had a little nosebleed is all."

"What guy?"

"Just some guy."

"Who?"

"I don't know. I don't know his name."

She closed her eyes, pinched the bridge of her nose with her fingers and sighed heavily. "If you get caught doing something you shouldn't be doing, they'll lock you up. Not in juvie either, but jail. Real jail. Maybe even prison. You're an adult now, and the courts are gonna treat you that way. Why can't you get that through your thick skull?"

"Nothing's gonna happen to me, Mom."

"I got enough to worry about," she said just above a whisper. "I don't need to worry about you, too. Least not any more than I already do."

I looked at her there in the near dark of the living room, forced myself to see her even though I knew it would rip me apart like it always did. The beautiful and vibrant woman my mother was in old photographs had been reduced to a junkie and an alcoholic on disability long ago. I'd been watching her die since I was a little boy, practically my whole life, as she rotted away, little by little, more and more every day, week, month, year. It wasn't a question as to whether she'd die young, only when. From the looks of her in the last couple years, prob-ably soon. It broke my heart, but there was nothing I could do. Like everything and everyone else in the city, she was what she was, and most days it felt like even an act of God Almighty Himself couldn't change that. I didn't know her any other way, so to me it was normal, I guess. You decompose in the dark long enough, eventually it gets so you find comfort in it, even if it's just the familiarity.

I barely remembered my old man, and although she'd had a series of boyfriends over the years, none had lasted, so, for the most part, it'd been just the two of us. I loved my mother, and she loved me. We didn't always like each other, that was the problem.

She stared at me, like she sometimes did, as if she'd never encountered anything quite like me and wasn't sure what to make of it.

"Go to bed." I reached out with my free hand and cupped

her cheek, stroked it gently with my thumb. "Try to get some sleep. We'll talk in the morning, all right?"

"You won't be here in the morning. You're never here in the morning."

I cupped her face a bit tighter, as if to assure her, but with another sigh, she turned, shuffled off down the hallway, and slipped into her room. The door closed quietly behind her.

Soaked in sweat, I stood there wondering if I'd ever see her alive again.

I set the small oscillating fan to high, smoked a couple cigarettes, finished the beer, and threw my headphones on. Rocking along with DIO for a while, I watched the shadows play along the walls and ceilings, the lights from passing cars on the street below gliding through the room like spirits, as lost and trapped within these walls as I was. Although it served as a sanctuary of sorts, my room was no different than the rest of the apartment: small, cramped, dusty, and old. The building was dying. Slowly. Just like everything else in this neighborhood. It wasn't much, but I was used to it, and it was the only room I ever remembered having, so I made the best of it. We'd lived in the building, in this same third-floor apartment, since I was five years old. People always told me nothing stayed the same. Here, nothing ever changed.

Tiring of the music, I turned my stereo off—a bunch of mismatched and in some cases homemade components I'd pieced together over the years—tossed the headphones aside, and selected a book from a squat bookcase against the wall. Mostly dog-eared paperbacks I'd already read, the middle shelf also housed my latest selection from the library, *The Beach of Falesá* by Dylan Thomas. I'd never read Dylan Thomas before, but while reading the book jacket I discovered it was a screenplay of sorts, published in book form, based on the short story by Robert Louis Stevenson. I was pretty sure I'd never read a screenplay either, but since I'd read and loved Stevenson's *Treasure Island* a few years before, I decided to give it a try.

After switching on the small lamp next to my bed, I lay back down and opened the book.

It is the hour before tropical dawn, on the hushed, grey open sea. A boat glides by like a shadow, the moon going down behind her tall sails.

I closed my eyes a moment, pictured such a setting as best I could.

A light knocking on the ceiling brought me back. I stared at the cracks in the plaster overhead. Woody, one of my neighbors, up on the roof, letting me know he was out there in case I wanted to join him, which I sometimes did.

A siren blared a couple blocks away then faded.

With a sigh, I read that opening sentence one more time then put the book aside and rolled out of bed. The window was already open, so I pulled up the old screen and stuck my head out into the night. Just as hot out there. I waited a few seconds and then there it was, the pungent aroma of pot wafting down from the roof.

I climbed through the window, pulled myself up by the ledge, and swung my legs around until I was straddling it. Dangerous, but I'd done it countless times. I rolled onto the roof, stood up, and wiped off my T-shirt.

Woody, slumped in one of two rusty metal lawn chairs he kept up there, puffed on a joint. At his feet, a bottle of tequila. "Richie," he said through a toothy smile. "What it is, young lion?"

"How you doin', Woody?"

"Couldn't sleep, my man."

"Me either. Too fucking hot. This is crazy."

"Allow the sweet leaf to be of assistance." He took a hit from the joint then held it out for me. "Dig my herb. You'll still be hot and drowning in your own sweat, you just won't give a shit."

"True enough." I took the joint, hit it hard, then handed it back. As I dropped into the lawn chair next to him, he passed me the bottle. I had a swallow. It burned but felt good once it was down. "Thanks."

"My pleasure." Woody smiled again with those giant white teeth. A Vietnam vet in his early thirties, he was a tall wiry dude with a handlebar mustache and long, dirty blond hair he kept pulled back into a ponytail. In cutoff jean shorts, sneakers, and a ratty, sleeveless Army jacket, he was unshaven and looked pretty worn down for a guy his age. He was on disability, but I wasn't sure for what, and had lived in the building for the last few years. We'd hit it off the moment we met, one night up on the roof. I often went up there to get away from everything and think, and Woody did the same. He was older, but cool, and never gave me shit about anything. Not to mention he had some of the best pot I'd ever smoked, and always had a bottle of booze handy. Unlike my friends, we also shared a love of books and reading. I could talk to Woody about things I couldn't with the guys, with no judgment or teasing, and sometimes that felt good. He was weird—*eccentric*, my mother called him—and stoned almost all the time, but he was a good guy, and really smart. I knew he'd been through a lot over in those jungles of Vietnam, but Woody hardly ever talked about those days in specifics. He didn't have to. His pain was obvious, his ghosts and demons carved directly into the lines on his face, their horrors forever haunting him, trapped in his sad brown eyes like the nightmares they were.

"Any new reads?" he asked.

"*The Beach of Falesá*," I said, unsure if I'd pronounced it correctly.

"You got it," he said, sensing my uncertainty. "Stevenson, yeah?"

"Dylan Thomas, based on Stevenson's story, I guess."

"Ah, Thomas." Woody stroked his mustache. "Even better. '*When one burns one's bridges, what a very nice fire it makes.*'

As one who has burned several bridges in his day, I'm here to tell you, ol' Dylan was correct."

I gazed out over the block and city streets below. Rows of nearly identical tenements lined the streets, bland, bleak and unimaginative buildings crammed together into neat rows I'd been surrounded by my entire life. "Most bridges I got I'm ready to torch to the fucking ground," I said.

Woody slapped his arm, squishing a mosquito against his bicep, then took a series of quick tokes from the joint and passed it to me. "Fuck it. Burn it all down. Don't much matter anyway."

"I guess." I took a hard drag on the joint, handed it back, then lit a cigarette. "Sometimes I'm not even sure it's worth the match."

A burst of laughter and pot smoke escaped him as he sat forward and coughed. Once it had passed, he hit the joint again and gave me a mock salute. "All this anger. We need to get laid, son."

This time I laughed. "Wouldn't hurt."

"No prospects? Young lion like you?"

"Been quiet lately," I told him.

"Nothing more from your girlfriend?"

"Nah, that's done." I thought about Mariana, wondered what she was doing at that exact moment in time. Her face drifted past my mind's eye, those big dark eyes, full lips, and that body—

"Shame," Woody sighed. "I know I only met her that one time, but she seemed nice."

"She was."

"Great tits." Woody laughed.

"Definitely."

I remembered how whenever her parents were out I'd sneak over to her apartment and we'd fuck on the floor in the den. She had this little dog that'd hop and bounce and bark at us from the doorway the whole time. I remembered the rug burns

I'd get every time, too, and how I didn't give a damn as long as she was squealing and wiggling beneath me, her fingernails dug into my back, ankles locked across my ass, heels grinding me deeper.

"Got to ask," Woody said, coughing out another cloud of pot smoke. "She dump you or you cut her loose?"

"Just sort of ended when she went to college."

"Happens."

He was right of course, and while I had feelings for Mariana, I'd never had any illusions of spending the rest of my life with her. She was my one serious high school girlfriend, but that was over now. We'd started dating halfway through junior year. Once we graduated, she worked for a year at the mall before going off to college. We kept dating, although it was mostly just going through the motions and counting down the inevitable by then.

"Mariana's goin' places," I said. "Where the fuck am I goin'? Plus, the whole thing with her family sucked."

Woody looked at me, puzzled.

"First-generation Portuguese. Her parents treated her like she was twelve years old. Even if they did let her date, sure as hell wouldn't be with a guinea like me. Had to be another *Portagee* or they wouldn't go for it. So we snuck around like little kids. Didn't mind at first, but a couple years in it got real tired."

"I can see how it would."

"It's better this way."

"You sure?"

"She's got big plans. Why should I get in her way?"

"Don't you have big plans, too?"

"Yeah," I scoffed, "sure."

"Don't let shit hold you back, Richie. Whole world out there, man. Go get you some. Nobody's gonna hand you a god-damn thing, you know that."

"Yeah. Figured that out a long time ago."

I stabbed the cigarette between my lips and left it there. Maybe so I wouldn't have to say anything else. Or maybe because the memory of that hippie lying in the street suddenly came back to me, and I wondered what Woody might think of me had he known what I'd done a few hours before.

"Something else bothering you, man?" he asked.

"Think Bronski came by to see my mother while I was out."

"Yeah." Woody winced, hit the joint, then had a pull of tequila. "I saw him around earlier."

I puffed my cigarette. Normally I'd have been filled with rage already, but the weed was making me so mellow I couldn't muster the anger. "Fuckin' guy."

"He's a parasite, Richie. A piece of shit."

"He'd leave her alone if she wouldn't let him in."

"Your mother's a good woman." He reached over, gave my shoulder a quick pat. "We all got our devils, man."

He was right, and I knew it, but it didn't help.

Another siren blared in the distance.

"Wish I could get us out of here."

"What's to say you won't?"

"No way out, Woody. Not for people like us."

Woody offered me the joint. I passed, so he hit it and seemed to think about what I'd said a while. "One thing I learned in the jungles," he said a moment later. "There's always a way out."

"Yeah, but—"

"No *buts*. There's always a way out, man. May not be clean, may not be exactly the way you want it, may have to pay a hell of a price for it—or someone else might—but there's always a way out. Always."

"Lived in this city my whole life," I told him. "Spent most of it trying to figure out how to be someplace else. Ain't found a way yet."

"Hey," he said through a big smile, "there's always the beach."

I smiled too. Didn't much feel like it but couldn't help it.

"Of Falesá?"

"You, me, your moms, couple hot little bikini bunnies. Sun, sand, beautiful healing ocean, stiff drinks, good food, and all the drugs we want. *Fuck* yeah."

"Nice dream."

He handed me the tequila. "Nectar of the gods, baby. Makes all your dreams come true, even if just for a little while."

We were a long way from paradise, but Woody was right. The weed and booze would get me there, if only in my mind. And on that unbearably hot night, up on that dirty old roof, in a dark city slowly choking the life out of me, that was close as I could get.

CHAPTER TWO

Richie?

I found her standing in the doorway to her bedroom in a T-shirt. Her short, thick hair was mussed, her face void of make-up, breasts full, nipples pressed against the thin fabric, her legs and feet bare. She held the bottom of the shirt just low enough to cover herself and smiled that sexy little smile of hers, her top lip curled like a snarl, her dark eyes alive and lusting.

Richie?

"Mariana…" Her name caught in my throat. "I…"

"I miss you too, baby." She leaned against the doorframe, cocked her head to the side and whispered, "C'mere."

Richie!

Mariana fell away to darkness as my eyes opened. Through a thick, hazy blur, I saw my mother standing over me with a stern expression.

"Will you wake up already? You got a call."

Realizing I had an erection, I pulled the sheet a little higher so she wouldn't see it. "Yeah," I said, coughing. "Okay. Gimme a minute."

As she left the room, I rubbed my eyes then swung my legs around onto the floor and coughed some more. Couldn't remember how late I'd been up on the roof with Woody, but from the way I felt, we'd gotten fucked up good. With a yawn, I grabbed a pack of cigarettes from my nightstand and shook one free. Rolling it into the corner of my mouth, I searched for a lighter but came up empty. Must've left it on the roof.

I struggled up out of bed, and since my hard-on was still raging I threw on a pair of sweatpants and padded barefoot down the hallway to the kitchen phone. It was hotter than hell, the humidity already through the roof. The wall clock next to the fridge read nine-forty-seven. The Mr. Coffee was on, and the whole kitchen smelled like freshly brewed. I ignored the rumbling in my stomach and grabbed the phone from the wall. "Yeah?"

"Hey." Aldo. "It's me."

"What's up?"

"Still sleeping? Lazy prick."

"Yeah, until you fuckin' woke me up. What do you want?"

"We're hitting The Park, you coming or what?"

I scratched my crotch, looked around for a lighter. "Yeah, of course."

"Ma should be here any minute. We'll head your way soon as he lands. Probably about ten minutes, cool?"

Snatching a lighter from the kitchen table, I sparked up the butt and took a long drag. "Nah, man, I got to take a shit and grab a shower," I said. "Make it twenty."

I hung up then went to the fridge. Not much on the shelves, but there was a small bottle of cranberry juice. I drank half of it then put the rest back, closed the fridge and leaned against the door, still groggy from sleep and still thinking about Mariana in that little fucking T-shirt. It was summer, I thought. Maybe she was home on break from school. Maybe I should call her, I thought, see how she's doing. Maybe she'd want to hang out.

After a quick piss, I stumbled back out into the kitchen and called her. Her mother answered the phone but she barely spoke English and I couldn't figure out what she was saying. I could tell by the tone of her voice she wasn't happy about a boy calling for her daughter, but I kept on it anyway. If Mariana was home, I wanted to talk to her. After a minute, she went quiet, and for a second or two, I thought she'd hung up on me. But then Mariana's younger brother Marcelo came on the line.

Even though he was two years younger than us, he'd always been a decent kid, and he'd helped keep our relationship quiet the entire time we were together. I didn't know him that well, but far as I knew, he was all right.

"Hey, Richie, what's going on? You looking for Mariana?"

"Yeah, I was thinking maybe she was home for the summer and—"

"She is, but..." He tried to cover the phone real fast, but I heard him arguing in Portuguese with his mother. When he came back on the line he was almost whispering. "You still there, Richie?"

"Yeah, what's up?"

"She's in Rhode Island for the next couple days."

"Oh yeah? What's she doing in Rhode Island?"

"Staying with a friend of hers from college."

"A girlfriend?"

"A dude. New boyfriend. Sorry, man."

I felt my face flush with embarrassment. "Hey, no problem, it's cool. I was just calling to say what's up, see how she was doing and shit. No big deal."

"Yeah. You want me to let her know you called?"

"Nah, man, don't worry about it. Thanks, I'll talk to you later."

Before he could say anything else and I could feel any worse, I hung up. My mother was waiting for me on the other side of the table, still in her bathrobe, a mug of coffee in one hand and a cigarette in the other.

"You gonna call Mr. Montero today?"

"Jesus H., what a haunt." I opened a cabinet, took out a mug and shuffled over to the coffee pot. "Yeah, if I get a chance, I—I don't know. Maybe."

"You got something better to do today?"

"Goin' over The Park with the guys."

"The Park. Hanging around there like hoodlums doing God knows what."

"Mom, I just woke up. Gimme a break, huh?"

She smoked her cigarette, watching me through the vines of smoke circling her. "What about that air conditioner?"

"Told you I'd take care of it, didn't I?"

"Why you got to talk to me in that tone of voice?"

I poured my coffee, sipped some. She was still staring at me. "I'll buy one today, all right? That's all I meant. Don't worry about it, I'll get one."

Her expression softened a bit. "You need a couple bucks? I don't have much, but I could give you a twenty towards it. Hit on a scratch ticket yesterday for fifty."

We both knew that was a lie. Bronski had given it to her. Broke my heart and pissed me off all at the same time. Like always. "It's okay," I said, moving toward the hallway. "You hang on to it."

She looked away, said nothing.

I gave her a kiss on the cheek then slipped down the hallway and into the bathroom. Collapsing onto the toilet, I smoked my cigarette, drank my coffee and tried to forget about Mariana rolling around with some Joe College asshole, and my mother rolling around with that pig Bronski.

Day hadn't even started yet and it was already shit.

I didn't know then it was only going to get worse.

Despite the heat, I wore a pair of jeans, high-top sneakers, a T-shirt and my black leather jacket. I had two jackets, one for winter and a lighter-weight one for spring and summer. We had a uniform for The Park, and it always included our leather jackets. It was our mark. Same way a gang wore their colors when they were at war. With us, it didn't make any difference. We were always at war.

At the corner, I waited for my ride, smoked a cigarette and replayed the conversation I'd had with Marcelo in my head eight or nine times. I felt like an idiot. Never should've called.

Then again, at least I knew now that Mariana had moved on. New boyfriend. Had I expected something different? Beautiful, smart and sexy girl away at school? I'd known it was over between us, and I was okay with that—or so I thought—but there was something final about this new information, the last nail in a crucifixion I had no control over. All I could do was hang up there on my cross a while and feel sorry for myself.

Just shy of ten-thirty in the morning, the neighborhood was still relatively quiet until Ma's IROC came flying around the top of the block, roared down the street and screeched to a halt not ten feet from me, an Iron Maiden tune blasting. From the passenger seat, Aldo leaned out a bit and grinned at me.

"Hey, slut," he said. "How much for a gangbang with me and my friends?"

"More than you got." I took a final drag on my cigarette then flicked it away. "Wop cocksucker."

"We got us a feisty one, boys."

"Open the fuckin' door, retard."

He did, and I climbed into the backseat. Fritz was back there, his black shades concealing his eyes as usual. I slapped hands with him then leaned forward and did the same with Ma, right before he rocketed out of there, flying through the streets of the city like the cops were chasing us.

"Where's Petie?" I asked, flopping back.

"Home," Aldo said.

Home was an apartment in the north end of the city where Petie lived with his grandmother, an ornery old lady who had raised him from the time he was in elementary school. His mother was serving a life sentence in Framingham for beating her then-boyfriend to death with a crowbar while he slept, after a weekend of drinking, drugging and fighting. Like me, Petie had grown up without a father. Only difference was, he had no idea who his was.

"Wanted to hang with Tammy a while," Aldo added.

"Have a little Bible study," Fritz said in his deadpan voice.

We all laughed.

"Said he might see us later at The Park," Aldo told me.

"What about you, Ma?" I asked above the blaring music. "It's Friday, no work today?"

Unlike the rest of us, Dino had a real job and had grown up and lived in a house with both his parents. He had two older brothers and one younger sister, and the IROC was his second new car since he'd gotten his driver's license four years before. His family owned a junkyard and scrap place on the outskirts of the city where he spent days tearing apart engines and appliances and heavy pieces of discarded machinery. We all worked out with weights a few times a week to stay in shape, but Dino stayed ripped by lugging all that shit around eight hours a day. "Good to be the boss's kid," he said, chuckling maniacally.

We left the city, flew toward The Park, which was technically two towns away but only about a five-minute drive from my door to the entrance. Lincoln Park, or just *The Park*, as we called it, was a giant old amusement park that had been there, in one form or another, since the late 1800s. Spread out over forty acres, there were numerous rides, food concessions, a midway of games and various exhibitions, a ballroom and all sorts of attractions. A huge Ferris wheel could be seen from a distance, but the main attraction was a giant, old wooden beast of a rollercoaster dubbed *The Comet*. For us, The Park was a regular hangout where we spent most of our time in the pool hall, a building that housed numerous bowling lanes and a large area for billiards.

For us, The Park had always been a fixture. We'd been going there our whole lives, and as kids, it was a treat if we got to go and ride the rides, see the sights, eat the shitty food and run around having fun. When we got a little older, we'd go see all the professional wrestling stars from TV fight in the ballroom or catch concerts from bands that were big once but fading fast, working the smaller circuits and milking whatever hits they'd had from years before. We didn't care. Tickets were cheap, when and if we actually bought them, and we walked around like we owned the place. Although our altercations usually took place in, or at a minimum began in, the pool hall or bowling areas, over the last few years we'd earned a solid reputation throughout The Park for violence and aggression. It wasn't much, but we considered The Park our turf, and if we had to fight to hang onto it or make examples of those who tried to challenge us, so be it. The regulars there knew that when we showed up, we were to be given a wide path, because it didn't take much to set us off, and once we went, things got ugly fast.

We'd usually hit the grounds in the morning and stay until closing later that night. It got tired sometimes, but there wasn't much else to do. We'd been banned from The Park at least four times in the last two years, but we just kept coming back. Sometimes one of the bigshot management guys would spot us and tell the cops working details there to get us off the grounds. If they could find us they threw us out, but The Park was huge, and on a busy day there were thousands of people milling around. Wasn't but five or six cops in the entire place. Few more once the sun went down, but even then it was hard to keep up with us. Most of the employees were afraid of us, so we had no problem getting in. Once on the grounds, we had lookouts that let us know if the cops were headed our way. If we got word, we'd screw, move to another section for a while—get something to eat, play a couple games of chance, whatever—then come back and shoot pool once the coast was clear again.

Like everything else, it was a routine that was getting old, but I went along anyway. This was my life and these guys were my crew, what could I do? If I was going nowhere fast, who better to go with than my best friends?

"Hey," I said to Aldo, leaning forward so he could hear me over the music. "I got to get an air conditioner. Promised my mother. She couldn't sleep last night."

"Hot as a fucker last night. Me and Candy couldn't sleep

either. Had to fuck the shit out of her a bunch of times until we were so spent we just kind of passed out. Blasted her in the face with a load so big, I actually kinda felt sorry for her."

Barely audible above the tunes, Fritz muttered, "His life is hell."

Aldo was the only one who didn't still live at home. He and his girlfriend Candy, a pretty blonde who managed a trendy clothing store at the mall, lived in a small bungalow owned by Aldo's uncle just outside the city. I'd have never admitted it to my mother, but she was right, Aldo's family *were* a bunch of criminals, and his Uncle Lou, in particular, was the worst of the lot. He had a hand in illegal activities all over the city, and connections to organized crime from Federal Hill in Providence all the way to the North End of Boston. I'd never had a whole lot of traffic with him, but I always liked the guy, and he'd always been nice to me. There were a lot of rumors about him, like he'd killed four guys when he was younger and earning his chops, or that one time he'd taken a guy's hand off with a hatchet for stealing from him, or that he could make one phone call and nobody'd ever see you again. According to Aldo, they were all true, and I had no reason to believe otherwise.

"Seriously," I said, "I got to get a hold of one today."

"No problem. We'll go see Chuckie D. later."

I sat back. "Cool."

A minute later, we pulled into the enormous parking lot. Dino parked and activated his car alarm. Rides like his were stolen all the time, and while anyone who knew Dino would never intentionally go anywhere near his car, most of the punks from Fall River, or beyond, who sometimes came this way to scour the area for potential jacks, didn't know him from a hole in the wall. So even with his reputation, their ignorance made him as vulnerable to those types as anyone else. Whenever he parked somewhere, it was a roll of the dice. Maybe his car would be there when we got back, maybe not. Usually at The Park it was safe, as enough people knew who the car belonged to, but there were no guarantees.

The Park already smelled like food. All the vendors were open and the hamburgers, hotdogs, fries, onion rings, and sausages with peppers and onions were grilling, the pizza was baking and the clams and scallops were frying, all of it wafting into the air and filling the area with the smell of greasy delicious. Little further on, the smells turned sweet from cotton candy whipping into pink clouds, recently prepared funnel cakes, ice cream delights and an array of other standard amusement park eats. We were all hungry, so we stopped at one of the booths we frequented and sat on the stools lining the front counter.

An eel-thin guy with leathery skin and a bulbous red nose we knew only as Pal ran the stand. A grumpy and grizzled old guy who'd worked there since forever, he manned the grill in whites and a paper hat, while a couple teenage girls waited on customers.

Aldo took the stool next to me and plucked a toothpick from a small plastic container on the counter. "Whaddaya say, Pal?"

Eighty if he was a day, Pal glanced over at us then waved with his spatula. Could never tell if he was saying hello or telling us to fuck off, and since his expression never changed there was no way to know for sure. Blinking his beady, deep-seated eyes, he scratched absently at his nose—which looked like some sort of mangled, giant red pepper—then returned his attention to the grill.

On summer days like this, things got busy early, and there was already a decent-sized crowd moving around. "Already hoppin'," I said, spinning my stool away from the counter so I could watch the passersby.

"Christ, it's hot," Dino groaned. "Makes me feel like fuckin' some shit up."

"Relax," Aldo said. "We'll get somethin' to eat, go shoot some pool and hang out a while, see what's what, then maybe we'll hit the beach."

"Hoi Richie!"

I spun back toward the counter. A girl our age stood with a small pad in her hand, her dark hair piled high on her head and held in place with a hairnet. Shawna Delgado. We went to high school together. Hooked up a few times at parties and dances sophomore year, but never officially dated or anything. By junior year Mariana and I were going steady, so messing around with Shawna was over before it ever got serious. Had never been an issue, really, but Shawna still had the hots for me and was anything but subtle about showing it. As the other guys realized who it was and did little to hide their laughter, I smiled and said, "Hey, Shawna. I didn't know you worked here."

"Just for the summer. Goin' to beauty school in September up in Boston. I got to go a year—just days—then I'm out, licensed and workin'!"

"So, like hairdressin' and makeup and shit?"

"Yeah, all that." Shawna batted her eyes at me. She always wore heavy eyeliner and gobs of mascara, which made her eyelashes look like inky little wings fluttering all around. "So, what you been up to?"

"Same old shit. You know how it is."

"Yeah. I heard you and Mariana broke up, huh?"

"While ago. She went to college and all, so, you know."

"Me and Bobby split up too." She let that information hang in the air between us for a while, before adding, "So done with that dick-weed. Actually, I'm not seein' nobody right now."

"Hoi Shawna," Aldo said suddenly, laughing as he mocked her accent.

She gave him a quick sideways glance and cracked the gum she was chomping on with a loud pop, his imitation of her going right by her. *"Hoi* Aldo," she said absently.

"Think maybe you could stop eye-humpin' the shit out of Richie long enough to take our order? We're freakin' starvin' over here."

The other guys laughed, but Shawna remained unfazed, staring at me like she was dying of thirst and I was a glass of ice water. "How about you, Richie?" she asked. "You seein' anybody?"

"Yeah," Aldo answered for me, "Mary Palmer and her five sisters."

Shawna winced then glared at him. "You're so gross, Aldo."

"*You're so gross, Aldo*," he mimicked.

"Come on, enough fuckin' around!" Dino slapped a beefy hand on the counter. "Four cheeseburgers with everything, large onion ring, large fry and four chocolate frappes."

Shawna jotted everything down, tore the slip from her pad and attached it to a spinning carousel contraption suspended between the counter and grill area. There were no other customers, so she made her way back to the counter.

"Workin' 'til six tonight," she told me. "Wanna do somethin' later?"

"Hey, Pal!" Aldo called to him. "Do somethin' about your employees, will ya? We're tryin' to have a conversation here."

He flipped a couple burgers, grumbled something about napkins then waved his spatula in the air again like a demented orchestra conductor.

"Anyways, I'll be around after," she told me with a wink.

"Cool. I don't really know if I will be, but if I am I'll come by and see what you're doing, all right?"

"Okay, Richie." She smiled wide, popped her gum again, then flipped Aldo off. Grabbing an empty silver holder from the counter, she brought it to an area behind the grill and began filling it with fresh napkins.

I looked at Aldo. He was still laughing. "What?" I said, trying not to laugh myself and feeling like a shit. "She's all right, she just likes me is all."

"Shawna likes everybody, bro," he chuckled. "She fucking *loves* you."

"What do you mean she likes everybody?"

"Dude, she's a slam-pig from way back."

I looked to the stool on the other side of me. Until he'd spoken, I hadn't even realized Fritz was sitting there. "That's cold, man. She's not that bad."

"Good thing you never fucked her," Dino said.

"Just fooled around a few times, was never anything serious."

"Don't never fuck that broad, dude," Dino warned. "She's so fuckin' hot for you she'll put those legs in the air first chance she gets. She'll lie, too, tell you she's on the pill or whatever. You'll get a look at that wet pussy, she'll be layin' there beggin' for your pecker and all of a sudden you got her feet behind her ears and you're bangin' that bitch like a porn star. Next thing you know, she's fuckin' pregnant and wantin' you to marry her ass. And that'll be that."

"Fuck you guys," I laughed. "Any one of you'd nail her ass in a heartbeat."

"We could get away with it," Dino said. "She don't want no kids with us."

"She don't want kids with me either, idiot. She just wants to hang out."

"She's-ah nice-ah girl-ah who wants-ah some-ah salami!" Aldo said in a bad Italian accent, laughing and spinning back and forth on his stool like a little kid on a sugar high. "*Hoi Richie! Hoi Richie!* Jesus Christ, imagine havin' to listen to that every fuckin' day?"

I shook my head, tried to ignore him. "Seriously, fuck is wrong with you?"

"Better get comfy," Fritz quipped. "It's a long list."

Aldo jerked a thumb at him. "Yeah, okay. Stevie Wonder's bustin' balls."

"The lights hurt my eyes. I'm handicapped, you fuckin' testicle."

"Only handicap you got is being a mental retard with a thumb dick."

"Sure, pick on the slow kid with the tiny meat."

Due to his quick wit and dry, often self-deprecating sense of humor, Francis "Fritz" Kohler was virtually impossible to make fun of, but even after all the years they'd known each other, Aldo never stopped trying. When it came to the sunglasses, Fritz claimed he wore them simply because he wanted to, and because he wore contact lenses and had really sensitive eyes. Truth was, he looked cool and kind of mysterious in them, but the real reason he wore them was to hide his eyes, not protect them. He had peepers the color of emeralds, and they were actually strikingly beautiful. I'm talking about the kind of eyes that are so pretty you can't stop looking at them. Only Fritz didn't want to be pretty. Those eyes were the first thing you noticed when he walked in a room, and with the blond hair and fair skin he didn't exactly give off a tough guy vibe. And in our neighborhood, that could be an issue. For years, as a kid, he took huge amounts of shit about his eyes. Right around eighth grade, he started covering them with sunglasses whenever he could. By high school, he wore them pretty much all the time, and since then the things never came off. I couldn't even remember the last time I'd seen him without them.

Dino was third-generation American, Aldo and I were second, but Fritz's family had been in the country since the 1800s. He claimed one of his great-grandfathers had been some sort of outlaw gunman in the Old West, but nobody knew if that was true. His father worked for the A&P supermarket chain, running the deli in one of their stores near Cape Cod. However he and Fritz's mother divorced when Fritz was little, so he didn't see much of him. They'd never been close. His mother was a lunch lady at one of the elementary schools in the city. Fritz lived in a modest apartment four blocks from mine, with her and her second husband, a fat mick cabbie named Shaughnessy. Fritz hated the guy and got into fistfights with him on a regular basis. Shaughnessy would throw him out, and Fritz's mother always took him back. Went on like that all through high school, and Fritz was always scheming, looking for an angle that would get him out of there for good. But until he could figure something else out, he needed the roof over his head.

"Funny, Ally, I didn't hear any complaints about my dick when your mom was sucking on it last night," Fritz said. "She kept saying how big and hard it was, how good it tasted in her slutty little mouth."

"In your fuckin' dreams maybe."

"The ones with your mother are my favorite."

"It doesn't count if it's just a dream, right?"

"Is that why you kept rubbin' my balls and tellin' me to go back to sleep?"

Thankfully, Shawna returned with our food, slapped cheeseburgers on paper plates in front of us then delivered our plastic baskets of fries and onion rings. Making sure the now-full napkin holder was ready for us as well, she hovered across from my stool, smiling at me. "Can I get you anything else, Richie?"

"Those frappes would be nice," Dino snarled. "Four chocolate ones if it's not too much fuckin' trouble."

She ignored him, just kept smiling at me.

"Maybe if we could just get those frappes," I said, smiling back.

"Comin' right up."

As she drifted off, the other guys burst out laughing through mouthfuls of cheeseburger, fries and onion rings. I felt bad for Shawna and was also a little embarrassed because I liked her, too. I didn't know her that well, but I knew her better than they did. She wasn't a bad person, and I was sure a lot of the things guys said about her probably weren't true.

Dino devoured his food the way he always did, killing his cheeseburger in three bites then grabbing handfuls of fries and onion rings and shoveling them in like the fucking things owed him money. By the time the frappes arrived, he was done eating, so he took his, stood up and drank it while watching the crowd.

"That boy eats like an animal," Fritz said in the most effeminate voice he could manage. "A *savage*, scary animal."

Aldo laughed, choked, and then spit out a mouthful of chewed lunch all over the pavement. A few people passing by gave him dirty looks, which only made him laugh harder and open his mouth wider so they could get a good look at the chewed food he hadn't swallowed yet. But Ma took offense, as Ma always did, and started after a middle-aged guy who'd stared with disapproval.

Before I could leave my stool, Aldo had taken him by the arm. "It's cool."

"You see that fuckin' guy?" He shook Aldo's hand loose.

"I was just goofin', man. Come on, relax, let's go shoot some pool."

Dino kept staring at the guy, who was now at least fifty feet away but checking back over his shoulder every few seconds. "Hey!" he called out to the man. "Yeah, you. You got a fuckin' problem, asshole?"

I ate faster.

"See?" Fritz sipped his frappe. "This is why we can't have nice things."

"Come on, man," Aldo said, guiding Dino back toward his stool but careful to not be too forceful about it. "Sit down and finish your drink, and we'll go shoot some pool. Fuck him, he's nothin', he ain't worth it. Don't worry about it."

Dino nodded, plunked down on a stool, and with his back to the stand, quietly finished his frappe like a kid who'd just been reprimanded by his dad.

Aldo flashed me a look of relief. It'd been close, and we all knew it. We also knew that was the kind of guy that'd probably land Dino in prison one day, because guys like that had no idea who they were messing with, and faced either serious injury or even death if he went off on them. Stupid bastard would've never known what hit him.

* * *

Unlike the rest of The Park, the pool hall wasn't frequented by the general public. It was the building most people glanced at and walked by quickly. There were no children in there, no families and very few outsiders. For the most part, the tables were occupied by regulars, guys and their girlfriends who'd been shooting pool there for years. It was a smoky joint The Park didn't seem to spend a whole lot of maintenance time on or pay attention to, a place where fights broke out all the time but were usually squashed afterwards, because while most of us weren't what I'd call close, we did know (or at least know of) one another, and at the end of the day, it was all about pecking order and respect.

We'd taken over as top dogs after the older guys ahead of us had either outgrown the place, stopped coming for other reasons, died or got locked up. No one handed it to us, though. We fought for it, earned it through violence and intimidation, because that's the way it was done and often the only thing guys like us (and them) understood. Our reign had lasted a couple years now, but it was always a relatively short-term gig. We were already on the way out at nineteen and twenty, and a whole new crop of young punks were lying in wait behind us, biding their time, hanging around and gradually making their mark, waiting for the right moment to either inherit the hall from us or to try to take it when and if they thought they saw an opening. It was no different than the streets we'd grown up on. Like swimming in shark-infested waters. Only we were sharks, too. You might not always get bit, but the chances were high it could happen at any time. Things could go from calm and friendly to explosive and brutally violent in the blink of an eye, and by the time most realized what was going down, they were already bloodied in the water. And blood in the water was a death that killed you slowly, left you wounded and vulnerable, and drew in more sharks looking to take you down and claim your little part of the sea. No matter how tough you were, every pack had their day, and ours was closing in. I could feel it even then, but I wasn't sure the other guys did. It sure as hell wasn't something you talked about or even openly acknowledged. You talked the talk and walked the walk until you decided it was time to move on or until somebody did it better and showed you the door.

Minute we slipped into the hall it was a bit cooler. Old fans ran in all the windows, and there were a few ceiling jobs working, too. Still hot and stuffy, but not as bad as outside. Even though it was early, a lot of the tables were already occupied. Black Sabbath tunes blared from a boom box on the snack bar counter on the back wall. Everybody acknowledged our arrival with nods or quick what's-ups, cool and controlled but respectful.

Experience had taught me to scope a room whether I was familiar with it or not. I'd been jumped more than once in my life so I'd developed a habit of checking out my surroundings thoroughly before settling in, no matter where I was. The others did the same. I locked on two things. First, a group of guys that didn't belong there. Four total, all white, all older than us, grimy biker types wearing jean jackets covered in patches, the sleeves cut off to showcase their heavily tattooed arms, and an insignia on the back that read: DEVIL RIDERS. Definitely out-of-towners, most likely from out of state and passing through, because I'd never heard of them. Good bet there were more of the skuzzy motherfuckers scattered all over The Park. Those types always had numbers.

Second, I saw our friend and sixth musketeer, Ray-Ray Smith, leaning against the far wall, the custom stick he always brought with him held behind his head and laid across his shoulders, like James Dean in *Giant*. Actually, Ray-Ray looked more like a cross between Rod Carew and Sugar Ray Leonard, only smaller. He was a laid-back, happy-go-lucky type. Until he wasn't. A former Golden Gloves bantamweight, Ray-Ray was known for quick hands and deadly accurate combinations that had left more than a few who thought they'd step to him unconscious in a pool of their own blood. A scar that began just below his hairline and snaked down across his cheek, over his jaw and halfway down his neck had come courtesy of a broken bottle a guy had nearly killed him with when he'd come home to find Ray-Ray on top of his wife a few years before. Ray-Ray was still in high school at the time, and the woman was in her thirties, some waitress from a diner in town Ray-Ray frequented. Ray-Ray knocked the guy so cold he was still goofy to this day. Smart, good-looking, and cool as the other side of the pillow, Ray-Ray was almost always in control and had a way with the ladies. But women were also his weakness, and often when it came to them, common sense and any smarts he had went straight out the window. He was the kind of guy that never had an ounce of fat on him and always looked ripped. In a tank top and shorts that showed off his thin but sculpted body, he saw us and nodded, then slid his eyes to the left, toward the bikers who were playing at the table in the center of the room. Our table. Anybody else would've cleared out the minute we walked in and handed the table over out of respect.

Not these assholes.

They'd seen us, too, and stopped playing long enough to laugh, mutter a few things to each other and then laugh again. They went right back to their game, making sure we understood how unimpressed they were with us.

I could almost hear Dino's rage building.

Ray-Ray casually scratched his scar, letting four fingers lay flat across his cheek for a couple seconds. That meant he was only aware of these four. No more of them in the bathroom or any who had come then gone and would probably be coming back any time. Once we'd seen that signal, he switched to two fingers then dropped his hand to his side and gave his hip a nonchalant pat, indicating a couple of them had small lengths of chain dangling from their sides in a loop. Then he slowly reached around behind him to his back, brought his hand back around and raised a single finger. One of them had a switchblade in the back of his belt. Ray-Ray returned his hand to the cue and looked away, as if nothing had transpired between us at all.

"The fuck are these clowns?" Dino growled.

"Anybody packin'?" Aldo asked quietly.

"Brass," Fritz said.

"Nobody get hot." Aldo shook his arms loose. "Not yet."

Dino was already frothing. "That's our goddamn table."

"Just stay cool. Let me try talkin' to them first."

"Yeah, good idea." Fritz smirked. "They look reasonable."

Aldo ignored him and turned to me instead. Gone was the silly kid spinning on a stool and acting the fool. He was our leader again. Just like that. "Richie," he said, "you come with me. Fritz, you and Ma go hang with Ray-Ray so they know we're together, makes it five against four. And watch the door for any more of these fucks."

They did as they were told, and so did I.

Aldo and I approached the table, slowly drifting across the room and coming up on them easy and laid back. Everyone else playing understood what was happening and either ignored the situation completely and kept playing and minding their own business or decided it was time to go and hurried out in case things got bad.

The head honcho biker, a guy with a long, unkempt red beard, a bandana and a huge gut, finished his shot then turned and acknowledged that we were there. "Yeah?" he said in a gruff voice.

"How you doin'?" Aldo asked, expressionless.

"I'm tryin' to play some pool, kid, you want something?"

"You almost done with the table?"

He squared his stance, his stick held in front of him, the butt end touching the floor. "We'll be done whenever we're fuckin' done. What do you give a shit? Fifteen other tables in here."

"Thing is, though, that one's ours."

They all laughed like that was the funniest shit they'd ever heard.

"You got some balls on you, boy," Honcho said, smiling with a set of broken and crooked brown teeth. He glanced over at Dino, Fritz and Ray-Ray long enough to let them know he was aware of them as well. "So, what we got here, huh? Few wops, whatever the fuck that asshole in the sunglasses is supposed to be and a skinny little nigger? That's it?"

Aldo and I stared at him.

"Look," Aldo said, the tone of his voice alerting me that he was running out of patience, "you guys finish your game and then we'll take the table and you can use another one, all right?"

Honcho leaned forward, as if we wouldn't be able to hear him otherwise. "Fuck off, Guido. And take these faggots with you, before you get hurt."

Over at the snack bar, the kid working it quietly locked the door on his little booth and pulled the security grate down over the counter. He got himself a Coke then watched through the grate to see what would happen next.

I didn't want to be there. I didn't give a shit about the table anymore. Few years before, I would've died to get it back. Now, I just wanted to get the hell out of there and do something—anything—else. But that wasn't going to happen any more than these dickheads were going to hand us our table, and that left only one way, one response. There couldn't be any other. People were watching, and if we let this slide we'd never recover from it. Those waiting to take our place would come out of the fucking woodwork to take runs at us, figuring we'd lost our will to fight for what was ours.

Subtly as I could, I quickly sized up the other three guys, looking for strengths and weaknesses. Like Honcho, two of them looked to be in their middle-to-late thirties. The other guy looked closer to fifty, thin but well-muscled, his silver hair pulled back into a long ponytail. In a leather vest with nothing under it, his chest and stomach were covered with numerous old and faded tattoos. A long bulge in his jeans, along his outer calf, let me know there was likely a knife, maybe even a gun, in his boot. Ray-Ray had missed that. The other two guys were bigger, not as big as Honcho, but good-sized, tall and rugged, men who had been brawling and kicking ass since we were in elementary school.

Aldo flashed Honcho his best shark grin and narrowed his eyes, but didn't say anything for several seconds. We all stood our ground, Black Sabbath screeching on the boom box behind us. And then, finally, Aldo leaned in just as Honcho had, and said, "Only ones about to get hurt in here are you and your girlfriends, you fat filthy cunt."

Like these things always did, it happened blink-of-the-eye fast, everything exploding at once and smashing together in a whirlwind of violence and mayhem.

Someone cranked the boom box just as Honcho swung the stick at Aldo's head. He ducked under it easily and hit him with an uppercut, a left hook and a straight right. Honcho's head snapped back as he stumbled away, his lower back hitting the pool table as a ribbon of blood flew through the air from his mouth. Aldo closed on him, leading with an elbow, swinging it around into his mouth. The guy's head snapped back again. This time he spit Chiclets.

Someone yelled something, then there was a flash of movement.

From the corner of my eye, I saw Dino fly through the air and kick one of the guys in the center of his chest, just as Fritz and Ray-Ray charged the other two.

The guy Dino kicked somersaulted backwards over the table and rolled off the other side, as I closed on Honcho from one side and Aldo got him from the other. I threw a right that caught him on the jaw, but he absorbed it without much trouble, and he and Aldo were suddenly wrestling, turning and spinning and throwing punches in a dervish. I closed, kicked my heel into the side of his knee as hard as I could.

He cried out and toppled over as his leg snapped. Didn't

matter how big or how tough a guy was, just like a clean shot in the balls, you kicked out their knee and down they went, usually crying like a little kid, because it shattered the knee and hurt like a motherfucker. Whatever fight was in a guy, once you kicked his knee out, it evaporated.

As Honcho fell, Aldo followed him, raining punches down on him, and then kicks. I joined him, kicking away with everything I had, my mind and vision blurred, everything working on instinct and experience.

Fritz cried out, fell nearby and slid along the floor, clutching his ear, which was bloodied. I spun, saw the older guy closing on me.

Next thing I knew, a sunburst exploded before my eyes and everything went dark. When I could see again, just a second or two later, I realized I was on the floor, too, and the old bastard was standing over me, his pool cue raised up over his head and on its way to my skull.

I brought a leg up into his crotch, and he doubled over and dropped the cue. Gave me time to scramble out from under him and up onto my knees.

As I did, another flash of color and blurred movement came at me from the right, followed by an impact that reverberated along my jaw and up into my temple. A sharp stabbing pain took the same route, settling behind my ear.

I fell over, rolled away and somehow regained my feet. My head was spinning, and the fucker that hit me was bearing down on me like a runaway train. Behind him, Dino screamed and lifted a guy into the air, slamming him down on the side of the pool table like he was tossing around a little kid.

I threw two punches, landed one. It stopped the guy long enough for me to circle to his side and clear my head a little. Adrenaline and instinct took the reins, and I bounced on the balls of my feet, faked another punch then kicked the guy in the side of the head.

It connected with his temple and fucked up his equilibrium.

He couldn't keep his balance. Looking at me, stunned, he staggered a little, then swung at me wildly just before he fell over onto his side.

Instead of getting the hell out of the way, I stood there admiring my work, and the looping punch connected, hitting me square in the nose. Pain exploded across my face and up under both eyes. I could already feel the blood coming from both nostrils, even as I took a couple steps forward and kicked the fuck in the side until he lay flat and went still.

To my left, Fritz was back on his feet, holding the older guy while Ray-Ray let loose with a furious series of combinations to his midsection and face.

I turned, saw Aldo was still stomping Honcho, working his other leg and midsection now. The biker was covered in blood and trying to crawl away, but Aldo stayed on him, stomping so bad I was afraid he might kill the sack of shit.

The music softened and groans of pain and heavy breathing aside, an eerie quiet fell over the hall. All four bikers lay either unconscious or unable to get up, bloodied and beaten.

"Everybody all right?" Aldo asked, winded. Not a mark on him.

"Fuckin' pussies!" Ma screamed, fists still clenched, eyes still wild. He had blood all over him, none of it his.

Fritz was bleeding from his right ear, where one of the bikers had evidently ripped his earring out, but was otherwise none the worse for wear. Ray-Ray was covered in sweat, spattered with biker blood and fine except for a couple bloody scratches, one on his neck, the other on his face. He smiled at me, nodded.

I nodded back, wiped my nose. My hand came back bloody.

"You good?" Aldo asked me.

"Yeah. I'm all right."

The kid at the snack bar lifted the grate, put five bottles of Coke on the counter. Fritz grabbed them, handed them out.

Suddenly Dino lunged forward. He'd seen the old biker stir, reach for his boot.

I called out, "He's packin'!"

Ma had hold of him before he could get whatever was in there out. Taking him by the throat with one hand, Dino lifted up and onto his feet.

The guy was so wobbly he couldn't stay up under his own power, so Dino held him upright by the throat and punched him in the face with his other hand. By the third shot, the guy had gone completely limp and unconscious.

Dino threw him back onto the pool table and the guy collapsed there like he was dead. His chest rose and fell slowly, so at least he was still breathing, but he wouldn't be right for a while.

Dino lifted the guy's leg, yanked his jeans up over his boot, reached inside and pulled out a long military style knife. He let the guy's leg go, held the blade up before him and studied it, turning it slowly beneath the dull fluorescent lights overhead. "Cool," he muttered, stuffing it into his belt.

"Make your call," Aldo said to the kid in the snack bar. "We weren't here."

"I didn't see shit," the kid said. "They must've fell or something."

Aldo motioned to the door and started back across the hall. We followed, soldiering behind him in single-file until we were back out in the sunshine.

Without a word, we disappeared into the safety of the crowd.

Five minutes away, in a Mobile station bathroom, I stood before the grimy mirror checking myself out. A bruise was already forming along my jaw, and it hurt when I moved it, clicked a little, but it was nothing serious. I got my nosebleed under control by jamming toilet paper into both nostrils and pinching the bridge for a couple minutes. I got my old man's nose, an Italian nose. Real Roman honker. Not exactly an Irish pug, if you get my drift. Thing is, by the time I was nineteen it'd been broken in fights so many times there was hardly any cartilage left. If I wanted to, I could press my nose down flat against my face, like a boxer. And there was a bump at the top of the bridge, courtesy of a baseball bat I got cracked with in a fight when I was sixteen. Doctor told me since it never healed right, it wouldn't ever go away. I didn't care about any of that, really, but I was a bleeder, too. I hardly ever got cuts; it was my nose that bled at the drop of a hat. One shot—wouldn't even have to be a hard one—and it started gushing.

Light spilled in from outside as the bathroom door swung open and Aldo sauntered in. He'd taken off his leather jacket. His white tank top was specked with blood. "You all right?" he asked, sidling up next to me at the sinks.

I pulled the toilet paper out of my nose. It was sopped with blood, but the bleeding had stopped, so I tossed it into a nearby trash bin and tried taking the toilet paper out of my other nostril. That side was still leaking, so I stuffed the tissue back up there. "Yeah," I said, "Just my nose."

"Caught ya good, huh?"

"Couple times. One of those fuckers hit like a brick, dude."

"Those lame-ass fucks?" He smiled at me in the mirror. "What, you slippin'?"

I shrugged. "Maybe."

"Don't sweat it," he said, playfully smacking me on the shoulder. "I'm just messin' with you. Thanks for the help back there. That fat bastard was strong, dude. You didn't take his knee out I'd still be rollin' around with the smelly fuck."

"Don't worry about it. How's Fritz's ear doing?"

"It's ripped up pretty good, but he'll be okay. Good lesson for him, man. How many times have I told that stupid bastard to take his earrings out if we're in a spot where shit could go down? How many times, Richie?"

I nodded. It was a lot. Although Fritz was the only one who had both ears pierced, we all had earrings, too, we just didn't wear them to The Park or other places where a fight might break out.

"Come on, let's get out of here," he said. "Place smells like ass cheese."

"I'll be right out, got to take a piss."

Aldo left me alone in the bathroom. I tried pulling the toilet paper again. The bleeding had stopped. I threw it aside and did my best to avoid making eye contact with myself in the mirror. Didn't work.

I looked like shit. And I felt worse. I held my hands up to the mirror. Skin broken, knuckles and fingers and wrists sore and pulsing, throbbing. What the fuck was I doing? I felt like going home, maybe read a while, escape to Falesá or sit up on the roof with Woody and get so high I didn't have to think about anything else.

Then again, maybe that was no better than this. Couldn't be sure anymore. Everything felt wrong. Hopeless. So when it was all said and done, what the hell difference did it make?

Not so long ago, this was me, this was my life, and while I always hoped for something different, I was okay with it. Sometimes I even reveled in it. And then somewhere along the line, things changed. I guess I changed. Things that never bothered me before ate away at me now. Things I'd found funny didn't make me laugh anymore, they just made me feel worse. Things it never occurred to me to question, now made me question *everything*. Maybe I was still changing. Gradually, the way night swallowed day. Maybe that's why I hadn't really noticed until lately. Same way it was dark before you knew it, the light gone before you realized it was dying. Maybe this part of me was on the way out, just like the light. But if that was true, then what was waiting in the dark to replace it?

I stared into my sad, glassy eyes reflected back at me in the dingy mirror.

Nothing, I thought. *Not a goddamn thing.*

* * *

We spent the next hour or so at the beach in Westport. Dino stripped down to his boxers like it was no big deal, made his way through the crowd, then crashed the surf, diving into the heavy incoming waves Horseneck Beach was known for. Ray-Ray peeled off his tank top and tucked it into his shorts, and the rest of us were down to our jeans. We sat on benches between the parking lot and start of the sand, letting the sun wash over us and the fresh sea air fill our lungs as we gawked at the girls in bikinis. Before long Ray-Ray was strutting across the sand to talk to a couple girls he'd been exchanging smiles with for a while. There were worse ways to spend a few hours in the summer, and if nothing else, everyone was cool. For once even Dino didn't seem to be looking for a fight. Minding his own business, he splashed around in the ocean, laughing as he met the crashing waves head-on, one after the next, diving into them again and again with the abandon and enthusiasm of a child.

"You all right?" I asked Fritz.

He'd finally gotten his earlobe to stop bleeding, but he'd thrown up twice at the gas station. "I'll live," he said. "One of those fuckers caught me with a couple good body shots. Right in the stomach. Didn't exactly go with the pile of Pal's fine cuisine already sittin' there, know what I mean?"

I nodded, pushed my hair back off my face. Like Aldo, I wore it a little long, almost to my shoulders, and in the direct sun and heat it had already gotten sweaty and tangled. "Anybody get a hold of Petie?"

"Yeah," Aldo answered, a pair of mirrored sunglasses covering his eyes so he could check out the women without getting caught. "Was a phone at the Mobile, had Ma call and tell him to stay clear of The Park for today. He said he'd catch up to us later."

I watched the people on the beach a while. Lots of families. White bread yuppie motherfuckers mostly. Made me wonder how they did it, how they got the lives they had, lives they seemed to take for granted.

"Hey," Aldo said, elbowing me and leaning in closer, "need to talk to you later. I got a thing."

"Yeah, all right. Don't forget about the air conditioner."

"I won't. We'll talk about it when we go get it, cool?"

"Cool."

He got up and stretched a little, showing off his physique in case any of the girls nearby were interested. "Check out Ray-Ray working these two bimbos," he said. "Five bucks says the sonofabitch fucks them both."

"May as well just give you the fin now," Fritz said.

"Gonna go see if I can get in on this action."

He left Fritz and me on the bench. I was still sore and knew Fritz wasn't feeling great either. "Could've lived without that rumble today," I said.

"They had it coming. Fuckin' wimps."

"I guess."

"You see Ma pick that one dude up and body slam him on the table? Jesus, thought he broke the guy's back." Fritz laughed lightly, shook his head. "Fuckin' animal."

"You ever get tired of all this shit, Fritzy?" The words left my mouth before I could stop them, and I immediately wished I hadn't said anything.

He didn't answer right away. When he did, he said, "I'm not even twenty for another two months, and I'm already running out of time. Won't be able to run around and do whatever I want forever, probably not even much longer. We're young and about as free as we're ever gonna be, Richie. Right here. Right now. Nobody tells us what to do, and we run the shit we want to run. It's fucked up, sometimes, I know, but at least it's ours. This is the only time our lives will be like this. Not too long, we'll be just like everybody else. Living in a shit place with a shit wife and shit kids, working a shit job for shit money and dragging our asses through shit lives. And that's if we're lucky. Most of us probably won't even have it that good. Look around.

Up the block, down the hall. Look. Nothing's hidin'. It's all right there. I don't know about you, man, but I'm in no hurry to get there."

In all the years I'd known him that was probably the most he'd ever said to me in one sitting. "You're an uplifting bastard, you know that?"

"Just sayin', I'm hangin' on to this as long as I can."

"Some days I'm not sure what *this* is anymore."

"That's deep. Very poetic. Don't go getting all goofy on me, Rich, huh?"

"Just keep wonderin' if it's worth hangin' on to so tight, you know?"

"What else is there? You gonna join the fuckin' circus? Be an astronaut?" He adjusted his sunglasses enough to wipe some sweat from beneath his eyes. "Remember when we were little kids and they'd tell us we could be anything we wanted to be, have any kind of life we wanted? They lied. It was bullshit. You get the hand you're dealt. That's it."

"Sounds great," I said through a heavy sigh.

"It's the life we got, Richie. That's all. No more, no less."

I closed my eyes, felt the sun wash over my face and chest as a warm wind blew in off the Atlantic, only making everything hotter, stickier, deadlier.

The heat had the whole city on edge, ready to blow. At least here, in the open, at the ocean, away from the confined spaces and concrete, the heatwave didn't feel quite as threatening.

When I opened my eyes, I was alone on the bench. Fritz was gone. He'd left without saying anything more and joined Aldo and Ray-Ray over on the sand, talking up the two beach bunnies.

I was on a beach with hundreds of people, and I'd never felt more alone.

* * *

"Get on the clock," Dino said, as he approached, drying himself off with his shirt. "Aldo and Ray-Ray got those two whores to invite us back to their house. Lakeville, bro, they got a pool and everything. Parents are at work until tonight. You know what that means."

It meant they'd scored a couple naïve teenage girls whose parents had money and a nice house in a nice town. It also meant while Aldo and Ray-Ray were fucking them, Dino and Fritz and I would rob them blind. Then Aldo and Ray-Ray would leave the girls, claiming they had to go to the bathroom, slip out of the house, join us in the waiting car, and we'd all get the hell out of there. By the time they realized what happened, we'd be back in the city getting paid. I threw my T-shirt on, dropped the cigarette I'd been smoking to the ground and stepped on it. My shirt stuck to me like a second skin, already wet with perspiration.

"They're riding with the girls in their car," Dino said. "You, me and Fritzy'll follow them in mine. Come on, let's go."

"Yeah," I said, looking around. "Okay."

It was a little over a thirty-mile drive from Westport to Lakeville, but both cars flew, so about twenty minutes or so later, we pulled into a driveway that led to a big, beautiful house set back from the road in a heavily wooded area. The closest neighbors were quite a distance away on either side, so it was perfect.

"Will you look at this," Dino muttered as we pulled in. "Jackpot."

"Fritz," I said, "there's always alarm systems in places like this, so make sure you check it out. Probably no cameras, but be sure, inside and out."

"Got it."

"And remember, no real names, don't forget and slip. All five of us will be riding back together, so there won't be any room in the car, and the trunk's not that big. Keep it to smaller shit. Small appliances and electronics, jewelry, cash."

We watched as Aldo and Ray-Ray got out of the other car,

trailing behind the two girls. Dino made a weird guttural sound and fiddled with his crotch.

"Jesus Christ, look at the ass on the shorter one. We should pull a train."

I put a hand on his shoulder. Not hard, but with enough force to get his attention. "Don't lose your shit, Ma. We're here to work. They're the ones fuckin' this time around, not us. They fuck, we shop. Got it? Eyes on the prize."

He looked at me as if he hadn't quite grasped what I was saying, but then it seemed to dawn on him and for a second or two I thought he was pissed and might grab me. Instead, a smile slowly broke across his face. "Okay, Richie," he said. "Whatever you say, buddy."

I slid my sunglasses on. "Behave yourself, you fuckin' degenerate."

He laughed maniacally and climbed out of the car.

Few minutes later, we were all sitting around an inground, kidney-shaped pool and having beers the girls raided from their parents' fridge. Ray-Ray was a huge cokehead and always had some on him. So after everyone got comfortable, he produced a small vial, laid out a few lines on the patio table, then he and Aldo and both girls snorted them. Dino did a huge cannonball into the pool while Fritz and I hung back, stretched out on chaise lounges in the sun.

The girls. Kristen and Amanda. Couple Catholic high school kids. Went to Bishop Stang over in Dartmouth. Both sixteen—almost seventeen they told us—between their sophomore and junior years. They were almost too perfect.

We'd pulled this scam a bunch of times before, and the marks were always the same. Money kids like this who wanted to be naughty and cut loose, run around with some bad boys for a thrill, spoiled brats who thought the world revolved around them, who'd been told their whole lives they were special and beautiful and better than everybody else, smugly convinced we were poor and stupid punks following them around like puppies hoping for a few scraps.

They never saw us coming, and these two were no different. Couple young girls in skimpy bikinis trying too hard to convince us what bad-asses they were, drinking and doing coke and claiming they did this sort of thing all the time, when in reality it'd probably been the first time they'd even seen coke, much less done any.

I drank the beer they gave me and tuned out. I didn't listen to their stupid stories, their incessant giggling or laugh at their jokes. They were both cute and had nice bodies, but acted like the high school kids they were, a couple squirts getting back at daddy by fucking a black guy and his guinea buddy from the wrong side of the tracks or whatever the fuck it was these types did. Even though I was only four years older than they were, the difference between sixteen and twenty was a hell of a divide. Almost as wide as our lifestyles. These were girls who skied in the winter, went to dance class and gymnastics, little princesses whose parents catered to their every whim. They had fancy parties for their birthdays and got extravagant gifts, cars and trips when they graduated high school, beautiful holidays with big decorated Christmas trees surrounded by brightly-wrapped presents, spreads of food and desserts and drinks on long, beautiful dining room tables like in the movies and stockings hanging from the fireplace. They had allowances and went on elaborate family vacations. They went to good colleges and partied on spring break in Florida, graduated and married men just like them, lived privileged lives and raised little bastards and bitches just like they were. I didn't hate them, but I didn't envy them either. They were alien to me, strange exotic creatures I had no connection to. We may as well have been different species. And in a way, we were. For them, we were the same, a distraction, slumming for fun to see what it was like to break the rules and run with guys like us. Only they had no idea who guys like us were. Not really. We were *things* to them, a dime a dozen, lesser beings both disposable and transient, nothing to take seriously or place any real importance in.

What they didn't know—what these types *never* knew—was that we felt exactly the same way about them.

Fritz had asked where the bathroom was earlier then gone inside. When he came back and sat down next to me, he said, "There's an alarm system with a keypad but it's not armed. No cameras in or out. Gorgeous fuckin' house. We're golden, Pony Boy."

I nodded, sipped my beer and tried not to laugh.

A Billy Ocean tune blared from a giant boom box on the counter of a tiki bar on the far side of the pool. Kristen, a petite brunette and the shorter of the two, was joking and laughing loudly with Aldo, who made sure she finished one beer then started right in on the next. Meanwhile, Amanda, a taller, curvy blonde, did another line of coke with Ray-Ray and started dancing by herself, shaking her ass, bouncing her tits and swinging her head back and forth, her long blonde hair flying around, wild and free.

Dino came up out of the pool, dripping wet in the sunshine, dressed only in his boxers, his comically giant cock visible and partially erect through the thin fabric as he eyed the girls and made his way back over to us.

"Jesus Christ," Fritz muttered, "can somebody buy this motherfucker a bathing suit so we don't have to see his dick floppin' around every goddamn summer?"

I chuckled but was worried about keeping Ma under control, so I gave Aldo the eye first chance I got, and he responded with a subtle nod.

Ray-Ray moved in behind Amanda, put his hands on her waist and grinded against her ass, his hands moving around and onto her stomach, pulling her closer. She fell back into him, grinding along with him, then slowly spun so they were facing each other. They began to kiss, and Ray-Ray slowly walked her back toward the sliding doors off the patio. In seconds, they'd disappeared inside the house.

One down.

Dino looked at me, started laughing and pointed to his dick, which was now fully erect and poking out through the fly in his boxers.

I shook my head, fired a towel at him. "Fuckin' asshole."

Aldo and Kristen were on the far side of the pool talking, and I could tell he was trying to get her to go with him as well, but she was holding back. This was her house, not Amanda's, but I didn't get the sense that was the problem. She looked more like she was chickening out and had maybe changed her mind about letting things go so far.

"Fuck's he doing?" Dino grumbled, wrapping the towel around him as he dropped down into a chaise lounge. "I'll take her ass in there if he wants to switch. Trust me, once I get her in and she sees *my* meat—"

"Be cool."

"—and his great big fireman's hat, she'll—"

"I said be cool."

He grabbed his erection, which was tenting the towel, and squeezed it. "I'm telling you, man—"

"Ma, just sit there and shut up before she hears you."

Dino frowned, laid back and let himself go. "Okay, okay."

I couldn't have stopped him, but there was a pecking order. Aldo was our leader, but then came me, and just like everyone else, Dino knew, accepted and respected that. There had to be order or everyone just did what they wanted, and that's how you got caught, how you made mistakes. So we waited. We nursed our beers and acted like we were enjoying ourselves.

Aldo kept working her, kissing her now and then, running a hand along her shoulder and down onto her waist, leaning in and whispering things in her ear. She'd giggle or smile but after several minutes they still hadn't gone anywhere.

The Billy Ocean song ended, segued into Madonna's "Lucky Star."

"Oh my *God*!" Kristen said, jumping to her feet. "I *love* this song!"

Seizing the opportunity, Aldo took her by the hand and started dancing with her. She responded, dancing close to him. When her back was to us Aldo gave us a knowing smile and a wink.

Madonna wrapped and was followed by Bananarama, which thankfully—oh my God—Kristen loved, too. Halfway through the song, Aldo got another line of coke into her, and by the time it was over, a fresh beer. She was staggering more than dancing by the time Prince was singing about crying doves, and Aldo slowly led her inside, assuring her everything would be okay, that they could just go to her room and talk a while.

Two down.

We gave it another five minutes.

Then we went to work.

CHAPTER THREE

I never liked stealing, but that didn't always stop me from doing it. I didn't feel good about it, never did, but I didn't give it much thought beyond the basics of the moment either. In the jungle we lived in, if something was there for the taking, and you didn't grab it, someone else would. Later, in the dark, when it was just you and whatever gods you did or didn't believe in, you could ask for forgiveness or rationalize almost anything. Didn't make it right, might have even made it worse, but that was one of the beautiful things about the dark. You could hide almost anything in it, including yourself, and after a while, all those things stayed hidden, even in the light.

Night hadn't fallen yet, but the day was almost over by the time we got to Chuckie D's place. He was a fence we'd gone to high school with and known for years. A guy that wore his blond hair combed straight back off his hawkish face and held in place with generous amounts of styling gel, rings on every finger, lots of gold chains, designer jeans, pastel T-shirts, white leather loafers and white dinner jackets with the sleeves rolled up, Chuckie was a hardcore criminal, extremely violent when necessary or angered, and generally crazier than a shithouse rat. But he was also someone we could trust and do business with. Later that same year, in September, the classic TV series *Miami Vice* would debut on NBC, and across the country, people would start dressing like its stars. Chuckie always took credit for the fashion trend, though, because he'd dressed like that since high school, years before the series had been invented or aired, and claimed the show ripped off his image and should therefore pay him royalties. Although he never did anything of the sort, he always said he was going to sue the show's creator and then go find Don Johnson and kick his ass. That was Chuckie. Nuts. But the best fence in the city.

He ran his business in an old and otherwise abandoned warehouse. Near the south end of the city, it had once been part of a larger cluster of buildings that constituted one of the numerous manufacturing companies in town. Empty for years, the surrounding area was a perfect buffer and hid his enterprise well. Besides, Chuckie had a deal with the bank that owned the place, paid them and the cops to operate without interference, kicked up what the mob boys needed to look the other way every month, and as a result, had himself a solid and very profitable business. Important, since he was also a degenerate gambler with a thousand-dollar-a-day cocaine habit and a penchant for banging expensive call girls four at a time, all of which required a good deal of continuous capital.

That night we found him zooming on coke, bouncing off the walls even more than usual as he wandered through his inventory, a clipboard in one hand and a pen in the other. A senior when we were freshmen, Chuckie was a few years older than us and into his twenties, but his lifestyle was already starting to take a toll on him. He looked ten years older than he was.

While the others waited in the car, once we were cleared by the goon working the entrance, Aldo and I went in with the merchandise. Chuckie smiled the minute he saw us, tucking his clipboard under his arm and extending his hand while still several feet away.

"Ally Genaro," he said with a wide smile. "How's it hangin', you piece of dog shit?"

"Low and to the right." Aldo took his hand and they shook. "Just the way you left it, Sally."

Chuckie put the clipboard down atop of a large box marked:

BLENDERS, and manically rubbed at his runny nose, as coke-heads tended to do. Once he'd finished with Aldo, he looked to me. We couldn't shake because I was holding a stack of electronics, so he gave me a playful slug in the shoulder. "How are you, Richie?"

"What do you say, Chuckie?"

"I say, nice as it is to see you mook bastards, you're not here to diddle my gonads, am I right? Let's do some busy-biz."

"I got two VCRs, really good shape," I told him, "and stereo components, amplifier, tuner, turntable."

Aldo handed him a pillowcase full of swag. "Plus some jewelry and silver."

"Barney!" he called out, his voice echoing along the high open warehouse ceilings. "Barn!"

Barney Fine, Chuckie's sidekick and right-hand man since their school days, emerged from a row of merchandise and sauntered over to us. Barney was in the same class with Chuckie, but he'd been held back four times, so he was twenty-two when he graduated high school and was now pushing thirty. Despite the inevitable nickname Barney *Fife*, he stood well over six feet, had a rugged build, wore sleeveless shirts to show off his sculpted arms, and had a droopy face like a hound dog. While Chuckie was the brains of the operation, Barney was strictly brawn. We'd always gotten along with Chuckie, but nobody liked Barney. He was a dick just for the sake of being a dick, and although he was a pretty tough guy, he wasn't anywhere near as intimidating as he seemed to think he was. Both Aldo and I had come close to fighting him many times over the years, but somehow it had never happened.

"What's up?" he said in his typical baritone, directing it to Chuckie.

Chuckie held a finger up for him to wait then quickly looked over the pieces I was holding. "I got VCRs coming out of my pooper, fellas. These are nice, though, so I'll take them. The components are *very* nice. Kyocera. And that's a Bang and

Olufsen table, definitely want that. Okay, yeah, we can do something here. Barney, take this shit and put it on my desk, then come back out and keep these nice young ladies company while I work some numbers."

Without comment or acknowledging us, Barney took the stack of items from my arms and strode off toward the back where Chuckie's office was. When he returned, Chuckie took the pillowcase from Aldo and carefully emptied it on top of the big box of blenders. This way there was no issue with what was in it. They'd both seen the items: a pile of jewelry and several pieces of fine silver from some sort of tea set.

Once Aldo nodded his approval, Chuckie swept it all back into the pillowcase. "I'll be back in two shakes of a hobo's dick," he said, bouncing away to his office. "Everybody play nice while I'm gone, don't make Daddy mad."

Barney stood before us, arms folded over his chest, staring at us like we'd just peed on his leg.

Several fans were blowing on high and positioned all over the place, but it was still hot there, and I just wanted to get paid and get out. I lit a cigarette and took a couple deep drags while Aldo and Barney eyed each other with disgust.

"Ain't seen you around in a while, Genaro," Barney said after a moment. "What you been up to? Still blowin' fishermen for twenties down Weld Square?"

"Yeah, worked the same corner with your mother last night. She said to give her a call, never hears from you anymore. I think that's what she said, anyway. She was taking this giant black cock in the ass and another one in her mouth at the time so it was hard to understand her. You know how it is."

Barney's droopy eyes slid toward me. "Hell you lookin' at, Lionetti?"

"Fuck's your problem, man?" I snapped. I was tired, sore, disgusted, hot, and not in the mood for his or anybody else's bullshit. "We're just doin' some business here, all right? Cool out."

"*Cool out*," he scoffed. "Listen to this fuckin' guy."

"Go fuck yourself."

"Calm down, Mary."

"How about you make me, fuck-head?" I dropped my cigarette to the cement floor and stepped on it. Aldo moved in front of me before I could get any closer to him.

The slightest twitch of a smile curled the corner of Barney's mouth. "Let him come, Genaro. Anytime, tough guy. Fuckin' guinea faggots are all alike. Bigger balls than brains."

Aldo turned toward him, still between us, and responded before I could. "Now that's some funny shit," he said, glancing back over his shoulder at me. "This fuck talkin' about brains. Hell would you know about brains, Barney? Only guy senior year with a wife and three kids."

"One of these days, Genaro, it's gonna be you and me."

"Now's good. I'm here now."

Barney stared at him, said nothing.

"Oh, that's right," Aldo said. "You don't do so much as scratch that pimple you call a dick unless Chuckie tells you to. I forgot. He told you to stay and you're staying. What a good *boy*."

Everybody remained quiet for a few minutes.

When Chuckie came back, he had cash in hand. "Okay, I can definitely move that jewelry, and I can melt those silver pieces down. Silver's high right now, getting good prices for it. I can go twenty-five hundred. *Cash moe-nay*, ya filthy cow-fuckers." He held out the pile of cash, but Aldo left it hanging there. "Problem-o?"

"Can't go an even three, huh?"

"If I could go an even three, I'd have an even three in my hand."

Aldo took a deep breath, let it out slow. "How's twenty-eight sound?"

"Like three hundred more than twenty-five."

"Tell you what. I'll take twenty-seven."

Chuckie dropped his hand to his side and seemed to think about it a minute. "I can maybe go twenty-six, but that'd be it. That don't work, gonna have to tell you to screw on this one."

"You got air conditioners?"

"Do I have air conditioners? I'm Chuckie D, of course I have fucking air conditioners."

"Well, Richie here needs one."

"Okay, but let's wrap this first. I'll go twenty-six, cool?"

"How much them air conditioners run, Chuckie?"

"Depends what size you want, I got two kinds. Big ones and little ones."

Aldo looked at me. "What size you want?"

"I don't know," I said. "What's the difference?"

"You want to cool off a room or a whole apartment?" Chuckie asked.

"Whole apartment, I guess."

"Then you want the big one. See how that works?" He rolled his eyes. "Six bills, retail. For you, a buck and a half."

"Tell you what," Aldo said. "You give us the twenty-five in cash and one of them big-ass air conditioners, and we'll call it even, yeah?"

Chuckie nodded. "Yeah, all right. That'll work."

"Cool." Aldo took the cash and pocketed it without counting it. He knew Chuckie would never stiff us, and counting it out would be seen as a sign of disrespect. "Good deal."

"Barnabas," Chuckie said, fiddling with his nose, "go get me an A/C."

Barney turned and disappeared between the rows of boxes.

"How's your uncle?" Chuckie asked Aldo.

"Mean as a motherfucker."

"Tell him I said hello next time you see him, huh?"

"Sure, no problem."

Barney returned carrying a large box, put it down at my feet, then moved back behind Chuckie and assumed the same stance he'd had before.

Aldo and I both shook hands with Chuckie, made sure to give Barney a couple dirty looks, then took off with our cash and an air conditioner still new in the box.

We all stood around Ma's IROC, outside Aldo's place, a small cottage in the woods of Westport he rented from his uncle, about ten minutes outside the city. Counting out the cash, Aldo divided it up into little stacks for each of us. Even though Petie wasn't on this job, he got a cut the same as the rest of us. It's how we did things. How we'd always done them. When one of us got paid on a job, we all got paid. Ray-Ray was the only one who didn't enjoy that perk, because while he was a good friend, and we had his back and he had ours, he wasn't really a member of our core group. On this one, everybody got four hundred and fifteen bucks. The extra ten dollars went to Aldo. As leader, he always took whatever overages existed once things were divided equally, the figures rounded up or down to make it easier. Besides, what kind of assholes stood around tossing coins and busting balls over a quarter here or a dime there?

After a few minutes of shooting the shit, Ma, Ray-Ray and Fritz took off, leaving me and my air conditioner alone with Aldo. We loaded it into the trunk of his car, a gunmetal gray 1976 Camaro he'd put a lot of work and money into, then sat on the front steps of his house. It wasn't dark yet, more like dusk, and although we weren't far from the city at all, it always felt like a whole other planet out this way. He'd only been living there a little over a year, but I'd been there a lot and always preferred it to hanging around in the city.

"Always so quiet here," I said.

"Took me a while to get used to it. The whole yard and trees and shit, all the privacy. Couldn't sleep at first without the sounds of traffic and all the other bullshit. But then I started likin' it, kinda came around, you know? It's peaceful."

"Peaceful works."

"Yeah, it's good. I mean, the place is a shoebox and it's older than dirt, but it beats a shitty apartment in some fucked up neighborhood in the city. No offense, but I already had enough of that to last me a lifetime."

"Me too." I lit a cigarette. "Candy out?"

"Yeah, she's closin' tonight, won't be home until around nine-thirty, probably, so after I drop you off home I'll go by Petie's and give him his cash, make sure things are still calm with him and Tammy."

"He'll wet himself."

"Always does."

"Better get your ass back here and take a shower before Candy gets home," I told him. "You smell like Catholic school-girl pussy."

"Best kind."

"You're an idiot."

"Idiot who got you four hundred bucks and a free air conditioner today."

"Just sayin', you got a girl like Candy who loves you, and you treat her like shit and cheat on her every chance you get."

"I don't treat her like shit, I just don't spoil her is all. You do that to a chick they start believing they're so special their pussy's lined with diamonds. Look how good you treated Mariana, and—"

"You really gonna bust my balls about her?"

"I'm just sayin', you treated her like a princess. How'd that work out for you? If you treat them too good, chicks get comfortable and either bail on you or stick around and start breakin' balls, tryin' to change you and make you into some sorta version of them with a dick. Like some kinda...what do you call those guys with no balls?"

"Eunuchs."

"Yeah. *Eunuchs.* I knew you'd know that, all the readin' you do."

"It's just a word, Ally."

"Well, it's a word I don't want anybody to think I am. I love Candy, I do, but things won't always be like this, man. Who knows what could happen, today, tomorrow, next week? Remember that asshole guidance counselor, O'Brien? *Where do you see yourself in ten years?* Ten years. Only place I see myself is right now, man. Right here, right fuckin' now. Figure even if I get lucky and don't wind up dead or in prison, one day it'll still be all over and I'll have to stop runnin' around anyway. I won't always have all this hair, this look, this body. I live long enough, I'll end up a fat, old bald-ass Italian fuck. Belly hanging down, dick all shriveled up, balls swinging down by my knees and shit. So fuck it, until then, I'm gonna have fun, and if that means I get a chance to lay somethin' down like that sweet little piece of ass today, then trust me, I'm layin' it the fuck *down*, man. Every time. Then I'll come home and be with Candy and sleep like a baby, because I know it's got nothin' to do with her."

"Hey, you don't have to explain yourself to me, dude. I'm just sayin' you should be careful. You lose Candy, you'll never find another one like her."

"She ain't goin' nowhere. I make her cum so hard she says she sees Jesus sometimes."

"Jesus?"

"The Christ."

"That can't be good."

"It's a religious experience, is what she's sayin'. You know, it's so good."

"She sees Jesus you should probably call an ambulance, bro."

"What can I say? My cock gives her near-death experiences."

"Fuck makes you think I wanna hear this shit?"

"Doesn't happen with the little quickies, only those big motherfuckers. You know, the ones where they shake and their eyes roll up in their heads? You touch and they start vibratin' all over the place, twitchin' and shit, can't talk, just lay there droolin'? First time she had one of those, I swear to

God, I thought she was havin' a fuckin' stroke, scared the shit out of me."

"Great. Next time she sees our Lord and Savior, tell her to tell Him I said what's up." I took a drag on my cigarette, exhaled through my nose. "So what'd you need to talk to me about? You know, besides your fuckin' crank and your girl-friend's magical twat."

"My uncle wants us to come by and see him."

"Us?"

"Yeah."

"We in trouble?"

"Nah, just said he wants to discuss an opportunity with us."

When someone like Aldo's Uncle Lou said he wanted to see you, you went and got seen. We'd done small jobs for him before for a few bucks now and then, but usually Aldo went to see him alone first. I'd come in on it afterward, once things were set. Me going along for the initial rundown hadn't happened before. Couldn't figure out if that was good or bad.

"He give you any details?"

"Nope. He'll get into it when we're there."

"You know anything else about it?"

"You know what I know."

I nodded. "Okay."

"I'll set it up." He gave me a slap on the back. "Come on, let's get out of here so you can get that air conditioner to your mom and I can get Petie his cash."

I looked to the sky. Couldn't see the sun anymore through all the haze, but it was still so hot I was sweating buckets. Part of me wished we could stay here for a while, go inside and play Aldo's Atari or something. Anything but going back to the city, going home, and whatever the hell was waiting for me there. Never knew what kind of shape my mother would be in, if I'd find that prick Bronski sniffing around or God knows what else.

"You ever think about just takin' off?" I asked.

"Where the hell am I gonna go, Richie?"

"Anywhere. Wherever. Just somewhere besides…here…"

"You all right?" he asked, brow furrowed. "What's the hell's the matter with you lately?"

I flicked my cigarette away and stood up. "Nothin'." I forced a smile and wiped my sweaty hair out of my eyes and back off my forehead. "Just talkin', that's all."

Aldo eyed me with suspicion. He'd known me a long time. "You sure?"

"Yeah," I said. "Of course."

But I wasn't sure. I couldn't even be sure at that point if it was him I was trying to convince or myself. Didn't matter, I guess, long as one of us believed it.

The old black-and-white flick playing on TV when I got there was still on. With the end table lamp and ceiling fixture off, that same console set we'd had for years provided the only light in the living room, except for what little bit of daylight was still hanging on and seeping around the sides of the drawn window shades. The sound was turned down, but I recognized the movie. *Key Largo.* I'd seen it a few times before. Good one. Humphrey Bogart, Lauren Bacall and Edward G. Robinson. I liked the old movies, and the local channel showed them every afternoon and early evening. At the beginning, the host, an older guy in a bad suit and hair dyed rubber-tire-black, introduced the films and shared trivia about the movies and stars. Midway point, during a commercial break, he'd be back, spinning a big drum full of cards viewers had sent in. He'd select one and announce the day's winner. They'd have until the end of the movie to call in and claim their prize, which was usually either cash or a gift certificate to a local store. When the movie was over he'd come back on and tell the viewers if the winner called in or not. Either way, there'd be another drawing and more prizes the next day. Now and then they'd play a good one, but the movies usually sucked. Most people watched for the prizes. My mother sent a card in every month for years, but the sonofabitch never picked her name.

The movie was almost over, and the scene playing reminded me of the time I watched *Key Largo* with Aldo. He rooted for Edward G. Robinson, the bad guy, through the whole thing, and was pissed when Bogart killed him and saved the day. He always sided with the villains. Even when we watched wrestling, from the time we were kids, he cheered for the heels and booed the good guys.

On the couch, my mother stirred, coughed a little, and came awake.

"Hey," I said, turning and crouching down next to her. She was still in her robe, but she'd kicked her slippers off. "You okay?"

She squinted, like she couldn't quite see me. "Richie…what's that noise?"

"It's your new air conditioner, Mom. I set it up in the window." I pointed to the far wall. "Left your bedroom door open, you need to do that when it's running and it'll cool off the whole place, okay?"

"Really?"

"Yeah. I told you I'd get one, didn't I?"

She was weak, but tried to get up. When she couldn't pull it off after two tries, I gently took her by the shoulders and sat her up. A bunch of empty beer bottles lay scattered across the floor, and her kit was on the table next to the couch. We both pretended not to notice.

"Wow, will you look at the size of that thing?" She squinted again. "It's kinda loud, though, no?"

"The real powerful ones make a little noise. We'll get used to it."

"How did you—"

"It's paid for. Fair and square, don't worry."

"Promise me you didn't steal it, Richie. Promise me right now."

78

"I promise."

"You know it's a mortal sin to lie to your mother. You know that, right?"

"Yeah, I know that. I'm not lying."

She smiled and wiped some spittle from her chapped lips. "I can feel it already."

"It's cooler, right? I got it set so in a little while the whole place will be nice and cool. We'll be able to sleep better now, huh?"

She took my hands in hers, gave them a squeeze, then pulled me in and kissed me on the cheek. "Thank you, sweetheart. You're a good boy."

Her hands were clammy. I gently put them back in her lap. "Did you eat?"

"No, I..." She rubbed her eyes. "Wait. What time is it?"

"Going on eight. Almost dark out."

She reached over to the table for her cigarettes and lighter, nonchalantly tossing a tissue over the syringe, spoon and ashtray. "You're never home before dark," she said, pushing a cigarette between her lips with a shaking hand. "What's the occasion?"

"I'm probably goin' back out," I told her. "I just wanted to get you set up and cooled down."

"Why don't you stay and we'll have dinner together, huh? We haven't done that in so long, Richie. We used to all the time when you were a little boy, remember?"

I nodded.

"Do you really? Do you really remember, Richie?"

"Grilled cheese and tomato soup," I said softly.

She lit her cigarette, took a hard drag and exhaled a stream of smoke across the room. "In the winters, that was your favorite."

"Yeah. Yours, too."

"Mine, too." She looked at me with eyes glassy, bloodshot, and full of love. "You were such a sweet little boy."

"What happened, right?" I winked at her.

"You're still my sweet boy," she said, the words catching in her throat. "You'll always be my sweet boy, my baby."

I wanted to cry, but didn't.

"How about I make us peanut butter sandwiches and some soup? I think there's a can of chicken noodle in there. We can watch TV and be nice and cool. Because, I don't know if you heard," she said, smiling playfully, "but my son got me a brand new air conditioner today."

I wasn't sure she could even get up yet, much less make dinner. "Tell you what," I said, giving her knee a pat, "I'll make it. Then we'll see what's on, okay?"

"Yeah?"

"Yeah, sure."

She noticed the TV behind me. The end credits were rolling. "Damn it, I missed the drawing."

"He didn't pick your card."

"Sonofabitch."

"Don't worry about it. Who cares about this mook and his prizes?"

"Me, that's who. One of these days he's gonna pick me, you'll see. He's gonna spin that drum, reach in there and pull out a card. And then he's gonna say my name."

"I hope so, Mom."

"You got to believe, Richie. You always have to believe."

She looked so sad in that light summer robe, her hair a mess and her face drawn and sickly. Made me want to burn the whole goddamn city down. Made me want to hurt somebody. The way she hurt. The way I hurt.

But when she looked over at that stupid air conditioner and smiled again, I let it all go. Even if just for a little while, we forgot the pain and disappointment, the addictions and destruction, lost dreams and hopelessness, the helplessness, the predators, the prey, the violence and sex, the coming night, the city, and the unbearable heat outside pushing everything and everybody to the brink. And then it was just the two of us, like when I was little and she wasn't quite so sick.

But like Bogie said in *Key Largo*, "When your head says one thing, and your whole life says another, your head always loses."

He was right.

The morning brought more heat, the humidity worse than the night before, and after having spent several hours in air conditioning, I was already spoiled. Stepping back outside was like walking into an oven.

Aldo called around nine, said he'd set a meeting with his uncle and would pick me up at The Corner at ten. My mother was out cold in bed and snoring softly, so I grabbed a shower, got dressed and headed out. Five minutes later, I was at the corner a few blocks away. Known facetiously as "Happy Corner" because of all the trouble that took place there over the years, it was actually just a corner of the city where a long, graffiti-covered cement wall was located on one side, and a place where teenagers had congregated for decades. We'd started hanging out there in junior high, and just like The Park, we'd eventually taken over. We didn't go as much as we once had, though, and a younger crop of kids was starting to take control. None of us particularly cared, as our time there was nearly over. No one over the age of twenty ever hung out there.

It was a little after ten o'clock, and the city was hopping. Since it was summer, there were already several kids congregating on the corner, some hanging on the wall, others just milling about, smoking cigarettes, maybe a joint or sneaking booze hidden in paper bags. Fights happened here frequently, but even alone I felt relatively safe on the corner. Everyone there knew and respected me and wasn't likely to even try fucking with me. Sad as it was, I was someone most of them looked up to.

I was still about half a block away when the kids there saw

me coming. A couple of the younger ones who were sitting on the wall jumped off to give their space to me, as a show of respect. I motioned for them to get back up there, indicating I had no intention of hanging around. Probably to play it safe, they waved back, but stayed on the sidewalk.

"What do you say, Richie?" a rugged kid in jeans and a Hulk Hogan T-shirt said, a cigarette dangling from his mouth.

Probably about sixteen, I knew him by sight but couldn't remember his name. "How you doin'?" I said.

"Sweatin' my balls off."

"I hear you."

The other kids there all acknowledged me with quick what's-ups or nods in my general direction. I strolled over to the edge of the sidewalk and looked down the street for Aldo's Camaro.

"You wanna toss some dice with us?" the kid asked.

"Nah, not gonna be here long," I told him.

"Cool, cool." He sidled up a little closer to me, looked around like he was about to tell me a secret, then said, "It okay if I ask you something, Richie?"

"Yeah," I said. "What do you want?"

"Thanks, man. I wanted to let you know," he said, lowering his voice, "that if you and the other guys ever need another guy or whatever, I mean, if I can do anything for you guys or—you know, you need me to do anything—I will."

"Good to know."

"Cool."

"All right," I said, and thankfully he was bright enough to realize he was being dismissed. "Take it easy."

"You too, man. Thanks, Richie, thanks a lot. I mean it."

"Yeah, okay."

He wandered back over to the wall, chest puffed and acting for the others like he and I were tight. I kept watching the street. Aldo was late, as usual.

Few minutes later, his gray Camaro flew down the street

and rolled to a stop at the corner. The kids all gawked and swooned over the car, calling out hellos to Aldo. I couldn't get in and out of there fast enough.

"You fuckers all behavin' yourselves?" Aldo called from behind the wheel.

The kids replied with a resounding communal, "NO!"

Aldo laughed, gave them the thumbs-up then pulled out, rocketing through the streets at speeds completely unsafe. I'd become accustomed to the way he and Dino drove and barely noticed it most days.

"How'd the air conditioner work out? Make your moms happy?"

"Yeah, works great, she loved it. You go see Petie last night?"

"Stopped by his place, but his grandmother said him and Tammy were out," he explained. "So I just left the cash in an envelope with her. Hopefully, the old bitch didn't steal it. Hey, listen, after we talk to Uncle Lou, figured we'd all hit the movies, yeah? That new De Niro flick's playing over Cinema 140, *Once Upon a Time in America*. Looks badass. Told the guys to meet us at the diner."

"Cool."

"All right. Let's go see what we can see with Uncle Lou."

We left the city, pulling onto I-195 and flying toward the neighboring town of Dartmouth. Aldo droned on, excited about the meeting with his uncle and going to the movies afterward. I stayed quiet, let him talk.

We'd been on the highway less than five minutes when some kid in a Mustang pulled up alongside us, keeping pace and giving Aldo the look.

Aldo turned to me, grinned his shark grin and pushed a cassette into his tape deck. Nazareth's *Hair of the Dog* began blasting from the stereo.

I pulled the seatbelt across my chest and buckled in.

In seconds, the race was on, and we were suddenly approaching and then blowing right by speeds of one hundred miles an hour. It felt like being strapped to a rocket, which in a sense, is exactly what it was. Since I wasn't driving and had no control, it only made everything more intense, but I'd been a passenger in many a race over the last few years—it was one of the things you got used to when you rode in cars like Dino and Aldo had—so I stayed calm but alert to what was taking place.

The Mustang was a bit ahead of us. Aldo kept his cool and his speed. As we came to the end of a long straight-away, the coming bend in the road flying toward us at blinding speed, the Mustang eased up a bit. But Aldo kept it pinned and rocketed right by him. I closed my eyes and hung on tight.

When I heard Aldo laugh and felt the car slowing, I opened my eyes. We'd made it. The Mustang was behind us. Dropping the window, Aldo put a hand out and waved to the driver. Then he closed the window, cranked the air back up and slowed enough to career off the highway and onto our exit ramp.

"God *damn*!" he said, laughing like a mental patient.

"Nice driving, man."

"Thanks! That's what it was too. Kid should've beat us easy. Newer car, more horsepower, I just outdrove him, that's all. That bend scared him."

"Fuckin' scared me, too. Think I left my spleen back there."

At sixteen, seventeen, eighteen and even nineteen, racing was cool and fun. Now it just seemed stupid and pointless. But I slapped his hand and acted like I'd enjoyed the race as much as he had.

Within minutes, we were driving at a normal speed along a suburban, tree-lined street, through a neighborhood of nice homes. When we got to Lou's house, a colonial with a two-stall garage and a big and beautifully maintained front yard, Aldo slowly pulled into the paved driveway and parked behind the other two cars already there.

Although Lou had a lot of money and did very well for himself, he tended to keep things low-key, like most guys in his world did. No reason to draw more attention to yourself than necessary, so he lived in a nice but modest home in a middle-class neighborhood typical of the area. He and his wife drove nice cars, but not too nice, and usually dressed in inexpensive clothes, again, not to draw attention. His house looked no different than any of the others, and unless you knew what he did for a living, you'd assume he was some sort of professional like everyone else on the street.

As we walked along the stone path to the front door, Aldo said, "Wouldn't mind having digs like this one day."

I didn't say anything. We climbed the three little brick steps to the front door and Aldo rang the bell. A few seconds later, I heard someone coming toward the door with loud, clunky steps.

The door swung open and we were greeted with the overpowering smell of heavy perfume and Aldo's aunt Vicky. In her younger days, she'd been a headlining stripper based out of Atlantic City, but now in her fifties, she looked more like a caricature of an aging exotic dancer still struggling to look twenty. In a skirt and blouse so tight they looked like they'd been painted on, she swayed before us atop a pair of six-inch heels. Squinting, she said, "Who's that?"

"Aunt Vicky, it's me and Richie."

"Ally?"

"Yeah, and my buddy Richie. You know Richie."

"Morning, Mrs. Genaro," I said.

"Oh, for God's sake, honey, I'm sorry. Hi, youse guys." She squinted again and smiled, revealing teeth smeared with the same clown-red lipstick she had on. "Can't see a goddamn thing, I ain't got my contacts in yet, I was just getting ready, I'm going out shopping with the girls. Anyways, I put my glasses down in the bathroom somewhere but I couldn't find them so I just came quick as I could. Lou don't like it when someone rings more than once. Irritates him something fierce, so I try to hurry and answer the door quick, like a bunny."

"Sorry if we bothered you," Aldo said in a far more pleasant tone than be usually had.

"Don't be silly, no bother." Moving a few strands of platinum hair out of her eyes, she stepped aside so we could enter. "Come in out of that awful heat, the central air's going. You boys want something cold to drink? You thirsty?"

"No, we're okay, thanks though," Aldo answered for both of us.

"You sure?"

"Yeah, thanks."

We stepped into a foyer, following Vicky as she jiggled her way across a living room, into the kitchen and finally to the head of a long hallway. "Go ahead in, Lou's waiting on you. I got to go put my eyes in and finish getting ready."

We followed the narrow hallway to the door at the end. It stood closed. Aldo wrapped his knuckles against it lightly.

"Yeah, come on!" a voice boomed from within.

Aldo opened the door and we moved into Lou's office, which was basically a midsized room with a huge mahogany desk, two chairs positioned in front of it, a leather couch on one wall, bookcases mostly full of books he'd likely never even opened, much less read, a carpeted floor and numerous shelves and glass cases that housed several pieces of expensive sports memorabilia. Behind the desk, two long windows overlooked a beautiful flower garden and a small patio beyond, outfitted with birdfeeders and a birdbath.

Lou was sitting behind his desk. He stood up as we entered. A short and rotund man with no neck and the build of an aging professional wrestler, he sported a greasy comb-over, dark eyes and tinted glasses with thick silver frames like something straight out of an Elvis getup. Along with a pair of stretch slacks, Italian loafers and a polyester shirt open to the middle of his hairy, gold-chain-laden chest, he looked like a cross between an old wise guy in a B-movie and the manager of a low-end used-car lot.

"Hey, Uncle Lou," Aldo said, extending his hand.

"You're late." He left Aldo hanging and instead reached across his desk to me with one of his huge paws. "How are you, Richie?"

As we shook, I watched my hand disappear into his and felt the pain of his grip. Trying not to react, I held tight and said, "Doing okay, Mr. Genaro, how are you, sir?"

He let go, motioned to the chairs in front of his desk. "Sit down."

I did, but Aldo remained standing, his hand still extended.

Lou gave a wry smile, clearly marveling at the balls on his nephew and finally shook hands with him. "I tell you to be here a certain time, Ally, that's when you get here, yeah?"

"Yeah."

Lou arched an eyebrow. "Huh?"

"Yes." Aldo dropped into the chair next to me. "Sorry, Uncle Lou. It won't happen again."

"See that it don't." Lou came around the side of his desk and sat on the corner closest to me. "You need to be more like this guy." He pointed a stubby finger at me. "Smart and respectful, like Richie, nice young man."

"This guy?" Aldo chuckled. "He's a chooch, trust me, a fuckin' horrible degenerate."

Lou jerked a thumb at him and leaned closer to me. "You gonna let him talk about you like that, Richie?"

I smiled but said nothing.

"What can I do?" Lou said to me. "His old man, my brother—rest in peace—we all loved the crazy bastard, but he got sent up Concord when Ally was just a baby, and he wasn't never coming out, except the way he did, feet first. I did the best I could to help his mother raise this little punk bastard, but Aldo don't always listen. Just like his old man. But you, you're smarter than that. You're a good listener, aren't you, Richie?"

"Yes, sir."

"Good boy." He dropped a baseball mitt hand on my shoulder. "See what Ally don't always understand is that you can't just be tough. Hell, we're all hard guys, right? But that ain't the thing. The thing is to be tough *and* smart."

Aldo slumped in his chair like he used to in high school. "Why you talkin' about me like I'm some sort of reject, Uncle Lou?"

"I'm tryin' to help you, son." He slid down off the corner of his desk, walked around behind me, then gave Aldo a pat on the shoulder, too. "Want to get your attention, because I need you to listen."

Aldo sat up straight.

"You guys aren't little kids no more." Lou moved back around the other side of his desk then looked out the windows at the birds, his back to us. "You need to start thinking about what you want to do with yourselves. The future, you see what I'm sayin'? Comes a time, a man has to make these decisions."

No one spoke for a while. I looked at Aldo, but he just rolled his eyes and shrugged, so I sat there and kept my mouth shut.

"You guys have done small jobs for me here and there in the past," Lou finally said. "Nickel-and-dime bullshit, stuff you give to kids nobody else wants to do, that kind of thing. But maybe you two want more than that, yeah?"

Slowly, he turned and faced us again.

"Yeah," Aldo said.

"Ally, you been after me to hire you and your crew for a while now." Lou plopped back down into his desk chair. "Thing is, you know I don't bring just anybody into my operation. You got to earn your way. Even you, Ally. *Especially* you, because you carry my name, understand? You can't be actin' like a goof and making me look bad, see what I mean? But if I was to give a couple young guys a chance, you two are it."

"What about the other guys?" Aldo asked.

"That Abruzzo kid's got potential, but personally, I wouldn't have him working for me. Too much of a hothead. All muscle, no brains."

"What about Petie and Fritz?"

"Petie? He's moron. I wouldn't let him empty my waste-baskets, what's wrong with you? And who the fuck is *Fritz*?"

"My buddy, the guy with the sunglasses."

"The blond kid with the earrings?"

"Yeah."

"I thought he was blind."

"No."

"Then why the hell's he wear those sunglasses all the time?"

"I don't know, he likes them, I guess."

Lou stared at him. "I got no interest in him either."

"What about Ray-Ray?"

"The nigger?"

"You don't got to call him that, Uncle Lou."

"Oh, I don't, huh?" Lou laughed harder than seemed necessary.

"Ray's black, what's the big deal? Who gives a shit? He's a solid guy. Ray-Ray's no punk, and he's no nigger."

"Good for you, Ally, stand up for your guys. I'm proud of you." Lou's expression slowly turned colder, deadlier. "Just not *too* hard, huh? Look, I got nothing against the coloreds and I got nothing against Ray. That kid could fight, but he's a druggie. Cost him a pro career. Now me, I don't give a damn what a man does with his free time, you understand, but I don't go in with no dopers. You want him on your crew, that's one thing, but not mine. Can't trust a doper."

"I'm just sayin'—"

"I want to talk to you and Richie," Lou interrupted. "That's why I told you to come see me. If I wanted to talk to those other mooks, I would've called them. Now you want to keep bustin' my balls or listen to what I have to say?"

"Not tryin' to bust balls, I just—"

"Look at Richie," he snapped, pointing at me. "See how he sits there and shuts the fuck up and listens? Do that."

Aldo slumped in his chair again and nodded.

"Here's the thing," Lou said, leaning back in his chair, "you guys need some work and I can bring youse on and see how it goes. I can't promise nothin', you got to prove yourselves, understand? But I always got work for a couple tough, smart young guys lookin' to make somethin' of themselves. I promised my brother I'd always look out for you, Aldo, and I always will. But I ain't handin' you nothin'. It's an opportunity, *capeesh*? A chance to come work for me, and we'll see how it goes. If it works out, you got a place with me. And let me tell you somethin', the guys that work for me, they work for me for the rest of their lives because they have security and a family around them they know they can count on and who can count on them. You know that better than anybody, Ally. You been around my guys your whole life. But it takes time, okay? You got to work your way in, it don't just happen."

"What would you want us to do?" Aldo asked.

"Whatever the fuck I tell you to do." He adjusted his glasses, pushing them higher on his nose. "To start, I'd give you basic shit, let you learn."

"Okay," Aldo said.

"Like I said, takes time. But that's what you want, no?"

"Yeah, you know I've always wanted to work for you for real."

"Things work out, *then* you bring your buddies in if you want. That way they're your responsibility. And it's your ass if they fuck up, not mine. They work for you. You work for me." Lou turned to me. "What about you, Richie? You want to come work for me, see how it goes?"

"I appreciate the offer a lot, Mr. Genaro," I said, hoping my voice wasn't shaking too badly. "But if it's all right with you, I'd like to think it over a little. I don't mean no disrespect, believe me. I just—"

"See?" Lou pointed to me again. "Smart."

Relieved, I smiled quickly and forced a swallow.

"The two of youse go knock it around and get back to me."

He stood up and motioned to the door, which was our cue to leave. "But don't take too long. I wouldn't want to think either one of youse was wastin' my time."

"Yes, sir," I said. "Thank you."

"All right, now fuck off. I got shit to do."

"Are you out of your fuckin' mind?" Aldo growled at me before we'd even reached the car. "My uncle offers us work and you tell him you got to think about it? You don't tell a man like Uncle Lou that. You tell him thank you, and you take advantage of the shot he's willin' to give you. Hell's the matter with you?"

"Just want to think about it, that's all."

"What's there to think about?" He grabbed my arm, turned me toward him. "You know how many guys would kill to get a chance to work for my uncle? You got any idea what kind of opportunity this is for us, Richie?"

I looked down at his hand then back at him. "You wanna let me go?"

"I want to put my foot in your ass, that's what I want to do."

"Seriously, man, let go."

"Fuck's wrong with you? This is our shot, man. We get in with my uncle, we'll be set. His guys are taken care of, believe me."

"Except for the ones in prison or dead, right?"

"That's where we're headed anyway," Aldo said evenly. "At least if we work for him there's a chance we might not end up either way. We'll have a real shot at havin' a life, Rich. Maybe it don't have to go down like everyone's been tellin' us it will since we were kids. We can be somebody, too."

"Let go of me, Ally."

Shaking his head, he walked around to the driver's side of the Camaro, then turned and looked at me over the roof. "What the fuck you think you're gonna do? You gonna go get some sucker job? Some straight job? Bust your ass down the fish houses or something like that? Make shit money the rest of your life? That what you want?"

"I don't know what the fuck I want. Okay?"

"Nah, man, it's not okay. We're twenty now. You heard what he said. We're not kids no more. And he's right, we got to make some decisions."

"You think I don't know that? I'm tryin', all right?"

"Problem with you, man, is you *think* you got options. You don't. You ain't gonna work some stupid job, and even if you do, you won't last. Know why? Because guys like us ain't got the temperament for crap like that, and it's only a matter of time before you'd fuck it up. Why wind up a petty criminal, out there on your own, when you could work for Uncle Lou instead? Don't make no sense."

I lit a cigarette; blew smoke out into the heat circling us. "I don't know."

"Look at me. Richie, *look* at me."

I did.

"You're like a brother to me. You're my boy. I trust you with my life. I'd die for you, Richie. I'd *die* for you. But you need to get your head straight, you understand me? You got to get your shit together, and you need to do it soon. You don't, you're gonna wake up in a few years and be everything you've always been afraid you're gonna turn out to be."

"Can we get out of here?" I asked. "Let's just get out of here, huh?"

"No smokin' in my car," he sighed, disappearing inside.

I dropped the cigarette to the pavement and stepped on it.

Looking to the sky, I saw a seagull gliding gracefully overhead, moving toward the nearby ocean, and in that moment, I'd have given anything to be able to fly away with him. But like everything else, it was impossible, out of reach.

I got in the car and Aldo sped off, Nazareth screaming from the speakers.

Neither of us said another word.

* * *

Aldo pulled up to a diner near the airport we frequented and parked out front. We sat in the car in silence for what seemed forever, the air conditioner fan the only sound. "You got any idea how long I've been asking my uncle for a break like this for us?" he finally said. "*Any* idea?"

"I'm not tryin' to be an asshole, all right?"

"Could've fooled me, man."

"I just want to be sure before I go all in."

Aldo looked at me, but I could tell it took considerable effort. "Richie, you think you're the only guy who ever wanted to change his life into somethin' else? You think you're the only guy that gets up every day to the exact same life he had when he went to bed, and says, tomorrow I'm gonna change it, start over fresh? You're not. Not by a long shot. And you know what happens with them types? Nothing. They just keep doin' the same shit over and over and bitchin' about how bad their lives suck, and they end up goin' to their fuckin' graves tellin' themselves they're gonna change shit. Look around, city's full of them."

"Maybe going to work for your uncle doesn't seem like much of a change."

"You serious? Changes everything. We'll have *real* respect, not just down the corner on The Avenue or at The Park. I'm talkin' big-time respect, good money—steady money—and we'll be part of somethin' nobody fucks with."

"It's the same shit, Ally, just a bigger scale, that's all."

"What the hell is wrong with you lately?"

"Why do you keep askin' me that?"

"You hear the shit comin' out of your mouth? Not for nothin', Richie, but you haven't been yourself in a while, man."

"You mean I haven't been the seventeen-year-old me or the eighteen-year-old me? *That* guy? You're right, I'm not him anymore."

"Then who the hell are you?"

"Maybe that's what I'm tryin' to figure out."

"Well hurry the fuck up."

"What, you got it all worked out at twenty, that it?"

"Did I say that?" Aldo drew a deep breath, sighed, and shook his head. He looked away, like he couldn't stand to make eye contact with me for even another second. "We been tight since we were kids, man. It's always been us, together, partners, thick and thin. We been through some shit over the years, but even when things were totally fucked, I always knew I could count on you."

"None of that's changed."

"Can I count on you to come with me on this then?"

"I didn't say no, all right? I just didn't say yes yet. Give me a little bit of time. That's all I'm asking, man."

"What's a little bit?"

"Couple weeks."

"Two weeks, Richie. Two weeks and I'm goin' back to my uncle and tellin' him I'm in. I hope you'll be there with me doin' the same thing, but I'm goin' with or without you. Understand?"

"Yeah, I do."

"Not bein' a dick, I'm being straight with you."

"I got it."

"We cool then?" He reached a hand out to me.

"Of course." I slapped his hand with mine. "We're always cool."

"All right," he said, finally smiling. "Let's go get some breakfast, then we'll go to the movies."

In the time we'd been talking, Fritz and Petie had showed up on foot and were hanging near the door to the diner, waiting on us.

"Get a load of these two," Aldo said as he got out of the car.

I got out and played along. "Give them a break, huh? Workin' girls gotta make a livin' too, you know."

"Hey, boys," Fritz said coolly. "Wanna date?"

Petie stepped forward, anxious and jumpy even for him. "Can I talk to you a sec? I need to talk to you, okay?"

"We can talk inside," Aldo told him. "I'm starvin', let's eat."

"No, I mean out here for a minute, I—I need to talk to you."

"You get that money I left with your grandmother last night?"

"Yeah. Thanks, man, thanks a lot. Had to give her some for rent I was so behind, but I got something else I need to tell you, man."

I joined Fritz over by the door. "Go do what you need to do," I said. "We'll meet you in there."

"You're gonna wanna hang around for this," Fritz said quietly. "Trust me."

"No, you too, Richie," Petie said, having not heard him. "I already told Fritz, but I need to tell you guys."

Aldo and I exchanged glances.

"What's up?" Aldo asked. "What's so important you can't tell me inside? It's hotter than Demi Moore out here."

Petie, beaming, rolled on the balls of his feet, hands in his pockets. He looked at Fritz then back at us. "Reason I wasn't home last night, is Tammy had somethin' important to tell me, so we went down to Buttonwood Park and fed the ducks and talked and...well...she broke the news. She's pregnant."

We all froze. I couldn't figure out what the hell he was so happy about.

"I'm gonna be a father," Petie said proudly. "So, we're gettin' married!"

"You *what*?"

"We're gettin' married, Ally. I want you to be my best man. And Richie, I want you and Fritz to be ushers in my wedding party, okay? Ma too, of course."

"Are you serious?" Aldo looked to Fritz. "Is he fuckin' serious?"

"Far as I can tell."

Petie was smiling so hard it looked like it was starting to hurt. "I wouldn't joke about somethin' like that, Ally. Come on, man."

"Petie..." Aldo put a hand on his shoulder. "Petie, listen to me. You can't marry this girl. Get your head outta your ass."

"What are you talkin' about?"

"You don't have to marry her just because she's pregnant."

"It don't matter. I love her anyways, man, I want to marry her."

"Shit, I got Candy pregnant twice already." Aldo dropped his hand. "My uncle knows a guy who can take care of this cheap."

Petie blanched. "I can't do that, man. I'm Catholic."

"So am I. Who gives a shit?"

"Me," Petie said softly. "I give a shit."

"Come on, how you even know it's yours?"

Petie stared at him. "Why you got to say something like that?"

"We're all thinkin' it, man. Somebody needs to say it."

"No, don't nobody got to say that."

"Tammy fucks around on you all the time. She just did with that hippie asshole we tuned up down by the waterfront. Hell's the matter with you?"

Petie turned away, his eyes moist. "That's all over now," he said. "Tammy and me had a long talk and we decided we need to do the right thing from here on out. She's gonna stop...doing that stuff and...and I'm gonna stop some stuff too, I—I'm gonna do the right thing."

"What are you gonna do, get a job?"

"Tammy's father, she said he's gonna be pissed at first, but once he calms down she said maybe he could get me in the union like him, and then I'd have steady work, you know?"

"Union? Doin' what?"

"He's a carpenter."

"Fuck you know about being a carpenter?"

"I could learn."

"Petie, you couldn't drive a nail with a gun to your head. You suck at that kind of thing, you always have. You're the only guy I know failed shop. You're gonna wind up down the fish houses or in one of the factories. Christ, maybe even Wendy's or McDonald's or some shit like that. You out of your mind?"

"It's not just about me now, Ally. I got a baby comin'."

"Baby, my ass. It ain't a baby yet. It's a blob, bunch of cells and shit."

"It's my kid, Ally. I ain't killin' it. Besides, Tammy wants to have it too."

Aldo turned to me and Fritz. "Little help, maybe?"

Fritz chucked and gave a theatrical shrug.

I wasn't sure what to say. Petie worshipped Aldo. If he wasn't listening to him he sure as hell wouldn't pay attention to anything I had to say. "Maybe you ought to, you know, think about it a little bit before you decide for sure what you wanna do."

"Yeah," Aldo agreed. "Richie's right, there's—what's the big rush, right? You need to think this through and—"

"I already did. Me and Tammy decided last night. We're gettin' married and we're havin' the baby." He looked down at the parking lot, kicked at stray stone with his sneaker. "Thought you guys was gonna be happy for us."

"Do whatever the fuck you want. It's your life." Signaling Fritz to follow him, he climbed the three steps to the front door. "You wanna fuck it up, that's on you. I'm goin' inside and getting somethin' to eat."

He and Fritz disappeared into the diner.

Petie looked at me helplessly, eyes brimming with tears.

"Take it easy, man," I told him, motioning to his eyes. "Wipe that shit up."

He did, standing there like a little kid that just found out Santa Claus is bullshit. "I'm tryin' to do the right thing, Richie."

"I know, man." I slung an arm around his shoulder. "Ally's just looking out for you. You know that. Don't sweat it, he'll come around."

He nodded.

"Come on," I said, turning him toward the door. "Let's go in and get some food and we'll get it worked out, all right?"

"What would you do, Richie?"

I stood there looking at him like a moron.

"If you was me," he pressed, "what would *you* do?"

"I honestly don't know, bro."

"You'd try to do the right thing. I known you since we were kids, you always try to do the right thing. It don't always work out, but you try." He offered up the saddest goddamn smile I'd ever seen. "Don't I got to try, too? Don't I got to at least *try* to do the right thing, Richie?"

The sun was already high in the sky and beating down on us without mercy. I was sweating and uncomfortable and wanted to get inside the diner into their crappy air conditioning and eat some breakfast and forget all this.

But like everything else in our lives, there was never a clear way out.

"The trick's all in knowin' what the right thing is," I said.

Petie's eyes met mine, and something passed between us. It wasn't anything new, just more intense and unnerving than it had ever been before, because now it was unquestionably real. He was doomed. Maybe we all were.

Nobody was getting out. Not without scars.

For guys like us, wasn't any such thing.

CHAPTER FOUR

We all sat in awkward silence in the booth, Fritz and me chain-smoking, our breakfasts long gone, plates stained with smears of egg yolk and littered with napkins and cigarette ash, whatever coffee still in our mugs long since cold. While we tried to pay attention to anything other than the tension hanging in the air like a funeral shroud, we did our best not to make eye contact with anyone else at the table. Aldo was working on his third cup of coffee and his second round of hash and eggs. Petie nervously looked to each of us in turn, then out the window at the traffic, then back to us, then back to the traffic. It went on like this for a long while, the drone of conversations from other patrons, the clanging of silverware on plates and the smell of grease and cigarette smoke filling the otherwise dead space.

"Ally," Petie finally managed, "you mad at me?"

Several seconds lived and died before Aldo answered him. But when he did, he kept his head down and his eyes focused on his food. "Nah, man," he said around a mouthful of corned beef hash, "I'm not mad at you. I just don't want to see you throw your life away."

Petie swallowed so hard it was audible. "What life? There ain't nothin' to throw away. This is the life I got. Maybe if me and Tammy get married and the baby comes she'll stop doin' what she does and we'll all be happy. A family, you know? A real family. Like other people. Why can't I have that, too?"

I took a drag on my cigarette, looked down the aisle toward

a middle-aged couple quietly bickering in a nearby booth and pretended I wasn't listening.

"Where you gonna live?" Aldo asked.

"My grandmother said long as we pay her rent Tammy can move in and we can live there with the baby until we're on our feet."

"You and Tammy and a baby are gonna live in one room?"

He shrugged. "Until we're on our feet. It'll be okay."

Aldo dropped his fork onto his plate, wiped his mouth with a napkin then finished off his coffee and sat back. "What if the baby's not yours?"

"Come on, man, don't—"

"No, fuck that, Petie, you need to get your head straight on this." He belched then leaned forward on the table, closer to Petie, who was across from him and next to me. "What then?"

"It is mine."

"You don't know that."

"And you don't know it's not."

"So, you don't care? You're cool with supportin' *Trampy* and some other dude's kid?"

"It's my kid, Ally. And you don't got to call her that, man."

"How do you know?" Aldo pressed.

"Tammy told me it's mine."

"Oh, well that's all you need because she never lies to you. You know, except for all the fuckin' time. She spends her life ridin' other guys' dicks."

"Jesus." Petie grabbed a napkin and wiped the sweat that had collected along his brow despite the air conditioning in the diner. "The fuck, dude?"

Aldo looked to Fritz and me for support but neither of us wanted anything to do with this. Realizing no more help would be coming from us, he returned his attention to Petie. "Look, I'm not tryin' to—"

"I love her, man."

"Yeah. I know you do."

"Then can you cool it with that shit? Please?"

Aldo sat back again, sighed and looked out the window a while. "I don't think you understand what you're gettin' yourself into here."

"I know what I'm doin'."

"No, Petie, you don't. That's the problem. You don't have a fuckin' clue."

"I ain't killin' it. And I ain't gonna make Tammy prove the baby's mine. She says it is then it is."

"How the hell can *she* even be sure?"

"Tammy said she ain't been with anyone else in the time when she would've gotten pregnant, so—"

"Are you out of your mind? In the last few months, you've caught her with two different guys!"

"Don't got to be so loud." Petie squirmed in his seat, looking like he'd come out of his skin at any moment. "I asked her about that, okay? And she said there wasn't no fuckin' with those guys. They did other shit but no fuckin'."

A slight laugh escaped Fritz, but he tried to cover it by coughing.

"This shit ain't funny," Aldo snapped.

"Something in my throat," Fritz said. "Sorry."

Aldo glared at Petie. "And you believe her?"

"Yeah, Ally, I do. Okay? I do. She promised me it was true. Just head."

"Unbelievable. Hey, don't worry about it, honey, we didn't fuck, I just sucked his dick. No biggie."

The table went quiet.

"Does this mean you won't be my best man?" Petie finally asked.

Aldo looked out the window again for a while. "Did I say no?"

"You didn't say yes."

"You're makin' a big mistake, Petie. But if this is what you want, I can't stop you. I know you really love this girl for some reason, but are you sure she loves you?"

Petie nodded.

Aldo looked at me. This time I met his gaze and gave him a subtle nod. I didn't agree with Petie marrying Tammy either, but it was heartbreaking to watch and listen to the poor bastard twist in the wind like this, and end of the day, he'd probably marry her no matter what any of us said anyway, even Aldo.

After more brutal silence, Aldo said, "You need a ring?"

A smile broke across Petie's face. "Yeah, ain't got much cash though."

"We'll go see Chuckie D. You scrape up whatever you can find or steal, and we'll get you somethin' decent, all right?"

"And you'll be my best man?"

"Yeah," Aldo said through a forced smile, "I'll be your best man."

"And you guys will be in the wedding party, right?" he asked Fritz and me.

"Yeah, sure," I told him.

Fritz finally let out a burst of laughter he'd been wrestling into submission for the last few minutes and said, "Petie, I wouldn't miss your fuckin' wedding for the world, my man."

"I'm gonna ask Dino, too. He's working today so I'll catch him tomorrow probably. Was thinkin' about asking Ray-Ray, but Tammy's father don't like black people."

"So?"

"So, he's paying for the wedding. At least Tammy said he will once we tell him and he calms down."

"Don't tell him Ray's black, let it be a surprise. Everybody'll be laughin' until the baby comes out looking like Magic Johnson. See how the racist fucker likes that."

We all laughed, even Petie, and things seemed almost back to normal.

Whatever the hell that was.

"Hey, could've been worse," Fritz said. "At least you didn't knock up Margaret Petrowski."

We all laughed again, remembering a girl Petie had dated in high school before Tammy. Margaret was actually a nice kid, but we'd always teased Petie about her relentlessly.

"You're right," Aldo said, "that would've been worse."

"What'd Margaret go?" I asked. "Six-six, six-seven?"

"At least," Aldo said. "Could've dunked on a ten-foot rim, I'll tell you that."

"She wasn't that big," Petie laughed. "Fuck you guys."

"Remember that bikini she used to wear?" I said.

"Oh Jesus, yeah," Aldo said, laughing. "The one with those huge granny panty bottoms."

"I still wake up at night screamin', thinkin' about those fuckin' giant trunks," Fritz said. "It was like, is this bitch getting ready to go to the beach or wrestle The Fabulous Moolah?"

"Didn't help that she looked like Frankenstein with blonde frizzy hair, huge tits and braces on her teeth," Aldo said. "Pretty sure that poor thing even had bolts in her neck, that's why she always had those fuckin' turtlenecks on, to hide that shit."

"Monster," Fritz said.

"You can say that again. Fuckin' beast."

"No, Frankenstein's monster."

"What?"

"You said she looked like Frankenstein."

"Yeah, she did."

"No, she looked like Frankenstein's *monster*. She looked like the monster. Frankenstein was the doctor that made the monster."

"Fuck are you talkin' about?"

"You said she looked—"

"Yeah, I know what I said, so what? Who the hell says *Frankenstein's monster*?"

"People who know what the fuck they're talkin' about?"

"I know it's the monster, dipshit, but who the hell says that?"

"People get that wrong all the time."

"They don't get it wrong, they just say Frankenstein and

everybody knows what they mean. You knew what I meant, didn't you?"

"Yeah."

"Then forget about it, who gives a shit?" He threw a crumpled napkin at him. "Ass."

"Guess it don't matter when it comes to Petie. He just called her *Frankie* when they were fuckin' anyway."

"You guys suck," Petie said, but it was through laughter. "I swear to God."

"How'd you really do her, though, bro?" Fritz asked. "Flashlight and a step ladder?"

"Let's get the hell out of here." I tossed some cash into the pile in the center of the table. "Unless you guys wanna see my breakfast again."

"Hurry," Fritz said, scooting out of the booth, "cocksucker had biscuits and gravy. Looked like vomit the first time through."

All of us laughed as we bounded out the diner and back out into the heat. It calmed us down quickly, brought us back to the furnace.

"Damn," I said, "this heat ever gonna quit?"

Aldo motioned to his car. "Come on, let's hit the movies, watch De Niro gangster-shoot some motherfuckers. Nice and cool there."

We piled into Aldo's Camaro and within a minute or two were racing along the highway toward the movie theater, laughing and having fun, heavy metal blasting from the speakers. I knew it would be back, but for the few hours that followed, all the other bullshit left us alone. We were free. Or something close.

After almost four hours at the movies, we finished watching Sergio Leone's epic *Once Upon a Time in America,* and returned to the heat. Pumped up from the violence in the film, but tired from the amount of time we'd spent sitting in the theater, we spent a few minutes in the parking lot, hanging around Aldo's car. It was much later in the day, nearly five. Petie had to go find Dino and give him the news, so the rest of us decided to hit Skinny Dave's, a grimy little arcade on The Avenue we'd been going to since we were kids.

We dropped Petie at his grandmother's apartment so he could call and set a meet with Dino, then rocketed through the city to The Avenue. Darkness was still a little way off, so everything was still in normal business mode, bustling and congested. The night people hadn't come out to play yet, but in another couple hours the entire strip would look and feel and sound different.

Once we got to Skinny Dave's, we hung out a while, played video games and a little air hockey, then sat at one of a handful of tables near the snack bar and had some Cokes. Although he seemed to be having a good time, Aldo had been bothered and distracted since he'd gotten the news from Petie.

"Don't let that other shit bother you," I told him.

"I know I was hard on him," Aldo said. "But shit, somebody's got to look out for the guy."

"Petie's Petie." Fritz sipped his Coke. "He's never gonna change."

"Maybe this'll change him," I suggested. "A kid can do that sometimes."

"You know, odds are that baby's not even his," Aldo said.

I nodded, distracted by a beautiful blonde girl playing pinball.

"Guy's life's over."

"You heard what he said." I watched the girl bounce herself against the machine, grinding her hip into it as bells sounded and lights blinked. "He knows he's got nothin', no life that's worth anything. Shit, who does?"

"We do, you fuckin' depressing asshole."

"How'd that thing go with your uncle?" Fritz asked.

"Good." Aldo eyed me quickly. "If we go to work for him

it'll be me and Richie first, then we can bring you guys in a little later on once we got things established."

"Cool," Fritz said, eyes hidden behind the dark lenses of his sunglasses.

"Problem is, Petie needs somethin' now, not later."

"Petie's not the only one," Fritz said. "I'm tired of this week-to-week shit, scrapin' and fightin' and stealin' for every little thing we got. It's gettin' old. *We're* gettin' old."

"Old," Aldo scoffed. "Shit, we'll never be this young again, Fritzy. Won't ever have time like this for the rest of our lives, time that's ours, know what I mean?"

"Yeah, I do, I was tellin' Richie the same shit down the beach, but not for nothin', that time's runnin' low, man. That's just being realistic. We're gonna make a move, we need to do it. Soon."

Aldo sat back and seemed to give this serious thought.

I sipped my Coke, watched the girl pumping her pelvis against the pinball machine and tried to ignore the erection pressing into my thigh.

"Maybe that's it," Aldo finally said. "We need a score. Somethin' real, though, no more nickel-and-dime bullshit, that's kid stuff. I'm talkin' about a real score, somethin' my Uncle Lou's gonna notice and respect. If we can show him, prove to him we can *all* be good earners for him, that we can get shit done as a crew, maybe he'll take us all on at the same time. Then—"

"That's the last thing Petie needs, man," I said. "He's gonna be a father, for Christ's sake, he needs to go get a fuckin' job. A regular job."

Aldo looked at me like I'd just dropped a steamer in the middle of the table. "Fuck are you talkin' about? I'm tryin' to set him and the rest of us up so we don't have to do that shit."

"What you're talkin' about is dangerous work."

"So?"

"So maybe since he's gonna have a wife and a kid dependin'

on him he should do something a little safer, where he knows he's gonna come home every night and be able to provide for them and himself."

A slight smile twitched across Fritz's face. "That sounded very convincing, Richard. You're a thoughtful, responsible, and mature young man."

"Go fuck yourself."

"Guess somebody's got to."

Aldo finished his Coke, crushed the can in his hand and tossed it onto the table. "Point is, you fuckin' clowns, he can do somethin' with himself—we all can—if we get in with my uncle."

"Just sayin'—"

"What, Richie? What are you *just sayin'*?"

"Nothin'. Forget about it."

I returned my attention to the girl at the pinball machine. The electronic music signaling she'd won a round went off, accompanied by rows of blinking lights. She jumped up and down, bouncing in all the right places, clapping her hands and smiling a big, bright smile. I imagined sauntering over to her, saying all the right things, then taking her by the hand and walking out with her. Her white painter pants couldn't have been tighter, and the harder I looked the more my imagination went wild.

"So, we need a score," Fritz said.

Aldo nodded. "A real one."

"I just don't wanna do any real time. I ain't built for that shit."

"It's no joke," I said. "Look at Benny Ravish."

Benny was a year older than us, a friend we'd all known and occasionally hung out with for years. Tough as nails, he was a serious second-story thief by the time he was sixteen, and at seventeen got into a fight with some kid outside Skinny Dave's, not even a hundred feet from where we were sitting. He knocked the kid out, and when he fell, he hit the back of his head on the sidewalk and cracked his skull open. The kid wound up in a coma for a month. When he came out of it, he recovered and was fine. But Benny got arrested, tried and convicted. Because the kid's old man was some sort of bigshot in the state senate, they threw the book at Benny hard and tried him as an adult. Gave him ten years in Walpole for attempted murder. He'd only served three and got paroled for good behavior just a few months ago. But he came back from prison a totally different guy. Quiet, subdued, timid. Not just broken. Destroyed.

"They split him up the back in there," Aldo said. "Wasn't much left of the poor fuck when he came home, and he was only inside a couple years. Benny was a tough sonofabitch, and they broke him like he was nothin'."

"He was a good kid," I said quietly.

I remembered the look in Benny's eyes. Once wild and full of life, when he came home they were empty and dead. Nothing there. No light, no spark. They'd killed it. He was still walking around, but his days of being alive were long gone. Thankfully, the blonde at the pinball machine was playing another round, so I focused on her instead.

"Come on," Aldo said, standing. "Let's blow this dump."

"You guys go ahead," I told him. "I'm gonna hang out a while."

"You sure?"

"Yeah, I'll catch you tomorrow."

We slapped hands and they left. I could tell Aldo was still annoyed with me, but I couldn't worry about that. Things were going to go the way they were going to go, no matter what I said or did. I'd either go along or I wouldn't, and at that moment, for the first time in my life, I wasn't sure which one I'd pick.

I stood up, straightened myself out, then drifted over to the blonde.

She was playing the machine at the end of a row, so I moved to the side and leaned against it, pretending to watch the game instead of her. I could feel the machine shifting and shaking as she bounced herself against it again and again. After a minute, she lost her last ball and the machine began a series of defeated tones and electronic music signaling the game was over.

"You were doin' pretty good there for a while," I said, smiling at her. "I was watchin' you play."

She smiled back, widened her blue eyes, and said, "I've only played a couple times, but it's really fun."

"Only a couple times, huh? You're a natural."

"Thanks." She combed a strand of her heavily teased hair behind her ear. "I'm Donna."

"Richie." I put my hand out. "Never seen you before. Live around here?"

She shook my hand. Her grip was barely noticeable, her skin soft and warm. "I'm from Rhode Island, just hanging out with a friend. He's in a band, they're playing tonight at a club not far from here."

"Cool." If she was going to a club she either planned to sneak in, had a fake ID or was older than me—at least twenty-one—but she looked a lot younger. "You wanna get a Coke or somethin'?"

Before she could answer, a pencil-thin guy in black eyeliner and mauve lipstick appeared at her side. In an outfit consisting of baggy silk pants and a checkerboard T-shirt, his platinum blond hair was wild and sprayed and moussed up into a series of crazy angles and shelves. "Problem here?" he asked.

"No problem."

"This is Richie," Donna told him. "Richie, this is my boy-friend Alexander."

"Her *boyfriend*," the guy repeated.

I looked at Donna instead of him. "Sorry, I didn't know you were with somebody."

"It's really not a problem, I—"

"Well, now you know," Alexander said in his best tough-guy voice.

"Take it easy there, Flock of Seagulls."

Donna laughed, but Alexander remained stone-faced. Stepping between us, he squared up like he was going to try to fight me. Unable to help it, I burst out laughing. Right in his face. I threw his girlfriend a quick wink, then turned and walked back out onto the street. Had it been a year or so earlier, or had the guys still been there, things would've gotten much worse. I was proud of myself. I could've crushed the kid but didn't.

I lit a cigarette and watched The Avenue a while.

The day was almost gone. Another one burned away, just memories now, most not even worth having, lost in the heat and slowly dying light.

For the next few days, I laid low. Spent time with my mother, partied some with Woody up on the roof and escaped to the South Pacific in the pages of *The Beach of Falesá*.

It was a Thursday night when the heat finally broke. It started to rain, lightly at first, more a mist really, and then the sky opened up and it poured for hours, as if trying to make up for all the time it had been gone.

That same night, the phone rang while I was lying in bed reading. It wasn't that late, but my mother was already sleeping peacefully on the couch, so I got to the kitchen fast as I could before it woke her, and snatched the wall phone from its cradle. The small clock on the stove read eight-forty-six.

"Richie?"

I recognized Candy's voice and knew immediately something was wrong. It sounded like she'd been crying. "Yeah, what's going on, Candy?"

"Something happened," she said, voice shaking and cracking.

"You guys all right?"

"No, I—well, I'm okay, I—I'm just upset. Aldo's hurt."

"What do you mean *hurt*? Hurt how? What happened?"

"Can you get down here? Please, Richie, I'm all by myself and—"

"Where are you?"

"I—I'm at the hospital. In the ER."

"What the hell happened?"

"We were having dinner a-and these three guys walked by our table and one of them said something to me he shouldn't have, so Aldo got up and said something back, and then they—they started fighting and they beat him up really bad. One of them was hurt, too." She was halfway through the sentence when she started crying again. "They brought Aldo here in an ambulance."

"Is he gonna be okay?"

"I don't know yet. Nobody's talking to me."

"Did you call anybody else?"

"No."

"You know his Uncle Lou's number?"

"I-I think I have it in my address book in my purse."

"Let him know, but whatever you do, Candy, *don't* call Dino, you hear me? I don't want him to know about this until we figure out what's going on."

"Okay, I won't. They beat him up really bad, Richie, it was awful, I—I've never seen anything like that before, I—"

"It's gonna be all right. Try to stay calm, okay? Sit tight, I'm on my way."

I threw on a pair of jeans and a T, pushed my bare feet into my sneakers, threw on my leather jacket and a Bruins cap, then headed out quickly as I could. I didn't have a car or any access to one at that point, so I ran a few blocks to where I could catch one of the late buses.

Adrenaline zooming, I waited at the stop, watching the traffic move through the darkness and rain. It was cooler now, and the rain felt good, but I couldn't shake the series of visions moving through my mind like a slide show. Pictures in my head of Aldo bloodied and battered. Three against one, she'd said. Aldo was a skilled fighter, but outside of movies and comic books, in the real world, those were bad odds no matter who you were.

Hang in there, man, I thought. *I'm coming.*

The bus pulled up about five minutes later. I was one of only five people onboard, so I grabbed a seat near the front. With so many emotions surging through me at the same time, it was hard to know which one to focus on, so I sat back and tried to calm down as best I could.

About ten minutes later, I was back on the street. I ran half a block then cut across a parking lot and sprinted toward the hospital lights burning brightly through the rain and darkness.

I found Candy sitting in a chair all alone in the ER waiting area. A few other people were there as well, but she was off by herself, the only occupant in a cluster of plastic chairs bolted to the floor.

She saw me coming, stood up and ran for me.

We hugged, and she held me so tight I could barely breathe. Her perfume wafted all around us, and I tried my best not to react to how strong it was at such close range. We'd hugged a few times over the years but never like this. She felt so delicate and fragile, like she might shatter into a thousand pieces if she pressed against me any tighter. I was drenched but she didn't seem to care.

"Richie," she gasped, "I don't—I don't know what to do, I—"

"It's okay." I held her close and rubbed her back. "Take it easy. Breathe. Come on, couple slow deep breaths. There you go. Easy now."

Once she let me go, I led her back to her chair and sat her down.

Crouching in front of her, I took her shaking hands in mine. The various bracelets on her wrists jangled as she trembled. "Have you heard anything?"

Candy shook her head no. "They said a doctor would talk to me soon."

"How long's he been here?"

She stared at me as if she hadn't understood the question,

then blinked and seemed to snap out of whatever trance she'd fallen into. "We, um, we—I don't know for sure," she said, glancing down at her watch, "I think I've been waiting about half an hour or so, I—I think, I don't know, I'm not sure, I—"

"Easy," I said, squeezing her hands gently. "Easy."

A woman so beautiful she literally stopped guys in their tracks, Candy prided herself on looking nearly flawless at all times—never a hair out of place, makeup perfect, never a wrinkle in her clothing, hands and feet always manicured and pedicured and polished—but on this night, she was unusually disheveled. Hair wet and flattened down from the rain, dress mussed and still soaked, pumps scuffed and her makeup smeared and running across her face like war paint, she clearly could not have cared less how she looked, and instead had a look of terror and helplessness in her eyes that scared the hell out of me.

"Stay here," I said, standing and putting her hands gently in her lap. "Let me go see if I can find something out."

I'd just approached the reception desk when the glass doors slid open and Aldo's Uncle Lou strode into the hospital with another guy at his side. I knew I'd met the guy once before but couldn't remember his name. I hesitated near the desk and waited until they'd joined me there.

I opened my mouth to greet him, but Lou pushed right by me and went straight for the woman behind the desk. The other guy held back a bit, closer to me. I acknowledged him with a nod as he eyed me with a dead stare, his face expressionless and deeply pockmarked along both cheeks. Probably fifty-something, he was tall and thin, with birdlike features and dark thinning hair. He looked more like a retired shoe salesman than a criminal, but then, lots of those older hardcore criminal guys did.

Within seconds, Lou turned back to us. "I'm gonna go back and see him."

"You want me to come with you?" I asked.

"You know what happened?"

I nodded.

"Tell me. His girl was so upset on the phone I didn't get much."

I relayed what Candy had told me.

"She all right?"

"Shaken up pretty bad, but yeah, she's okay."

"All right," Lou said, turning for the door to the ER. "Wait here."

Since his buddy wasn't exactly the talkative type, I went back over to the chairs and sat next to Candy. She grabbed my hand the minute I sat down. It was still shaking.

Lou was gone less than five minutes. When he came back out I met him by the reception desk.

"He'll be all right," Lou told me. "They tuned him up good, though. Ribs are bruised, and he's cut and swelled up pretty bad, but he'll be fine. Gonna be hurting for a while, that's for sure."

I stood there, unsure of what to say but grateful to hear Aldo hadn't been seriously hurt.

Lou turned to his friend. "Happened over at Madam Ling's."

That was a small Chinese restaurant about five minutes away.

"They're friends," the guy said, which I knew meant they paid protection.

Lou moved closer to me, lowered his voice. "I think it'd be better if you and your guys handle this, yeah? I don't want to get involved. Might embarrass Aldo, you know? If he was hurt real bad, that'd be one thing, but like this, it's small potatoes. Better for you guys to take care of your own business."

"Whatever you think is best, Mr. Genaro."

"Like I said, smart kid." He smiled and gave my shoulder a squeeze. "Aldo's sitting up, waiting for them to release him. Go see him, I told him you were out here. But don't take all night. When you come back, we'll talk more."

"Okay." I motioned to Candy. "What about—"

"I'll talk to her." He looked over at her. She was crying

quietly, a tissue held to her nose. "No wonder he has so many problems when he's out with this broad. Look at her."

"Yeah, lots of guys hit on her."

"Why wouldn't they? Face on her like an angel and a body straight out of Hell. You don't never get tired of bangin' somethin' like that." He let out a burst of laughter, seemed to remember where he was, then cleared his throat and nonchalantly adjusted his crotch. "Okay, go do what I said."

With that, I ventured through the door and down a hallway that led to a nurse's station. Everyone there ignored me for several minutes until a nurse asked if she could help me. I gave her Aldo's name and she brought me to a room where he was waiting to be discharged.

Aldo was sitting on the edge an examination table, legs dangling just above the floor. Dressed in jeans and a sleeveless T-shirt, both were sprayed with blood. When he looked up as I came in the room, I saw the horrific condition of his face. He had stitches across his forehead, his lips and both eyes were badly swollen—the right one nearly shut, just a slit—his nose was covered with scrapes and dried blood around the nostrils while long black bruises streaked across one of his cheeks and down across the side of his neck and throat.

"Jesus," I said. "You all right, man?"

He nodded and tried to smile, but it was too painful. I could tell he was embarrassed. Aldo had lost a couple fights here and there, but he'd never taken a beating like this. "Thought my nose was busted," he said, his swollen lips slurring his words, "but they said it's okay. Ribs are bruised up but no broken bones. Hurts like a motherfucker when I breathe, and I got a headache that won't quit. But I'll live."

"Three on one, huh?"

"We were sitting there minding our business, having dinner. These three cowfuckers walk by our table and one of them looks at Candy and says, 'Hey, baby, wanna go for a ride?' Candy blows him off, and I tell the guy to screw. So then he says, 'On my cock?' I get up and throw. Hit him right in the face, perfect shot. He goes down, but the other two jump me. I got some shots in, believe me, they all know they were in a fight tonight. But once they got me down I was fucked, couldn't get back up with both of them on me. Stomped and kicked me so long I thought they were gonna kill me, bro."

"Sounds like they tried."

"Feels like it, too. Candy still out there?"

"Where else would she be? She's shook up bad, though."

"Scared her, she's never seen shit like that." He adjusted his position and moaned a little. "Christ, my whole fuckin' body hurts. I need to get out of here so we can take care of this."

"You're in no shape right now to do anything. They're gonna let you out in a few minutes. Go home, get some rest and heal up. I'll handle it."

Aldo hung his head.

"Don't worry about it," I told him. "I'll take care of it."

"I know," he said quietly. "I know you will."

"You worry about yourself. And Candy, too."

"Wanted to tell you, I been thinkin' about that other thing."

"What other thing?"

"The score."

"We'll talk about it later." I held my hand out and we shook. His knuckles were scraped and stained with dried blood. "Don't worry about it now, okay?"

"Okay," he sighed.

I left him sitting there, looking as beaten and defeated as he was.

Back through the doors and into the waiting area, I found Lou and his buddy standing over by the entrance talking with a couple uniformed cops.

I went over to Candy and suggested she go in and wait with Aldo until he was discharged. Dabbing at the tears in her eyes with a tissue, she thanked me for coming then disappeared into the ER.

When Lou was done with the cops, they all laughed and shook hands and the officers left. Realizing I was back, he and his buddy walked over to me.

"Richie," Lou said before I could say anything, "you remember my friend Jimbo, yeah?"

"Yeah, sure." I nodded to his friend. Now I remembered. The guy's name was Jimbo D'Amata. "How you doin'?"

He nodded back but said nothing, just looked at me with the same dead stare that never seemed to change.

"I straightened shit out with the cops," Lou explained. "Aldo don't want to file no charges and neither does the restaurant. So, no worries from them. Besides, those two are payroll guys and just wanted to help. They went to Madam Ling's. Turns out these scumbags paid cash for their meal, but one of the waitresses got a license plate on the car they left in. They ran the plate and got the name. Officially, nobody saw nothin', so no worries, no way to trace anything back to you. They did a quick run on the sonofabitch, though. He's got a sheet a mile long, mostly drugs—possession and intent to distribute—and a couple A&Bs. He's done time in county a couple times, but not in a while. He's a little older than you fellas, so watch yourself, yeah? Got no idea who the other two are, but this piece of shit ought to be able to lead you right to them. Just needs the right kind of incentive, know what I mean?"

"Yeah, I do."

"Don't play around with somebody like this. You hit 'em, hit 'em *hard*."

Jimbo held a small piece of paper out for me, so I took it. The name *Jeffrey Collins*, along with an address in the city was written on it.

"Okay." I put the paper in my pocket.

"Now if nobody minds, I'm gonna go home and watch *Cagney and Lacy* with the wife then give her the high hard one before she gets pissed about me being out so late and I got to listen to her bullshit." Lou winked at me and motioned toward the exit in a slow, sweeping motion. "You got what you need. Go forth, young man, and *do.*"

We'd all been arrested before. We'd all been convicted of crimes. But they were mostly A&B's, B&E's, robberies, disorderly conducts—that level of crime—and none of us had been arrested as adults, at least not yet. All our charges had been as minors, and at eighteen, those records were sealed and it was the same as having a clean slate. Problem was the cops still knew who we were and what we were about, and never forgot or gave us a chance to be anything else. Once they saw you as a criminal, that stuck. For me, I grew up around cops and criminals and never saw much difference between the two. One side got to wear badges and carry guns and pretend they were better than everybody else, superior somehow, because they were cops, but they did more or less whatever the hell they wanted, especially when dealing with guys like us, were as deep into corruption and crap as the worst elements the city had to offer, and didn't pay any more attention to the law than criminals did. So I learned very early on that there were three sets of rules in this life. One for cops, one for everybody else and a third one everyone knew existed but hardly ever talked about. That was the rule for *some* criminals. Guys like Lou Genaro could get away with a whole lot more than someone like me or anyone on our crew because he had the green to make things happen. Bread made cops and judges and lawyers and politicians look the other way. Lots of bread made them your business associates and golfing buddies. In all three worlds, guys like us were small change, expendable and not at all important. I remember a cop once telling me that I could die or rot in a prison cell for the rest of my life and no one would even notice I was gone, much less care. I didn't matter, I had no value. So I understood Aldo's desire to move up, to become more closely affiliated with his uncle and to begin what he hoped would be the next step toward being one of those guys who *did* matter. His uncle ran this area, which made him a very big fish in a medium pond, and for guys like us, that was good enough.

Still, the last thing any of us needed at that point was a pinch, and since I was in charge of handling the guys who'd tuned up Aldo, I knew I'd have to orchestrate things carefully. Dino was the wildcard, as usual. From the second he knew what happened, there'd no stopping him. Nobody'd be able to call him off, pecking order be damned.

So, the following night, when I found myself waiting on the corner smoking a cigarette while Fritz and Petie broke into, hotwired and stole a car a few blocks away, I was still working out exactly how we were going to do this in my head.

Through the darkness at the end of the street, I saw Dino emerge, strutting with purpose down the sidewalk, like the Hulk, hands clenched into fists and hanging at his sides, bouncing against the outside of his legs as he walked.

"Parked a street over," he said flatly, eyes on fire.

"Need you to be cool tonight," I told him.

He nodded, but I knew he wasn't listening.

"Ma, I'm serious."

"So am I. Their asses are grass."

"Yeah, but we're gonna do it smart, understand?"

"I just wanna smash these faggots. You see Ally's face?"

"We all did. I know you're pissed. So am I. So are the other guys. You'll get your chance to bust heads, but you need to listen to me and do what I say."

"Richie, not for nothin', but I don't got to take orders from you, man."

"Who runs our deal?"

"This ain't the time for this bullshit."

"Dino, look at me." I squared my stance but tried not to appear too aggressive. If he turned on me I was in trouble. "Who runs our deal?"

"Aldo," he said through a sigh.

"Who's number two?"

"You."

"That was Aldo's decision, yeah?"

He nodded sullenly.

"So while he's down, I run this shit, just like he wants me to. So yeah, you *do* take orders from me tonight, got it?"

Dino chewed his bottom lip. "Yeah, I got it."

I held my hand out.

"You know I always got your back, Richie." He shook my hand quickly. "I'm just fuckin' pissed."

"Forget about it. We'll make it right."

An old, nondescript Chevy rounded the corner and pulled over. Fritz was driving. I took the passenger seat and Dino hopped in back with Petie, who held a large canvas duffel bag across his lap.

"Ray-Ray in on this?" Dino asked.

"He's been taking heat for a drug buy the other day," Petie said, "so he's sitting this one out. But he said if we need him tomorrow he can probably move then, figures the cops won't be watching so close if he's cool tonight."

It was only about nine o'clock, but the streets were quiet. While the rain had stopped that morning, the heat was back, just as bad as it had been before. Fritz already knew the address, as he'd spent the day before doing recon and casing Jeffrey Collins's apartment, which was in a crap building adjacent to one of the worst housing projects in the city.

"Okay," I said, "here's what we know. This Collins piece of shit lives with another guy and maybe a chick now and then, we're not a hundred percent on her though. Now, we don't know if Collins's roommate is one of the three we're looking for, but there's a good chance he is. Aldo told me what all three guys looked like, and from what Fritz saw yesterday the other asshole coming and going from that apartment is probably one of them. Either way, these two are gonna tell us where to find the third guy, and then we'll handle him too."

Everyone went quiet.

As we rolled into the neighborhood, the city turned darker, and an eerie fog drifting in from the nearby ocean covered everything in a spooky haze. Most streetlights had been busted, shot out or simply didn't work in the area, so we had to rely largely on the headlights. They revealed those moving through the night, occupying the corners and standing around fires in barrels burning through the darkness and sending sprays of sparks high into the air. Drug dealers and pimps huddled at the mouths of alleys and in doorways, shooting the shit with exhausted-looking hookers, drug addicts, winos and other dregs of society. None of us came from what would ever be confused for good or even particularly safe neighborhoods. But this area was far worse. It was also Black Mamba territory. They were the largest, most organized and violent street gang in the city. Consisting of close to one hundred members, all poor and pissed-off young black guys, nobody fucked with the Black Mambas.

As we moved by one section of projects, a bunch of them were standing around on the street in their leather vests, eyeing our car with suspicion.

I looked into the backseat at Petie. "Ray-Ray made that call, right?"

"Yeah, told me he talked to his cousin."

Ray-Ray had two cousins who were Black Mambas, one of them high ranking. You didn't roll onto their turf and cause shit without a permit, regardless of the situation or even if it was justified, without having to answer to them, so his call granted us safe passage.

"We got a pass to handle our business tonight and tonight only," Petie said, "and only at that one building."

"Good," I said, "we shouldn't have any trouble from the Mambas then."

Fritz pulled the car over and parked on the street next to a vacant lot covered in debris and overgrown grass surrounded by rusted chain-link fence. He pointed a black-gloved finger across the street at a small apartment building on the corner. "That's it. First floor, second door on the right."

Adrenaline firing, I took a couple deep breaths. "Okay," I said, "me and Dino up front. Ma, you're the first one through. We get in, get it under control and lock it down."

Petie unzipped the bag on his lap, removed four black ski masks, slipped one on himself, then handed out the other three. Once we'd donned them, he removed three pieces of lead pipe, handed one to me, one to Dino and kept the third for himself. Fritz produced his usual brass knuckles from the pocket of his leather jacket, slipped them on, then gave us a nod.

"Car stays runnin'," he said. "We don't have an extra guy to stay with it so hopefully it's still here when we get out. This neighborhood, who knows?"

"It'll be here," Dino said, as if willing it to be so.

"If it's not, we stay together." I pointed to the lot. "Head that way."

"Come on," Dino said through gritted teeth, his eyes wide and white against the black mask. "Enough of this sittin' around talkin' shit."

"Easy." I pulled the ski mask down over my face. It smelled like mothballs and made my cheeks itch. "Straight shot, no stops, no hesitations. Once we're inside, if we hit anything we're not expectin', be cool and follow my lead, got it?"

Everyone nodded.

"All right." I drew a deep breath, looked over at the squat two-story building, then opened the car door. "Let's go."

We crossed the street in single-file, moving quickly but not running, a snake-like shadow of four guys in black, blended into the night and moving through it with singular purpose. Within seconds, we'd closed on the building, entered the small vestibule and positioned ourselves on either side of the second door on the right.

Dino reached a gloved hand to the doorknob, tried to turn it on the off chance it might be unlocked. He looked at me, shook his head no. I quickly scanned the door for locks. Looked like a single deadbolt and there was almost certainly a chain as well, but if there was more, and we couldn't break through right away, it'd give whoever was inside time to prepare for us. I held my hand up, signaling Dino to hold, then gave him a quick nod.

He knocked on the door.

It seemed to take forever to get a response. We stood there in the filthy little lobby, the tiles beneath our feet cracked and stained, the ceilings above covered in watermarks and cracks, the painted walls around us chipped and battered. The smell of urine filled the air, mixed with what might have been vomit.

Dino knocked again, little harder this time.

"Yeah?" a male voice on the other side answered.

"Hey, is Tiffany there?" Dino asked.

"Who?"

"Tiffany."

"No Tiffany here."

He looked at me. I nodded.

"Hey, fuck you, man! I know she's in there! Open up!"

"Fuck off."

Dino knocked again, hard enough to rattle the casing. "Tiffany!"

The deadbolt turned. We readied ourselves.

"Motherfucker, there's no Tiffany here, now fuck off or—"

As the door swung open, Dino braced himself then kicked it with everything he had. It burst back into the guy, knocking him to the floor and swinging the door so hard it almost came off the hinges.

Dino was the first one through. I followed, the other guys behind me. We rushed into the apartment, a small little dump that looked like it hadn't been cleaned in months. The whole place stunk like weed and booze and piss, and the only light was from a small lamp in the corner.

Petie was the last guy through, so he closed the door then headed straight for the back part of the apartment with Fritz.

The guy who'd answered the door was good-sized but so shocked at what had happened he didn't have time to react before Dino stomped him in the balls, stomach and chest. Any fight he might've had in him was gone as he rolled around on the floor moaning and clutching his genitals.

I heard commotion from the back, but I moved through the main room to the kitchenette. No one there. The kitchen table was covered with drugs and paraphernalia, the sink full of dirty dishes and covered in scurrying roaches.

In the center of the table was a revolver.

On the counter was some sort of makeshift little altar constructed from small animal bones, black candles burned halfway down on either side of it and a pentagram written on the wall behind it in what looked like blood.

Turning back, I saw Dino lift the guy up by the scruff of his neck and push him down into a threadbare chair. The guy gave no resistance, still reeling from the attack. To keep it that way, Dino swung the pipe down across the guy's shin, and then the other. He yelped and fell out of the chair. Dino put him back, pressed the pipe against his chest and held him there.

Fritz and Petie returned from the rear of the apartment with a couple they'd found in one of the bedrooms. The guy was bloodied around his eyes and the girl was screaming at us, trying to figure out what was going on. Both were nude.

"Fuck are you pricks doin'?" the woman, a skinny brunette with track marks up and down her arms, screamed. "You motherfuckers think you are? I got a nigger pimp that's gonna kill you fuckin' faggots when I tell him—"

Petie grabbed her by the throat and yanked her in close to him. "I ain't gonna tell you again to shut that *fuckin'* cock-sucker of yours. Say one more word, and I'll jam this pipe so far down your throat it'll come out that dirty, giant snatch. You understand me, bitch?"

Eyes wide, she nodded as best she could with his hand around her throat.

"What's goin' on?" the guy with her said. "What's this shit?"

Fritz answered him with a lead pipe to the gut. With a grunt, the guy doubled over, dropped to his knees and vomited all over the floor.

"Looks like somebody had pizza," Fritz quipped. "Anchovies. Gross."

Petie pushed the woman down onto a dilapidated couch next to the chair and told her to stay put. She did, covering herself as best she could.

"Which one of you is Jeffrey Collins?" I asked.

Neither answered.

Dino raised the pipe and smashed it down on the guy in the chair. It struck his shoulder and he cried out, immediately grabbing at it and writhing around in the chair.

"Jesus—fuck—okay, okay!" the guy said. "I'm Jeff, all right?"

I pointed to vomit boy. "He with you at Madam Ling's the other night?"

He looked at me, and I knew then what the answer was. I also knew he now understood why we were here. "I don't—what are you talkin' about?"

Dino slid the pipe into the back of his pants, grabbed Collins and yanked him up onto his feet. While Petie kept an eye on the other two, Dino, Fritz and I all beat on him until he was lying on the floor in a puddle of his own blood and piss, crying and choking about an ambulance.

Then we turned to the other guy.

"I bet that shit hurts, huh?" I asked him, still trying to catch my breath. "I'm thinking that many hits with a pipe his legs and ribs gotta be busted, right? Three on one, bad odds, not really fair."

The guy looked around like the cornered rat he was. "The fuck, man, it—it was just a fight, we didn't—"

"I'm gonna ask you this one time," I told him. "You make

me ask again and we're gonna take these pipes and split your fucking skull with them, you understand me?"

"Yeah," he said softly. "Yeah, I do."

"There was three of you. Who's the other guy?"

"His name's Tim."

"Tim got a last name?"

"P-Patrick."

"And where does Tim P-Patrick live?"

After a few seconds, he hadn't answered. Dino stepped forward and punched him so hard in the mouth the guy spat out four teeth in a drool of blood and spittle then collapsed, face-planting on the floor. He didn't move for a while and the girl on the couch started to cry.

Collins, still rolled up in a ball a few feet away, said something, but I couldn't make out what it was.

I looked at Dino. "Crack his fuckin' head open."

"Wait!" the girl said. "Just wait, okay? I know where Tim lives, he—he lives over on Brock Avenue."

That wasn't far.

I noticed an old blanket over the back of the couch. I pulled it free and threw it at her. She wrapped herself in it but said nothing more.

Dino had drifted into the kitchenette. "What's all this Devil shit?"

"It's our way," she said, a sick gleam in her glassy eyes. "Our truth."

There was a lot of Satan worship in the area, lots of people were into that kind of thing, and there was a large hardcore cult in the area that operated throughout the city and reached all the way to Fall River. Mostly drug addicts and hookers, they held ceremonies in the Freetown State Forest, were known to be violent, and were mixed up in all sorts of sick shit.

And then Dino saw the gun. He picked it up, studied it a minute. "Let's do these evil fuckers," he said. "Let's do all three of them."

"Hey, I—I didn't do nothin' to you guys!" the girl said.

We'd already been there longer than I wanted to be, and now Dino handling a gun was the last thing we needed. I ignored him, hoping that might work. "What's Tim Patrick's address on Brock Avenue?" I asked the girl.

"You ain't got to worry about it," she told me, eyes still trained on Dino. "He's supposed to be comin' over any time."

"He drive or on foot?"

"He drives a piece of shit blue Mazda."

Dino tipped the kitchen table over, dumping drugs and the rest across the floor with a resounding crash. Then he made his way to the counter, and using the gun, smashed the little altar to pieces. With a quick look back at the girl, he hocked a loogie all over the pentagram then strode back closer to me.

The girl said something in what sounded like Latin, muttering it beneath her breath like a prayer while staring at Dino the entire time.

"Fuck you say to me?" he moved toward her. "You tryin' to put some sorta hex or shit on me, you fuckin' whore?"

To my right, I heard Fritz quietly say to me, "We need to go."

The girl laughed at Dino and wrapped herself tighter in the blanket. "Fuck you, man. Fuckin' retard."

Before I knew what was happening, or could do anything about it, he'd begun pistol-whipping her.

Fritz and I grabbed him, pulled him off her. But he'd already hit her several times, and her face was a bloodied mess. She slumped back against the couch and didn't move, twitching as if she were being shocked.

"Go!" I said, pushing Fritz into him. "Get him out!"

Petie stood staring at the girl, eyes wide and in full panic mode, peering out through the holes in his mask.

"Hey," I said, not wanting to use his name.

"Fuck," he said. "Is she dead?"

"*Hey!*"

He looked at me.

"We're out. Let's go. Move."

Petie brushed by me and left the apartment.

Collins muttered something again, so I kicked him until he shut up.

The other guy still hadn't moved since losing his teeth. The girl had stopped twitching and her eyes were open but rolling around in her head like she'd lost all control of them. Blood leaked from her hairline, painting her face in crimson. She tried to sit up but moved like she was boneless, flopping over forward and crashing to the floor in a heap.

I backed out, closed the door, then turned and hurried back across the street. Drawing a deep breath of night air, I fast-walked toward the car, just as a Blue Mazda pulled up in front of the building.

The headlights hit me and I froze.

Suddenly, the other guys appeared out of the darkness and closed on the car. They pulled the driver out, threw him to the ground and began kicking and stomping him. Then Fritz pummeled him with his brass knuckles until he lay still.

We were all back in the stolen car and driving through the fog within seconds. No one said anything. Breathing heavily, I pulled the mask off, as did the others, and we returned them, along with the pipes, to the bag. Once we'd cleared the neighborhood, Fritz pulled into a convenience store and Petie tossed the bag into a dumpster in back.

Five minutes later, we were at the water. I asked Dino for the piece and he handed it over without saying a word. It was slick with blood and had several long strands of hair stuck to it. I walked it out to the end of a stone jetty, careful not to slip on the slick rocks in the dark, and tossed it into the Atlantic.

Then I lit a cigarette and smoked it a while, breathing in the sea air and letting the breeze blow over me, a light spray from the ocean misting all around.

Unusually deserted and covered in fog and darkness, the city seemed like a whole other planet that night, like some alien world we'd stumbled into in the dead of night. It didn't feel like home anymore. It all faded away into a blur of distant city lights barely visible through the fog, and all I could think about, all I could see, was that girl covered in blood.

She and the others had paid a heavy price for what had happened to Aldo.

Now all I could do was hope we wouldn't pay an equal toll for what we'd done to them.

CHAPTER FIVE

For the next few days, everybody laid low. Nobody talked, nobody hung out. We all went our own ways and stayed quiet. I mostly drank and smoked up on the roof with Woody, tried to keep things light and myself as high and drunk as possible, so I wouldn't think about things or remember that night. Not that I could ever forget the sound of that gun cracking against that woman's head. But the booze and the weed helped numb it all. The pain and fear were still there. I just didn't give a shit.

Until the attack made the local news, and then I knew it was time to sober up. The assault was reported and believed to be a drug-related dispute between rival dealers, but police said there were no solid leads on the actual perpetrators. Collins and his two buddies had all gone to the hospital with broken bones and various injuries, a couple fairly serious but none life-threating. I thought maybe we were out of the woods, and then they reported that the woman, identified on the news as Joanna Holt, was in a coma. Doctors weren't sure if she'd pull through.

Christ, I thought, *we're all gonna burn for this.*

Couple days later, soon as he was strong enough to drive, Aldo called, told me to meet him at the corner, then drove over and picked me up.

He started yelling before I'd even gotten in the car.

"The fuck happened?" he said, spitting the words at me.

"Dino went crazy," I told him.

Aldo drove to Buttonwood Park and pulled in over by the

duck pond. He closed the windows, cranked the air conditioning, and didn't say anything for a long time. We just sat there.

"Should've never brought him with us," I finally said.

"None of you could've stopped him from going."

I was glad Aldo at least acknowledged that much. "You
know how he gets. He was so pissed, all he wanted to do was
bust heads. It was all goin' fine until that chick laughed at him."

"Laughed at him?"

I explained what had happened.

"Jesus," Aldo said through a sigh. Wincing, he gently
rubbed his ribs. "So, she says some Devil shit to him and then
laughs right in his face?"

"I didn't have time to get him out of there, Ally. Before any
of us knew what was happening, he was poundin' on her with
the gun. I should've grabbed the piece when I first saw it, but I
didn't know Ma was gonna go in the kitchen and find it. I was
tryin' to keep things under control and still watch everybody. I
wanted to get in and out, quick, you know? Just didn't happen
that way."

"I talked to Uncle Lou."

"And?"

"Obviously, he don't want anything to do with this, but he
got some information from some of the cops on his payroll. End
of the day, nobody gives a rat's ass about these fucks. They're
all scumbags. Cops aren't gonna waste any time worrying
about those losers. The problem's the chick. If she dies, then
they got to do something. And Uncle Lou says they'll come
looking for us."

"Why us?"

"Because Collins has been talkin'. He told the cops the guys
who attacked him mentioned Madam Ling's, so he knew you
were there because of what they did. They can already trace it
back to me. And once they trace it to me, won't take long to
trace it to all of you." He rubbed his eyes, like a headache had
settled behind them. "I got an alibi, was home with Candy the

whole day and night, never left the house, and as a favor, because you guys were lookin' out for me, Uncle Lou's putting together an alibi for all of you too. He's got enough places on protection, one of them will claim you guys were there when the attack went down. Besides, the pigs can think—hell, even know—it was you guys, but they can't prove shit. You left nothin' behind at the scene and nobody there can do positive IDs on any of you because of the ski masks."

"Then we're okay?" I asked hopefully.

"Not yet. If that Holt chick lives, they won't even bother followin' up, the guys my uncle knows on the force already told him that."

"And if she dies?"

"They'll round you guys up and try to squeeze you."

"Shit."

"Nothin' we all haven't been through before."

"Stakes are little different this time around."

"Long as everybody sticks to the same story and uses the alibi my uncle gets you, we'll be fine. Like I said, they got nothin'."

"But if they know—"

"They can know whatever they want. Only thing that matters is what they can *prove*. And they got jack shit for proof."

I looked over at the pond before us, and all the ducks gliding around. "If the cops pull us in, Fritz and me can get through it no problem. It's Petie and Ma I'm worried about. You know how the fuckin' cops are. Once they start double-talkin' and bullshittin', Petie's gonna get confused."

"He'll be fine. He's been squeezed before and got through it. We just got to coach him, keep it real simple and make sure he knows exactly what to say."

"What about Dino?"

"What about him?"

"If they piss him off—and they will—there's no tellin' what he'll say or do."

"Neither one's gonna rat."

"Not on purpose."

"We'll worry about that if we have to. Right now, that bitch is still alive."

I nodded. "Either way, I'm not about this shit, man."

"What's that mean?"

"The hell you think it means?"

Aldo adjusted his position in the seat despite the obvious pain it caused him and slung an arm across the steering wheel. "I don't know, Richie, why don't you tell me?"

"Means I'm there if we ever need to kick ass, but I don't beat on women, and far as I knew, until the other night, neither did anybody else on our crew."

"Ma lost it. He hates that Devil shit, and then if she laughed at him the bitch was askin' for it without even knowin' it."

"I'm not gonna be runnin' around killin' people, man."

"Nobody was tryin' to kill anybody."

"She could die."

"Who gives a shit?"

"She could *die*, Ally."

"If she kicks, we'll deal with it."

"And she'll still be dead."

"We're talkin' about a lowlife piece of shit, just like the rest of them."

"Doesn't mean it was cool for Dino to do what he did. She had nothin' to do with what happened to you."

"Are you defendin' this skank?"

"I'm sayin' Dino was wrong, and his bullshit may have finally ended up killin' somebody. And you know what? I'm not burnin' for that motherfucker."

Aldo stared at me as if he'd never seen me before and was trying to figure out how I'd gotten into his car. "Fuck did you just say?"

"You heard me."

"Are you sidin' with her over him?"

"Don't be an asshole."

He arched an eyebrow.

"Ally, come on. No, of course not, don't even ask me shit like that."

"Then I'm still listening."

"I'm sayin' I can't defend what he did."

"So who's askin' you to?"

"If you were there you'd understand what I'm sayin', you—"

"I'm not defendin' it either, all right? But that don't mean—"

"It was a crazy-ass fuckin' *psycho* move, Ally. Completely out of control. It's the kinda shit that's gonna get us all killed or behind bars for the rest of our lives, you understand what I'm tellin' you here?"

"I get it. I do, okay? But we need to stick together."

"I'm not sayin' we don't. But if she dies we're—"

"We stick together. *Especially* if she dies."

"Of course." I nodded, but wouldn't look at him. "You're not hearin' me."

"You sayin' you'd rat him out if some fuckin' hooker steps off?"

"I'd never rat anybody out," I told him. "You know me better than that."

"Then what are you sayin', Richie?"

"If that woman dies, my days of runnin' with Dino Abruzzo are over. You hear me? They're fuckin' *over*."

"You're gonna cut him loose? Just like that? Over some dirty whore you don't even know? A bitch that'd cut your throat without even thinkin' about it?"

I pulled my cigarettes out, remembered I wasn't allowed to smoke in his car then put them back. "You know I spent a few nights in lockup here and there, and what have I always said? That was enough, right? I'm not goin' to prison."

"Dino would die for you. You know that, right? He'd take a fuckin' bullet for you without even thinkin' about it."

"You think I wouldn't do the same for him?"

"You got me wonderin' now, you wanna know the truth. If it was you got jumped, Ma would've been right there, beatin' their asses just the same as he was for me."

"Ally, he's crazy."

"We're all crazy, brother."

"No, I mean it. He's fuckin' nuts. He's insane. If we hadn't been there to pull him off—"

"But you were."

"And he still might've killed her."

"Yeah. He just might've. Shit happens, people die sometimes."

"Tunin' somebody up's one thing, but I'm not some stone psycho. That's not me and it's not gonna be me."

"Ma told me himself he didn't mean to hurt her that bad."

"You weren't there."

"Been with him a thousand other times on a thousand other nights. Same as you. Ma's just Ma, that's all. We'll get him through this, just like he'd get us through it. And we'll do it *together*, yeah?"

"You really think you got to tell me this shit?"

"It's all for one, man. Can't be no other way."

"I got Dino's back," I said. "I got everybody's back. Always have, you know that. You fuckin' *know* that. We don't need to be havin' this conversation. I just can't keep runnin' with somebody that unpredictable."

"Can't? Or won't?"

"What the hell difference does it make?"

"A lot, especially since it seems like you're driftin', Richie, changin'."

"You don't trust me, is that where this is goin' now?"

It took a while before he said anything else. "That ain't the question."

"What's the question then?"

"Do *you* still trust *me*?"

"Why are you askin' questions you already know the answers to?"

135

"Let me put it this way. Candy knows I love her, right? But sometimes she still wants to hear me say it. Know what I mean?"

"Of course I trust you, ya fuckin' moron."

"Okay, then it's squashed right now, ya dick." Aldo faced the wheel, his entire demeanor back to normal. "I gotta get Petie, bring him over to Chuckie D's and see what we can do about a ring for Trampy. You wanna come?"

"Nah, you guys go ahead."

"All right, I'll drop you back home."

"Don't worry about it," I said, pushing open the door. "I'm gonna hang around a while, feed the ducks."

Once I was out of the car, Aldo leaned over and put his hand out. "Be cool," he told me. "We'll get this worked out. Trust me."

I shook his hand. His grip seemed a little tighter than usual. "Always do," I said. "I'll catch up to you guys later."

I closed the door, lit a cigarette, took a few needy drags, and walked over to one of the benches on the grass. A young couple a few years older than me stood on the banks of the pond with a toddler, a little girl with pigtails who kept laughing hysterically every time her parents tossed feed to the ducks.

It was the most beautiful sound I'd ever heard.

I don't how long I sat on that bench smoking cigarettes and watching that family play with the ducks, but eventually almost everyone else was gone and I found myself alone in that part of the park. The heat kept rising, so I took my leather jacket off, slung it over my shoulder and walked up the path past a big playground and eventually to the entrance to the city zoo. Various versions of it had been there for years. I remembered my mother taking me there when I was little, but I hadn't passed through the gates for more than a decade. I didn't go in that day either, I just sort of rubber-necked it for a while. I always liked animals, but even as a little kid the place made me sad. All those animals in cages and corrals, behind glass or in water tanks. They didn't seem to like it any more than I did. Same as them, I knew nothing alive ever wanted to be trapped.

For hours, I walked around the park and surrounding neighborhoods, heading toward Dartmouth, which was only minutes away even on foot. I moved along the narrow sidewalks, watched the traffic and remembered walking the same route just a couple years before when I was in high school. I'd often skip school, walk to the mall and spend the day there. Early in the morning, the only other people there were usually senior citizens, oldsters in sweat suits exercising and walking from one end of the mall to the other, then back again. And of course, there were the mall cops, usually older guys with wrinkled uniforms and caps askew, who'd stop and ask me what I was doing there on a school day. All I had to tell them in those days was I went to private school, and they automatically assumed I was on a different schedule than the public-school kids and left me alone. I'd sneak into the movies, get a slice of pizza or a hot dog, or maybe if I had more cash than usual, I'd treat myself to a burger, fries and milkshake at Friendly's or a hot turkey dinner at the lunch counter at Woolworth's, then spend hours wandering the mall, looking at all the shit I couldn't afford, occasionally shoplifting what I could get away with, checking out the pretty girls who worked in all the stores or killing time playing video games for quarters at a little arcade over by the movie theater called The Dream Machine.

When I got to the mall that day, it was busier due to the summer season, the place already hopping and loaded with people milling about. I drifted around, hid in the crowd and tried to blend in, to forget everything I knew and all the visions in my head.

I'd been there maybe an hour when I saw her.

Mariana. Standing in front of Child World toy store with her new white bread boyfriend. In a striped rugby shirt, chinos and loafers, he looked like he'd fallen out of a JC Penney catalog. Mariana saw me right about the time I saw her, leaned over and said something to the guy, who responded with a nod then ran a hand through his perfect short hair and gave her a quick peck on the cheek he wanted me to see.

She left him there and approached me cautiously, which hurt, but she looked good. Really good.

I smiled. "What's up?"

"How are you, Richie?"

"You know how it is."

She tossed her hair off her face and looked at me with eyes that used to melt me into a puddle with a blink or two. "How's your mom?"

"Same."

"My brother said you called the other day."

"Yeah, just wanted to say hi, see how you were doin'. No big deal."

"That was nice."

"I have my moments."

"Yes, you do." She smiled, subtly cocked her head toward her boyfriend. "Can't talk long, Rory and I are going to the movies in a few."

"*Rory?*" I chuckled, even though I didn't really find anything funny about it. "Who the fuck is named *Rory?*"

Her smile vanished. "My new boyfriend. Don't start, all right?"

"College boy, huh?"

"Yeah, that's what they got at colleges."

I looked past her at him, smiled and waved. He waved back. "What'd you do, try to find a guy as different from me as you possibly could?"

"Pretty much."

"How's that workin' out?"

"Just fine. He's a sweetheart. He's smart and witty and—"

"Witty?"

"It's like funny."

"I know what it means."

She shrugged. "Anyways, I'm doing good. *Well*, I mean. I'm doing very *well*, thank you. I love it at school."

"I'm happy for you." I lit a cigarette. "I mean it."

"Do you?"

"Just said I did, didn't I?"

Neither of us said anything, and I thought back to not long after we'd first started dating. We'd usually go to a movie or out to eat or something, then find a place to make out. Lots of times we'd end up at a Friendly's not far from her house. Seemed like every time we went there we'd run into this guy Wayne, a stocky dude in his early twenties Mariana had known since they were kids. I was cool to him the first time we met, shook his hand and even invited him to sit with us. But he acted like a smug dick, ignoring me or rolling his eyes whenever I said anything, while grinning and winking at Mariana every few seconds then looking over at me, like there was some joke they were in on and I wasn't.

First time, I let it go. Even when we sat in the same booth and he sat on her side instead of mine. He put his arm around her and smiled at me the whole time, like I was some stupid kid. At sixteen, I guess that's what he figured me for. She removed his arm and told him to behave himself and I gave him a look but didn't do or say anything else about it until later when we were alone.

"Fuck is that guy's problem?" I asked.

"Wayne's just goofin', Richie, I've known him since we were kids. He lives a couple houses down from me. He always flirts and stuff, but he's just kidding."

"Didn't look like he was kiddin' to me. How old is he?"

"Few years older than us. Twenty-two, I think."

"Did you and him have a thing?"

"Ew, gross. No way."

"Well, he was awful cozy with you, puttin' his arm around you and shit."

"Don't be jealous."

"Of that clown? Not jealous, but if he puts his arm around you again I'm gonna say something to him."

"He's harmless."

"Yeah? Well, I'm not."

We didn't talk about it again, and I'd forgotten all about the bastard. A couple weeks later we ran into him at that same Friendly's. This time we said a quick hello and got our own booth.

Hadn't even gotten our food yet when the fucker came over and sat in our booth, again, sitting across from me and right next to Mariana. He put his arm around her and smiled at me like an idiot.

"Hey, pal," I said, "don't put your arm around my girl-friend, all right?"

"She don't mind," he chuckled, pulling her closer. "Do you, hon?"

Mariana blushed but didn't say anything.

The waitress arrived, delivered the two coffees we'd ordered then moved away.

I put both hands on my mug, felt the warmth coming through. "Tell you what, *Wayne*," I said, smiling back at him. "I mind."

"Relax, tough guy. Just snugglin' with my girl."

Mariana looked like she was about to lose her mind. She knew I was close to going off on this moron.

"I'm only gonna say it one more time. Move your arm. Now."

"Oooo," he said, mock shivering. "You're scary!" He looked at Mariana. "He's scary!"

"You got no fuckin' idea."

Wayne took his arm from her shoulder and leaned forward, both hands on the table between us. "Easy," he said in a low voice. "Just havin' some fun, bud. You don't want no fuckin' problems with me, junior. I ain't one of your punk friends. You fuck with me, I'll beat your ass six ways to Sunday."

"Wayne, he's just—"

"Shut up, Mariana." He leaned closer to me. "You hear me, punk?"

I threw my coffee in his face. It was scalding and he screamed and brought both hands to his eyes as Mariana slid as far away from him fast as she could.

Jumping out of the booth, I grabbed Wayne by his hair with one hand and smashed the mug down across his head with the other. It shattered and cut his scalp open. As he continued to yelp and cry out, I yanked him the rest of the way out of the booth and onto the floor, where I punched him in the face until I was exhausted and he was no longer moving, just grunting and making weird gurgling sounds.

Mariana, in tears, ran out while the other patrons all looked on in horror, and the manager came to tell me he'd called the police.

As Wayne lay there crying and holding his bloodied and burned face, two of his teeth on the floor next to pools of his blood and the spilled coffee, I lit a cigarette and sat back down in the booth.

The cops picked me up about five minutes later. I wound up going to court and having to pay a hundred-dollar fine on an A&B. I never did a day in jail or juvie, except for the night I was arrested.

Mariana didn't talk to me for a week. But the next time I saw her, she fucked me like she hadn't had sex in a year. From then on, our relationship was never the same, and to this day I wasn't sure if that was good or bad. I turned her on, but she was afraid of me too. Not that I'd ever do anything to her, of course, but she knew that at any moment I could become extremely violent if I felt I had to. She'd heard about me and my friends, but until then had never seen us do anything. Now that she had, she realized it wasn't just high school boys talking big and trying to act tough. I remembered feeling strange after that, like she'd seen a different part of me that, until then, I'd tried to keep hidden. But she didn't break up with me. From then on, whenever we ran into Wayne, he'd look away and keep his distance. Mariana always seemed confused, like she couldn't quite understand who the hell I really was or what made me tick.

Now, years later in the middle of the mall, while her new boyfriend waited on us to finish our conversation, she was still looking at me the same way.

After a few awkward seconds, she said, "So what have you been up to?"

I took a drag on my cigarette, exhaled through my nose and tried to think of a decent answer. "Just hangin' out. Same shit as before."

"That sounds exciting."

"Sorry I'm not fancy enough for you anymore, there, college girl."

I could tell from her expression the words had hurt her. "It's not like that, Richie," she said. "Really, it's not. I just want to make something of myself. I want to go places and see things and learn about the world and everything in it. I want to have a life. A real life. I studied and worked hard to make it to college, and I plan to make the most of it. What, am I supposed to apologize for that?"

"Of course not."

Her posture relaxed. "Rory calls it *expanding my horizons*."

"Worldly guy, huh?"

"He is, actually. He's a junior."

"Wow, he must know a lot then, huh?"

"Why do you have to be so nasty?"

"I'm just kiddin'."

"No you're not."

"Okay, I'm not."

"If you want to know the truth, I've learned a lot from him already."

"I bet."

"Not like that," she said with a smirk.

"So where's he from? Beverly Hills or some shit?"

"Yeah, Richie, he's from freakin' Beverly Hills." She seemed to realize she'd forgotten her new persona and let slip the old Mariana, but got hold of herself quickly. "He's from Connecticut, actually."

"That explains the outfit." I took a couple steps closer to an ashcan positioned next to a wooden bench, flicked my cigarette then had another drag. "Anyway, I gotta get goin'. Nice seein' you."

"You too," she said, but didn't move. "Richie...are you okay?"

We'd known each other too well for too long. I pushed away memories of being in bed together, wet and exhausted from fucking and fooling around for hours, wrapped in cool sheets, holding each other tight and talking about a future as a couple we'd never know.

"Yeah," I lied. "Sure."

Her eyes gave her away. They always had. "You look tired."

"I'm all right."

"You still running with Ally and the guys?"

"What else would I be doing?"

She looked disappointed but not surprised. "Too bad."

"You used to like those guys. You used to like me."

"I'm in college now. I'm not a kid anymore. And neither are you."

"What am I, an old man now?"

"No, but you're still doing the same stuff you were before."

"So what?"

Mariana steeled herself, like she often did when she was working her way toward saying something she considered important. "So, the whole leather jacket tough-guy bad-boy thing was hot when we were in high school. But you're supposed to outgrow that stuff."

"That what happened?" I asked. "You outgrew that stuff?"

"I outgrew you, Richie."

I couldn't really blame her, but part of me wanted to.

"I got to go," she said.

"Take care of yourself, huh?"

"You too."

I watched her walk back to her boyfriend. He slung an arm over her shoulder and together they drifted off, swallowed by the crowd and on to better things, a better life. I stood by the bench smoking my cigarette, feeling like the idiot I was and wondering if I looked the part too.

People kept moving. The world kept spinning.

And somewhere, not very far away, a young woman was fighting for her life, with mine likely hanging in the balance right along with her.

Dusk was settling in by the time I rounded the corner of my block. The humidity was still bad, but the latest heat wave seemed to be pretty much over. Jacket slung over my shoulder, I wearily climbed the steps to our building. At the doors, I stopped and looked back at the street. The block was empty. Not even any cars passing by. A strange feeling crept through me, as if someone was watching me. I scanned the buildings across the street and down the block. Nothing. The feeling shifted, became more an instinctual sense of danger.

In the foyer, I checked our mailbox. Bunch of bills and a magazine my mother liked. Once up the stairs and down the hallway toward our apartment, the feeling grew stronger.

By the time I could see our door, I knew why.

Bronski, the super and landlord, was knocking lightly, a big bottle concealed in a wrinkled paper bag in his other hand.

This fuckin' guy, I thought. *Just what I need.*

A short and stocky bastard, but still ripped from hours of manically lifting weights in his first-floor apartment, Bronski was always sniffing around my mother. "Honey?" he said, softly as his gravelly voice would allow. "You in there? I got a present for you, open up."

Part of me wanted to turn around and leave. The other part wanted to beat him to death right there in the hallway. I wasn't sure I could do either.

"Hey," I said. "Fuck are you doin'?"

Bronski turned to me, his beady little eyes blinking rapidly. "How's it goin', kid?" He wiped some spittle from the corner of his mouth with his free hand then stood up straighter, pushing out his chest and widening his stance. "Whattaya want?"

"I live here."

He laughed, but it quickly turned to a gurgling cough from all the cigars he smoked. Perpetually tanned to the point of looking like cracked leather, he adjusted the muscle shirt he had on—some T-back number with a monster truck or some bullshit on it—and shuffled his booted feet like a bull getting ready to charge. "Your mother home, kid?"

"She's always home."

He jerked a thumb at the door. "Ain't answerin'."

"Probably sleepin'. Or maybe she don't want to see you."

He smiled, revealing crooked and nicotine-stained teeth. "Can't be that," he said, running his hand through his silver hair. "She's always happy to see me, kid."

"Yeah, well not tonight." I stepped toward the door, but he didn't move. "You wanna get the fuck outta the way?"

"Hey, who are you to talk to me like that, huh?" He poked a stubby finger into my shoulder. "You watch your mouth, kid, you know what I mean?"

"Touch me again and we throw. Right here."

He laughed in my face, which just made me want to smash his even worse.

"Tough guy, huh? One of these days, kid, I'm gonna show you what a real tough guy can do." He straightened his posture again, hiked his jeans up a little higher then held the bottle out. "How about you let me in and we all sit down and have a couple drinks, huh? Be friends."

Before I could tell him to go fuck himself, I heard locks disengaging, and the door opened enough for my mother to peek out.

"Hey," Bronski said, turning his back on me. "Got a present for you, honey."

My mother looked at me, and I could tell she was embarrassed and didn't want me there. "Richie, what—what are you doing home?"

Bronski looked back over his shoulder at me and grinned like the imbecile he was. "Yeah, go play, kid."

I stepped toward him.

"Richie," my mother said. "Don't."

Bronski laughed again, opened his arms as if to hug me. "Come on, kid."

I looked at my mother.

"It's okay," she said awkwardly. "It's...it's okay. Just go hang out with your friends or something for a while, okay?"

I handed her the mail then walked back down the hallway to the stairs.

Behind me, I could hear them whispering.

I never looked back.

Few minutes later I found myself downtown, outside the bus station, smoking a cigarette while a bum old enough to be my father leered at me like the pervert he was. A bank of pay phones lined the outside wall of the terminal. I thought about calling the guys, but I didn't feel much like hanging out with them. Not tonight. I wanted to go home and forget about everything for a while, maybe smoke some dope. Going back to the apartment wasn't an option for at least a couple hours. Nothing good would come of it anyway, not as long as Bronski was there. It was a miracle we'd never come to blows, and while I knew we probably eventually would, I wasn't looking forward to it. He was old but still strong and in incredible shape. I could tell he was a man who'd been in his share of fights over the years too, a man for whom violence was still more or less recreational sport. I was confident I could get the better of the old fuck, it was something of a no-win situation. If I won, I'd be accused of physically abusing a guy more than three times my age. If I lost, I'd never live it down. Plus, Bronski would be in control. Then again, in some ways he already was. After all, my mother sent me away, not him.

Bills had to get paid, addictions had to be fed.

Choking back bile, I noticed a bus headed toward SMU, a college just outside the city. Every now and then I'd go to the Southeastern Massachusetts University campus and walk around, kill time and check out the college girls. The whole place, with its gray futuristic buildings and large open lawns, reminded me of something straight out of a science-fiction movie or some horror flick set in the near future. They also had a great library, much better than the local public one, and long as I kept a low profile, most just assumed I was a student there. In the last few years, I'd read a lot of books I found in that library. Didn't have a card or anything, I just stole what I wanted. But since I usually brought them back, I didn't really consider it stealing. *Creative borrowing*, Fritz called it.

"Got another cigarette?"

The bum was close enough for me to smell him. I handed him mine.

He took the cigarette with grimy fingers, smiled lasciviously and tried to convince me to join him in the bus station restroom for a few minutes, explaining he usually liked his boys a lot younger than me but I was so cute he'd be willing to make an exception. The luck. It just kept falling my way.

He muttered something about my ass, but I was already walking away.

I hopped the bus, dropped into a seat near the back and closed my eyes.

Last thing I saw was that filthy old bum staring at me from the curb, puffing on the cigarette I'd given him and rubbing his crotch.

Darkness crept closer as I walked the SMU campus, doing my best to behave like I belonged there, despite my rough look. Every now and then people eyed me with suspicion, but I learned that if I smiled and acted like I was just another student, they usually bought it.

I made my way along the cement paths toward the library looming in the distance like some secret laboratory from a science-fiction thriller. There weren't as many people around during the summer months, but they did have a summer session and other things happening, so there was still enough activity for me to get lost in the crowd. No one checked anything, I was allowed to walk right in, so I did, and made my way to a section I usually looked through first. On the second floor of the library, there were several freestanding spinning racks that housed old paperbacks. I'd found a lot of good stuff there in the past, and they seemed to change them up every few months, so I put my jacket on the back of a nearby chair at an unoc-cupied table and started browsing the titles.

As usual, my eyes wandered. A few kids sat at tables, study-ing or reading, but the place was mostly empty. Even those here during the summer session looked wildly foreign to me. I won-dered what it was like to go to college, to live in a dorm, not to have to worry about anything but going to class and doing what-ever the hell else it was they did all day and night. Go to parties, play sports, read, watch movies, listen to music, fuck, study, learn. Repeat. Then graduate and go out into the world with that piece of paper and a shot at a real fucking job. No, a career. Guys like me got jobs. These people got careers. And much as I made fun of them when I was with my friends, I envied them. I couldn't even imagine a life where you got to come to a place like this free and clear and live your life study-ing and having fun and learning everything you could, all so at the end of it you could walk into a life that'd carry you the rest of the way. It was like their whole lives were set out for them, while I had to fight for everything, steal and scrape and always look over my shoulder. Didn't seem fair. Because it wasn't.

Rather than continue to feel sorry for myself, I returned my attention to the racks, eventually settling on a badly worn copy of Dostoevsky's *Notes from the Underground*. Hadn't read that one yet, but I'd read *Crime and Punishment* when I was in high school and liked it a lot. According to the back cover, this one had been written prior to that.

"I am a sick man...I am a spiteful man..."

With an opening sentence like that, I wasn't about to leave it there, so I took it over to the table, sat down and decided to give it a try.

That's when I saw her.

Standing at the end of a nearby aisle was the most beautiful woman I'd ever seen. I just sat there staring at her like a goof, mesmerized, my mouth hanging open. Flashes of the bum from the bus station blinked across my mind's eye, and I straightened up. If she saw me, I didn't want her to think I was some ogling degenerate. But she didn't see me. She didn't notice me at all.

In that strange moment, I watched her while trying to appear as if I wasn't, and noticed in her a seemingly innocent and beautiful young woman who had likely come from a world vastly different from my own. Normally that would've caused me to immediately put up a wall or to run to a list of defensive reasons as to why she was, or should be, of no interest to me. I'd been here plenty of times, seen countless attractive college girls, and outside of physical attraction, never felt connections to them whatsoever. But she was different. She was graceful without being studied, genuine and real and about as girl-next-door as anyone could get. Maybe not next door in my neigh-borhood, but still. There was an effortlessness about her, as if she were wholly unaware of how enchanting she was. None of the darkness I swam in, that touched and soiled me and everyone I knew, seemed to have anything to do with her. She was free of it. I could tell. And that made me hesitate. I suddenly felt like someone with a contagious disease. Did I have any right to infect this poor girl?

Shit, did I even stand a chance?

I noticed she was holding a book and flipping through it casually. Every now and then she'd stop, read a bit of it, then continue flipping through. I tried to see the cover or binding, but couldn't make them out from that distance.

If I didn't at least try to talk with her, I knew I'd spend the rest of the day, possibly the rest of my life, regretting it. There was something there, something drawing me to her, something telling me I needed to act on this. Unlike anything I'd experienced before, I just went with it and hoped for the best, and before I knew it, found myself standing and moving toward her.

"Hi," I said softly, as I sidled up next to her.

She looked surprised by my sudden appearance, but not threatened or put off by it. Her big blue eyes, brimming with equal parts beauty and intellectual curiosity, blinked languidly. "Hey," she said, smiling to reveal perfect teeth.

"How's it goin'?" I asked, shuffling about like a nervous kid.

"Fine, thank you." She held my gaze, obviously waiting for me to offer some sort of explanation as to what I was doing there. "What's up?"

"Anything good?" I pointed to the book in her hand.

"Well, it's a classic." She held it up so I could see the cover. D.H. Lawrence's *Sons and Lovers*. "Trying to decide if it's right for me."

"Have you read any of Lawrence's stuff—*work*—before?"

"I read most of *Lady Chatterley's Lover* while I was in high school."

"Most?"

"You know." She smiled a little wider and blushed. "The good parts."

"You mean the dirty parts."

She laughed and looked away as her fair skin continued to turn a deep crimson. I laughed too. Partly because I didn't want her to feel alone in her embarrassment, and partly because her admission and subsequent reaction was possibly the cutest thing I'd ever seen.

"I've read that one." I pointed to the book in her hands. "It's good."

"Yeah?"

"Yeah."

She noticed the book I was holding. "What are you reading?"

"Dostoevsky." I showed it to her.

"I haven't read him yet."

"He's cool. Bleak, but cool."

We stood there a few seconds, neither of us saying anything.

"I'm Richie," I finally managed. I put my hand out.

She shook it. Gently. "Holly Hannah."

"Holly Hannah. I like that."

She brushed a wisp of dark blonde hair from her eyes and smiled coyly. "I didn't have anything to do with it, but thanks."

"You're not from around here, are you?"

"Is it that obvious?"

"Maybe a little."

"I'm from Iowa, actually."

"Really?"

"Uh-huh."

"Never met anybody from Iowa before." Truth was, I only vaguely knew where the hell Iowa was, and probably couldn't have found it on a map if I tried. "Must be a big change for you, huh?"

"Pretty big. I'm still getting used to it. The accents around here crack me up. No offense."

"Yours is cute, too."

"I didn't know I had one."

"You just don't sound like you're from around here, that's why I asked."

"I'll be starting sophomore year this fall," she said. "You?"

Afraid she might not want to keep talking with me if she knew the truth, I considered lying but decided to roll the dice and be honest. "I don't go here," I said. "I just like the library. It's a lot better than the public one."

"Oh." Her demeanor changed, became more guarded suddenly. "So where do you go to school?"

"I don't. I mean, not anymore. Not since high school."

"You don't go to college?" she asked, as if such a concept was beyond anything she could imagine.

"No, I—I mean I thought about it, I wanted to, I guess, but it wasn't really in the cards."

Holly arched an eyebrow. "In the cards?"

"It's an expression. You know, like it didn't work out, wasn't meant to be."

"How come?"

What might've been intrusive or rude from someone else, came off as innocent and honest from her. "Not enough money and my grades weren't good enough for scholarships."

"So, what do you do? Work?"

"Yeah," I lied, my mind racing and finally settling on the last real job I'd had back in high school. "I work for a shipping company. Unload trucks."

"Well," she said, holding her book up again, "since you recommend it, I'll give this a try."

"Just the dirty parts or the whole thing?"

The sound of her laughter made me feel valuable somehow.

"I'll be sure to try to whole thing," Holly assured me.

"So..." I frantically searched for something that might allow me to keep the conversation going. "Why are you here during the summer?"

"I came in a couple months early," she explained. "There were some courses they were offering in the summer session I wanted to take advantage of so..."

I had a feeling there was more to it than that, but let it go. "Cool."

"Yeah. Well, anyway, I—"

"Hey, do you think maybe I could get your number? You know, so you can tell me what you think of *Sons and Lovers* once you read it." I grinned playfully. "You don't want me to spend the rest of my life wondering if you liked it or not, do you?"

"Clever."

"I do my best."

She smirked but it was playful. "I don't have a phone in my room," she said. "But there's one in the hallway."

"Hallway?"

"In the dorm. Where I live."

"Oh. Yeah, sure. Right. Cool, I'll take that then."

Holly pursed her lips, as if she couldn't quite figure something out. "Do you really want the number or are you teasing me?"

"Depends."

"On what?"

"Do you want to give it to me?"

Another smile crept across her face. "What if I do?"

"Then I definitely want it."

"And if I don't?"

"I still want it."

We both laughed, mostly because we were so awkward.

"Seriously, I don't want to creep you out or anything," I told her. "I just thought maybe we could go out sometime, maybe get to know each other. We already have reading and books in common, right?"

"Thanks, Richie, but I don't know you. And you don't go to school here."

"I'm twenty years old. I have a job. I still live with my mom, which is always a big hit with the ladies. And as you can see, I'm not only funny and super charming, but incredibly handsome."

"And *so* modest!"

"What else do you need to know?"

She looked away, uncomfortable.

"I'm just playin'. Tell you what, do you have a piece of paper and a pen?"

She motioned for me to follow her over to a table where she'd left a notebook of lined paper. I recited my number to her and she jotted it down.

"If you ever want to get a cup of coffee or something or maybe go see a movie or get something to eat or whatever, I— just—you know, gimme a call." I shrugged clumsily. "If you want."

"Okay," she said, smiling. "Thanks."

I stood there like a goof. I didn't want to leave her. "Are you busy now?"

"Are you serious?"

"Sorry. It's just…"

"What?"

I swallowed. Hard. Fuck it. "You're the most beautiful woman I've ever seen."

"Oh my God." She laughed, whirling away. "Okay, I—"

"And you seem really nice," I added quickly. "And I—I'd really like to get to know you better. You know, if you'll let me. Seriously. I know we don't know each other at all, and I'm probably not exactly the kind of guy you go out with but—"

"What kind of guys do you think I go out with?"

"I don't know. The kinda guys they got in Iowa."

I could tell she was trying not to laugh again. "You mean like farm boys?"

"Is that what they got there?"

"Mostly."

"Okay, then yeah, that's what I mean. Do they have Italians in Iowa?"

"Three. We keep them on eight-hour shifts so there's always one around."

"Look at you." Chuckling, I pointed at her. "Good one."

"I don't even know your last name."

"Lionetti."

"Lion like the animal or lion like a no-good lyin' dog?"

"You should take this on the road, you've got a solid standup act."

Holly picked up her notebook, put the Lawrence novel atop it then pinned them both to her chest. "I have to go. It was really...*interesting*...meeting you, Richie."

"Call me sometime. If..."

"I know. If I want."

"Yeah. If you want."

"Bye, Richie."

"Bye, Holly."

She walked away. I watched her go, still hooked.

At the top of the stairs, Holly stopped and looked back just long enough to flash me another gorgeous smile. Then she was gone.

With *Notes from the Underground* tucked under my arm, I walked back over to the table where I'd left my jacket, sat down and began to read. After a few pages, I still couldn't get Holly out of my head, and decided I was in too good a mood for Dostoevsky, so I returned it to the rack. Besides, I hadn't finished the Dylan Thomas yet, and escaping to a tropical paradise beat the hell out of a depressed and sick old Russian dude any day of the week.

Jacket slung over my shoulder, I left the library and headed for home.

* * *

A week came and went. I spent my time doing what I always did, running with the guys and hanging out, reading, doing my best to take care of my mom and getting high and drunk with Woody up on the roof whenever I could. Mostly though, I thought about Holly and wondered if she'd ever call me. For some reason, I couldn't get her out of my head. In the background, where I'd pushed it down like a trash bin I didn't want to empty and just kept forcing deeper, my thoughts focused on Joanna Holt. There hadn't been any news, which I tried to convince myself was a good thing, but she was still in a coma, and from everything I'd heard, doctors still weren't sure she'd ever come out of it. Sometimes, when I poured myself into bed in a drunken and stoned stupor, I'd remember Ma whipping her with that pistol, the sound it made as it cracked against her skull and the way she whimpered with each blow, before going quiet and still, her face a mask of blood.

Meanwhile, life went on. Aldo arranged for Petie to get himself a nice ring from Chuckie D at a good discount. Petie gave it to Tammy and moved forward with his plans to marry her in the next couple months. He was still around but not as much, as he spent most of his time with her, trying to keep it all together and his fiancée out of other guys' cars and beds. Dino worked at his family's place and hung out when he could. Aldo and Fritz and me did the usual, shooting pool at The Park, hanging on the corner and dealing best we could with the heat and a city that always seemed on the edge. Ray-Ray was around, but not a lot. He was up to something and promised more news on it soon, hinting that if things went the way he thought they might, that score Aldo was looking for might fall right into our laps. He wouldn't go into detail until he was sure, so I didn't think much of it. But Aldo seemed locked on, like he knew more than he'd told me. Like it was almost a sure thing. I couldn't be sure if it was just wishful thinking on his part—Aldo being Aldo, always so certain he could will anything into reality as long as he strong-armed it enough—or something real.

The money from the score at the house in Lakeville was starting to run low, so I knew we'd need to make some moves soon. But I didn't push it, I just let things roll like usual. When another opportunity presented itself, I'd be ready.

Like always, there was a whole lot of nothing going on for a while. And then all hell broke loose. Everything came down at the same time, like one of those sudden summer storms where it goes from sunshine to black clouds and downpours in a matter of minutes.

It was a Friday when Aldo called a meeting. I knew it was important because he'd said we all had to be there, no exceptions, no excuses. I caught a ride with Dino, and we met the others at Ally's house in the early afternoon.

With the exception of Dino, who chose to stand, we all sat around a picnic table in the backyard. Candy was working, so we had privacy. The yard was a modest area of mostly crabgrass surrounded by woods. Candy had put a couple bird feeders and a cement birdbath up, and in the sunshine, an assortment of colorful birds chirped and hopped around, bathing themselves between snacks. It was all so peaceful, seemed a shame to ruin such beauty and tranquility with the likes of us.

"All right, everybody shut the hell up and listen to what the man has to say." Aldo motioned to Ray-Ray. "Go."

Ray-Ray scratched at the deep scar along the side of his face. "We been looking for a major score," he said. "And I found one. Truth be told, it found me. Couple weeks ago, I'm mindin' my own business, sittin' out front of my house smokin' a branch, and Grady, this broke-down old bastard I know from the neighborhood, come up on me talkin' about he needs my help. I'm high as a motherfucker, so I told him to sit his black ass down and tell me what he needed." He put his hands together, cracked his knuckles. "Now I known Grady near my whole life. He worked construction for years, then hurt his back and couldn't work no more, so he got on disability. He got nothin' to do all day, so he starts gamblin'. Gets hooked. Bad. I'm talkin' about a fucking degenerate gambler here, man, kinda dude gets his monthly disability check on a Thursday, goes right out and drops half of it on scratch tickets, blows the other half at the track and he's broke by Sunday mornin'. *Every* goddamn month. That's why he lives in shit, has nothin' and barely keeps a roof over his head. This asshole sees two ants walkin' across the sidewalk he'll bet you which one makes it to the curb first. Can't help himself. Fuckin' drunk-ass motherfucker, too. Likes the Mad Dog."

"Oooo," Fritz said. "Classy."

"Couple years back," Ray went on, "Grady's over at the track in Raynham, and he's losin' bad, like Grady always does, so he takes a break, figures he'll go get himself a hot dog, a Coke and a smile. But some motherfucker spilt ketchup on the floor, left a big ol squirt of it by the counter, and didn't nobody that work there see it. Ol Grady comes hobblin' over, slips and falls right on his old ass. Hurts himself. Bad. Already had a fucked-up back, now it's worse, and his neck's all fucked up too."

"There's a lawsuit," Petie said.

"Exactly." Ray-Ray smiled, bright and wide.

Fritz bummed a cigarette off me, so I had one too.

"So," Ray-Ray went on, "Grady goes and gets himself a lawyer, and that lawyer sees nothing but dollar signs. Grady's in the hospital for months, gettin' operations and treatments and shit, all kinds of bad news. Even when they finally got him patched up enough to go home, he's still a goddamn mess. Poor bastard can hardly walk now, needs a cane and shit, and his neck ain't never gonna be right. Pain and sufferin', my brothers, it's a beautiful thing, music to a lawyer's ears, and Grady's lawyer hears that band playin'. He goes and tries to get the track to settle outta court, but they say no and take their chances. Takes forever but it finally gets to court. Now Grady got himself one of them ambulance-chasin' motherfuckers, and this bastard goes for the throat. Long and short, Grady wins in court, gets a big-ass payday. 'Course it gets appealed and that bullshit goes on and on for almost four years. Then finally, after all the paperwork's done and all the right people got their scoops of honey from the pot, it's Grady Time. His piece is comin'. And it's a big motherfuckin' piece."

"How big?" Dino asked.

"Brother's never walkin' right again. Two hundred and fifty thousand. And that's after everybody else got paid. Even the commonwealth."

"Jesus, that's a lot of bread."

"That's bread with butter and gravy, baby." Ray-Ray chuckled. "Grady been waiting on this cash for years, and he finds out it's finally coming his way real soon. Nigger like Grady's got no idea what the fuck to do with that kinda green, right? So, he figures he'll put it in a safety-deposit box at the bank. First National, downtown. He's got some checking account there or some shit with probably fifteen fuckin' cents in it, so he goes and tells the bank he's got this money comin' and can they cash his check and let him rent a box? Bank manager tells him since it's so much money they got procedures and shit they got to follow, for his safety and theirs. She tells him they need two weeks to put it together and to bring in that much cash for him. Now, since he's old and shit, they look into that too, make sure nobody's scammin' him or nothin', because most folks, not being fuckin' morons, are gonna deposit the check and invest it or whatever, right? Usually one of those deals where the cash is there but ain't nobody ever gonna actually see it. But Grady, he don't want that kinda deal, don't trust it. He's old-school, wants the money. *Cash* money. He figures he puts it in a safety deposit box, he can go in and take a little out here and there when he goes to the track or wants to buy somethin' or whatever. Rest of it's safe, nobody got a key but him and the bank, it's all good."

"All right, so he gives them the check for a quarter of a million," I said, "and they cash it then walk it across the bank and put it in a safety-deposit box?"

"Yeah, but they ain't gonna do that shit during regular business hours. Too dangerous. They told Grady they'd do it right before they open. They had a bank security guard there, and they even brought in an off-duty pig for extra security. They escort him and the cash to the room where the boxes are. But Grady don't know these motherfuckers, all these white folks smilin' and talkin' about his money, so he comes to me. Tells me the whole story, asks me if I'll go with him and be *his* security. He knows me from the neighborhood and shit, knows I can handle my business, so I'm cool. All I got to do is go down there with him, keep him safe until the money's in the box, and he'll pay me a thousand in cash for my troubles."

"Sweet," Petie said. "Shit, that was easy money."

"Yeah," Aldo said, "that's the whole point. It's all easy money."

"No such thing," I said.

"Let the man finish." Aldo flashed me a look.

"I go on the job with Grady a couple weeks back," Ray continued. "Whole thing goes off without a hitch. Grady takes out five grand, gives me one, sticks four in his pocket and stuffs the rest—banded bills in ten-thousand-dollar stacks—into one of them big-ass safety-deposit boxes. Two hundred and forty-five thousand dollars. *Cash*."

"Christ," Dino said, arms folded across his chest. "That's a lot of green."

Aldo nodded. "Just shy of a quarter million waiting for us to take it."

"I'll hear from Grady any day now," Ray explained. "He'll be back there grabbin' more, and he'll want me with him. That's when we take him down."

"You're talkin' about robbing a bank," I said.

"No," Ray-Ray said. "I'm talkin' about robbing somebody *in* a bank."

"What kind of security?"

"One broke-down old-ass guard near the bank entrance, that's it."

"Armed."

"Yeah," Aldo said, "but we'll be armed too."

I laughed nervously. "Oh, *we* will?"

"What's your beef?"

"This isn't like knocking over a store or stealing from some-body's house, Ally. This is a fucking bank we're talking about. What the hell do we know about robbin' banks?"

"Ray just got through tellin' you it's not the bank we're robbin'."

"Candy from a baby." Ray-Ray grinned from ear-to-ear. "And tax-motherfucking-free. Can't pull this off alone, though, so we all go in, we all win."

"Except for Grady," I muttered.

"Stupid old nigger's just gonna blow it anyhow," Ray-Ray snapped. "Better in our pockets than the track's. Besides, he's in his seventies and drinks like a fish, won't be alive long enough to spend it even if he wanted to be."

"And you don't think this shit's gonna come back on you?" I asked.

"No reason to look at me, I was there to help. We just make sure I get a good knock on the head. Unless somebody makes one of you, you'll be good."

"They'll tie us to it through you, Ray."

"Won't be no reason to suspect me is what I'm tellin' you."

"They'll narrow it down. How many people could've known about this?"

"They can narrow it down all they want, blood. Grady's a drunk with a big mouth. Ain't no secret in the neighborhood he got hurt at the track, sued their asses and won. Lotsa folks know he got a big payday. Could be any one of them that hit him. That's why I go with him from his front door to the bank and back. He's more afraid of being robbed in his own neighborhood than anyplace else."

"Besides," Aldo added, "the cops won't even look at us for something this level. And even if they do, we'll all have alibis ready to go."

Fritz drummed his fingers on the table. "Okay, break it down."

"The total take's two-hundred-and-forty-five thousand," Aldo explained. "Usually we'd have to move the money through somebody, take cents on a dollar because of the serial numbers. But we're not robbing the bank, we're robbing a customer. That money's likely clean and not logged, so right off the top, we take ten grand and I give it to my Uncle Lou as a tribute. Shows him we're a crew that can earn. He wants to bring me and Richie in to start, but if we can show him our crew has this kind of balls and can make him money, he'll let me bring you guys in too."

No one objected or asked any questions, so he continued.

"Givin' him that money's an investment in the future. Our futures. Next is Ray's end. This is his deal. Without him bringing it to us, we'd have nothin'. He wants an extra bump, and that's only fair, wants to walk with fifty grand. That leaves a hundred and eighty-five thousand. Split up equally five ways, that's thirty-seven thousand apiece."

Petie stood up too, smiling like an imbecile. "That—that's almost forty grand, man! Holy fuckin' shit. I've never even *seen* that much cash. Not all at once anyways."

If the whole thing hadn't been so crazy, I'd have laughed.

"How long would it take you to make that, Ma?" Aldo asked.

Dino shrugged. "A year, maybe a little more."

"Petie," Aldo said, turning to him, "that kinda score could really help with the new family, no?"

"Are you kiddin'? It'd get us out of my grandmother's place. I could do all sorts of shit I can't afford now, for me and Tammy, the baby too. Hell yeah."

"Fritzy, you could get your own place too, get away from your mother's asshole husband, buy enough sunglasses to last you the rest of your fucking life." Aldo's gaze finally settled on me. "And you could get yourself some wheels, Richie, and still have plenty of money left over to take care of your moms and buy as many books as you want."

"Yeah," I said, "because it won't be too suspicious at all that this guy gets robbed then a bunch of mooks like us are flashin' money all over town."

"We give my uncle his cut, but I'd hold the rest for a while somewhere safe until the heat cools down. That way we don't get stupid and spend it right away. Richie's right, we don't want to draw attention."

Everyone stayed quiet. A gentle breeze kicked in, rustling the trees and sending several of the birds into flight. I couldn't help but think about the cash and the freedom it could give me. I wasn't about to say it, but I knew it was enough to get me out of there. I could take it and run, go wherever the hell I wanted and try to start over. But it could also land me in prison or the morgue.

"And the best part is," Aldo finally continued, "it opens a door for us with my uncle. It gets us in, sets us up. Then we'll be earnin' regular for him and makin' good money. Steady money. And we'll have *real* respect."

"It's dangerous, though," Dino said.

I was glad he'd said it before I could.

"We'll be in and out in less than three minutes," Aldo answered.

"So, we just go in like it's a bank robbery?" Fritz asked.

"Here's how it goes down," Ray said. "I walk in with Grady, we get the manager. She walks us over to the safety-deposit box room in the right back corner of the bank. She unlocks the door, her and Grady and me go in, they both use keys to open the unit, then the manager leaves. Grady pulls the box and I go wait outside the door while he does his thing. Now once that door closes, it locks. He can open it from inside, but nobody outside can get in without a key."

"Then how do we get in?" I asked.

"When I leave to wait for him outside, I don't let the door

close all the way. I hold it open just long enough until you guys get there."

"And you think the authorities won't figure that out?"

"Not if we time it right. If you guys rush me right when I'm comin' out the door, knock me out and rob poor old Grady, it'll look like me and him never had a chance."

I looked to Aldo. "You're talkin' about storming the bank."

"We go in there fast and loud, with plenty of firepower."

"And where are we supposed to get heavy artillery?"

Aldo hesitated before answering. "The Stork."

The Stork. Real name, Teddy Lewis. A freak we'd all known since junior high. Known for being a self-taught chemist, kind of kid who could build you a bomb from shit you found under your sink at home, wire a car to blow up with homemade explosives or make you a chemical cocktail that could burn and eat its way through steel, cement or damn near anything else. Kind of kid who'd done a bunch of stretches in juvie for blowing shit up by the time he was ten. Brilliant guy, but an absolute nutcase, he lived in a shitty little cottage down by the beach with his parents, a couple old hippies. Senior year of high school, his parents took off to some place down in South America to avoid drug charges and never came back, leaving him the cottage. Far as I knew, since graduation Teddy had stayed out of jail and mostly spent his time playing with his chemicals and explosives down at the beach, drinking cheap beer and tequila, ingesting insane amounts of drugs and working on solving any number of conspiracy theories he studied and raged about constantly. In addition to charging for his rare talent, he also ran guns, which made him more than enough money to live life the way he wanted.

"Are you kidding me?" I asked. "The fucking Stork?"

"Who else?"

"It's just one more person involved, one more person who knows—"

"The Stork ain't gonna know any specifics, and he won't say shit."

"First place the cops are gonna go lookin' once they realize there were big guns used is The Stork's place."

"Cops are over there questioning him all the time, who gives a shit? Without any proof, they can stick it up their asses. And you know The Stork's not gonna rat us."

"You sure about that?"

"He's crazy, Richie, not a snitch. Besides, like I said, he won't know details."

"The Stork's never ratted nobody out," Petie agreed. "Teddy's all right."

"You think we can count on that guy? He's fuckin' insane."

"There's nobody better, and he's got inventory like nobody else."

"I didn't say he's not good at what he does."

"All he'll know is we need firepower, nothin' about the job."

I shrugged, looked down at the table.

"Now," Aldo said, moving on, "the security guard's an old fuck but he carries a piece, a revolver probably older than he is. We swarm on him with enough firepower so he don't even pull it out of the holster. We move in fast and loud and clean. Ray-Ray says Grady likes to go early, so it'll be in the morning, could be busy, no way we can control that, so we can't worry about it. Whether there's three or thirty people there, we handle it the same way. Shock and fear, fellas, they're beautiful things."

"How's it actually goin' down?" Dino asked.

"Two of us secure the tellers and customers," Aldo said, "make sure everybody's shittin' their pants and cooperating while two more head straight for the safety-deposit box room and take out Ray. We make it look as good as we can, really crack him, he can take it. Hopefully, we don't have to hurt the old dude, but we rush him, empty the box of cash and we're out. Just like that. The guard, staff and customers are gonna stand there with their hands up while we snatch the cash and—

poof—just like that, we're gone."

"That's if everything goes perfect," Fritz said.

"No reason for it to go any other way if we follow the plan."

"Fritz is right," I said. "There's a lot that can go wrong."

Aldo sighed, rubbed his eyes. "Not if we do what I'm sayin'."

"What if the security guard decides to be a hero?"

"He won't."

"What if he does?"

"Richie, he won't."

"You got no way of knowin' that for sure."

"He'll be surprised, and when he sees us runnin' up on him in scary masks with huge firepower, nobody in there's gonna do shit. Trust me."

"It's not you I'm worried about."

"End of the day, it's not even the bank's money. Why be a hero?"

Ray nodded. "Nobody gonna get killed for some tired old nigger's cash."

"How come you get to say that word all the time but I can't?" Petie asked.

"Sit your cracker ass down and listen," he said.

"Not sayin' I want to, but how come—"

"Cracker-ass cracker."

"See, now that shit's racist."

"Black man can't be racist, dumbass."

"Oh," Petie said, rolling his eyes, "here we go with this horseshit again."

"Black man can be *bigoted*," Ray-Ray said, "but not racist. Racism comes from power, brother, the powerful subjugating the vulnerable. Racism got power behind it, the power to take the bigotry and implement it in real-world ways, you see what I'm sayin'? Black man don't have no power like that. Read a fuckin' book now and then you don't gotta color, you might understand some of this shit. Ignorant motherfucker."

"Listen to you. Who taught you all them fancy words, Ray?"

"Your grandmother, last time she was *subjugating* my black cock, right before I *implemented* it in that fat old milky white ass."

"Why's everyone always shittin' on my grammy?"

"Old bitch is a freak, that's why."

Everyone laughed, and for a couple seconds, things seemed normal again. But this was real. We were really talking about robbing a man in the middle of a bank, in the heart of the city.

"Okay," Dino said, bringing us all back, "who does what?"

Aldo answered. "The way I figure it, Petie, you drive, which means you'll be waitin' just down the street. Ma, you and Fritz handle the guard, then once he's disarmed, you make sure the customers and the tellers are in cooperation mode. Me and Richie hit Grady. I'll take out Ray. Once he goes down, me and Richie crash the room, grab the cash and we're gone. Thing is, on this one it's all or nothin', fellas. We're all in or nobody's in. If one of us wants out, we're all out, and Ray-Ray just goes and does his thing on the up-and-up for Grady now and then and makes himself a quick couple bucks. We're all in or it don't happen. Period."

"Dangerous shit," Dino said in an uncharacteristically soft tone.

"If we follow the plan, everything's gonna go smooth as silk. It's the score we've been waitin' for. The score that'll put us on the map and get us to the next level. No more nickel-and-dime bullshit, running around like punk kids." He stood up, walked a few steps away, toward the birdbath, then turned back, hands on his hips. "Obviously, me and Ray-Ray are in, so it's down to you guys. What's it gonna be? Ma?"

Dino stood there like a granite statue, his sculpted arms still folded over his big chest. Frowning, he seemed to think long and hard for several seconds, and I thought it was all going to die right there, with his bowing out.

"Fuck it. I'm in."

Aldo nodded. "Petie?"

"If you say this is gonna work, then it'll work. I'm in."

"Fritz?"

He was the only one still sitting at the table, his eyes concealed behind the dark lenses, his expression unreadable. "Can you come back to me?"

"Stop fuckin' around. In or out?"

Fritz let out a long and heavy sigh. Then he took a deep drag on his cigarette and exhaled slowly, through his nose. "In."

I'd hoped Fritz would end it. He was smarter than the others, and I could tell he had serious reservations about the whole thing. But that's not how it played out. It was all coming down to me. I felt Aldo's eyes on me even before I saw them. Everyone was looking at me, waiting to see if I'd put a stop to this or if we were really going forward. I wondered how many of them secretly wished I'd say no. Probably Fritz. Petie worshipped Aldo and went along with anything he wanted. And Ma likely didn't give a shit either way.

"Anything goes wrong," I said, "we'll be lookin' at prison time. Not juvie, not jail. Fuckin' prison. And that's if nobody gets hurt. That security clown pulls his piece and starts shooting, we—or he—could end up dead."

The mere mention of the word reminded me of Joanna Holt.

"Like I said about a hundred fuckin' times now, if we follow the plan nothin's gonna go wrong. But that ain't the question. In or out, Richie?"

I wanted to say I was out. And I should've.

But I didn't.

CHAPTER SIX

I walked the city for hours, aimless and frustrated, my thoughts and fears rattling around in my head like a bag of hammers crashing a skull. Reminded me of the Hall of Mirrors at The Park, where everything was distorted and crazy, and no matter which way I turned, there didn't seem to be any way out. City wasn't so different, really. All the streets and parks and alleys—everything—all looked like more of the same, an endless maze where the only escape was feet first, zipped up tight in a body bag.

The sky opened, dousing the city in a warm and steady rain. I was on my way home by then, but still a few blocks from my building. Different than most summer downpours, this was a quiet, whispery rain. A sad rain. A lonely kind of rain. Made me feel as if it was falling just for me, to comfort me somehow, maybe to let me know I wasn't quite so alone in my grief. But I was alone. Even in the middle of such an old city, with all its ghosts and desperate souls, I'd never been more alone in my life.

I stood by the steps a while, letting the rain wash over me as I dug my cigarettes from my jacket pocket. Cupping the flame, I sparked a butt.

Smoking in the rain, I watched the traffic glide past like phantoms, the people on the street hurrying and scrambling about for cover as if acid were falling from the sky. A couple people eyed me with suspicion, a few others like there must be something wrong with me, but I stayed where I was, puffing away on my soggy cigarette and letting the rain do its thing.

Once in the foyer, I shook the rain free then wearily climbed the stairs.

The minute I got inside, I heard my mother's voice. I closed the door and followed the only light—from the television—into the living room. It was cool in there, she had the air conditioner blasting. I don't think she'd turned the thing off since I brought it home. Couldn't wait to see what the electric bill was going to look like.

At first, I thought she was talking to the television like she sometimes did. But as I crossed into the room I saw her stretched out on the couch, her kit on the floor next to her. She was watching one of her soap operas. "Hi," I said. "You say something?"

The show went to a commercial, and she finally looked at me with her bleary eyes. "What happened to you? You look like a drenched rat."

"Got caught in the rain is all. What were you saying when I came in? I couldn't hear you with the air conditioner on."

"Nice and cool in here though, huh?" She smiled lazily.

Over the years, I'd learned to be patient when my mother was flying. "Yeah, it's real nice."

"You had a call while you were out."

"From who?"

She smiled and wiggled about on the couch, adjusting her position. "Some little girl looking for you."

"You write it down?"

"On the pad in the kitchen. Holly something."

"Yeah?" *Fuckin' A*, I thought, smiling. Felt good to smile. Felt even better to know she'd actually called me. I could hardly believe it. "When she call?"

"Little while ago," she said dreamily. "An hour, maybe, I don't know. Said you could call her back if you wanted. Number's on the pad."

"Thanks." I hurried back to the kitchen and looked at the

paper. Sure enough, despite her condition, my mother had gotten it right. The name at least. I could only hope the number was right too. I remembered Holly saying she didn't have a phone, so I'd have to call the pay phone in the dorm hallway, and figured this was likely the number she'd given. I waited until the soap opera was back on and my mother would be distracted and not listening in, then dialed.

It rang about twenty times before someone picked up.

"Hello?"

Female, but I couldn't be sure it was her.

"Holly?"

"No, it's Theresa."

"Is Holly there?"

"I'm not sure if she's in her room. Hold on."

"Thanks, can you tell her it's Richie?" I said, but she was already gone.

After a few minutes, I was ready to hang up. I couldn't even tell if the call was still connected. My excitement waning, I decided to give it another minute or so when someone suddenly came back on the line.

"Hello?"

"Holly?"

"Yes."

"Hey, it's Richie."

"Hi, Richie!"

"Hey. Got a message you called."

"Well, you said to call if…"

"Yeah," I said, clearing my throat. "Definitely. What's up? You wanna go get a bite to eat or somethin'?"

"Well, actually, there's a movie playing not far from campus I kind of wanted to see. Would you like to go with me?"

"Are you nuts? Of course. Yeah."

She laughed. "Okay. It's tonight. There's a seven-thirty-five showing and one at nine-forty-five. I was hoping to catch the early one, is that okay?"

171

"It's great. Yeah, for sure. Should I come get you or did you wanna meet there or what?" There was a pause, and I thought maybe I'd blown it with a stupid question. "Either way's cool," I added. "I want you to be comfortable."

"Thanks. You can come by and get me if you want."

"Sure." I checked my watch. It was a little after four. "Did you wanna get something to eat first or…"

"Maybe after?"

"Cool. I'll pick you up about seven then. Which one's your dorm?"

"Let's just meet out in front of the library, okay?"

"You got it. See you then."

I hung up, feeling like a million bucks. I hadn't been on a real date in a long time and already worried I was a little rusty. There was something about this girl that made me nervous and off my game. Usually I was confident with women, but Holly made me feel like some nervous schoolkid.

Shit, I thought. *I got another problem.*

I called Aldo. "Hey, man, it's me. What are you doing?"

"Just pinched off an anaconda shit. Now I'm scratchin' my balls."

"Jesus, sorry I asked."

"Livin' large, motherfucker, it's a full afternoon. What's up?"

"I need wheels."

"When?"

"Now."

"Now?"

"Yeah, now. I got a date in three hours."

"A *date*? Like a real date?"

"Yeah, a real date."

"With a girl?"

"No, with a fuckin' elephant."

"Who you got a date with, you sex machine?"

"Your mother, what difference does it make?"

"Aw come on, man, you promised you'd stop fuckin' my mother."

"You don't know her, all right?"

"Then how do *you* know her?"

"What are you, the fuckin' date police? It's a girl I met, who gives a shit?"

"All right, all right, take it easy. You wanna borrow my car?"

"Either that or we gotta clip one."

"Takin' a girl on a date in a hot car's actually pretty fuckin' funny, dude."

"Don't make any difference to me, man, I just need wheels. Fast."

"Borrow mine."

"Thanks, bro."

"You know the rule, though. No party-humpin' in my car."

"Yeah, I got it."

"Don't need to be spongin' your filthy fuckin' nut juice off my seats."

"Don't worry about it. She's not that type of girl."

"They're all that type of girl, *paisan.*"

"Not this one."

"Listen to this fuckin' guy, he's already in love. You sound all excited and shit, like a little girl going to her first real dance."

"Suck my dick."

"Aw, don't be mad, it's adorable. You and Sister Whoever-thefucksheis, go have a good time."

"I'm not saying she's a nun, she's just not some pig, all right?"

"You tryin' to tell me she's a nice girl?"

"Yeah, that's what I'm tryin' to tell you."

"Nice girls fuck too, Richie. They just do it politely and with more of a classy hip motion. Usually, they lay a towel down first too, which, you know, is kinda nice."

"You're a piece of work, you know that?"

"Hey, at least I got wheels, you broke-down walkin'-ass motherfucker."

"I got to pick her up at seven, Ally."

"Where?"

"SMU."

"College girl, huh? Fuck you doin' trawlin' college pussy, you bag of shit?"

"I gotta grab a shower and clean up. Pick me up at six-thirty, cool? That should give me plenty of time to run you home then go get her."

"I'll be there."

"Thanks, man. And hey, about today, I—"

"Don't talk about that shit over the phone. Never know."

"Just wanted to let you know I wasn't bustin' balls is all."

"I never thought that. You know what it is, dude? It's business, that's all. Somebody's gotta ask the questions. Better you than anybody else. You're smarter than the rest of us. You always question shit. That's a good thing, Richie, keeps everybody on their toes, including me. Don't apologize for it."

Goddamn Ally, always knew what to say and when to say it. "All right, man," I said. "See you in a couple hours."

"You got it."

"And, Ally? Thanks, man. Seriously."

"One for all, bro."

"Yeah," I said. "All for one."

As planned, I met Holly in front of the library. After a few awkward moments of small-talk, we walked back across campus to the parking lot and Aldo's car. I admitted the car wasn't mine, but a friend's I'd borrowed, which she found odd, so I explained how some people in the city didn't have cars.

It was different in the small Iowa town she came from.

"Everybody has a car," she said. "Even if it's a crappy one.

Back home it's more open. Everything's farther away."

Conversation came relatively easy from there, as I mostly let her talk about her hometown and family. By the time we got to the theater, I knew she had an older brother who was an accountant, two younger sisters—one in junior high and the other in high school—her mother was a nurse and her father owned a hardware store, and that she'd been a cheerleader and an honor roll student throughout high school. It all sounded so perfect and nice I wasn't sure if I should be envious or suspicious.

The movie was *Racing with the Moon*, starring Sean Penn, Nicolas Cage and Elizabeth McGovern. Set in the 1940s, it was about a couple guys in a small town living out their last days before being shipped off to fight in World War II. I hadn't heard of it or seen any ads for it on TV, but I didn't care. I would've gone to see anything with her, whatever she wanted. Rather than playing at the mall or bigger theaters in the area, it was showing in a small art-house theater in Fairhaven, about ten minutes from the city. I'd been there a few times before, by myself, since none of the guys ever wanted to see the kinds of films they played there, and it wasn't exactly the best place to bring most of the girls I dated.

Besides Holly and me, there were maybe another six or seven people there. The rest of the seats were empty, but the tickets were cheap and the popcorn was hot and fresh, so it wasn't all bad.

Once the movie started, I got into it.

We didn't talk much, although now and then Holly would lean close and whisper to me about one of the characters or comment about the plot. She smelled like baby powder and some sort of heady soap, like she'd just stepped out of a shower. Her hair was pulled back into a ponytail, held in place with a colorful cloth band, and she was dressed in designer jeans, a frilly white blouse with padded shoulders and a pair of brown suede boots. Her clothes were nice and new and probably expensive, and she looked really nice. I'd done my best to clean up, but there was only so much I could do with an old pair of Levi's, a sleeveless Alice Cooper concert T-shirt, a leather jacket and scuffed boots.

At a particularly romantic part of the movie, I slowly dropped my hand onto hers. She didn't object, so I left it there, slowly rubbing the top of her hand with my thumb. After a moment, she turned her hand over and took mine in hers.

We held hands until the credits rolled.

Once the lights came up and we were walking back up the aisle and out the exits to the street, conversation became an issue again. I was still having trouble talking to her, still nervous and uncertain around her, frantically searching for things to say and afraid no matter what I came up with would sound stupid or be of no interest to her. "That was pretty good," I said, as we reached the car.

"I liked it too. Kind of sad, but romantic."

I unlocked the door and held it open for her. "Like life."

Jesus. You did not just say that, you fucking moron.

Holly gave a coy smile. "True."

She got in, and as I closed the door and rounded the front of the car, I felt like I'd dodged a bullet.

"So, do you want to go get something to eat?" I asked, sliding behind the wheel. "What are you in the mood for?"

In just the dashboard light, she had a strange green tint to her, but she still looked gorgeous. "I'm not super hungry," she said. "Are you?"

"Not really." I was starving. "But I could eat, I guess. Up to you. You wanna maybe get some coffee, something like that?"

Holly sat forward and seemed to think about it a moment. "Maybe a slice of pizza and a Coke?"

Damn, this girl just keeps getting better.

"You have the best pizza here," she said. "Much better than back home."

"I know a place." I started the car. "Best pies around."

"*Pies*," she said through light laughter. "I love the way you guys talk."

"You guys?"

"Around here, I guess. Sometimes it's like an entirely different language."

"Sometimes it's like an entirely different world." I winked at her.

She self-consciously adjusted her hair. "I didn't—I—I'm sorry, Richie, that didn't come out the way I wanted it to. I didn't mean it in a superior way or—"

"I know. It's cool. Don't worry about it."

Holly reached over and squeezed my shoulder. "Thanks."

"For what?" I asked, doing my best to ignore the sensation firing through me that her touch had left behind.

"Being such a sweet guy."

"Yeah, that's me. I'm known for my sweetness."

"I bet!"

She laughed, and I felt a rush. I was becoming addicted to the sound of her laughter. And the way she looked. And the way she smelled. And the way she talked, I—Christ—I could've just sat there and listened to her talk for hours. None of the other shit in my life mattered at that moment. It was still there, hiding, but it had no power over me. For now, that belonged to Holly.

For once, without having to do drugs or drink myself into oblivion first, it felt like maybe life wasn't all that bad. More than constant struggle, violence and darkness, it was beautiful too. Because if I could feel what I was feeling when I was with her, then it *had* to be beautiful too. There was no other word for it.

A big smile on my face, I pulled out and headed back to the city.

From the street, and to the uninitiated, Dominic's was an unremarkable little pizza parlor downtown, crammed in between a dry cleaner and a joke shop, it only had a few tables and was mostly a takeout place, but they had great food. The place had been there since before I was born, and although Dominic's son Dom Jr. had run things for the last several years, the old man still made pies a few nights a week, tossing and spinning the dough in a window facing the street. It was a performance, watching the old guy work, and before we even got inside, Holly stopped to marvel at his skills. I'd been watching the guy do his thing since I was a kid, so it was no big deal to me, but Holly was impressed. Dom winked at us, recognizing me and gave a big smile.

Once inside, we grabbed a table for two near the door and I went up to the counter and ordered a couple slices and two Cokes.

"How you been, Richie?" Junior asked, grabbing the slices from a fresh pizza just out of the oven and sliding them onto paper plates. "Ain't seen youse in a while."

"Been around, doin' okay." I motioned to his father. "Got the old man workin', huh?"

"Can't keep him outta here, what am I gonna do? Where's the boys tonight?"

I jerked a thumb behind me at Holly.

He grinned, bounced his eyebrows comically. "Hot date, huh?"

"Yeah, don't worry about it." I scooped up the plates with a playful smirk. "Lotsa ice in them Cokes, yeah?"

"You got it."

Once I'd paid, I delivered everything to our table and sat down across from Holly. "Careful, it's real hot," I said. "Gonna want to give it a sec to cool down some."

"These slices are *huge*," she said. "Even for around here."

"Couple of Dominic's slices are like a meal, you know?"

"Looks really good. Smells good, too."

I grabbed a small glass shaker of parmesan and another of crushed red pepper. Even before I sprinkled my slice with both I could feel her watching me. "What?" I asked, making sure I had a smile on my face.

"Nothing. Just never saw anyone do that before."

"Put cheese and hot pepper flakes on a slice?"

"Nobody does that where I come from. It's okay, I think it's cool."

"You wanna try it?"

"No."

We both laughed.

"What can I say?" she chuckled. "Even the pizza's boring in Iowa."

I shrugged. "Sometimes boring's nice."

She watched me a moment, like she was weighing the validity of what I'd just said. "Maybe sometimes it's not so bad."

I blew on the slice then took a bite. Delicious as always.

Holly had some of hers. "God, that *is* good."

"Best around. Been comin' here since I was a kid." I sipped my Coke. "You sure you don't want nothin'—*anything*—else? They got fries and shit—*stuff*, sorry—and salads, subs, whatever."

"This is fine," she said, taking another bite. "Thank you, though."

We ate without talking for a few minutes.

"So," I eventually said, "you like goin' to college?"

"I do, yes."

"What are you goin' for?"

"Teaching."

"Cool."

"I'd like to teach at the elementary school level."

"Lucky kids."

She smiled, but it was laced with caution.

"If I had teachers looked like you, I would've paid a lot more attention."

"You didn't like school?"

"Not really. You?"

"It was fun, but once high school was over I couldn't wait to get out of there. I didn't even care where, really, I just wanted to get out of town and out of Iowa. It's not so terrible there as I make it out to be, it's my home and I love it, but it's *so* boring, and everybody's more or less the same. I've always wanted to see and experience more of the country, more of the world. I want to know people from all over, to learn from and experience other cultures and places and people, you know? Hopefully, once I'm established professionally, I can travel, see the world, before marriage and family and all that comes along and makes it harder, if not impossible."

Wow, I thought, *this is one smart chick*. I loved it and related to what she was saying a lot more than she probably knew. "Sounds like a plan."

"Most people where I'm from never go anywhere. They graduate high school then either go to a local college or get a job in town. They spend their whole lives there, and unless they go on a vacation or something, they never know or see or experience anywhere or anyone else."

"Not so different here," I said. "Most people stay where they grow up, I think. It's what they know. Feels safe. Even when it isn't."

"I just don't want to be most people."

"I don't think you have to worry about that."

"That's a compliment, right?"

"Forget about it."

She arched an eyebrow, confused by my response.

"That means definitely."

"Well, thank you then."

"You're welcome. Now me, I'm about as typical as they come."

"Oh, I seriously doubt that."

I had another bite of pizza. "I never been anywhere."

"Do you want to stay here the rest of your life?"

"Shit, I don't want to be here now."

She laughed lightly. "Where do you want to be?"

"I dunno."

"Haven't you thought about it?"

"Sure, but..." I wanted to be careful not to say the wrong thing and insult her, but not all of us had parents who could afford to send us across the country to go to college. Most days, my mother didn't have enough green to send me to the corner for a loaf of bread and a pack of cigarettes. "It's complicated."

"Most things in life are. Especially if they're worth anything."

"Yeah," I said. "Got a point there."

"You don't want to unload trucks the rest of your life, do you?"

"No."

"Not that there's anything wrong with that, it's an honest living. But there must be something else you'd rather do."

"Try anything else."

"Seriously, Richie, if you could be anything, what would you be?"

"Batman."

"Okay, besides Batman."

"You said anything, goddamn it. I want to be Batman."

She shook her head, had another bite of pizza. "You're funny."

"Yeah, but looks aren't everything."

I thought she'd laugh. Instead, she said, "I actually think you're really cute."

"Well, since I'm already good-looking, then I want to be rich and famous."

"Okay, now that we've established how dreamy you are, seriously, answer the question."

"Jesus, maybe you should be a lawyer."

"I'm sorry, I was just—"

"It's cool, I'm only teasin'."

"I really am curious, though."

I finished the slice, sat back a bit in my chair and had a swallow of Coke. "So, you mean, what do I want to be when I grow up, is that it?"

"Yes, that's what I mean."

I liked her even more. She didn't back down or take any shit, but she did it with grace and humor.

"I don't know," I told her. "That's the truth. I got no idea. Pathetic, huh?"

"Not at all. You just haven't figured it out yet."

"I guess I just want somethin'...I don't know...regular... normal."

"Like?"

"Good job, nice place to live, somebody to be with. Maybe a couple kids one day. I want a dog, too. I like dogs. Maybe a cat. They can be dicks but they're mostly cool, I think."

"That's it?"

"Told you I was typical."

"There's nothing wrong with wanting those things, Richie. I want them too, I just want to experience the world a bit before I settle down, that's all."

"Maybe when you grow up with that stuff you're used to it, so wantin' it doesn't seem like much. But if you've never really had it..."

"I wasn't putting you down."

"I know. It's okay."

"I'm sorry if I—"

"You didn't, and don't be sorry."

She had another bite of pizza then delicately wiped at her mouth with a napkin. "What kinds of things do you like to do?"

"You mean like hobbies?"

"Whatever interests you. I know you like to read."

"Love to read. Doesn't fit when you look at me, I know, but—"

"Why do you put yourself down like that?"

"I don't know." I felt myself blush. "Just tryin' to be funny, I guess."

"How did you get hooked on reading?" she asked. "My

mother read to me from the time I was really little, always encouraged reading, got me interested in books at a young age, and I took to them."

"My mom used to read to me, too," I said, barely able to remember those days. "But only when I was real little. I got serious into books when I was in junior high. Got into a fight with this kid and got a detention. Couldn't do anything but sit there or read. Only two choices they gave you. I was bored, so I went over and picked out a book that looked cool, started readin' it."

Holly let her elbows rest on the table and sat forward, listening intently. She looked like she'd never heard anything so fascinating. And she was serious.

"Anyway, it was some Western thing—cowboys and Indians stuff—a short one from like the 1950s or somethin'. I don't remember the title or the writer, but I liked it so I kept goin', finished it in a couple hours. Got me to thinkin'. I liked the way a book could take you to other places and times, and...well... sort of like what you're talkin' about. I couldn't get out of here on my own, but books were a way out in a way. Does that make sense?"

"Perfect sense."

"I been readin' ever since."

"What else do you like to do?"

"I hang out with my friends, go The Park, go to movies sometimes, just—you know—usual stuff."

"Do you like sports?"

"I like hockey. I watch boxin' sometimes too. Got a friend that boxes."

"In Iowa, everyone's a huge football fan."

"You guys don't even have a pro team."

"College football rules there, it's like a religion. Baseball's big too."

"I watch the Sox sometimes. Football, too."

"What do your parents do?"

I cleared my throat, tried my best not to appear too awkward. I figured the question was coming, I just always dreaded answering it. "My father died when I was four."

"My God, I'm so sorry."

"Nah, it's okay, you didn't know, and besides, it's—"

"I shouldn't have assumed. I'm really sorry."

"It's okay, you got to stop apologizing all the time." I smiled. "It was a long time ago, it's okay, I—I barely remember him." I dug my cigarettes and lighter out of my jacket pocket, lit one. "He had a bad heart, only nobody knew it, and one day he just fell over. That was that."

"How awful. Did your mom remarry?"

"No, it was just us, mostly. She had a few boyfriends here and there but nothing too serious, and none of them were all that crazy about having a little pain-in-the-ass ankle-biter runnin' around." I forced a smile, but I could tell all she saw was the pain. "Anyway, my mother has health problems too, been on disability for a long time. It's why I still live at home with her. She needs me, so…"

"You take care of her?"

"I try."

"Your father would be proud of you, I bet."

I knew she meant well, and I liked her even more for it, but my old man would've been anything but proud of me. "Yeah, I don't know," I said. "Maybe."

"I hope you don't think I'm prying, I—"

"Nah, it's cool."

"—just want to get to know you better, that's all."

"Yeah?" I smiled again. "I want to get to know you better too."

She watched me a while. It was the second time she'd sized me up since we'd sat down. "Why do I get the feeling you're not telling me something?"

"I could say the same thing about you."

"Really?" She seemed genuinely surprised.

"Well, why are you here in the summer when you don't have to be?"

Something shifted, changed in Holly's eyes, and I knew I'd hit a nerve.

"Every time I go back there," she said softly, "I'm afraid."

"Why?"

"I'm afraid I'll never leave. It's silly, I know, but...but it's like I'm afraid something will happen, and I'll have to stay there and..."

"What's gonna happen?"

"Nothing, I just worry something might, and I'll end up stuck in that town for the rest of my life. I'll be like everybody else there." She blinked, seemed to snap out of her trance. "I know I sound terrible, like I think I'm better than everybody else, but—"

"I don't think that."

"No?"

"No. I get what you're saying. Believe me."

"I do." She twisted a napkin in her hands absently, like she didn't know she was still holding it. "That movie tonight made me think."

I drew on my cigarette, exhaled through my nose. "About what?"

"Lots of things, but mostly about what it must've been like for kids back then, with a war on. So many went off to fight and never came home. So many died before they ever got a chance to live. They were just kids, most of them. And here we are, we don't have anything like that hanging over our heads. We have advantages and opportunities they never did. It's criminal to me not to take advantage of them. They died so we'd have them. How dare we waste them?"

She was right, of course, but I could've told her that in my world lots of kids still died before they got a chance to live, that those opportunities and advantages she was referring to didn't necessarily exist for people like me, and that there were different kinds of wars, all of them with victims. I would've been right too, had I told her that. But I didn't, because in that strange moment, in that nearly empty little pizza joint, I was too busy wondering if I was already falling in love with her.

"You wanna get out of here?" I asked. "Maybe go someplace else, I—I could take you to The Park, if you want."

"It's kind of late to go to a park."

"No, I mean Lincoln Park, the amusement park. You ever been?"

"Oh. No, I've never been there, actually."

"Then let's go. They're still open. Come on, I'll win you a stuffed animal. A big one."

Holly smiled, and I'm certain it was the most beautiful thing I'd ever seen. "It's okay, I should probably get back anyway, it's getting late."

"You sure? They got all sorts of cool rides and lots of stuff to do."

"Is it expensive?"

"Nah. Besides, don't worry about it, I got us covered."

She tried to hide it, but I could tell by her expression what her hesitation was. It had nothing to do with me. Holly was thinking I was some poor sap who didn't have much, so she was trying to come up with ways to keep the date from costing me too much. I wondered if that's why she'd opted for a slice instead of a regular sit-down meal at a restaurant, and why she'd chosen a smaller film in an old theater with ticket prices well below those of the multiplexes. Usually, it would've pissed me off, but with her it didn't. It just made me feel bad, like I wasn't good enough, a novelty act, somebody she could add to her list of people she'd met and experienced. Or maybe it wasn't anything that shitty. Maybe she was just a sweet person who was simply trying to be considerate.

"Why don't we go next time?" she said. "Make a night of it."

"Good to hear there's gonna be a next time."

"If you want there to be, sure." Her skin flushed. "Do you?"

"You out of your mind? Of course."

She laughed. "Me too."

"Good. It's not as much fun if I have to drag you kicking and screaming."

"Thanks for the pizza. And the movie."

"Don't forget the amazing conversation and the great jokes."

"Those too."

"My pleasure." I grabbed our plates and cups, dumped them into a nearby trash bin, then sat down and finished my cigarette. "You wanna go get an ice cream or something on the way back? I know a place."

"I'm sure you do, and it probably has the best ice cream on the planet. But I'm stuffed." She reached across the table and put her hand on mine. "Thank you, though. I had a really nice time tonight."

Out of the corner of my eye, I saw Dominic Sr. come out from behind the counter and close on the old jukebox in the corner. He made a selection then looked at me, winked and gave me a thumbs-up. That's when I realized we were the only two in there now.

"Me too." I crushed my cigarette in an ashtray next to the napkin holder. "Come on, let's get out of here. I'll take you back."

The old Bobby Darin song "Somewhere Beyond the Sea" kicked on, and I smiled. I owed Dominic one. Bastard knew how to do it.

I took Holly's hands in mine. "Right after this dance."

Genuinely surprised, she started to laugh as we rose from our chairs and headed to the center of the small floor. "*Here?*"

"Sure," I said, spinning her slowly. "Why not?"

Neither of us said a word for the rest of the song. We just looked into each other's eyes like a couple love-struck kids, which I guess in a way, we were. Holly felt good in my arms, like she was meant to be there.

Everybody's got those moments, those seconds where life means something more, when you feel alive in a way you didn't even know you could, moments you never forget and that hold their power even years later. That's what that dance was for me. I'd never been happier or more content in my life. I didn't know exactly what the feeling was, because I don't believe I'd felt it before, but as I embraced it—and her—I realized what it was.

Peace. I was at peace.

When I dropped Holly back at school, she let me walk her to the steps of her dorm. I'd never been on the campus that late. It was even spookier than normal, deserted and deathly quiet. But when we said goodbye, she hesitated, and I leaned in and kissed her.

I don't know how long we kissed, but we eventually ended up on a bench a few feet from the entrance, holding each other and making out like a couple crazed high school kids.

"I should—I—I really have to—"

"It's okay," I told her, coming up for air just long enough to speak.

"Richie," she said a moment later, pulling free. "We need to stop."

I nodded, cleared my throat and tried to stop my hands from shaking. "Okay, sorry, I—"

"You didn't do anything wrong, it's all right." She straightened her blouse and stood up. "We just got a little carried away."

I sat there looking up at her, wanting nothing more than to take her back in my arms and make love to her right there. "I didn't mean to..."

She smiled, and there was more than a hint of mischievousness in it. "Call me?"

I stood up, took her hands in mine. "When? Tomorrow?"

Whatever cool I'd had, or thought I had, was gone. And I didn't care, I just wanted to be with her.

"Sure."

"Yeah?"

"Yeah." She pushed herself up onto her tiptoes and gave me a quick peck on the cheek. "Thank you for tonight, I had a really nice time."

"Me too."

When she pulled away, I let her hands go, watching as she skipped up the steps. At the doors, she stopped, looked back, smiled again and blew me a kiss.

I caught it, put it in my pocket.

Beaming, Holly disappeared inside.

My head was so far up in the clouds I didn't even remember walking back across campus to the parking lot. Outside Aldo's car, I smoked a cigarette and thought about the evening, Holly and everything we'd done. Crazy. I'd never experienced anything like this—like her—and I just stood there a while beneath a streetlight, smoking my cigarette and grinning like a clown.

I drove back home, found a space on the street and parked. Normally I would've brought the car back that night, but it was already after eleven, so I decided to return it in the morning.

What I hadn't expected was to find Aldo sitting on the steps to my building, huddled there, like he'd been waiting a long time.

"Hey, man. What the hell you doin' here?"

The moment Aldo looked at me, I knew something was wrong.

Very wrong.

"Had Candy drop me off. Been waitin' on you a while," he said.

"It's late, figured I'd bring the car back in the morning."

"It ain't about the car, Richie."

"Okay," I said, moving closer. "What's it about then?"

He sighed and looked away, as if the answer was somewhere down the block, hidden in the dark.

"*Ally*," I said. "What's goin' on?"

"That broad Ma tuned up, Joanna Holt," he said softly, his dark eyes locking on me again. "She died."

CHAPTER SEVEN

We gathered down by the water, along an empty stretch of pavement leading to the wharf, where numerous boats, mostly fishing vessels, bobbed and rocked in the early morning breeze. The sun was still coming up, breaking over the horizon, and several boats were already underway, chugging out into the Atlantic. Others had crews just arriving and boarding, readying their vessels, while others sat empty and dark. The whole area reeked of fish and hard, backbreaking work. It had been a long time since I'd been up that early. In fact, I hadn't slept at all, opting to roll with Aldo back to his place, where he called the rest of the guys and arranged the meet.

For the first few minutes we all just stood there, shuffling around like zombies waiting on a goddamn bus or something, no one sure what to say or how to say it. Dino moved off by himself, maybe ten or fifteen feet from the rest of us, and stared out at the ocean, the breeze blowing through his hair. I'd never seen him so quiet and detached.

"All right, listen up," Aldo finally said. "Here's how it's gonna go. I talked to my uncle. We'll be okay, but we got to do this right."

"*Okay?*" Petie said, his voice barely containing his panic. "How the fuck is this gonna be okay, Ally? Ain't nothin' okay!"

"Shut your mouth and listen."

Petie's body deflated, his shoulders slumping and his chest

caving as if someone had punched him dead in the gut. He looked to me, hoping for support, but I had none to give him just then. Ally was right, we needed to listen.

"I was home with Candy and in no shape to do much of anything that night," Aldo said. "Her pain-in-the-ass mother even stopped by with soup, so I got her as a witness to back my alibi too. Now…"

A couple burly older guys walked by, on the way to their boat. Once they'd moved out of range, Aldo continued.

"The rest of you were down at the Lobster Villa that night havin' dinner."

"Lobster Villa?" Petie threw his hands in the air, let them fall and slap down against the outside of his thighs. "I fuckin' hate seafood, Ally, why would I be there? That don't make no sense."

Aldo drew a deep breath and pinched the bridge of his nose with his fingers, up near his eyes, like a headache was setting in. "I swear to Christ," he said through a long exhale, "you need to shut the fuck up and listen to me or I'm gonna strangle you with my bare hands and throw your ass right off that wharf. You understand me?"

"Sorry," he said softly.

"No," Aldo said, stepping closer. "Do you *understand* me?"

"Yeah, I—yes—I understand."

Aldo relaxed his posture a bit then continued. "The rest of you were there havin' dinner that night. You didn't leave until late, so you couldn't be at the scene. Uncle Lou owns some stock in the joint, okay? The hostess workin' that night, two waitresses and a busboy are all gonna swear you guys were there at the right times, but it ain't gonna be that easy. The cops are still comin' for you. They're gonna round you up and lean on you, but they got nothin'. Zero, you hear me? These guys and this Holt chick were mixed up in all sorts of shit. Real scum-bags, makes us look like choirboys, yeah? Nobody gives a squat about any of them. But the cops got to go through the motions, they got to make an effort, and if they squeeze somethin' out of one of us, then they'll have to follow through."

"And if they don't?" Fritz asked.

"Then they drop it."

"A homicide," I said. "They're just gonna *drop* a fuckin' homicide."

"My uncle has guys on the inside that feed him info, I told you that. They don't give a fuck about this bitch. They know it was you guys—I told you one of the fuckers said the guys that attacked them mentioned Madam Ling's, so it don't exactly take Columbo to figure this shit out. Thing is, all they got is what some drug addict piece of shit said. No proof. His word against ours. And it's not like he can ID any of you. You had masks on. All they got is somebody mentioned the place I got jumped. So what, who cares? No way to pin it on you guys. Only way they can get to you is if you crack. Stick to your story, and don't change it. You don't answer questions. You don't have conversations. You tell them where you were and when, and then you shut your fuckin' mouth. You don't let them get to you, you don't let them confuse you. You keep it simple and you stick to the story. Nobody gets hot. Ma, I'm talkin' to you especially. You hearin' me?"

Dino, who was still staring out at the water, nodded but didn't turn around or say anything.

"We've all been through this kind of shit before, for other stuff," Aldo reminded us. "Act like it. This ain't the first time we've had cops leanin' on us with their bullshit. Stakes are higher on this, but you do what I'm tellin' you and it'll all be over in a few days."

"Okay," Fritz said, arms folded across his chest.

"Dino?"

He nodded again.

"I understand," I said before Aldo had to ask.

"Petie." Aldo put his arm around him. "I know you're nervous and worked up, all right? I'm gonna sit down with you, and we're gonna go over this shit, just you and me. And we're gonna keep goin' over it until you got it down and don't have to worry about nothin', *capeesh*?"

Petie stared at him like a little kid that had come up out of a nightmare and wasn't sure if he was awake or still dreaming.

"You trust me, don't you?"

"Of course, Ally. Always, man."

"Then trust me on this. It's gonna be fine. *You're* gonna be fine."

"When you figure they'll be coming?" Fritz asked.

"It'll be soon, and they're gonna lean hard, fellas, so be ready."

I moved away from the others, closer to Dino. "Hey," I said quietly, "you all right, man?"

He finally turned his attention from the ocean and looked at me, his eyes dull and blank. "I knew it was gonna happen one of these days," he said. "Just never thought it'd be like this, you know? Didn't think it'd be some fuckin' girl."

"It was an accident, Dino."

He stared at me with those empty eyes.

All the things I'd said to Aldo about Dino I regretted. I couldn't desert him, not now. We had too much history, too many years, and I owed him. He'd saved my ass more than once in countless scuffles. I put a hand on his shoulder. "You never meant for her to die. None of us went there to kill nobody."

"It don't matter now, Richie."

"We got you, man," I told him. "Feel whatever you need to feel."

"That's the part of this I never saw coming," he said through a heavy sigh. "Figured when it happened I'd feel like shit. I thought—fuck—I didn't know what I thought, I just...I thought I'd feel real bad, you know?"

"It's all right to feel bad, man, you didn't mean for this to happen."

"That's the thing, though. I don't feel bad. I don't feel

anything." Dino gazed back out at the water, his face stone. "Not a goddamn thing."

I felt a chill course through me, as if it had surged directly out of him and into me. I dropped my hand, unsure of what to say. So I didn't say anything. I stayed quiet and watched the boats.

"The next day or two are gonna be a bitch," Aldo said, drawing our attention back to him. In his leather jacket, no shirt underneath, jeans and a black bandana tied around his head, he looked ready to brawl, but something in his voice was different that morning. He was worried. He was doing his best to hide it, but I knew him too well. None of this was over until we'd made it through to the other side, and he knew it. "Let's not make it easy for the pricks. Spread out, make the fuckers work for it."

"I'm gone," Dino said. "You want a ride?"

"I'm okay," I told him. "Thanks."

He gave me one of his playful punches to the shoulder, but for the first time in all the years I'd known him, it had nothing behind it. I watched him walk back across the loading and parking area to his IROC, unsure if he was still the guy I knew or if he'd become something else now, a stone-cold killer with no remorse or conscience. We'd always known how violent and crazy Ma could be, but it was real now. It wasn't a brawl, an ass-whipping he'd put on some poor bastard or even one of his crazy escapades. This was murder. He'd finally done it, just as we all knew he would one day. He'd killed someone, and there was no way back. Not from that. He was the first one through, from this life to that one, and we were all stumbling along right behind him.

I looked to Fritz. "Go with him."

Ever the good soldier, Fritz gave a quick nod and headed after him.

Aldo sidled up next to me. "I'm gonna go sit down with Petie and get him ready," he said quietly. "You all right?"

"Yeah," I lied.

"You want me drop you back home?"

"Nah, go ahead. Just make sure he's ready, man."

"Forget about it. When I'm done with him, he will be."

"He fucks up, he takes us all down with him."

"He'll do fine. You worry about you, yeah?"

"Yeah."

"We got this, bro. Don't worry."

"Me?" I forced a smile. "Worry?"

"We'll talk when it's over."

"Yeah."

Aldo strode back to his car, and he and Petie drove off.

Alone on the wharf, I watched the boats a while longer. Wouldn't be so hard to get a job on one of those crates. I knew a bunch of guys who did that sort of work. Almost all of them were hooked on drugs within the first couple months—painkillers and uppers mostly—and always had huge wads of cash when they came home. They'd hit shore, blow all their money on cars, jewelry, clothes, fancy stereos and whatever else they could find, pay a few bills, toss a couple bucks to their landlords, girlfriends or wives, then drink and drug the rest away and wind up back out on another trip so they could do it all over again. By the time most had been in the trade a few years, they were burned out, sick and on disability. Young guys with back braces and other ailments, hooked on prescription drugs and hobbling around like grizzled old men.

Everywhere I turned was a goddamn dead end.

I lit a cigarette, then headed for home.

The stench of something burning hit me even before I got the door open. Once inside, the kitchen was filled with smoke and I could hear whatever had been left on the stove crackling and popping. Waving at the smoke and hurrying through the room, I closed on the stove, saw a frying pan on the right burner, which was glowing bright orange, and what were once two eggs and some bacon burned to a crisp. I grabbed the pan, dropped it in the sink and ran some cold water over it, then switched the stove off, turned on the overhead fan and made for the nearest window. After I'd pulled it open, I called out for my mother, who wasn't on the couch in the living room or in her bedroom.

Waving at the smoke, I ran to the closed bathroom door. "Mom!"

I pounded on the door then tried the knob. It was unlocked. I threw the door open and found her slumped on the toilet, the rubber tubing still tied off above her elbow and the syringe dangling from the bend in her arm.

"Jesus Christ." I grabbed her shoulders and propped her back up. Her head lolled about like her neck was broken, and her eyes rolled around in her head as if she'd lost all control of them. "Mom! Mom, are you all right?"

"Stop yelling," she said, slurring the words.

"Look at me, you—Christ—don't move."

I reached down and carefully removed the needle from her arm then tossed it into the sink. Blood spurted free, spraying across the front of me before dying down to a slight dribble. Grabbing a hand towel, I pressed it against the wound and bent her arm up, pinning it against her chest. "Hold this here," I told her. "Mom, can you hear me?"

"Huh?" Her eyes focused a bit and she squinted at me like she couldn't quite see me yet. "What are you doing?"

"Hold your arm up against your chest, like this." I took her free hand and pressed it against her arm, then undid the rubber tubing and threw it aside. "Come on, I need to get you up."

I lifted her up off the seat. She was remarkably light, but because her body was so limp it was difficult getting her to walk. Struggling with her through the door and back into the living room, I sat her down on the couch.

Combing her hair from her face with my fingers, I cupped her face with my hands and held her steady. "Look at me, Mom."

She did. Slowly, she smiled dreamily. "Hi, baby. My baby boy."

I kissed her forehead and gently rested her back against the couch. Heart still smashing my chest, I opened another window then grabbed a can of spray from beneath the sink and sprayed freshener around.

"You burn something, Richie?" she asked.

I returned to the couch with a small glass of orange juice. "Here. Take a sip of this."

"What is it?"

"Just drink some, it's orange juice."

She had a swallow then coughed, dribbling a bit from the corner of her mouth and down across her chin. I wiped her clean with my T-shirt. "Stinks like a fire in here." She sighed. "What'd you do?"

"You were cooking eggs and bacon and forgot," I told her.

"Yeah?"

"You're not supposed to use the stove when you…you're lucky you didn't burn the whole building down." I checked her arm. The bleeding had stopped. "You all right?"

"Peachy keen." She managed a crooked grin, like she'd had a stroke and could no longer move her lips normally.

"Are you still hungry? You want me to make you something to eat?"

She shook her head no.

The smoke had mostly dissipated, and she was high but seemed okay, so I relaxed and gave her a hug. "You got to be more careful, Mom."

"I can't be saved."

I let her go, looked into her shadowy eyes. "What?"

"It's true, baby. I can't be saved."

"It's gonna be okay."

"Why's the windows open? Got the air conditioner going, you…you need to close the windows or it won't work right, Richie."

"Okay," I said. "I'm on it."

"I'm tired. I'm so tired, Richie."

She closed her eyes and her head slumped forward, her chin resting on her chest as both arms fell to her sides and she began to tip over, sliding onto her side. I took her by the shoulders and gently guided her until she was lying down, then took her feet and put them on the couch so she was stretched out.

I closed the windows and came back to check on her. She'd drifted off so fast and so soundly, at first I thought she'd died, but ever-so-slightly, her chest rose and fell with a steady and consistent rhythm.

Back in my room, I changed my bloody shirt, collapsed on my bed and lit a cigarette. Smoking, I stared at the ceiling and did my best not to let the emotions exploding through me take control. I wanted to smash something. Everything. I wanted to scream at the top of my lungs, to rage against the whole goddamn mess that was my life. I wanted to cry. I wanted to run. I wanted Holly.

I finished my cigarette, rolled out of bed and went to the phone in the kitchen. The number rang forever. Nobody ever answered.

I found enough in the fridge to throw a bologna and cheese sandwich together, ate it standing at the counter and drinking milk from the carton, then went back into the living room and checked on my mother.

Her eyes fluttered and opened. "Hi."

"You all right?"

"I'm always all right. Even when I'm not."

I stared at her.

"Yeah," she said. "I'm okay."

"I got to go."

"Where?"

"Out."

She nodded as her eyes slid closed again.

"Don't use the stove until I get back," I said, but the only response I got was a soft snoring sound. I leaned over, kissed her on the cheek and ran my hand across her forehead a few times. I felt like a little kid, that same scared and lost little kid I'd always been, hoping my mom was going to be okay and all the while knowing she wasn't, that one of these days she wouldn't wake up, she wouldn't come back to me.

I told her I loved her even though she couldn't hear me.

The phone rang, taking me away from her.

"Yeah?"

"It's going down," Aldo said. "Just got word the cops picked up Fritz at The Park. They brought Dino in about ten minutes ago, went right to his house. I dropped Petie at the arcade. They grabbed him the minute I pulled away. If the fucks aren't already comin' up your stairs they'll be there soon, man."

They were bringing us all in at once, which meant they planned to work us against each other, keeping us in separate interrogation rooms while they went from one to the next then back again. Fucking cops, always so predictable.

"Call you when I can," I said.

The line went dead. I hung up, grabbed my jacket and hurried out. I didn't want the police in the apartment, and I didn't want my mother to know they were picking me up. I figured I'd go hang on the corner and let them get me there.

I hadn't even reached the end of the block when an un-marked car pulled up alongside me and a detective I recognized stepped out of the passenger side. Detective Almeida, a gangly, forty-something bastard with a thick shock of black wiry hair and a penchant for polyester slacks and cheap sports jackets, he'd arrested me at least three times in the past.

"Hold up there, Richie."

I stopped, looked at him.

He pointed to the hood of his car. "Come on over and assume the position. You know the routine."

"I didn't do nothin', why you hasslin' me?"

"Move your ass."

I strolled slowly as possible over to the car and placed my hands on the hood. Behind the wheel was another detective I recognized, a fat little black guy named Mendes. He smiled at me the way cops do, all bravado and bullshit superiority.

Almeida frisked then started to cuff me.

"You arrestin' me?" I asked, turning toward him. "For what?"

Next thing I knew I was kissing the hood. His hand was clamped on the back of my neck and I was pinned against the car.

"What was that?" he asked. "You say something, Lionetti?"

I shook my head no as best I could.

He pulled me back up and cuffed me. "You're not under arrest at this time. The cuffs are just for your protection and mine."

"What do you want? What's this all about?"

"I think you know what it's about, dipshit. Need you to come in with us for some questioning. You know how this works, you been through it enough."

"Could've just asked me, why you got to be an asshole about it?"

He spun me around then got right in my face, so close his nose kept brushing against mine. "You and your little punk-ass friends fucked up good this time, *Guido*. You're in a world of shit, my friend."

"I don't know what the hell you're talkin' about," I said. "But if you got any Certs on you, pop a couple, huh? Your breath smells like linguica and knob."

Suddenly I was lying in the gutter, pain booming into my shoulder and neck. I managed to roll onto my back and saw Almeida standing over me with a look of fake concern.

"You okay, Richie? Got to be more careful, bud, these sidewalks can be tricky." He reached down, grabbed me by my hair and pulled me back to my feet. It hurt like hell, but I didn't give him the satisfaction of reacting. I just bit my tongue and took the pain.

I *fell* one more time on the way to the backseat, but Almeida was nice enough to help me up. Once in the car, he buckled me in then joined his partner in the front seat. As we took off, I closed my eyes and did my best to breathe and ignore the pain in my wrists and shoulders. The asshole had purposely put the cuffs on too tight, so they'd hurt more than normal. As we roared through the streets of the city, I could hear him babbling to Mendes, but between the partition and the crackling bursts from the radio, I couldn't make out what he was saying.

Five minutes later he parked out front of the precinct, dragged me out of the backseat, and he and Mendes escorted me inside. I'd been there before, but it was usually busier. Mendes said something to the cop working the main desk as Almeida pushed me across the lobby and down a hallway, where he made sure I tripped into both walls a few times on the way before finally bringing me into one of interrogation rooms.

Same as always, it reeked of body odor, cheap aftershave and cigarettes mixed with some sort of industrial cleaner. A two-way mirror on one wall, couple chairs, a table with an ashtray in the center and the biggest goddamn phonebook I'd ever seen lying next to it. In one corner, on the floor, was a roll of paper towels. I'd been down this road before plenty of times, enough to know a phonebook and paper towels in an interrogation room was never something you wanted to see.

Almeida roughly pushed me down onto a chair. "Gonna leave the cuffs on while we talk, Richie. Just a safety issue."

"Yeah, all right, whatever, but can you loosen them up?"

"Why? Are they hurting you, precious?"

"Little tight is all."

"Okay, hold on a sec. Let me see if I care." Almeida put a hand on his chin, narrowed his eyes and looked off to the side, like he was giving it some thought. "Nope, don't give a shit."

He sauntered out, left me there for what seemed like an hour but was probably only about ten or fifteen minutes. Was hard to know for sure because these rooms never had clocks in them, and with my hands pinned behind my back I couldn't check my watch.

I knew what they were doing, of course. After watching me through the two-way to see how I was reacting, they'd started in on the other guys. I also knew they'd be back to me with their lies and intimidation soon enough.

They didn't disappoint. This time, when Almeida returned, he had Mendes with him. He stopped at the table long enough to plunk down a cassette recorder with a microphone attached to it, then he moved over to the far corner of the room and stood there with his arms folded over his gut. He didn't give a shit that my cuffs hurt either. That'd come later, when it was time for him to play the nice guy. It was always the same crap with these guys, like watching a movie you'd seen a bunch of times.

I noticed Almeida didn't bother turning the recorder on, and instead turned the other chair around and sat in it backwards, leaning across the back of it and leering at me from the other side of the table. It went on like this for two or three minutes, and we all did our little routines, the two of them glaring at me and not saying anything and me sitting there, quiet and expressionless, like none of this fazed me in the least.

"There's two ways we can do this, Richie," Almeida finally said. "One, we can talk like men and cut through all the horseshit and get on with it. You can be honest with me and I can be fair with you. Or two, you can be a fucking lowlife dildo and I can be the biggest asshole you ever met."

"Don't sell yourself short. You're already the biggest asshole I ever met."

"I bet you'll be a real laugh riot on the cellblock, faggot. At least when all them hardcore convicts aren't corn-holing your pucker, huh?"

"What am I doin' here?"

He shook his head with disgust. "Unbelievable. You think

this is your typical petty bullshit, Richie? That what you think, you fucking jackoff?"

"I don't know what to think. I got no idea what I'm doin' here."

After a dramatic pause, Almeida threw the date and hours at me, as I knew he would. "Where were you on that night, during those hours?"

I pretended to think about it a minute, then asked him to repeat the date and time. He did, even though he knew I was fucking with him. "Yeah, I was at The Lobster Villa, down the south end, havin' dinner."

Almeida laughed lightly, under his breath, like he knew the answer before I'd given it to him, which after talking to the other guys, I'm sure he did. "Uh-huh. Alone or you have somebody with you? Anybody there see you?"

"Waitress. Other people. I don't know. I was there with my friends."

"Which friends, who?"

"The guys you got in the rooms down the hall."

This time his face was set in stone. "I asked you a question. Answer it."

"Petie Trezza, Fritz Kohler and Dino Abruzzo."

"And what were four street rat douchebags like you doing in a nice place like that, huh?"

"Havin' dinner. Hell you think we were doin'?"

"This is no joke, Richie. A woman's dead, asshole."

I shrugged. "Somebody died?"

"Yeah, you little piece of shit, somebody died."

"What's that got to do with me?"

Almeida drummed his fingers on the phonebook. "We already know you and your buddies were there, Richie. Jeffrey Collins said in his statement the guys who attacked him and his friends told him it was payback for what happened at Madam Ling's. Now, we know your boy Genaro got his ass kicked there, and we know you, Abruzzo, Trezza and Kohler went after Collins and his friends to get revenge, settle that score up, yeah? Only things got out of hand, and now a young woman's dead, Richie. Murdered." From a manila folder, he produced a black-and-white photograph of a battered Joanna Holt in the hospital, lying in bed with tubes and wires coming off her like some sort of cyborg. He slapped it on the table and slid it over to me. "Take a good hard look, punk. This is serious shit, so I suggest you get your head out of your ass and start cooperating, and maybe—just *maybe*—you won't spend the rest of your miserable life in a fucking cage."

I stared at him.

"Well?" he pressed.

"I don't know what the hell you're talkin' about."

"Jeffrey Collins—"

"I don't know no Jeffrey Collins."

Almeida's face turned hard, and I knew then what was coming.

"You gonna waste my time? That's how you wanna play it, fuck-face?"

"I don't understand," I said. "Are you accusin' me of a crime?"

With speed I didn't realize he possessed, Almeida stood up, grabbed the phonebook and swung it at me all in one fluid motion. It landed on the side of my face with such force the blow knocked me out of the chair and onto the floor. Colors exploded before my eyes then cleared, and suddenly I was looking at the table legs. My head was spinning and the right side of my face was throbbing, but before I could think much about it, I heard his chair squeal along the floor and felt him lift me back to my feet.

"What's the matter with you?" he asked. "You forget how to sit in a chair?"

"Thought I had it down."

He sat me back in the chair, straightened my hair and smiled. "All better?"

I looked over at Mendes. He was still in the corner, staring at me.

Almeida returned to his chair and sat down. "Let's try again."

"Look, I don't know what you want me to tell you."

"I want a statement, Richie. I want to know what went down there that night and how it ended up with Joanna Holt dead. There's no way out of this, you understand me? You and your reject friends are fucked. Only chance you got is to talk to me, boy. I'm the only one who can help you."

The pain in my face had faded, but my head was still ringing. "How am I supposed to give you a statement if I don't know what you're talkin' about?"

"We know you were there, asshole!" Almeida pounded the table with his fist and sprang up out of his chair again. "We got a witness that'll testify they saw you and those other retards leaving Collins's place."

Typical cop bullshit tactic number one, pretend they have a witness. I made sure my expression left no doubt as to how unimpressed I was with this latest alleged development.

"We know you were there, Richie, and we know what you did. The only thing we need to know now is which one of you clowns did her." Almeida sat back down and seemed to calm somewhat. "Right now, it's looking like you."

Again, I remained silent.

"You know we got your buddies here too. We picked everybody up. And I got to tell you, I respect a man who doesn't rat out his friends, okay? I get it. I do. But the way I see it, if one of those guys rats you out then why should you still be loyal to them?"

"Even if somebody did rat me out, which they didn't because none of us did anything or were even there, doesn't mean I'd roll over on them. I'm not a rat. Period. I don't give a shit what somebody else does."

"You're a real tough guy, Lionetti, we're all impressed. But it gets worse."

"Always does."

"Yeah, keep makin' jokes, wiseass. We pressed your boys too, and one of them claims it was you who did it, Richie."

Typical cop bullshit tactic number two, pretend one of your accomplices are fingering you.

"Did what?"

"Beat Joanna Holt to death."

"I got no idea what you're talkin' about. Zero."

"You know we can put you in a lineup and have you speak while Collins and the others listen, right? They can ID you by voice."

"Good luck with that. Meanwhile, I don't know who this Collins guy is, I don't know no Joanna Holt, and I don't know nothin' about any murder."

"What about Madam Ling's?"

"Best Peking ravioli in town. I also recommend the pan-fried noodles."

This time he just slapped me across the face with an open hand. It stung, and was humiliating, but I'd take it any day over the phonebook.

"What about it?" I asked. "Aldo got into a fight there, so what?"

"Not much of a fight from what I heard. Got his guinea ass kicked."

"Hey, win some lose some, what can you do, right?"

"You're forgetting we know you clowns, Richie. Shit, I been arresting you myself since you were twelve and knocking over old ladies so you could steal their purses. You've always been a fucking loser, a little punk who don't give a goddamn about anybody or anything. You're a fucking disgrace, and you and your buddies are all huge pieces of shit with extremely violent tendencies. So, you know what? Don't go trying to tell me you and those other cretins didn't go after Collins and his friends for what they did to Genaro."

"How could we do that when Aldo didn't even know who the guys were? We probably would've if we knew who did it, but we didn't."

"In his statement, Collins specifically—"

"How many fuckin' times I got to tell you? I don't know this Collins dude."

Phonebook time again.

The first blow snapped my head back and bloodied my nose. The second not only took me out of the chair, it sent me halfway across the room. The whole point of using a phonebook was it didn't leave marks. Usually, cops hit you in the body with it or the back of the head, but Almeida was cracking me full in the face with the fucking thing. Not that it made much difference. Nobody gave a shit if somebody like me left a police station bloodied up.

Almeida grabbed me, yanked me back to my feet and slammed me against the wall so hard all the air flew out of me in one violent rush. "You think I'm fucking around with you, you punk-ass little cocksucker? You think I'm playing games and got nothing better to do with my time? We're talking about murder, Lionetti, you hear me? *Murder!*"

He spun me around and dropped me back into the chair. I sat there, blood running from my nose and dripping onto the table as he straightened his clothes and calmed himself.

"I tried to help you," he said, pointing a finger at me. "I tried to give you a break, and you wanna act like an asshole? *Fuck* you, dickhead. You're gonna burn for this, kid, and I'm gonna love every goddamn minute of it."

Tough-guy, movie-of-the-week cop talk. Only ones who ever said shit like that was the police. I'd heard it all before, meant shit to me. They had nothing, just like Aldo said. And while I was worried if they leaned on Dino too hard he might go ballistic, and Petie could easily break or fuck up under pressure, I knew neither one of them would ever finger me. And Fritz was likely being his usual wiseass self and getting the phonebook routine even worse than me. If they had anything at all, I knew they would've already read me my rights.

"Fuck this clown." Almeida stormed out, slamming the door behind him.

Right on cue, Mendes came out of the corner, grabbed the roll of paper towels and placed it on the table. Then he moved around behind me and took my cuffs off.

My shoulders were sore and the cuffs had left deep marks on my wrists. I rubbed them, trying to get the circulation going again. "Thanks," I said quietly.

Mendes grabbed the other chair, but rather than sit across the table from me, he placed it next to mine then sat down. He motioned to the paper towels. "Clean yourself up, son."

I tore a sheet off, wiped my nose. The bleeding had all but stopped, so I used another one to wipe up the small puddle I'd left while bleeding all over the table.

From his shirt pocket, Mendes produced a pack of cigarettes and a Zippo, which he placed on the table. "Have a smoke," he said. "Relax."

Kents. Who the fuck smoked *Kents*? I took one from the crumpled pack anyway and fired it up. Tasted like an ashtray full of ass but gave me the nicotine I needed. Snapping the lighter shut, I tossed it back onto the table then exhaled a stream of smoke at the ceiling.

"Richie, this is serious business, you understand? We're not talking about boosting a car, robbing a house or knocking over a Cumberland Farms or some shit. We're not talking assault or a disorderly here. This is a homicide, son, the big leagues. We're talking going up Concord or Walpole for this, you understand? This is a murder rap." He took a cigarette for himself, lit it. "Look, we know you were there, but we don't think you did it, Richie. We figure it was probably Abruzzo. Now let me explain something to you. If you cooperate and tell us what happened, tell us who did Joanna Holt, give us a sworn statement and agree to testify, I'm telling you right now, you'll get maybe a couple years of probation. Odds are you won't do a day in the joint. It's not you the DA's gonna want. Other side of the coin is, you can keep playing the tough guy and you'll take the rap for something you didn't do because your buddies don't have the same level of loyalty you have. And if that happens, we're talking twenty years or more, Richie. And you'll serve it, trust me, won't be no walking out in a couple years for good behavior. Not for murder. You'll get thirty-to-life, I promise you, and you'll serve at best—at *best*—twenty of it. We're talking about walking in at your age and not walking out again until you're in your forties or fifties. And that's if you survive. Big *if*. You know what that kind of time does to a person? You think you can pull that kinda time? Not in juvie or county. Prison. You know what they do to young guys like you up Concord or Walpole?"

I smoked my cigarette, nodded.

"You got a chance here to do the right thing, the smart thing. You can save yourself and get a second chance. Do it, Richie. Do it."

I took a couple more drags before I spoke. "I can't give you somethin' I don't have. I'm sorry some chick died, I am, but I had nothin' to do with it. I don't know anything about it. You want me to lie, make shit up?"

Mendes shook his head. "Come on, man. I'm trying to help you, you got to see that."

"You asked me about this stuff and these people, and I answered you."

"You prepared to take a fall for this? Your friends are selling you down the river on this one, Richie."

"No, they're not. And you don't have any witness either."

"That's one hell of a gamble you're taking."

"Nah, it's a sure thing. None of those guys would make shit up like that, and I wasn't there and had nothin' to do with it, so your witness, which doesn't exist, is full of shit."

The photo of Joanna Holt was still on the table. Mendes

tapped it with his finger. "Take a good look, Richie. Look at her face, the damage. She's dead. Twenty-three years old, and now she's dead because one of you guys took a blunt object and beat her with it until she slipped into a coma and eventually succumbed to her injuries. Think about that a minute."

"I don't need to think about it. I'm sorry somethin' happened to this chick, but it's got nothin' to do with me."

"What the hell is it with you guys? What's wrong with you? What's broken in you that makes you this way? I grew up here too, not far from where you live. I didn't have shit either. But I made something of myself. You guys, you really don't give a shit. My partner's right, you don't care about anybody or anything, do you? Not even yourselves."

"You're not so different than me," I told him. "You just got a badge."

"You can tell yourself that all you want, son. It don't make it so."

"Detective, I've answered your questions honestly and told you everything I know about this, which is nothin'. If you're accusin' me of a crime, then arrest me and let me get a lawyer. If not, then we're done here, because we're just goin' around in circles, and I got nothin' else to say."

Mendes gave a sad nod. "I thought you were the smart one of the group."

I took another drag, crushed the cigarette in the ashtray. "I am."

Outside the police station, I stopped at the curb and looked back to make certain they weren't following me. All clear. I crossed the street, maneuvering between cars as best I could until I'd safely reached the other side, then I waited and looked around. None of the guys were on the street. They'd cut me loose first. My whole face hurt, I had a bit of a headache, and although my nose had stopped bleeding, both nostrils were crusted with dried blood. I couldn't shake the memory of that photograph of Joanna Holt, dead and battered in that hospital bed, and was sure I never would. It brought me back to that night, the sounds and sights—even the smells—of that shitty little apartment, and dragged my regrets back to the surface and into the light. I'd been running things that night. It was my job to make sure we pulled it off without any problems, and I'd not only failed, a woman had died because of it.

I'd have given almost anything to change that, but it was too late.

Moving along the street, I ducked quickly into the first alley I came to and threw up. Hacking and emptying my stomach next to a dumpster that smelled like old gym socks and ball cheese, I noticed a homeless guy a few feet away. In rags, he was sitting on a big piece of cardboard and gobbling down a Slim Jim while firing me a look of disgust. I was offending the guy who lived outside in his own filth, shit in abandoned cars and reeked of urine and pit stench. Still, I really couldn't blame the poor bastard. I wouldn't have liked some asshole staggering into my living room and ralphing chunks all over the place either.

"I'm eatin' here!" the guy moaned, holding up his meat stick. "I'm eatin'!"

"Yeah, sorry, bro." I wiped my mouth, spit a couple times then walked back out to the street, my stomach muscles sore and twitching with little spasms.

There was still no sign of anyone, so I turned and walked away, back toward home. I'd only made it about a block when I had the overwhelming urge to run. I increased my speed to a fast-walk, and then a jog. A block later I broke into a full run. Pushing hard, I felt like a little kid again, dashing through the streets like I once had. I hadn't run like that in a while, at least not that far, and though my lungs burned and my eyes watered, I kept going, fast as I could, forcing myself to go harder and harder, faster and faster. By then it felt like a fight, which I guess in a way it was. I reached deep inside for all the rage, then ripped it out like that old magic trick, where the guy pulls the line of handkerchiefs from his sleeve and they just keep coming. The more anger I pulled loose the stronger I got, the harder I ran, all of it building and getting worse with each stride, with each block that passed, the city and people and all else around me nothing more than a peripheral blur.

When I finally came to a stop, exhausted, I leaned against a big blue standing mailbox on the corner and tried to catch my breath. Bathed in sweat, I ignored the looks of passersby and held tight to the box. I hadn't slept, and it was catching up to me. I was exhausted before the run, and now I was so completely spent it felt like my legs were going to give out and I'd slip into unconsciousness at any moment.

The sky had turned red, like a warning. Like blood.

I needed to go home, to fall into bed and pull the covers up tight over me and forget everything. I needed to sleep for hours, days even. I needed the dark, the quiet, the safety of night.

But I didn't go home. Instead, once I'd gotten my breath, I lit a cigarette, coughed out a few drags and kept walking. Eventually, I found myself on The Avenue, and after wandering a while longer, closed on a small little dumpy porn theater that had been there since the 1960s. That kind of place wasn't my thing, but I was old enough to get in and I knew it'd be dark inside and mostly empty this time of day. After showing my ID and tossing some crumpled bills at the bored chick working the box office, I moved through the tiny lobby, past a display of XXX VHS rentals then through a battered swinging door and into the darkness of the theater.

There were only a few other people in there, all guys much older than me. Huddled in the shadows, they moaned and groaned and breathed heavily while they played with themselves in the dark. The floors were sticky and probably hadn't been cleaned in years, and the whole place smelled like jizz and bad decisions. I found a seat as far from the others as I could, dropped into it and pulled my jacket in tight around me.

Up on the old screen was a scratchy film of some middle-aged broad with really bad skin and frizzy hair prancing around nude and yelping like a puppy. A pasty bald dude with a crank the size of my fucking arm chased her around what I guess was supposed to be some sort of doctor's office.

Thankfully, by the time he caught her, I was gone, lost in sleep...

The beach was unlike anything I'd ever seen. Beautiful white sand stretched far as I could see, the ocean clear and still, like tinted glass, and all of it bathed in a bright full moon hung in the blue-black sky like a medallion of bone, a talisman of night watching us all and casting its spells of good and evil both.

Maybe it was Falesá, I thought. Maybe I'd finally made it.

My mother was there too, sitting at the base of a palm tree, watching me. She wore a light, flowery dress and a dainty pair of white sandals, her hair full and clean and pulled back away from her face. But as I got closer, I realized despite how good she looked, she wasn't happy. She stared at me, eyes filled with fear and sorrow.

"What is it?" I asked, crouching next to her.

"I had a terrible dream, Richie."

I smiled. "We're still dreaming, Mom."

She slowly shook her head no. "Only you, baby."

I took her hands in mine. They were soft and warm, and the track marks that once littered her arms and legs were no more. "Tell me what's wrong."

"I dreamed you were dying, Richie."

"I'm right here."

"You were lying in the street, on your back, and there were flames, these...these horrible flames. You were in so much pain, bleeding and crying out for me and—"

"It's okay," I assured her. "It's okay."

"There was so much blood, and you were lying in the street."

"I'm all right, Mom, I'm not bleeding."

"The blood looked almost black. Your blood, Richie."

"Mom—"

"You cried out for me, and I wasn't there. I'm so sorry."

"It doesn't matter. You're here now. So am I. And everything's okay. Look how beautiful everything is."

She smiled, but it was a smile of sorrow and regret. "Run, Richie. Run."

I closed my eyes, held her hands tight.

"Did you see how beautiful that moon was?" she asked.

"Yes."

"Don't stop until you see that moon again, Richie. Don't stop until you catch it, until you can reach up and pluck it right out of the sky."

I felt her hands slip from mine. When I opened my eyes, she was gone, and the beach and the palm tree and the ocean and the moon were gone with her. All that remained was a strange and otherworldly fog drifting all around me. I tried to see through it, but all I could make out was a vague figure in the distance. Draped in fog and shadow, I couldn't tell who it was, but I knew—somehow, I knew—it wasn't human.

At my feet, the gentle waves lapping shore turned to blood, and where a beautiful moon once resided, there was now a blistering sun, burning the vision from my eyes, leaving me blind in the fog and ankle-deep blood.

I couldn't see her, but I knew who was there with me now, her face battered and brutalized, her body broken and cold, slick and dripping blood.

She whispered demonic prayers in my ear, her lips so close I could feel her breath—icy and foul and void of anything alive and healthy and clean—as it stroked the side of my face.

I jerked awake, slamming my feet onto the floor and clutching the sides of the seat, certain I was falling.

"Jesus, you all right?"

A young girl sat next to me, her hand on my shoulder.

"Get the fuck off me!" I shrugged her hand off and leaned away from her, recoiling until I realized where I was. Pawing at my eyes, I drew a deep breath and glanced around at the faces scattered in the darkness and glaring back me for having interrupted their masturbatory fantasies.

On the screen, a muscular black guy was fucking the daylights out of a pale little redhead who looked like she hadn't eaten in a month. "You like that, baby?" he bellowed in a booming baritone.

She nodded and kept telling him how much she loved it, but from the looks of her, the poor thing probably would've preferred a sandwich.

"Take it easy," the girl next to me said, reminding me again that she was there and had been touching me while I was asleep.

I quickly checked my back pocket to make sure my wallet was still there, and from the look on her face I knew she realized what I was doing and didn't think much of it.

She rolled her heavily made-up eyes. "Yeah, like I'd roll you. Come on, I ain't like that."

"Fuck you want? Why you sitting so close with all these empty seats?"

Grinning, she winked in a way she seemed to think was sexy but was really just kind of sad. She looked so hard for such a young girl—she couldn't have been more than sixteen—and I knew what she was, but it was hard not to feel sorry for her.

"Need a date?" She ran her tongue over chapped lips. "I can help you out while you watch the movie. Okay, Daddy?"

Somewhere beneath all the ridiculous makeup, the bruises and grime, beyond the bleary, drugged-out eyes, B-movie lingo, platform shoes, costume jewelry and thrift store skin-tight miniskirt, there was a teenage girl, a kid who should've been in high school, whose biggest worry should've been that night's homework and who was going to ask her to the next dance. There wasn't that much left of this one, though. She'd been at the game a while, few years at least from the look, which meant she'd be dead or busted out or broken down beyond repair by the time she was twenty, and there was no stopping it. Even if I'd tried to help her, if I had the vaguest idea as to how, she'd refuse it, fight me, call me an asshole and run right to her pimp, claiming I tried to fuck with her or rip her off. I'd seen it all before, grown up around it. There was never a shortage of girls like this, the street just kept taking them and spitting them back out. The Devil never let go, not once he had his claws in your ass.

"Just leave me alone," I said. "Okay? Don't make me be an asshole."

"You don't have to be like that. Come on, I can make you feel real good for twenty. *Real* good. Right here, okay?"

She reached for me and I stood up. "Fuck off."

"Fuck you then." The girl slinked away into the dark. "Pussy-ass faggot."

I moved into the aisle and hurried back up and out into the light.

Outside, even the shitty air full of exhaust fumes on The Avenue felt and smelled good after the stank of that shithole. Until my eyes adjusted, I didn't realize how much later in the day it was. I'd slept a few hours away in there and somehow hadn't been robbed or molested, I couldn't believe it. I lit a cigarette and stood on the curb smoking it, watching the cars and people go by, and the night slowly rolling in across those still red skies.

A police car slinked past, slowing enough for the cop in the passenger seat to take a good hard look at me. I stared back, puffing my butt, until they pulled away and were absorbed into the rest of the traffic cruising The Avenue.

Across the street, a city bus rolled to a stop at the corner. I flicked my cigarette away and headed for it. It'd drop me closer to the station, where I could grab another bus that could get me to Holly. I needed beauty and laughter, some good in all this bad, some light in all this darkness, tenderness in all this violence and filth. I needed *her*. And I could only hope that just then, she needed me too.

The campus was quiet and mostly empty. I went straight to Holly's dorm building, hung around the base of the stairs and smoked a cigarette. I'd never been inside a college dorm before, and I wasn't sure how they worked or what the rules were. I wanted to walk right in and find her so we could talk, but I wasn't sure if that was allowed. I didn't give a shit about me, I just didn't want to get her in trouble.

A moment later, the doors opened and a couple girls came down the steps talking. They noticed me right away and moved to the far side of the steps to avoid me. I smiled and tried to appear harmless as possible.

"Excuse me," I said. "Do you guys know Holly Hannah?"

The girls exchanged troubled glances, and the taller of the two asked me who I was and what I wanted. I told them I was a friend of Holly's, but I could tell they weren't sure whether to believe me.

"She's out," the girl said.

"Do you know where she went?"

"No, she went out with some friends a while ago."

"You got any idea when she might be back?"

"No."

The two girls hurried away, one of them looking back at me nervously. So much for fitting in. This time around I was apparently standing out like a neon fucking sign. I finished my cigarette then sat on the bottom step, unsure of what to do with myself. She'd be back sooner or later, I figured, so I decided to just wait it out.

I don't know how long I sat there, but it seemed like hours before I finally saw her approaching from one of the pathed walkways with a small group of other kids. I stood up and straightened myself out as quickly and best I could, but even before Holly and the others had reached me, I could see the apprehension of those with her.

"Richie," Holly said, breaking from the others, smiling brightly. "What's up, you—"

Before I could speak I saw her face fall. The closer she got to me the more concerned she looked.

"My God, what happened to you?" she asked.

"What do you mean?"

She pointed at my face. "You—your face, it's all bruised and scraped and—is that *blood* dried around your nose?"

I took her hands in mine, but all I felt in them was tension. "It's okay, it's nothing, I just needed to—"

"Did you get into a fight?"

"No, not really."

Holly looked at her friends, who had now joined us—three other girls and a guy—and smiled nervously. "It's okay, you guys, this is a friend of mine."

They all looked at me like I was some sort of zoo animal that had escaped, some exotic creature they'd heard about, read in books and seen in movies, but had never experienced in the wild. The guy, a thin dude with curly hair and glasses, looked at me like he smelled something bad.

"What's up?" I said to them. "How you doin'?"

The girls smiled, but I could tell they were uncomfortable around me and maybe even trying not to laugh. Arms hooked, they told Holly they'd see her later and hurried up the steps and into the building. Curly stayed where he was, a couple books tucked under his arm and that same condescending look on his face.

"This is Richie," Holly said to the guy. "Richie, this is my friend Robin."

I put a hand out. "How's it goin', man?"

"Ah...yeah," he said, looking to Holly and not bothering to shake my hand. "Um, you *know* this guy?"

I slid between the two of them. "You got some kinda problem, chief?"

The guy stared at me as if he couldn't quite figure out whether to run or laugh. "Looks like you've already got enough for both of us," he said.

Holly took my hand and tried to move me back toward her and away from him. "It's okay, Robin, just go inside."

"Yeah, *Robin*, just go inside. While you still can."

He looked to Holly. "Are you sure? I mean, if you want I can stay and…"

"And do what?" I asked.

"Relax, *Fonzie*, there's no need for threats of physical violence, okay?"

I shook my hand free of Holly's and stepped closer to him. "What the hell did you call me, you little fuckin' pussy?"

"Robin," Holly said, "go inside. Now."

"You sure you're okay?"

"She's fine," I answered for her. "Fuck off."

"Richie—"

"Nah, fuck this guy," I said, squaring on him. "Walk. Before you get hurt."

Robin moved away and started up the stairs. "Oh, he's *charming*, Holly."

I started after him, but Holly grabbed hold of me again.

"Richie, stop. What's wrong with you?"

"What's wrong with *me*? That guy's a dick."

"Robin's a friend of mine. He's actually a really good guy, he just uses sarcasm and humor as a defense. You probably scared him to death."

"Good."

"No, it's not. I go to school here, Richie, I live here. Those are my friends. You can't just show up here looking like you just had a brawl or something and acting aggressive and violent like that. That's not how things work here."

I nodded. She was right. "I'm sorry," I said. "I just needed to see you and I've had a really bad day and the last thing I needed was your friends looking at me and treating me like I'm a piece of shit."

"They're just not used to…"

"Guys like me."

"Yes, okay? They're not used to guys like you."

"Are you?"

"I'm trying, Richie, but you acting like this doesn't help." Holly combed a strand of hair from her eyes and took a couple deep breaths. "What's going on? Why are you here?"

"I came to see you, I…I needed to see you."

"What happened?"

"It don't matter, I—"

"It does matter. Have you seen your face? Are you all right?"

"Yeah, I'm fine, don't worry about it."

"Don't worry about it? You look like someone beat the hell out of you."

I took her hand again, and I was glad she let me. "I'm okay, I promise. Let's go someplace and talk, huh?"

"I really wish you'd called me first, I—"

"I'll take you anywhere you wanna go, but can we just get out of here?"

"Richie, I've got plans tonight."

"Oh." I stood there like a moron. "You mean like a date?"

"No, with friends. I'm sorry, I wasn't expecting to see you today."

"I just wanted…I got to talk to you, Holly."

"I'm right here."

"Not here, I…"

"Look," she said, taking her hand back and wandering over near the steps. "Richie, I had a really nice time the other night. Matter of fact, it was one of the nicest dates I've ever been on, and I like you, I like you a lot. But we hardly know each other, and you show up here looking like this, threatening my friends and embarrassing me like—"

"I embarrass you?"

"I didn't mean it like that, you just can't come around here looking and acting like a maniac. You're scaring everyone, me included."

I would've rather taken all the beatings the cops wanted to dish out than to absorb a single blow from her. And she hadn't even hit me. Didn't have to, her words slammed me in the gut worse than any punch I'd ever been hit with. In that moment, I remembered I was somewhere I didn't belong and never would.

"Richie," she said, "I'm not trying to hurt your feelings, it's just—"

"Yeah, I get it. It's okay. I made a mistake. Sorry. I'm really sorry."

In that moment, the same old feelings I'd been wrestling with my whole life came flooding back. Fight or flight, it's all I knew, all I'd ever known. Who the hell was I to think I could change anything, have anything different?

"I'm going inside," she said. "Go home and clean yourself up, calm down and maybe give me a call in—"

"Sure." I leaned in and quickly kissed her cheek, then turned and walked away. "Have fun tonight, huh?"

"Richie?"

I wanted to turn back, to put my arms around her and feel her arms around me. I wanted her hair on my face, her body against mine. I wanted to scream, to rage, to cry, to tell her I thought maybe I loved her and please love me back, to collapse and drop to my knees and beg whatever gods out there were listening to help me. I wanted her to tell me everything was going to be all right, and that the whole goddamn world wasn't burning down, and me along with it.

But I just kept walking.

* * *

I rode the buses for hours. Didn't even care where they were taking me, I just rode bus after bus, going from one end of the city to the other then back again, slumped in a seat and blankly staring out the windows, seeing nothing and feeling even less. Now and then, I slept.

It was dark by the time I got off the last bus and found myself back on The Avenue. It was hopping by then, the lights shining bright, the streets packed with cars and people everywhere. It was a sticky, muggy night. The heat just kept rising. I made my way a few blocks over to a package store on the corner. Joey Berrone, one of the guys who worked there, was the older brother of a guy I knew and had gone to school with. He'd sell me booze out the back if nobody was around. Luckily, he was on, working the counter. I tapped the glass and he glanced up, saw me, then cocked his head toward the back.

Slipping into the alley, I met him at the back door, a large and battered number he pushed open with his shoulder.

"What do you say, Richie? Jesus, somebody tuned you up good, huh?"

"I fell."

He shook his head. "Fuckin' cops, man. *Fottuti stronzi.*"

"I'm all right. They hit like little girls."

"Atta-boy, don't take no shit from those cocksuckers."

"How's your brother doin'? Haven't seen him a while."

"God gimme strength. He's *deficiente*, this kid, a freakin' moron. But what am I gonna do? He's my blood." Joey rolled his eyes. "What do you need, pal?"

"Let me get a fifth of Jack and a couple packs of Winston Lights, huh?"

Joey disappeared back inside then returned seconds later with a brown paper bag containing both items. He handed it to me, and I gave him the same amount of cash I always did when we did this, twenty bucks. Didn't matter what I wanted, long as it was a fifth and cigarettes, the price was twenty dollars. I was underage, so I couldn't exactly be choosy, and Joey didn't give a shit because he pocketed the cash anyway.

"*Grazie*, man."

"Always a pleasure, Rich. You take care of yourself, huh? Put somethin' on your face, it's gonna swell up somethin' fierce. You know what works good on that?"

"Steak?"

"Only if you can't find fresh pussy."

He was still laughing as he slid the door shut. Fucking degenerate.

I emptied the two packs of cigarettes from the bag, pocketed them, then cracked open the Jack Daniel's and took a long pull. Wandering back out onto The Boulevard, I kept the bag down by my leg and away from traffic, so when the cops drove by they couldn't see it. Between the car stereos blasting and all the talking and yelling and laughing, it was really loud on the street, and within seconds my headache was back, pounding behind my eyes and temples like a bass drum. Still, The Avenue was always a good place to get lost in the crowd, especially on a busy night like this. As I walked, I took a swig of JD now and then, and just like I knew would happen, I hadn't even made a block when some asshole noticed what I was drinking and started bugging me to share. I wasn't in the mood for any bullshit and gave him a look a blind man would've understood. Thankfully, he was bright enough to drop it, leave me the fuck alone and move on. I had no idea where I was going, but until I figured it out I wanted to keep moving, so I didn't let him or anyone else slow me down.

By then I knew Aldo and the other guys were probably losing their minds wondering where the hell I was and trying to figure out what I was doing. The normal move was for us all to hook up after the police station bullshit, and I'm sure the other guys had, assuming there hadn't been any fuckups. But I just couldn't do it that night. I needed time away from everything, including them.

Once I'd reached near the end of the bustling part of The Avenue, I crossed the street, slipping between the endless cars packed tight and rolling so slowly I could've outrun them if I'd had to. Some girl drunk off her ass and sitting on the back of a convertible with another other big-haired metal chick pulled her tube top up and flashed me, laughing and screaming at the top of her lungs.

Amidst the hoots and applause of the countless other guys who had seen what she'd done too, I made it to the other side of the street. I took another long pull of Jack, then turned and headed back in the direction from which I'd come.

After a few blocks, I leaned against an iron security grate covering a closed shoe store, had some more to drink and watched the sights.

As I lit a cigarette, my mind drifted back to Holly. I'd fucked that up good. Idiot. She probably thought I was some sort of punk now, a lowlife piece of shit that went around fighting and stealing and drinking from a paper bag on the street. Turned out I was exactly all the things she likely feared I might be. I had no right to drag a nice girl like that down into the gutter with me. I should've known better, I thought, should've stayed away from the beginning and just admired her from a distance. I should've realized she lived on a different planet, and crawled back to my fucked-up shit-swamp life where I belonged.

I drank some more. It burned really good, but goddamit, I couldn't shake her. She kept haunting me, watching me from the shadows in my mind, the taste of her lips and the feel of her tongue against mine, the way she'd felt and the look in her eyes when we danced together.

"*Hoi* Richie!"

I was well on my way to drunk, but knew immediately who it was.

Shawna Delgado and another girl stood a few feet away, looking at me like they'd appeared out of thin air. Shawna was wearing a low-cut belly shirt, a pair of pink shorts and matching high-top LA Gears. Her hair was down and teased out like a model in a Mötley Crüe video, and she had on her usual copious amounts of makeup, her lips colored circus red and her eyes all black liner and inky eyelashes. Long and colorful feather earrings dangled from her lobes, and a gold crucifix hung between the tops of her breasts, which had been pushed up and together to showcase her generous cleavage. I recognized the girl with her, a tiny blonde with hair teased to the moon, but couldn't remember her name.

I raised the bottle. "Hiya."

"What are you doin' out here by yourself?" Shawna asked, chomping the gum she always seemed to be chewing. "Where's your boys?"

"Flyin' solo tonight. What are you two up to? No good, I bet."

"You know it." Shawna smiled wide and adjusted the black suede fringe purse on her shoulder. "We're just hangin' out, seeing what's goin' on."

"Cool." I took another pull. "Me too."

"You remember Melody from school?"

Melody. Right. In high school, everybody called her Mel.

"Sure." I smiled. "Hey, Mel."

"Hey, Richie."

Shawna leaned in and said something to her I couldn't make out. At first, Melody looked upset, but then her expression changed and she smiled and nodded. I had no intention of getting in the middle of it, so I just stood there drinking until Shawna finally moved over closer to me and put a hand on my shoulder.

"Richie, are you okay?"

"You know me, baby. I'm always okay."

"I'm serious."

"Why, don't I look okay?"

"My dad's working the night shift tonight, won't be home until tomorrow morning, and my mother's gonna be asleep soon," she explained. "You wanna come back to my house for a while and hang out? Got my car, it's parked a couple blocks from here."

I drank until it seemed like a good idea. Wiping my mouth, I blinked in an attempt to clear my slightly blurred vision. The bottle was already more than half-empty. "What about Mel?"

"She can come too," Shawna said, snapping her gum and smiling at me.

I took a longer look at Melody. Skin-tight Capri-style jeans. White patent leather heels. A faux-torn KISS half-T-shirt, one shoulder exposed, the undersides of her small breasts peeking out.

"Yeah?"

Shawna slowly licked her bright red lips. "Yeah."

I wanted Shawna to be Holly. I wanted to be back at Dominic's having slices and dancing and listening to her tell me about Iowa. But I was already shitfaced, Shawna and Melody were the only ones there, and they both looked good. Really good.

"Come on," Shawna said, taking me by the hand. "It'll be fun."

Who was I to argue with fun?

CHAPTER EIGHT

I'd known Shawna since junior high, and we'd fooled around a few times in high school, but I'd never been to her house and had no idea where she lived. Drunk as I was by the time we reached her car (an old Dodge Colt the color of baby shit), I was relieved when she drove away from all the noise and mayhem of The Avenue.

We ended up in a quiet neighborhood full of neat little houses, the tiny front lawns fenced with chain link, and the narrow driveways paved. I knew we were somewhere near Buttonwood Park, but couldn't see straight enough to make out any street signs. All I knew for sure was this was a street in the city I'd likely never been to, and I couldn't have been happier about that.

Shawna slowed when we neared her house, drifted into the driveway, then killed the headlights. Once she'd hustled me inside, the three of us crossed through a kitchen, and after a harrowing minute or so negotiating an open wooden staircase, I found myself in a small but finished cellar.

"By now my mother's probably shitfaced as you—if not worse—and already asleep or passed out or whatever," Shawna explained. "She always gets wrecked when my dad works nights, and between the booze and the downers she takes when she goes to bed, she sleeps like the fucking dead, so it's cool. But if some sort of miracle happens and she wakes up, all she'll do is open the door and call down here to me, she won't do those stairs."

"I don't blame her," I muttered. "Who built those, Irwin Allen?"

"Who's Irwin Allen?"

"The disaster-movie guy. You know, *Towering Inferno* and shit like that?"

Shawna looked at me like I'd grown a huge floppy cock out of the center of my forehead while no one was looking.

"I seen that movie," Mel chimed in. "Steve McQueen's in it. I love him."

"Yeah," I said, nodding. "McQueen's the man. *Bullitt*? Shit."

"He's old but he's wicked cool. And *so* hot."

"He's dead, Mel."

"Steve McQueen's dead?" She put her hands on her tiny waist. "No way."

"Died a few years ago, yeah."

"Okay, so *anyways*—" Shawna groaned through a dramatic sigh, "—back in *Who-Gives-A-Shit Land*, where everybody else lives, if my mother calls down, just be quiet and let me do the talkin', okay? She'll never know you were here."

"That'd be best." I stood there with my bottle and looked around. It wasn't bad. Beanbag chairs, a coffee table and a couch, a small fridge against one wall, a stereo system on the other, the walls covered in posters and nice plush wall-to-wall carpeting on the floor. "Pretty cool setup you got down here, Shawna. Could use a bar, of course, but looks good."

Shawna tossed her purse onto the coffee table then went to the fridge and grabbed two bottles of St. Pauli Girl. She handed one beer to Mel then opened hers and drank nearly half of it in a single shot. "All right," she said, smiling bright. "Let's get this party goin'."

On a coffee table I noticed a huge glass bong, rolling papers, an ashtray and a lava lamp. Trippy. Woody would've loved this place. I staggered over to the beanbag chairs, then rethought it. In my condition, if I dropped down into one of those fucking things I'd never be able to get up. Opting for the couch instead, I lowered myself down onto it carefully. The room spun a little then settled.

Mel switched the stereo on. "I've got some mescaline," she announced, dancing with herself as Journey's "Send Her My Love" played from the standing speakers bookending the stereo. "I fucking *love* mescaline."

Hadn't done that in a while. "That'll work," I said, firing up a cigarette while watching her little ass sway back and forth.

Shawna plopped down next to me on the couch, grabbed a Frisbee from the floor and began deseeding some weed. She smelled really good, but her scent was quickly overpowered by the smell of pot. "This is really good dope," she said, winking at me. "*Really* good."

"Cool." I sat back, watched the room slowly drift, tilt, then right itself. I felt her leg and side against me, and she felt good. Between her proximity and Mel's dancing, my jeans were getting tighter by the second. I smoked my cigarette, had another swig of JD and tried to play it cool.

"Let's get fucked up!" Mel laughed, spun away and kept dancing.

At the outskirts of my blurred mind, the guys lingered, angry with me for disappearing without any word. Numerous huge bong rips and the rest of the Jack took care of that, though, and once Shawna and Mel started dancing together, I didn't much give a shit about anything else. They wanted me to join them, but I was so fucked up I couldn't get off the couch, so I stayed where I was and took in the show like that's what I'd meant to do all along.

As I butted my cigarette in the ashtray, Mel kicked off her heels and danced barefoot, her body moving to the music. Her torn KISS T-shirt shifted and rode up along her belly, revealing half of her breasts. She wasn't wearing a bra. Shawna saw I'd noticed, so she reached up under her belly shirt, unhooked her bra in front, and with a wiggling and gyrating motion that was truly amazing, somehow freed herself of it without losing her top. Suddenly her bra was swinging from the tip of her finger, whirling around over her head and flying through the air at me as she danced and laughed.

It landed on top of my head, the cups hanging over the sides of my face. They smelled like sex, so I left the bra there for a few seconds before pulling it off and tossing it onto the coffee table with a mischievous grin.

The Journey medley had ended and segued into Bad Company's "Feel Like Makin' Love" by the time Shawna and Mel faced and held each other, their bodies crushed together and swaying to the music.

I responded with a heartfelt golf-clap. Faced with that level of magic, there was really nothing else to do, and luckily, three or four songs later, I had my legs back enough to stagger to the fridge and grab us all fresh beers.

With Aerosmith's "Toys in the Attic" speeding from the speakers, we all sat on the floor in a circle, hit the bong several times then did the mescaline.

Like always, it took forever to kick in, but once it did, all I remember is a couple hours of laughing so hard my stomach muscles hurt. Everything was hysterical on mescaline. Everything.

Later, in a fog of booze and drugs, and no longer concerned with having to stand or get up, I collapsed into a beanbag chair. Everything looked like I'd smeared Vaseline on my eyes. As I pawed at them, my body tingled and my mind drifted, but I didn't give a shit about anything.

Bowie's "Fame" was playing, freaky and cool and trippy.

Shawna fell across the beanbag chair on one side of me, and Mel did the same on the other. I put my arms around them and we all just lay there, listening to the music and being still.

Despite the sexual tension, there was something pure about the whole scene, a kind of primal closeness that came with a strange understanding and appreciation for the altered consciousness we'd achieved together. We were one, if even for just a short time, in that dimly lit little cellar, and it was good. No darkness, only light.

Shawna kissed my cheek, licked my ear. Mel nibbled my neck.

Then they leaned across me and kissed each other.

I stroked their hair as they made out, and as their intensity and passion surged, I broke into the middle of their kissing with some of my own.

We became a tangle of flesh and heavy breathing.

They held on tight.

I did too.

With Shawna at my side, a bag of McDonald's in one hand and a cardboard tray holding two large coffees in the other, I shuffled across the small paved lot to a series of benches facing the water. Behind us, the New Bedford-Fairhaven Bridge loomed over the Acushnet River. Whenever ships passed through, the old bridge would open to let them pass, holding up traffic. But this early in the morning, there wasn't much activity, and everything was relatively quiet.

We found a bench and sat down.

"Got a freakin' headache that won't quit," Shawna said, her eyes covered with large black sunglasses.

I handed her the bag. "That makes two of us."

She reached in and pulled out two breakfast sandwiches. I traded her a coffee for one then set it in my lap while I popped the lid off the coffee and attempted a sip. "Christ, that's hot."

Shawna opened a small cream and poured it in hers. "You don't take milk or sugar?"

"Black."

After mixing her coffee, she blew on it a bit then took a sip.

I unwrapped the sandwich and tore off a big bite. I needed the grease, and it not only tasted pretty good, it helped combat the rancid taste in my mouth.

"Sorry we had to leave so early," Shawna said between a bite of English muffin, egg, sausage and cheese. "I'd still be sleepin'."

I nodded but felt like shit. My whole body was sore, my vision fuzzy and my head was pounding. I'd gotten maybe three hours of sleep before Shawna shook me awake, explaining we had to get out of the house because her father would be home any minute. We were in her car and pulling out before I realized Mel wasn't with us. She'd left at some point during the night, but only lived a few doors down, Shawna told me, so it was no big deal.

All I remembered was Mel nude and on top of me, riding my dick while Shawna crawled over and sat on my face. When they switched, Shawna fucked me so hard it hurt, and as Mel ground herself into my face, the taste of her pussy mixed with what Shawna had left behind. I could still feel the weight of them, the feel of their bodies, how wet they both got, their smells and taste, the feel of their tongues and mouths on me as one sucked while the other licked, then switched.

A smile curled my lips.

"What?" Shawna asked, eyeing me.

"Nothing," I managed. "I think I'm still drunk."

Shawna laughed. "Me too. I'm definitely still a little high."

We sat there quietly a few minutes, eating our sandwiches and sipping our impossibly hot coffees while a highlight reel from the night before continued to play in my mind. I wolfed down my sandwich then lit a cigarette and sat back, stretching my legs out in front of me. I really wanted to leave, to head home and just crash in bed for a few hours, but I didn't say anything.

"That was fun last night," she finally said.

"I'm not gonna argue that one."

"I don't—I mean, I never really did anything like that before, I—I mean, me and Mel get fucked up sometimes and maybe, you know, a little, but—"

"Don't worry about it," I said, though I didn't believe her for a second. I reached over and gave her hand a quick pat. "It's cool."

Shawna smiled and nodded. "We should go out, Richie."

"Sure," I said. "I'll call you, we'll go to the movies or somethin'."

"No, I mean like *go out*. With each other. Like, steady."

I cleared my throat, coughed and took another drag, leaving the cigarette dangling from my lips as I exhaled through my nose. "I like you, Shawna, but I just got out of the thing with Mariana, you know?"

"So?" She took her sunglasses off and let them rest on top of her head. "I just got out of a relationship too."

"Just not lookin' for anything too serious right now, that's all," I told her as gently as I could. "But if I was gonna be with somebody, it'd be you."

I could tell by the look in her eyes she believed me, and it made me feel even worse. "I always liked you, Richie. Had the hots for you since forever."

"I always liked you too."

Shawna threw the remains of her sandwich into the bag, crumpled it up and tossed it into a nearby trash bin. "We could be good together."

I smoked my cigarette and feigned nonchalance best I could. "Probably."

"We could have a lot of fun."

"That's definitely true," I said, winking at her.

"Don't you ever think about stuff like that?"

"Stuff like what?"

"I dunno," she said, shrugging. "Having a real life."

"Some days I'm not even sure I know what that is anymore."

"Like, a good job, maybe a house or nice apartment, some-one to share it all with you can care about and who cares about you. Maybe some kids."

Rather than make eye contact I kept staring out at the water and smoking my cigarette. "I guess one day, maybe, yeah."

"But not now?"

"Come on, Shawna, at our age? You want all that already?"

"Maybe not all of it just yet but...I wouldn't mind startin' a more serious life, buildin' and workin' toward that, you know what I mean?"

"I guess."

"My father works at one of the ice houses," she said, referring to the ice factories in the city. "It's union, a good job. I bet he could get you in there if you wanted."

"Yeah?"

"Uh-huh. I mean, he's never met you, but I know he'd like you if he did. Well, maybe not at first, he don't like any boys I like, but you know what I mean. Once he stopped bein' an asshole he'd like you just fine. Anyways, he does really good." She put her hand on mine, left it there. "The money's good and there's benefits and—"

"Shawna," I said, sitting up. "I don't wanna work in an ice factory."

"What *do* you wanna do?"

I want to go home, I thought. *I want to go home and go to sleep.*

When I didn't answer after a few seconds, she said, "I just don't want to be one of those people, you know?"

"What people?"

Shawna looked down into her coffee cup. "The kind that runs around being crazy and a kid too long, and then one day you wake up from all the parties and good times and you're older and alone and all used up. I see it, Richie, you do too. You know what I'm talkin' about. One of those worn-out old party bitches with four kids hangin' on them and no man in sight, livin' in the projects on food stamps and welfare checks, tits hanging down, belly all saggy and fat."

"Jesus, Shawna, why would you end up like that?"

"I'm just sayin' it scares me is all." She looked away, out at the water, and combed her hair from her face with a finger, hooking it behind her ear. "We could be really good together, Richie, and I'd be really good to you."

I flicked my cigarette away, put an arm around her, and pulled her over against me. "None of that shit's gonna happen to you. You'll find somebody a lot better than me, and you'll have a nice life with some kids and a house, the whole bit. Don't worry about it. You'll be all right."

She pulled away. "But not with you."

I finally looked her in the eye. I had to. "Shawna, I—"

"Yeah, I know. Whatever."

"Don't be pissed, I like you a lot. I just—"

"I swear to God, Richie, I don't get you. What do you want?"

"I don't know. Just not…"

"Me?"

"It's not that."

"What then?"

I stood up, unsure of what else to do. "I don't even know if I'm gonna be around here much longer, okay? If it wasn't for my mother I'd probably be gone already."

"Gone where?"

"I don't know. Someplace. Anyplace but here."

"What's so bad about here? This is our home."

"I just want out, okay? I'm not shittin' on things. There's lots of good people here and a lot of great things about the city, okay? That what you want me to say? There is. But it's not what I want. You asked me what I want. That's what I want. Out."

She looked up at me with her sad eyes. "I like to travel too."

"I'm not talkin' about travelin'."

I turned, looked at the city limits. A stretch limo pulled over a few blocks away. Two women in their early twenties crawled out in short skintight dresses, both barefoot, their spike heels and little glitter purses in hand. Although they were a fair distance away, one of them saw me watching, widened her eyes comically, stuck her tongue out and flicked it at me while she and her girlfriend laughed and scurried off down a side street. Call girls being dropped off after an all-night party, no doubt, beautiful and young and about the saddest thing I'd ever seen. We'd probably gone to high school together, a couple seniors when I was a freshman. I looked in the other direction, focused on a strip club across the street, now closed. More young women slinking around, these holding coffees and carrying big bags full of costumes on their way to work for the early morning crowd. Grizzled and tired men who'd soon show up to eat a horrendous but cheap breakfast buffet while watching women even more bored than they were dance and shake their tits.

"You mean movin' someplace else?" Shawna pressed. "Why?"

"Why the hell does everybody I know keep makin' me have this fuckin' conversation?"

"I'm not makin' you do anything. Why are you bein' an asshole?"

"I'm an asshole because I don't want the life I have?"

"You don't want the life you have, you don't want the life I'm talkin' about, what the hell kind of life *do* you want?"

"I'm twenty fuckin' years old, how the hell am I supposed to know? I just know what I don't want, okay?" I motioned to the city. "This isn't what I want."

Shawna took a sip of coffee then dropped the cup in the trash. "That's the problem with you, Richie. You always think you're better than everybody else."

"Here we go with this bullshit."

"It's not bullshit. You think you're above the rest of us. Like we're all pathetic losers or some shit, but you're so much better than that. Than us."

"I don't think any of that. I just don't want to be here."

"You wanna run away, that's all."

"Yeah," I said, tossing my coffee away too. "I do. I wanna run. And I want to keep runnin' until I can't run no more."

Shawna didn't say anything else. She just looked at me a while. Not with anger, more confusion, and finally, with what I'm pretty sure was sympathy. I saw in her what my future would be—at best—if I stayed here. I'd be her father. Working some backbreaking union job that'd make me old before my time, struggling to pay the mortgage on my neat little house, mowing my neat little lawn, Shawna at home and a bunch of kids running around. Gerbil on a fucking wheel, drinking too much while she took pills and watched soap operas, all of us existing and running like maniacs but never actually getting anywhere, never really living. Dead before we even had a chance to live.

Or I could follow Aldo and be a criminal the rest of my life, for however long that lasted. Probably busted down in some cell or dead in the gutter before I was thirty.

Maybe Shawna was a savior and I didn't realize it. But I didn't feel enough for her to gamble my life on it.

"I got to go," I said quietly. My head was pounding again.

Shawna leaned in and kissed me.

I was shocked. Maybe it was her way of saying goodbye, or maybe she was just a better person than I was, better than I'd given her credit for.

"Come on," she said, holding out her hand, "I'll drop you home."

Together, we walked back to her car.

I never saw Shawna again.

When I got home, my mother was still asleep. The apartment was nice and cool. Quietly as I could, I slipped into bed, and before I remember my head hitting the pillow, I was out, spiraling down into a deep and dreamless sleep.

Hours later, I woke to the muffled sound of voices beyond

my bedroom door. I lay there a moment, staring at the ceiling and listening. I was sure it was my mother talking with someone. Bronski. His gravely tone was unmistakable.

I rolled out of bed, threw on some jeans and a T-shirt, stepped into a pair of ratty sneakers and headed out into the kitchen.

Barefoot and in a sheer summer nightgown, my mother was at the door, her back to me as she spoke. Through the partially open door, I saw Bronski standing there trying to work his way inside.

"Mom," I said evenly.

She turned and looked at me over her shoulder, smiling nervously. "Richie, you're up. I, um, I'm just talking with Mr. Bronski for a second, okay?"

"No, it's not okay." In two strides, I was at the door too. She tried to palm it best she could, but I noticed the baggie clutched in her hand. Bronski, in a sleeveless tank top, shorts and flip-flops, stood in the hallway holding a big bottle wrapped in brown paper.

"Hey, kid," he said, smiling like the imbecile he was.

"Move out of the way, Mom."

"Richie, don't."

Taking her by the elbow, I gently moved her out of my way, stepped into the hallway and closed the door behind me. Bronski was so close I could feel his hot stank breath on me.

"What are you doin', huh? We ain't done talkin'."

"Yeah, you are." I stared into his beady eyes. "From now on, I'll bring the rent down to you when it's due, got it? No need for you to come around here unless somethin' needs to be fixed."

Bronski pointed at me with the bottle and laughed. "You makin' the rules now, tough guy?"

"Stop givin' my mother that junk."

"What are you talkin' about? I don't mess with no junk."

"No, but you make sure she does, don't you?"

He puffed his chest up. "Me and your mother's friends, kid. She asks me to help her out, I help her out, see? She likes to dope up, so I help her dope up, that's all. She's fun when she dopes up, kid, know what I mean?"

"You need to get out of here," I told him.

"Oh yeah? You're the boss of me? That it, kid?"

"Stay the fuck away from my mother." My hands were clenched into fists but I kept them at my sides. "Or I'll put my foot so far up your ass your dentist's gonna have to work around it."

He laughed his gurgling laugh.

"I'm not playin' with you, motherfucker."

"You don't call me that, kid." He put the bottle down. "I don't like that."

"I don't give a shit what you like, you fuckin' moron. Stay away from her. I'm not tellin' you again."

Rocking slowly on the balls of his feet, Bronski slapped his right pec with his left hand then switched and slapped his left pec with his right. He reminded me of me of a gorilla, only nowhere near as intelligent. "What happens if I don't, huh? You think *you're* gonna set me straight, kid?"

"I catch you anywhere near my mother again," I said evenly, "I'll kill you wherever I find you."

He glared at me for a few seconds, as if he hadn't understood what I said, then slowly, a smile broke across his weathered face. "You crack me up, kid. You got balls on you like fuckin' grapefruits, I'll give you that."

Retrieving his bottle, he turned and clomped down the stairs, laughing, coughing, shaking his head and mumbling indecipherably.

As I turned, my mother opened the door. I could tell by her expression she wasn't pleased. I walked by her and into the kitchen in search of coffee. There was half a pot left but it was cold, so I poured a mug and microwaved it.

"Why you got to fight with him all the time, Richie?"

"He's a piece of shit."

"He…"

The microwave beeped and I snagged my coffee. "I don't want to talk about it. He just needs to stay away."

"He helps me, Richie."

"No. He doesn't."

"He—"

"He's a pig and he's using you, has been for a long time now."

She leaned against the counter like if she hadn't just then she would've toppled over. Maybe so. She looked rough even for her.

"You think I don't see the shit in your hand?"

With a sigh, she turned and shuffled off down the hallway to the living room. "Aldo's been calling since yesterday afternoon looking for you," she muttered. "Call him back so he's not bothering me all night."

I grabbed the wall phone, dialed. As it rang, I checked the clock. It was almost six o'clock. I'd slept the day away.

"Yeah?"

"Ally?"

"Richie, what the fuck, where you been?"

"Been around, I—"

"You all right?"

"Yeah, I'm good."

"Where the hell you been?"

"Ran into Shawna Delgado down The Avenue."

"Fuck are you talkin' about? Nobody knew where you were, man. We thought they still had you, were holding you for some reason."

"Why would they do that?"

"You tell me."

"Fuck's that mean?"

"You just disappeared on us. What's wrong with you?"

"When I got out of the precinct I waited around a while but

241

nobody else came out, so I took off. What the hell you think I was doin'?"

"I had no fuckin' idea, Richie, because you weren't around, not like I could ask you, right? We thought they had you, were pressurin' you maybe or maybe they somehow got you to talk or somethin'."

I gripped the phone so tight it hurt my hand. "You thought I fuckin' talked?"

"I didn't say that. Did I fuckin' say that?"

"Pretty goddamn close to what you just said, isn't it?"

"We were worried, man."

"About me or that I talked?"

Aldo breathed into the phone a few times, and I knew he was trying to calm down before answering. "About you, asshole."

"I took off for a while, went down The Avenue, got a bottle and hung out. Ran into Shawna, like I said. I went back to her place for the night and got fucked up. She dropped me home this mornin' and I grabbed some sleep. I got up a few minutes ago, and here I am, all right?"

"You should've called to let me know you were out."

He was right, and I knew it. "Sorry, I—you're right. Sorry, man."

"That's all I'm saying, and besides, I—wait—you spent the night at Shawna's?"

"Yeah, with her and Mel."

"Who the fuck's Mel?"

"Remember the skinny little blonde from school? Melody Mitchell?"

"Tiny little thing, tits like softballs, raisin-on-a-cracker nipples, likes KISS, does lots of mescaline?"

"That's her."

"She blew me sophomore year under the bleachers."

"Shocking."

"They fuck you?"

"Hard. I'm still sore."

"No shit, dude, *both* of them? Please tell me they did each other too."

"Yup. Mel had half her fuckin' head up there. It was a good night, bro."

"Motherfucker. Good for you. Finally tagged Shawna. When's the wedding?"

"Fuck off. We all set or what?"

"Yeah, we're good."

"Everybody made it?"

"Everybody got through it fine. Even Petie didn't fuck up, stuck to what I told him even when they knocked his ass around."

"I got the phonebook too."

"No-good fucks."

"How about Ma?"

"Believe it or not he kept his shit together. We're home free, man. Cops did their bit, went through the motions, got nothin'. Unsolved drug-related homicide. We're clear."

"Hope so."

"Forget about it. Now, you dressed or lyin' around naked?"

"Always naked for you, baby."

"Filthy whore."

"Yeah, I'm dressed. Why?"

"I'm comin' to pick you up."

"Gimme half an hour. Where we goin'?"

"We got a date with The Stork."

"The Stork?" My stomach dropped. "We're still doin' the job?"

"Of course we're still doin' the job. I'm not gonna let this one get away. What's the matter with you?"

"Me? What's the matter with *you*? We're gonna make these kinda moves with all this heat on us?"

"Ain't no more heat. It's off, just got through tellin' you that."

"Still, might be better to wait a while."

"Nope, now's the time to jump, bro. Trust me."

"If you say so."

"Meet me at the corner in twenty."

The line clicked, died.

I hung up and walked into the living room to see if my mother had eaten anything all day. I found her on the couch, fixed and on her way to Neverland.

Leaning down, I kissed her cheek then went into the bathroom and turned on the shower. Sitting on the toilet, I smoked a cigarette and tried to clear my head. But the storms had just started, and we were heading straight into another one. The biggest and most dangerous I'd ever encountered.

I took a shower as cold as I could stand, though I couldn't help but wonder if all I'd done was scrub myself clean for the slaughter.

Purple Mohawk glistening with gel, The Stork moved from the counter of his messy kitchen to the table where Aldo and I were sitting. Equally messy, the table was covered with old magazines, papers and strange metal canisters, glass tubes, spools of wire and assorted bottles and cans of household substances. The cottage was small, cramped, cluttered and smelled of chemicals, marijuana, cigarettes, sulfur and food gone bad. Outside, through the open screened windows, the sounds of ocean lapping shore brought with it a breeze that, despite the heat, kept the place relatively cool. A huge, battered boom box atop an ancient and rusty refrigerator played a mixed tape featuring haunting Gregorian chants interspersed with songs from punk bands like The Plasmatics and The Sex Pistols. Standing before us in jeans, jackboots and a sleeveless Dead Boys T-shirt, Teddy Lewis—*The Stork,* as he was known—with his wild hair, numerous piercings and thick-lensed, black plastic eyeglasses, looked like a cross between a nerdy mad scientist, a rooster on LSD, and a berserker you'd find atop a roof with high-powered rifles, picking people off for the fun of it. Six feet tall, he was lanky and shockingly thin, his long skinny arms covered in tattoos of skulls and devils and grim reapers.

"You ask me," The Stork said in a soft, whispery voice that didn't fit him, "unless it's something you absolutely got to do, then don't. Because if you show up to party with the kind of muscle you're asking for, you need to understand there's no way back."

"We get it," Aldo said. "But like I told you, we need serious firepower."

"And that's cool." The Stork fumbled a cigarette from a crumpled pack he found amidst the debris on the table. "It's just that The Stork feels a sense of civic and moral obligation to at least attempt to sway young men from the evil they sometimes feel the need to do, you understand."

Aldo grinned at him. "What, are you a priest now, Teddy?"

He pulled a silver Zippo from his front pocket, flipped it open, fired up the cigarette, then snapped it shut. "Merely a prophet, here to do God's work as best I can." He exhaled a stream of smoke then smiled back, revealing mostly brown teeth. "A conduit, as it were. You see, if a man goes into a hardware store and purchases a hammer, goes home and bashes his little lady's skull in with it, that's not the hammer's fault, and it sure as hell isn't the guy who sold him the hammer's fault. But that guy who sells it to him does have a moral obligation to, at a minimum, be vigilant. The Stork and his goods are no different. They're simply tools you desire that I provide. How you use them isn't my concern. But I deal in danger, baby, and sexy as that may be—it's only right to let guys like yourselves know that if there's any way you can achieve your goals without these goods, then you should do so. If not, then here I am, here you are, here *we* are, and it's time to do some *bid'ness*."

We'd been there less than five minutes and I was already itching to get the hell out. Teddy had always been peculiar, eccentric and creepy smart, but he'd lost his goddamn mind since high school, out here all alone on the beach in his little cottage, with his explosives and firearms and drugs.

"We appreciate your concern," Aldo said. "But we need what we need."

"Then you shall have it." He craned his neck, suddenly eyeing a small metal canister on the table next to me like he'd just noticed it was there. "Quick side note, don't touch that."

About the size of a mug, it was rusted and worn, with what appeared to be some sort of wick extending from a small hole in the top. "Okay."

"Yeah, it really shouldn't be out like that."

I slid my chair back a bit. "Is it dangerous?"

"If you touch it. That's why I said don't touch it."

"I'm not gonna fuckin' touch it, Teddy, what the hell is it?"

"An explosive device, what do you think? You touch that shit, *if* we wake up at all, it's gonna be on the fucking moon."

I held my hands up. "Christ, what's it doin' there then?"

"Must've been trippin', man. Normally I'd never leave something that unsafe out in the open." He chuckled, shook his head. "Anyway, be right back."

As he left the room, Aldo and I exchanged uneasy glances, but I could tell he was trying not to laugh. I slid my chair closer to his, dug my cigarettes out and lit one. "You realize he's completely out of his mind, right?" I whispered.

"Fuckin' Stork, man." Aldo shrugged. "We knew that before we got here. Minor detail."

"Minor, my ass."

"It's just business, Richie."

"Guy belongs in a padded cell."

"Don't worry about it." Aldo waved at the air between us as if he were trying to knock my words away. "Teddy's bat-shit crazy, but he's a professional, and you know well as I do, he'd never cross us."

"You better be right."

"Not about right or wrong, man. We were never here."

"Where'd you get the money for all this?" I asked.

"Gonna take almost every dime I have. Emptied out the savings."

"Candy's gonna crown you."

"She won't even know it's gone."

The Stork returned carrying a large canvas duffel bag. He pulled a chair out from the table and placed the duffel on it, then swept his arm across that end of the table and cleared all the junk there onto the floor. Unzipping the bag, he reached inside and came back with a stick of dynamite. "The fuck that get in there?" He looked at Aldo. "Did you say you wanted a stick of dynamite too?"

Aldo shook his head no.

"Huh." The Stork tossed it onto the counter then returned to the duffel, and this time, pulled out a gun and placed it on the space he'd cleared on the table. "Okay, moving on. This beauty is a standard model, stainless steel Tec-9 semi-automatic assault weapon. Technically it's an assault pistol. Little less bread and a lot lighter than an Uzi, it'll deliver the punch you're looking for, trust me, and the fucker's as durable as they come. It can jam now and then, of course, but generally speaking, it's highly reliable. Clip holds thirty-six rounds. Whole thing disassembles in two steps for easy cleaning or break down. You combine the ergonomically-designed grip with the light weight and you've got a piece that's easy-peasy to handle but still has big swinging nads. It's the kind of weapon people see you waving around, they not only piss their pants, they shit them, too. There's two of these babies in here for you."

Aldo nodded, and The Stork returned it to the bag.

Next came a large black shotgun, which he held up, the butt resting against his hip, the barrel pointed at the ceiling. "Mossberg 500 shotgun. Known as *The Persuader*, and for good reason. Some Johnny Dildo decides to play tough guy and fuck with this fine instrument of destruction, and it'll *persuade* his ass right into another fucking dimension. Pump action, twelve-gauge, five-plus-one-round capacity. Barrel's just under nineteen inches, so it's good size. Not super heavy, but it's not light either. Fine gun, though, and it'll fuckin' stop anybody in their tracks. You want to put somebody down, this'll get the job done. Reasonably priced, always reliable. You said you wanted maximum scare, well, between the Tec-9s and these mothers, whatever job you're doing, they'll see you mean motor scooters coming. If they got any kind of functioning brains in their heads, they'll get real cooperative, and quick. Got you two of these bad boys too."

Again, Aldo gave a nod, and the shotgun was returned to the bag.

"You also said you needed a handgun. Could've gone more low-end with this, but I went with something a lot nicer because a bunch of them recently became available at a premium price and I'd like to move them soon as possible. The goodies that fall off the backs of trucks never ceases to amaze." The Stork pulled another weapon from the duffel, held it up. "Gentlemen, this is a Glock 17 semi-automatic service pistol. Lot of pigs are starting to carry these, and they're popular in the military too. Weighs about a pound and a half, has a seventeen-round detachable box magazine. Range is about a hundred and sixty, hundred and sixty-five feet or so. Excellent up close and at medium range. Reliable and durable, easy to use. Solid piece."

A smile broke across Aldo's face. "This is why we came to you."

"Hey, you can buy some piece of shit revolver from any snot-nosed kid in the projects or you can hit up that fucking used-car salesman Chuckie D if all you want is a gun. But if you're looking for professional goods for professional needs, you come to The Stork. Now, you sure you guys don't need explosives?"

"Just the guns and ammo."

"You need to burn anything? I got chemical burn products that'll—"

"Just the guns."

"Cool." He put the handgun back then zipped closed the duffel. "Ammo's in there. Probably gave you more than you'll need, but better to have too much than wind up with nothing but your cock-a-doodle-doos in your hand, right?"

Aldo stood up, so I did too. "All right, what are we talkin'?" he asked.

"Normally I'd be looking for at least two grand, but for you, The Stork can go an even twelve hundred. Includes the ammo, because I like you assholes. I'll even throw in the duffel. For these goods, that's a deal, Mr. Man, trust me."

Aldo pulled a wad of cash from the side pocket of his jeans, peeled off twelve hundred dollars and handed them to The Stork. He counted it quickly, holding the cash up to his thick glasses, then tossed the cash on the counter and handed Aldo the duffel.

"You guys need any blow? I got some serious Peruvian blow."

"We're good."

"Working on some killer acid too. Making it myself. It's off the charts, this shit. You wanna see God? Because I can set up a meeting."

Aldo put his free hand out. "Always a pleasure, Teddy."

"Isn't it, though? I'm so much fun." They shook hands, then The Stork reached for mine and we shook too. "And you, Richie, lighten up, you need to relax. You're wound up tighter than a baby's butt, looks like you haven't had a decent shit in days. You need to drop a plop? Toilet's down the hall on the left. *Mi casa es su casa*, dude."

"We got to go," I told him, "but I'll mail you my next one."

"I've gotten worse deliveries."

I gave him an obligatory smirk. "Good to see you, Stork."

"I don't know what you're talking about," he said, smiling

as he let my hand go. "I haven't seen either one of you pricks since high school."

Back at Aldo's house, we inspected the weapons more closely. Holding them made everything real. The weight, the feel, the smell, there was no mistaking what they were, what they were for, and what they'd make us once they became part of what we were about to do. The Glock and shotguns weren't that big a deal. Hadn't done it much, but it wasn't the first time we'd held or even used those sorts of things. But the Tec-9 was something else. Except in movies and on TV, I'd never even seen anything like that before, much less held or fired one. Just the same, we went through the weapons quietly and carefully, like we knew what we were doing, checking them over and making sure they were in good working order as best we knew how. Once satisfied, we returned everything to the duffel and stashed it in a small padlocked utility shed at the rear of the property.

For the next few hours we did recon work, and that became the pattern for the following three days. All I did was eat, read, sleep and watch over my mother as best I could. Rest of the time I was with Aldo, parked down the block and across the street from the bank. From early morning until midafternoon we watched the neighborhood, got a feel for the area, the comings and goings, and took note of both consistencies and anything else we needed to look out for. The cops passed by at the same times every day. Two in a cruiser passed the bank every thirty to thirty-five minutes or so, and one cop walked a beat that covered approximately a four-block area. Little overweight, he was a middle-aged guy but was one of those grizzled veterans who'd been walking that neighborhood for years, and he made good time. It took about twenty minutes for him to complete one time around, unless he stopped and spoke with someone or was distracted in some way. The good news was that not once had they both been on the block at the same time.

Unfortunately, there was no way to know for sure the exact time we'd hit the bank, but if everything went our way, the cops would be nowhere around when the job went down. Worst-case scenario, we'd know how much time we had, when and from which direction they'd come, and how many we'd have to deal with.

As for the bank, the manager, a woman in her fifties, got there first each morning. It varied by one or two employees depending on the day, but there were always anywhere from four to six tellers working once the bank opened. There was also a receptionist at a desk not far inside the front entrance. The manager and two loan officers had cubicles toward the back of the bank, and the safety-deposit room was on the right, toward the rear. One guard, older than fucking time and armed with a revolver, nightstick and handheld radio, sat on a stool just inside the entrance. There was only one floor, and it was a relatively small space, so at least on paper it didn't seem like controlling things would be all that difficult. Aldo kept assuring me everything would go fine as long as we did our jobs and followed the plan.

"In and out," he kept saying. "We're gonna hit them so fast and so loud and hard they're gonna fill their pants. By the time they figure out what's going on, we'll be gone."

On the fourth day, Petie announced that his wedding to Tammy had been moved up to the following weekend. Apparently when her father heard the news that she was pregnant, he demanded they be married soon as possible or he'd have nothing to do with his daughter and future son-in-law again, so the date was set and we all went and got tuxedos at a local place downtown.

A small store that'd been there forever, it was owned and operated by an older guy with a pompadour dyed tire-black, enough gaudy jewelry to make Sammy Davis Jr. jealous, and the smallest feet on a grown man I'd ever seen.

I'd never worn a tuxedo before, but once I was all dressed

up I looked pretty good, and so did the other guys. Dino, Fritz and I all wore black, as did Aldo, while Petie went with a white jacket and black pants combo.

"Tammy said the white jacket's gonna make me stand out," Petie told us.

"Makes you look like James Bond," Fritz said.

Petie beamed. "Really?"

"Yeah, if James Bond was a giant scrotum in a cummerbund."

Everyone laughed except for Petie, who looked like he might start crying. Fritz immediately grabbed him, threw an arm around him.

"Come on, man, I'm just playin' with you."

"Yeah," Petie said, forcing a smile. "I know."

"What's the matter with you?" Aldo asked.

Petie shrugged. "Just nervous, I guess."

"Hey, look at me." Aldo took him by the shoulders. "You look awesome, man. You look, ah...fuck's the word I need, Richie?"

"Suave?"

Aldo snapped his fingers and pointed at Petie. "Suave. You hear that? You look fuckin' *suave*, bro."

"The hell's that mean?"

"I got no idea. But whatever it is, it's good and that's what you look like."

Fritz glanced at me and shook his head. "This conversation's actually happening, right?"

"Far as I can tell," I said.

"Okay then." Fritz started back toward the dressing rooms. "I'm gonna go watch Ma try to tie his bowtie again. It's like Ray Charles working a fuckin' Rubik's Cube, I'm tellin' you, it's not to be missed."

Aldo walked Petie over to a series of mirrors. "Look at you, you look badass. Tammy's lucky to have you. You're gonna be fine. You're the man, and you got this. You hear me?"

252

Petie nodded.

"Richie," Aldo said, "am I lyin'?"

"Nah, you're not lyin'." I smiled, but I was worried about the poor bastard.

The owner showed up, looking a bit agitated and pointing toward the dressing rooms. "Excuse me, but the large gentlemen that's with you, he—he's having trouble with his tie and getting very angry and the—the young man in the sunglasses is making fun of him, which only seems to be making it worse."

"Hey," Aldo said, ignoring what he'd said and pointing to Petie. "How good does he look in this get-up, huh?"

"Oh yes, very handsome." The man smiled politely. "I'm afraid your friend may break something if he doesn't calm down and I—I don't want any trouble."

"Don't you worry, I'll take care of that rude bastard." Aldo left Petie, put his arm around the man, and began walking him back toward the front of the store. "Let's talk money for now though, huh? You know who my uncle is, right?"

"You get a load of the feet on that guy?" Petie asked.

"Oddly fuckin' small."

"Like little kid's feet. You'd think he'd tip over, no?"

"Yeah, he's not a big guy, but I don't see how the hell he stays upright."

"Richie, my hands are bigger than his feet. That's fucked up. I bet he's got like little baby toes too, huh?"

"I don't really want to talk about dude feet, bro."

"Fair enough. Come on, let's get these monkey suits off."

Later, on our way back to the car, I took Aldo aside. "Listen, man, why don't you let Petie sit this one out?"

"This shit again, really?"

"We don't even need him."

"He's part of the crew. Can't leave him out. I wouldn't do that to him."

"Ally, he's got a kid on the way."

"He's drivin'. He's not doin' anything else."

"But something could go wrong."

"It won't, but even if it does, it'll go wrong for us, not him. He can just drive away. It'll be like he was never there."

"He won't leave us behind. No matter what happens. You know that."

"I got it worked out, taken him on recon same as I did with you and the other guys. Only we covered the route in and out, must've been fifty times now. He gets us in, waits and watches, then gets us out of the city and back on the highway. Route we got worked out takes less than a minute and a half, and we're home free. If I was gonna put the best driver on it, I'd have Ma behind the wheel, right? I put Petie there because it's the safest job. Now stop jinxing us with all this bullshit and drop it, all right?"

I wanted to push it, to remind him that Petie would do anything Aldo told him to do, including sitting the job out. He'd be upset at first, but he'd deal, and when it was all said and done, he'd be safe. But I didn't say anything more. I just stood there and went along with it.

"Let's talk about something important," Aldo said. "How'd I look in there all decked out?"

"Like a fuckin' guinea in a tuxedo."

We both laughed, but like everything else in those days leading up to the job, it was laced with tension. Arms around each other like the old friends we were, we headed for the car, and the others waiting on us.

The next day, Aldo got word from Ray-Ray. He'd be accompanying Grady to the bank for a withdrawal from his safety-deposit box on Monday morning at eleven o'clock.

We were a day away from Petie's wedding and reception.

And three from a move that would change our lives forever.

CHAPTER NINE

The wedding was held at Saint Anthony's, a beautiful and ornate church that had been there since the eighteen hundreds. I hadn't stepped foot in the place since I was a kid, and far as I knew, neither had the other guys, but for a few minutes at least, things felt right. Petie looked good, happier than I'd ever seen him, and despite the jokes Fritz couldn't help himself from mumbling about her white dress, even Tammy looked nice. Everyone behaved, more or less, and we all did our thing, escorting and seating those in attendance while Aldo hung with Petie and tried to keep him calm until Tammy arrived and it was time to get on with the show.

It was a nice ceremony, and except for getting tongue-tied during the nuptials, Petie handled himself pretty well. Because Tammy's father insisted on a full Mass, the whole thing took a little over an hour, but due to the heat and the endless droning of the priest, it felt more like two or three.

The reception took place at a hall belonging to a social club about five minutes away. There were maybe forty people there. I knew about ten. I was paired with one of Tammy's bridesmaids, some chick named Anita I vaguely remembered from high school. I tried to be nice, but she acted like it was a huge effort to be around me the whole time, and whenever she spoke to me she made sure I knew she had a boyfriend. By the time the ceremony was over and we were back at the reception, I'd stopped paying attention to her and focused instead on the open bar and free chicken dinner.

Once dinner was over, and all the formal dances, cake cutting, garter and bouquet-throwing bullshit was done, people took to dancing and drinking. While Petie went table to table with his new bride, thanking people for coming and talking everybody up, the rest of us hung at the bar, taking advantage of the fact that it was a private party so we could drink legally.

"You think they got more of that chicken?" Dino asked me.

I sipped my Seven & Seven. "You get one plate, you fuckin' pig."

He chuckled. "That shit was good though, no?"

"Yeah, tasty." I turned in my stool, leaned back against the bar and watched the dance floor. Aldo was out there with Candy, while Fritz was dancing with the bridesmaid he'd been paired with, some friend of Tammy's nobody knew. Unlike Dino and me, Fritz hit it off with his bridesmaid immediately and they were having a great time. I thought about Holly, wished I could've brought her here. That was over though, at least for now. I knew that, had to accept it. There was no room for that, no room for her or the feelings that came with her.

"Hey," Dino said, elbowing me. "What'd you get them for a present?"

I glanced over at the table displaying all the wrapped gifts. "A blender."

"For what, like milkshakes and shit?"

"Whatever you got to blend, I guess." I lit a cigarette, let it dangle. "Chuckie D had a ton of them for cheap. Why, what'd you get them?"

Ma took a pull on his beer, belched. "Car stereo. Nice one. Pioneer."

"Petie don't have a car, though."

"I know." He shrugged, slumped back against the bar, his tie undone and his shirt sleeves rolled up to the elbow. He'd taken his jacket off the moment they'd gotten there and left it on the back of his chair. "Figured they could put it in Trampy's."

"I don't think she's got one either."

"You serious?" He squinted at me, as if he were losing sight of me. "How the hell was I supposed to know that? How come nobody fuckin' told me?"

"Don't worry about it. They're havin' a kid, they're gonna need a car sooner or later. When they get one, they'll have a stereo, right?"

"I guess." He took another swig of beer. "Tried to get him speakers too but I couldn't get the fuckin' things out, and then the car alarm went off and I had to screw."

"You stole a car stereo and gave it to them for a wedding present?"

"I put it in a box and had my mom wrap it first. What am I, an asshole?"

The band kicked off another tune, and most on the dancefloor stayed there. To my right, I noticed a young guy coming toward me. He was friends with Tammy's family, and while he looked familiar, I wasn't sure who he was.

He leaned in so I could hear him over the band. "You friends with Ray?"

Since I didn't run with this dude I wasn't committing to anything. "Who?"

"The black cat."

"What about him?"

The guy jerked a thumb at the restrooms on the far side of the room. "He's in the men's room."

"So?"

"So, you better go have a talk with him. He's in there doing shit he shouldn't be doing, if you get my drift, and if Tammy's old man or one of his friends catches him, it's not gonna be pretty. Trust me on this."

I nodded but stayed where I was. He moved down the bar and ordered a drink as Dino slapped my arm and asked what that had been about.

"Nothing," I told him. "I'll be right back, got to take a piss."

I dropped down off my stool and headed toward the men's room. I kept looking out at the dance floor until Aldo noticed me. I signaled him by cocking my head in the direction I was headed and made sure he could tell by the look on my face that it was important.

Before I'd reached the door, Aldo was at my side.

"What's up?"

"Ray's doing something in there that's getting the wrong kind of attention."

"Like what, a giant spatter shit?"

"No idea."

"Knowin' Ray, he's probably got one of the waitresses bent over in there."

"Wouldn't surprise me."

Together, we stepped into the restroom.

It was empty, but there were three stalls along the back wall. Two were closed, the third was open, and slumped on the toilet was Ray-Ray. I knew right away what I was seeing, but it was a couple seconds before it registered with Aldo.

"Jesus Christ," he said. "Stay by the door, don't let nobody in."

I moved back to the door, leaned against it and smoked my cigarette.

Aldo crouched down in front of the toilet and slapped Ray across the face none-too-gently. "Hey! Wake up, asshole!"

Ray's head lolled around like his neck was broken, his glassy eyes rolling. He'd used his necktie to band his arm, and the needle was still in his vein, the syringe hanging there. "What's up, baby?" he asked dreamily.

"Fuck are you doin', man?" Aldo unfastened the tie, pulled it free and stuffed it into the pocket of Ray's jacket. Then he plucked the needle free and tossed it in there too. "You're *shootin'* this shit now?"

We all knew Ray-Ray did lots of coke and even snorted heroin now and then, but we'd never known him to spike. I stood there blocking the door and smoking my cigarette, sweating like a pig, visions of my mother filling my head.

"Relax, Holmes." Ray seemed to come around a bit, straightened up and rolled his sleeve back down, but he was still groggy. "It's under control."

"Yeah, fuckin' looks it." Aldo stood up, walked out of the stall, then started back like he was going to swing on him. Apparently, he thought better of it at the last minute and walked back out, pacing over by the sinks. "Christ, Ray. You can't be doin' this shit. Not here. Not now. Hell's wrong with you?"

Ray-Ray pushed himself up and onto his feet, then shuffled over to the sinks. "I'm a grown-ass man, motherfucker, I'll do whatever the hell I want, wherever the hell I want, whenever the hell I want."

"At Petie's fuckin' *reception*? Trampy's old man's the type that'll call the cops over this kinda shit. The fuck, Ray?"

"Relax. I got the situation well in hand."

"We got a job to do," Aldo reminded him. "Don't need any fuckups now."

"Yeah, we got a job. A job I dropped in your lap. *I* dropped. Me. So be cool. I tell you I got this, then I got it."

"I got to be able to rely on you, man. Come on, this is business."

Ray ran the water, splashed some on his face. After glancing at me in the mirror, he turned to Aldo with one of his typical bright smiles. "Nigger, we at a party. Ain't no business happenin' here. I'm just havin' fun, celebratin' with my boys at Petie's wedding. What's wrong with that?"

"You're spikin', that's what's wrong with that."

"Ain't no thing."

"Ain't no thing?"

"That's what I just fuckin' said."

He and Aldo squared on each other, and for a minute I thought they were going to go. But neither man made a move, they just stared at each other for what seemed forever. Eventually, Ray-Ray put a hand out palm up and smiled.

"It's only now and then, brother-man. I got this."

It took a few seconds, but Aldo eventually slapped his hand and nodded.

Someone pushed on the door, hitting it so hard it knocked me off balance. I stumbled forward and Fritz stuck his head in.

"Fuck you guys doing in here?" No one answered, so he came in, letting the door close behind him as he looked from one of us to the next. "I swear to God, if you're having gay bathroom sex without me I'm gonna be pissed."

Aldo moved over to us, leaving Ray at the sinks. "Just talkin'."

"Everything good?"

"Yeah," Aldo said through a smile. "Everything's good, Fritzy."

"Cool, because I'm takin' off with my new lady friend, Babs. She's got her daddy's convertible, wants to drive down the cape. Girl's got a thing about fuckin' on the beach at night she'd like to discuss with me in detail."

I winked at him.

"Nice," Aldo said. "Congratulations. Dry spell's over, huh? About time."

"I'm gonna do some seriously fucked-up shit to that poor girl." Fritz ambled over to one of the urinals, pulled himself free and began to urinate. "I'm already deeply ashamed."

Ray-Ray laughed and walked out.

I exchanged a troubled glance with Aldo, but neither of us said anything.

Fritz flushed, quickly washed his hands, then headed for the exit. "Don't wait up, whores."

Once the door closed, Aldo ran his hands through his hair and let out a long sigh. "Jesus Christ," he said just above a whisper. "The fuck?"

"This is bad."

"No shit."

"What if he's high Monday?"

"He won't be."

"But what if he is?"

"You heard him. Business is business."

"I don't know, man. I don't like it."

"Me either, but it's still Ray we're talking about. He'll do the right thing."

"Getting high's all right, but putting a fucking spike in your arm's somethin' else, Ally. It's a whole other ballgame. Shit, we don't even know how long he's been doin' it, but if he couldn't stop himself tonight then it's bad. Real bad."

"Yeah, but—"

"I know what I'm talkin' about when it comes to this shit."

Aldo's dark eyes turned sympathetic. "I know, bro." He put a hand on my shoulder. "It'll be all right."

"Can't trust nobody on the horse."

"One job, Richie. Just one. Whatever he does after, that's his business, I don't give a shit. Long as he's doin' junk, I won't work with him again. None of us will. But we got to get through this first. He'll do the right thing. You know he will. Ray's no punk. It's business and he knows how to do business. Come on, man, we've known him forever. We've gone to war with him."

"You put that shit in your veins, it changes everything." I took a hard pull on my cigarette. "Makes him vulnerable, man, and that puts us all in danger. This is a major problem, Ally."

"That's why after this, unless he's done with that shit we're done with him."

"He can make mistakes even after the job that'll sink us."

"I'll handle it." Something changed in him just then, in his expression and posture. Something from deep inside him. "We just got to get through this job and we'll be all right. Okay?"

I stared at him. I had nothing else. Didn't matter anyway. Nothing was going to sway Aldo from this heist. Nothing.

"*Okay?*" he asked again.

"Okay."

"Come on," he said, turning me toward the door. "It's Petie's night. Let's get shitfaced, have some fun. Besides, I think I'm supposed to make a speech or some shit."

"Try to remember not to call her *Trampy*, huh?"

"I'll do my best."

Back at the reception, Aldo kept dancing. Ray-Ray acted like nothing was wrong and Dino eventually found some drunk-ass aunt of Tammy's old enough to be his mother to dance with. They ended up out in her car. Petie sat at the head table holding hands with his bride and looked like he couldn't possibly be happier.

I parked myself at the bar and kept drinking until none of it mattered.

My fondest memory of the whole thing was a group photo we all posed for not long before the reception ended. Unfortunately, Fritz had already taken off, but the rest of us huddled around a table, Aldo and me in the center, arms slung around each other, and Dino next to us, holding up a bottle of beer in one hand and flipping off the camera with the other. To his right, Petie and Ray-Ray leaned into the shot, goofing for the camera and holding up their drinks too. We were all laughing when the shot was snapped, and it looked like none of us had a care in the world because that whole goddamn world was ours. The here, the now, the future and even the past. All of it, ours. And maybe it was. For just that quick second it took to snap the picture, maybe it really fucking was.

Then, like everything else, it was gone. Smoke drifting into the night, spiraling away into nothing, nowhere.

Petie and Tammy headed out for an overnight honeymoon of sorts at a fancy hotel in Boston, Dino and Tammy's aunt left together and Aldo and Candy took off not long after.

Outside, on the corner, I leaned against the building in my rumpled tuxedo and smoked a cigarette. Looking like some low-rent lounge singer on break, I watched the city a while through bleary, drunken eyes. It pulsed all around me, like a heartbeat, the lights twinkling and almost beautiful in the heavy summer darkness. I tried to imagine what Holly was doing and if she was thinking about me too. Did I haunt her the way she haunted me?

Didn't really matter.

I threw my cigarette into the gutter and shuffled off toward home.

I made it home later that night but never went inside. I stood down on the street, looking up at the apartment and picturing my mother up there either so high she wouldn't know where she was or rolling around with Bronski. Maybe both. I don't know how long I stood there, but it was a long time. Eventually, I made it down to the wall, where a bunch of younger kids were still hanging, despite the late hour. They paid their respects and asked why I was dressed the way I was. I explained, hung around a while and smoked a couple joints with them, had a few pulls from bottles wrapped in brown paper, then drifted off and found myself walking the city.

When the sun finally broke, I was sitting on the steps of Holly's dorm. I'd been there a couple hours and still couldn't convince myself to go inside. I was exhausted, hadn't slept at all, and was still a little drunk, but I had to do this or I knew I'd regret it for the rest of my life. I knew it was over before it had even really started, but I couldn't just walk away and never see her again. Much as it was going to hurt, I had to be near her one more time, to see her face, to hear her voice, to maybe even kiss her one last time.

"Richie, what are you doing here?"

Startled, I looked behind me. About halfway down the steps, Holly stood in a lightweight bathrobe and slippers, her hair mussed and her eyes still heavy with sleep. "Hey," I said softly.

"Are you okay?"

I struggled to my feet. "How'd you know I was here?"

"Someone saw you out the window. How long have you been here?"

"I don't know. A while."

"You're lucky campus security didn't see you."

"I'm not worried about it."

"I'm sure." She combed her hair with her fingers. "I look awful, just rolled out of bed."

"You look beautiful."

"Real funny." She made a playful face then realized her mistake. "My God, you're serious, aren't you?"

"No reason to lie."

She looked at the ground. "Thanks."

"Now me, I look like I been run over by a dump truck. Maybe two."

I hoped she might laugh. Instead, she stayed where she was, pawed at her sleepy eyes and said, "I'm sorry about the other day."

"Me too. I acted like an asshole."

"I didn't mean things the way you took them, I—"

"It don't matter."

"Of course it does. I'm trying to tell you I..." She seemed to notice what I was wearing for the first time. "Why are you in a tuxedo?"

"Friend of mine got married last night."

"Really? Neat. Did you have fun?"

"I'm not sure."

Holly smiled, like she couldn't help it. "Have you been out here all night?"

"I don't know, maybe. It was dark when I got here."

"Jesus, Richie. You could've—"

"Yeah, I know, I'm lucky the college rent-a-cops didn't find me."

"You really are."

"I didn't want to bother you. Plus, I was pretty drunk."

"Why were you drunk?"

"Not much to do at a wedding reception besides dance, eat and drink."

"True, but there's such a thing as moderation."

"What the hell's that?"

Holly laughed lightly. "Do you want to come up for a while?"

"Nah, I don't want to scare nobody."

"Then don't be scary."

"I came to say goodbye."

She seemed genuinely surprised. "Why goodbye?"

"I got some things goin' on. I don't know if I'll be around anymore."

"You're leaving?"

"Maybe. I don't know yet. It's just...a lot of things could happen."

She came down the rest of the steps, stopping just short of me. "Are you in some sort of trouble, Richie?"

"I was born in trouble."

Suddenly her hand was cupping the side of my face. I had to stop myself from falling into her, from grabbing hold of her. Afraid I'd never be able to let her go if I did, I stayed still, closed my eyes and let her touch me, her soft palm warm against my cheek.

"You really were, weren't you?" she whispered.

"I got to go."

"No, you don't."

I opened my eyes, looked into hers. "If I don't, I never will."

"What's wrong with us? I mean we—one date—for God's sake, we..."

"Don't worry, when you look back, I'll just be some guy you knew for a little while a long time ago, that's all."

"What about me?"

"What about you?"

"What'll I be when you look back?"

"Same thing you are right now. Girl of my dreams."

"I've never met anyone like you, I...I've never felt like this about..." She shook her head, as if it were all too much. "I want you to be safe, but I—I know you're not. I don't even know why exactly, I just know I don't want you to be afraid, and I don't want to be afraid for you. You're so sweet and you...why does this have to be so hard? Why can't we just..."

I took her hand and slowly brought it to my lips. I kissed it softly. Once, then again. "Let go. I'm not worth it."

"What if you are?"

"I'm not."

"Am I?"

"That's why I have to go."

"Shouldn't that be a reason to stay?"

Before I could answer, she fell into me, her head against my chest and her arms wrapped around me. I held her tight, remembering what her body felt like in my arms, the way she smelled and the way she breathed in quick little shallow breaths. I wanted to remember all of it, forever, because I knew then I'd never experience it—her—again.

"We never even got a chance to know for sure," she said.

I didn't answer. I didn't need to.

"Maybe we really could've loved each other, Richie."

"Maybe we already do."

"Sometimes it happens that way, doesn't it?"

We kissed, and in that moment, I'd never felt such warmth and beauty.

"Are you really leaving?" Holly asked a moment later.

"Yeah. Some things are happenin' I can't get into with you, but..."

"What kind of things?"

"Nothin' good."

"Then why are you involved in them?"

"I don't really have a choice."

"We always have a choice."

"Don't matter. Forget about it."

"It's not that easy."

I nodded. She was right. But no matter what happened, I wouldn't be around. If things went bad, I could die, and even if they went perfectly, once we had the score, I'd either take my cut and leave the city or let Aldo talk me into going to work for his uncle. No matter what, it was all dangerous, and no place or life for someone like Holly.

"Even if I run," I said, "what the hell am I runnin' from? A whole lot of nothin', Holly. You'd be runnin' from better things, because you got everything to lose and a chance at a life you'd never be able to have with me. Guy like me, it don't matter if I live or die, stay or go."

"That's not true."

"Yeah, it is."

"If you asked me to come with you...it's crazy and off the wall and makes no sense but...right at this moment...I'm not sure I'd say no."

"I wouldn't do that to you, much as I might want to. You got a shot at a real life, a good life." I leaned in, kissed her forehead. "Go get it, live it. There's nothin' for you with me."

She looked up at me with eyes filled with tears I hadn't noticed until just then. "Am I ever going to see you again, Richie?"

I answered her the only way I knew how. "Think about me sometimes, huh?"

We kissed again. I tasted her tears. Or maybe they were mine.

Neither of us spoke again. We just held each other for a long time.

Then I walked away.

A memory. A ghost.

* * *

In those last days before the heist, and even on that last day, Sunday, a lot of things changed. Maybe it was too late to make much difference, or maybe it was simply an illusion, a wily trick of misdirection life had thrown my way, the way living things saddled with incurable illness often rebound and seem to get better, just before they die. I'd never been the type that scared easily, but on that Sunday, in those hours spent with my mother at home, silently counting down the minutes until I'd be trapped in something I couldn't escape, something beyond anything I'd done before, I was afraid.

My mother looked better than she had in months. She was bright-eyed and almost giddy that I'd decided to stay home and spend the day with her. We hadn't done that in a long while. I pretended not to notice when she slipped into the kitchen and quietly made a phone call. I knew she was telling Bronski to stay away, and thankfully, he did. She showered and dressed in something other than her pajamas, a nightgown or bathrobe, and she seemed genuinely happy, bopping around in anticipation of our afternoon together. It reminded me of when I was a little kid and still felt like I could count on her, like she might somehow be able to save me and protect me from harm. But there was no going back. Those days were gone, if they'd ever really existed at all, so instead, I grabbed hold of these new memories, the ones of this last day we'd share before everything went down and changed forever.

Despite my nerves, it turned out to be as nice a day as we'd hoped for. She made some Jiffy Pop on the stove then poured it into a big bowl, buttered it and sat with me on the couch munching popcorn while we watched a movie. It wasn't really my kind of thing, some sort of romantic comedy with Audrey Hepburn, but it was pretty good, and besides, my mother was enjoying herself and she was sober, and that was all that mattered. Later, we played board games and just talked, like we hadn't in a long time. No bitching at each other or arguing, no judgments, just conversation. And then I ordered us a couple nice dinners from a local restaurant that delivered, and we ate them together at the table. "Like normal people," my mother said, laughing and so full of life.

But no matter how clean she was for the moment or how happy she was with me, the day, and all that was happening, she was still my mother. She'd made me, brought me into this world, and she knew when something was wrong.

"What's bothering you?" she asked.

"Nothin', I'm fine."

"Tell me, Richie. It's okay. What's wrong? You look like you got the weight of the world on your shoulders."

I took her hands in mine, gave them a kiss. "Don't worry about me, I'm okay. I'm havin' a nice time. It's been a nice day."

"It has, hasn't it?"

"It's good to see you happy."

"You too." She smiled. "You know, when you were just a baby, Richie, sometimes you'd be in your crib, and you'd clench your little hands together into fists and cry really hard. I'm talking so hard your face would get all red. It was scary, and your father and I weren't sure what was wrong with you, so we took you to the doctor and had him examine you." She sat back, lost in the past. "We thought you must be in pain, but they ran all these tests, and nothing was wrong."

"Why was I doing it, then?"

"That's what your father asked the doctor, and he wasn't very nice about it either." She took on a voice I guess was supposed to sound like my father's. "'*Well there must be something wrong with the kid, he's crying and clenching his fists and kicking his legs all the time, that's not normal.*' He got upset, your father, but it was only because he was so scared for you. He used to do that. If he was scared, he got mad, it was just his way of showing he loved you."

I felt myself smile. My mother seldom spoke about my father, and I'd never heard this story before.

"Anyway, the doctor looks at us and says, '*Mr. and Mrs.*

Lionetti, there's absolutely nothing wrong with your baby, he's in perfect health. He's just mad.'"

"Mad," I said, chuckling.

"Yeah, and your father says, *'Mad? He's a baby for Christ's sake, what the hell's he got to be mad about?'* And I just laughed and laughed. I couldn't stop. You were mad, that was it. Our boy, our son, our little man. There wasn't anything wrong with you, you were just pissed off."

We both laughed a while, and it felt good. I hadn't seen my mother laugh so hard in years.

"Your father took you out of my arms and held you," she said once our laughter had quieted. "And he said, *'What's the matter, Richie, why are you so mad, little fella?'* And you looked up at him with those big, gorgeous brown eyes and smiled. Every time you did it after that, if he was there, he'd do the same thing, and you wouldn't be mad anymore. You'd smile that beautiful little smile of yours and sometimes you'd even giggle, you know how babies do, best sound in whole world, and after a while, you got mad less and less."

Laughter had turned to silence.

"He was a good man," she said softly. "And he loved you very much, Richie. The sun rose and set on his little boy, believe me."

"I wish I could've known him."

Eyes filled with tears, she smiled and said, "Me too."

My mother still missed him, still loved him, and in my own way, so did I.

"So, I was born angry, huh?"

"I think it's because you're so smart. You were just raging against things you couldn't control and didn't understand."

"Sounds familiar."

"You can't fight the world, Richie. We can't even fight ourselves, not really, even though we do. It's not a fight we can win. Sometimes, you got to let yourself be, you know what I mean? You have to learn to leave yourself alone a little, to just let yourself *be*."

"I'm tryin', Mom."

"I know you are, sweetheart. So am I. I promise you I am."

"You need to get help."

"I know. I'm sick."

"You got to stay away from that pig downstairs."

She nodded, looked away. "I don't want to...let's not talk about this."

"You're right," I said. "Come on, let's go out."

"Out? Where, I—"

"Let's go get an ice cream, it's hot."

"We got ice cream in the freezer, I think."

"Shit's older than I am. Come on, put your shoes on, I'm taking you out for an ice cream. You never go out."

It took some convincing, but eventually she did her hair, put some makeup on and relented. I couldn't remember the last time we'd taken a walk together, much less gone anywhere, but I knew I'd never forget that night even then. In those days, most things weren't open on Sundays, so the city was quiet, not a lot of traffic or people on the street. It was like the whole world had taken a breath, just for us.

When I think of it now, I remember my mother sitting on a stool at a local ice cream parlor not far from our apartment, smiling from ear-to-ear and eating a big sloppy double scoop of maple walnut ice cream. She was still far too tired and worn down for a woman her age, but the track marks that populated her arms and legs were mostly hidden, and she looked happy. And I think, for a little while at least, she genuinely was.

"Thanks, Richie," she said. "Thanks for making me come out."

"You should do it more often."

"*We* should do it more often."

"Yeah. We should."

I'd never been so happy to be with my mother. And never so heartbroken.

Later, after we'd gone home, she stayed up a while to watch

TV and I went into my room and collapsed into bed. I didn't sleep for a long time, I just lay there staring at the ceiling and running a million different scenarios in my mind of how the next day might go. In some ways, my whole life had led to this moment, this one day, and in a matter of hours I'd find out if that was good, bad or somewhere in between.

For the first time, I had a glimmer of hope that I might actually be able to get us out of here. My mother was so happy on our walk and at the ice cream parlor. If the job went right, I could afford to get us to a place where she could get well, and I could do something else with my life, something better.

I read a little more from *The Beach at Falesá*, and while the mysticism and magic of the story, coupled with the exotic location, distracted me a while, the constant conniving of the white traders scurrying around for profits like rats pissed me off. The spiritual versus the material. Even in paradise, the disease that is Man spread.

Maybe that's all I was, all the guys were. Rats running around looking to steal other people's crumbs, and biting anyone who got in our way or tried to stop us, filling our pockets while spreading disease.

I tossed the book aside, thought about the people who worked in that bank. They all had families, hopes, dreams, fears. They were going to get up and go to work like any other day, with no clue what we had in store for them. I thought about Grady, poor old bastard, and how even though he'd finally gotten a break in his miserable life, guys like me were going to come along and take it all away from him. Then again, if we didn't do it, somebody else would. Why not us then? Why not me?

It was all excuses, of course, bullshit to make me feel better about being a lowlife asshole, and I wasn't fooling anyone, not even myself. While I knew the guys rarely, if ever, thought about the victims of our crimes, I usually did. On some level, that made me worse. I cared, it mattered to me—they mattered—yet I did it anyway. Cornered, I was going back to what I knew. And what I knew was survival. Mine.

Now it came down to the guns. I wondered if I could use one on someone if I had to. While I'd never gotten off on violence like some guys did, I had no problem using it if necessary. I was also good at it. Leveling a gun on someone and pulling the trigger was a hell of a lot different than beating the Christ out of someone though. If I had to, could I really do it?

Lying there, what disturbed me most wasn't the question, but the answer.

I'm sure I drifted in and out of sleep after a while, but I don't remember sleeping that night. A couple times, my mother's story about my anger as a baby replayed in my mind, and I wondered why she'd never told it to me before.

I noticed my fists were clenched.

Born angry, I thought.

Tomorrow, I hoped I wouldn't die that way too.

CHAPTER TEN

That morning, the heat broke again. What began as a gentle rain turned to a thunderous summer downpour that just kept coming. A literal storm had settled over the city, raging and soaking everything down.

We met at a predetermined location about ten minutes from the city as Aldo had instructed. Behind an abandoned and burned-out factory in Fall River, amidst the debris and piles of bricks that had once constituted buildings, in a small parking area still surrounded on three sides by rusted chain-link fence, we parked and began to prepare. The old lot was tucked nicely behind and into the shadows from the looming giant shell of what had once been a textile factory years before. Just over the Braga Bridge, it was right off Interstate 195, hidden from both the access road leading to it and the highway.

It was still relatively early in the morning, only a little after ten, but due to the weather it looked more like early evening. Fritz and I came with Aldo in his car. Dino and Petie followed in a stolen four-door Jeep Cherokee Aldo had clipped in the early morning hours of the night before. The idea was for Petie to drive the vehicle there so he could get a feel for it. When the job was over, we'd return here, switch vehicles, burn the Cherokee and be back on the highway home, gone before anyone even saw the flames. Because of the rain, and because the forecast called for downpours to continue into late afternoon, we'd brought a can of gasoline, which we left in Aldo's trunk.

Aldo got our outfits for the robbery from Chuckie D, identical gray-blue jumpsuits, the kind mechanics sometimes wore, black work boots and black leather gloves. The masks were identical as well, the killer from the *Halloween* movies.

"We look like sick fuckin' rigs in these," Dino said, chuckling as he pulled his mask on over his head. "Those bank assholes are gonna shit when they see us comin'."

"Yeah," Petie said, studying his mask. "One Michael Myers is scary enough, but we're bringing five."

Ma started signing the piano theme from *Halloween* in a falsetto that normally would've been funny but came off even more disturbing than the original. "*Deh-neh-neh, deh-neh-neh, deh-neh-neh, deh-neh-neh, deh-deh! Deh neh-neh, deh-neh-neh, deh-neh-neh, deh-neh-neh, deh-deh, deeeeeeh!*"

Leave it to those two to be laughing and babbling just minutes before we were taking off. He was doing his best, just like the rest of us, but it was obvious Petie was terrified. He always talked too much when he was frightened. Ma, on the other hand, was actually enjoying himself. No one else said anything. Even Fritz was unusually quiet and reserved, keeping mostly to himself. As I pulled on my jumpsuit, buttoning it up to the neck, I realized that despite the rain, Fritz still had his sunglasses on. I thought about putting my mask on, but stuffed it in one of my pockets instead. I was already having enough trouble breathing normally, and once I was under that thing it'd only get worse.

I looked over at Aldo. There was something wrong, something bothering him, I could tell. He was nervous just like the rest of us, but there was something more gnawing at him.

As the others finished dressing, I pulled him aside. "Everything okay?"

"Better be," he said quietly.

"There somethin' else going on I should know about?"

When his dark eyes found mine, something had changed in them too. There was a coldness, a distance. And there was something he wasn't telling me. "Just do your job like everybody else and we'll get through this without any problems, okay?"

I nodded. "Yeah."

He produced the Glock and held it out for Petie. "Probably won't need it, but just in case. Don't even touch the fucker unless you have to. You pull it out it's because you need to use it. No other reason, you read me?"

"I know, man, you been over this with me a hundred times."

"Don't *I know* me, Petie. Do you *fucking* read me?"

"Loud and clear, man." Petie checked it over quickly then slipped it in his side pocket. "Loud and clear. I promise."

"Where's the rest?" Dino asked. He was the only one who had already put his mask on, and between that and the rain, his voice was muffled.

"Already in the Cherokee," Aldo said. "You'll get them once we're rollin'."

The rain was pouring, but we'd managed to shield ourselves from the worst of it under an archway, the door on the other side of which led to what had once been loading docks. We stood there in the rain. Nobody said anything for a long time. I leaned against the old brick wall along the back of the building and listened to the rain and the hum of traffic rushing past along the nearby highway. My heart was thudding in my chest, pulsing in time with the throbbing in my temples, and for a minute I thought I'd lose it and call the whole thing off.

"Breathe," Aldo said, sensing my panic.

"I'm all right," I told him.

"You sure?"

"I'm sure."

He turned to the others. "Everybody good?"

No one answered.

"Any problems or questions, now's the time."

Again, silence.

"Okay then." Aldo checked his watch. "It's ten-thirty. We're ten minutes out on a good day, but the rain's gonna slow everything down some—and Petie, I want you drivin' the speed limit or under the whole way, no exceptions—so we're probably lookin' at landin' right around ten-forty-five. That'll put us fifteen minutes in front of Ray and give us enough time to scope everything out one last time. Anybody's havin' second thoughts, this is your last chance."

No one objected.

"All right," he said. "Then let's go."

We piled into the Cherokee. Petie slid behind the wheel, Dino took the passenger seat, and Aldo, Fritz and me jumped into the backseat. As we pulled out, Aldo removed the Tec-9s and handed one to Fritz and the other to Dino. They immediately began checking them over, then held them down in their laps, below window level. The shotguns came next. I took mine and laid it across my lap. Aldo did the same with his. We said nothing more.

The drive back over the bridge and to the city was only about ten minutes or so, but it felt like hours, like time had slowed to a near stop. No radio, no talking, just the sound of rain and the wipers surging back and forth across the windshield.

Eventually, we reached the city.

Petie found a space diagonally across the street from the bank and parked, purposely moving up enough into the space in front that no one else could park there and block us in. There was a car parked behind us, but that wasn't a problem. One in front of us would make it more difficult to get out and possibly slow our escape. Petie kept the wipers going, but through the side windows, it was tough to see much, except for First National's sign, which they'd kept lit due to the darkness caused by the storm. It shone through the rain like a beacon, a white box with fancy blue lettering.

"Rain makes it hard to see much from here," Petie said.

"Drop your window if you have to," Aldo told him. "Keep

it runnin' and don't move an inch until you see us comin'."

"You got it."

"We got less than fifteen minutes before Ray gets here with Grady," Aldo said. "Everybody sit tight. Ma, take that fuckin' mask off. They go on when we move, not until then. There's hardly anybody on the street with all the rain, but we don't need to draw attention."

Dino did as he was told and pulled his mask off. He looked like a child who'd been reprimanded, and it made me think about when we were all a bunch of kids running in the streets, stealing bicycles and snatching purses, shoplifting comic books, professional wrestling magazines, candy bars and Slim Jims from stores all over the city. We stole everything we could get our grimy little punk hands on, and we'd stand and fight with anyone—other kids or even adults—who dared get in our way or try to stop us. Sometimes we'd win, sometimes not, but we always stuck together and lived or died as a group. And now, here we were, in a situation where that concept had become literal, sitting in that Cherokee in our jumpsuits and boots, holding weapons that could easily kill everyone in the bank and then some. There was no way around it now. The minute we stepped out of this vehicle we'd become something else and there'd be no way back. This is who we'd be. This would be our lives now, our livelihoods.

"Think I'm in love, fellas," Fritz said with a sigh.

No one said anything.

"Best night of my life down the cape," he continued. "I got sand in places I didn't even know I had. Her name's Barbara. I'm gonna get a place and move in with her, I think. Never met a girl like this before, I mean, she's—"

"Fritzy," Aldo finally said. "Shut the fuck up."

He looked out the rain-blurred window but didn't respond.

"What's this waitin'-around shit?" Dino growled, fidgeting in his seat. "Job like this you gotta get there and go. Go fast and get the hell out."

"Yeah," Petie said, "Ma's right. Where the hell's Ray-Ray?"

"Everybody be cool," Aldo snapped. "He's due any minute."

I stayed quiet, but I knew what Dino meant. Waiting gave us time to think about what was coming and what we were doing. In that strange moment, I needed to either get out and do this or drive away. What I didn't need was to keep sitting there with a shotgun in my lap and a Michael Myers mask in my pocket, remembering everything that had led us to this point.

"Cop should be passing by now," Aldo said, checking his watch again.

"In this rain?" Dino said. "Fat fuck's probably standing around in a store talkin' some chick's ear off."

A few minutes came and went, then Aldo sat up a bit and checked his watch a third time. "There's the cruiser," he said. "Right on time. Won't have to worry about those douchebags for another half hour or so."

We all watched through the blurred glass as the cops drove by.

"Still no sign of that fucker on foot though," Petie said.

"Fuck it," Aldo said, "we go anyway. Can't wait on him. Hopefully, by the time he comes around the corner, we'll already be gone. If he shows, just be cool, he'll probably walk right by without even knowin' what's happenin'."

"What if he doesn't? What if he goes to the bank for some reason?"

"He comes in the bank, Petie, we'll handle it. Just make sure this thing is runnin' and ready to go the minute you see us come through those doors."

Dino clutched his shotgun with both hands but kept it on his lap. "This is bullshit, man, I can't keep fuckin' sittin' here like this!"

"Shut your mouth and mask up." Aldo pulled his mask on. "They're here."

Fritz took his sunglasses off and placed them on the small section of seat between us, then slipped his mask on. Ma hastily put his on as well. I was the last one, and after a quick glance at Ray's piece-of-shit car pulling into a space across the street, I slipped mine on as well.

It smelled of rubber and glue. Wasn't easy to breathe and each breath was loud and labored, but I could see well through the eyeholes. My hands shook, so I gripped the shotgun hard as I could, drew a deep breath, then let it out slowly. My hands went steady, my mind went blank. I felt nothing.

As Ray-Ray and Grady hurried through the rain and into the bank, we waited for the last time, counting down the few minutes it would take for them to get the bank manager over to the safety-deposit room.

All I heard was rain pounding the roof, blood pulsing in my ears and my slow, steady breaths beneath the mask.

"Move," Aldo said suddenly. "Go!"

We did.

Get down on the floor!

I don't remember everything, some of it's just flashes and blurs, but I do remember how everything was both muffled and amplified beneath the mask, from my breathing, to the rain, to our heavy footfalls against the wet pavement.

Close your eyes!

I remember the guard just inside the entrance, and how impossibly old he looked—all wrinkles and white hair and liver spots, like some decrepit grandpa—and how by the time he saw us coming through the doors and realized what was happening, it was too late. He tried to fumble for his revolver as he rose from his stool, but Dino slapped him with the Tec-9 so hard it sent the poor bastard halfway across the lobby. Though Aldo and I were already making a beeline for the safety-deposit box room, I remember the sound it made as it cracked against that guard's skull. I heard him grunt and fall to the floor, the revolver bouncing and sliding away along the highly-polished floor.

Don't fuckin' move!

I heard Dino yelling at the few patrons who were there, telling them to get down on the floor while Fritz ordered the tellers to raise their hands and step back from their drawers and any silent alarms they might trip.

"Let's go!" Fritz yelled, moving to the swinging half-door that led behind the counter, waving his shotgun and ushering all the tellers out from their windows and down onto the floor with the patrons. "Everybody out, right now! Come on, move your asses! And keep your hands up nice and high!"

"Everybody quiet!" Dino screamed from somewhere behind me.

I remember seeing the bank manager come through the doorway of the safety-deposit box room, Ray-Ray close behind her as Aldo and I closed on them, leveling the shotguns. The manager looked confused at first, then terrified, raising her shaking hands and mumbling something about cooperating and there being no need to hurt anyone. Aldo ordered them to the ground and I stepped around him quickly, preventing the door from closing behind them by blocking it with my foot.

My head was on a swivel. Everything was heightened—sights, sounds, colors, everything—and all of it experienced from beneath the claustrophobic cover of a cheap rubber mask. I was sure my heart would explode any second.

The manager dropped to the floor and sprawled out on her stomach as Aldo instructed. Just as we'd planned it, Ray refused.

"I said down, asshole!" Aldo smashed him full in the face with the butt of the shotgun. "Down!"

Ray staggered back and dropped to his knees, blood already gushing from his nose and mouth. "Jesus Christ! You mother-fucker!"

"Shut your mouth!"

I moved into the room, my shotgun leading the way.

It was brighter in there, smaller and cramped. I found Grady standing at a table in the center of the room, a long open metal box before him, and a look of horror on his weathered face. "No," he whispered. "*No.*"

I motioned with the weapon for him to step back. He didn't. "Move," I growled. "Now. I'm not playin' with you, old man."

Grady squinted with moist, bloodshot eyes. "You ain't takin' my money."

I produced a canvas bag from inside my jumper, tossed it on the table then jammed the shotgun under his chin and against his throat, forcing him back until he was pinned to the wall. "Blink and I'll be the last fuckin' thing you see."

"Let's go!" Aldo yelled from beyond the doorway.

Keeping Grady in my sights, I stepped back, turned the box over and emptied the banded cash onto the table. Tossing the box aside, I swept the pile of cash into the bag. A few banded stacks fell to the floor but I left them there.

"God*damn* you," Grady said in a rumbling voice. "Goddamn you to hell, boy. I find out who you is, I'll kill you myself."

I punched him in the gut with everything I had. He gasped, doubled over and collapsed, lying there holding his stomach and writhing about on the floor. His body bucked and I thought he might be having a seizure, but then he vomited and lay still, weeping softly. The idea of executing him crossed my mind. I'd never experienced anything like it, yet for a moment I felt myself beginning to bend to it.

Put this lame-ass motherfucker's brains all over the floor.

Grabbing the bag, I quickly left the room, closing the door behind me and nodding to Aldo that we were good to go.

As I moved by him and toward the exit, I saw Aldo still standing over Ray, who was on his knees, hands pressed to his face in an attempt to stop the flow of blood from his nose and mouth. Through the holes in the mask, I saw Aldo's dark eyes staring at me. He blinked. Slowly. Like a reptile.

Then he turned back, racked the shotgun, placed it against Ray's forehead and pulled the trigger.

It nearly took his head off as his face exploded and his

brains and the back of his skull sprayed the air in a disgusting mist.

Unable to believe what I'd just seen, I stood paralyzed, ears ringing from the blast, which echoed through the open space and up along the high ceiling.

What did you do? What—What did you do?

"We're gone," Aldo said flatly. "Move."

When I didn't, he grabbed me by the front of my jumpsuit, shook me like a child, then pushed me toward the doors. "I said *move!*"

Given the signal, Dino and Fritz began backing toward the door, their Tec-9s still trained on the tellers and patrons.

The rest was all automatic pilot. Whatever control of myself I'd had to that point left me in those last moments. It was like walking through a dream, a lucid nightmare where I was helpless and could do nothing but watch in horror as it played out.

We'd been inside the bank less than three minutes, and in those few seconds before we got back out through the doors, with the sounds of people whimpering and crying somewhere at the very edge of my senses, I'm sure I thought we'd made it, that Ray was dead but we'd made it, and soon we'd be back in the Cherokee and on our way to a clean getaway.

I should've known better.

Sometimes you get away, but it's never clean.

We hit the air and the rain, moving quickly but not running, the weapons down by our sides as we stepped off the sidewalk and started across the street to the Cherokee. I was still watching Petie slowly pull out to meet us when I heard someone screaming.

Ma saw him first. The goddamn beat cop, walking his beat in the rain, had turned the corner just as we'd emerged from the bank. And from the sounds of sirens in the distance, he'd already called for backup.

I couldn't make out what was being yelled, but as I looked back without stopping, I saw the cop in a firing stance, his gun out in front of him, one hand locked on his wrist as he ordered us to freeze and drop our weapons.

Aldo was ahead of me, Dino and Fritz behind me. No one stopped, but Dino spun, and while still moving backwards, raised and fired his Tec-9.

The cop fired too.

Instinctually, I ducked, dropping low into a crouch. Aldo did the same.

Both Dino and the cop missed, but the cop fired again, and this time Dino jerked to the side and spun like a top, a tear appearing in the shoulder of his jumpsuit. He grunted and dropped the Tec-9 as his arm went limp.

Fritz grabbed him, pulling him back toward the Cherokee, and Aldo slid back around behind me, leveling his shotgun, racking it and firing again and again, walking right toward the cop as he did so.

The cop flailed and yelped, tumbling to the sidewalk in a spray of blood as the rounds blasted into him. Aldo kept walking and firing until he was within a foot or so of the man, then turned and started back toward the Cherokee.

That's when I heard the screech and saw the cruiser fishtail at the top of the block. Two cops jumped out, positioned behind the open doors. One had a pistol, the other a shotgun. They offered no warnings, they just opened fire on us. I never thought about it, I just dropped the shotgun, grabbed the Tec-9 Dino had dropped and stood up firing back, spraying the area and riddling both doors, the hood and windshield with bullet holes.

"Go!" someone yelled. Aldo, I think.

But Fritz was down. The cops had hit him and he was lying in the middle of the street, his knees drawn up to his chest and his hands clutching his midsection. He was crying out, saying something, but I couldn't hear him over the rain and ringing in my ears.

I ran for him as Dino grabbed my shotgun with his good hand, held the butt against his thigh, racked it, then fired at the cruiser.

Fritz was covered in blood and making a horrible gurgling sound. His eyes, through the mask, were wide and terrified, and he tried to say something but only managed a raspy whimpering noise. It was the worst fucking sound I'd ever heard.

"It's okay, it's okay," I told him. "You're gonna be all right, I got you."

Grabbing him by the back of his collar, I ran for the car, literally dragging him behind me as I went and firing the Tec-9 at the cruiser with my free hand.

The cop with the shotgun went down in a spray of bullets.

But not before he'd hit Dino.

Last thing I saw was Ma vaulting backwards into the air, hit in the chest by the shotgun blast. He landed on his back, arms out at his sides and legs stretched out straight like a bloody snow angel.

He was dead before he hit the ground, the mangled hole where his chest had been a bloody horrific mess, the shotgun lying in a puddle of rain and gore next to him. That ridiculous mask still covered his face.

Aldo was in the Cherokee first, and as I got there, I crouched and lifted Fritz up and onto the seat. In what was only a second or two but felt like hours, I contemplated trying to get to Dino, but there was no way I'd make it.

The last cop kept popping up over the open car door and firing at us, but had stopped to reload, and the sounds of approaching sirens had grown louder.

Aldo put a hand out. I took it, and he yanked me up and into the backseat.

Petie hit the gas and sped past the cruiser, and although he was screaming incoherently and crying, he got us through a set of lights, onto the ramp and to the highway within seconds.

We pulled the masks off and I looked at Fritz. His was still on, so I took it off gently as I could. He was lying across Aldo's lap, his legs on the floor. Although Aldo was holding him and slowly rocking back and forth in the seat, he didn't look at him. He just stared out the window, saying nothing.

The minute I pulled the mask free, I knew Fritz was dead. I looked away, tears filling my eyes. This couldn't be real. It couldn't be happening, not like this. But it was. Ray was dead in the bank, Dino was dead in the street, and Fritz was dead in Aldo's arms.

"Nobody on us," Petie mumbled, glancing maniacally at the rearview every few seconds. "There's—there's nobody on us, I—I think we're out, I—"

"Just drive," Aldo said evenly. "Get us there."

Petie nodded, his entire body shaking.

Fritz was covered in blood. He'd bled out all over the seat and us. I'd never seen so much in one place. Then came a terrible stench, and I knew he'd vacated his bowels.

Aldo leaned forward and threw up on the floor, retching so violently I almost joined him.

We reached the lot in Fall River without further incident. The one cruiser on the scene had been disabled by the gunfire, and by the time the others had gotten there, we were gone. But they'd certainly called in a description of the vehicle, so we knew we didn't have much time to dump it and switch cars.

The three of us stumbled from the Cherokee and into the rain.

"Come on," Aldo finally said, "we got to go, move it."

We all pulled off our jumpsuits then tossed them into the Cherokee along with the masks.

Aldo handed me his shotgun. "Make sure they're all in there. Burn them."

I took it, then took the Glock from Petie, who was still crying, and moved back to the Cherokee. As Aldo grabbed the gas can from the trunk of his car, I tossed the Tec-9s and shotgun into a pile on the floor. I gave a quick look and realized no one was watching me, so I tucked the Glock into the front of my jeans then pulled my T-shirt down over it.

Fritz's sunglasses lay on the seat. Like everything else, they were covered in blood. I cleaned them off as quickly and best I could then put them on him. I don't know why, it just seemed like the right thing to do.

Tears streamed my face. I angrily wiped them away.

"Douse it."

Aldo stood next to me with the gas can. I took it from him and splashed gasoline all over the interior of the Cherokee. Then I tossed the can in too, peeled off my gloves, collected theirs as well, and added them to the mix.

"Why'd you do Ray?" I asked him. "The fuck, man? He was our friend. You been to war with him. How many times did he have our backs over the years? He was one of us, and you did him like he was nothing."

"Y-You killed Ray-Ray?" Petie asked through his sobbing.

Aldo ignored him, dealt with me instead. "You think I wanted it to go down that way? I did everything I could to find a way around it, but we couldn't risk it. I couldn't trust him anymore."

"*You* couldn't trust *him*? He trusted you, and you put his brains on the wall."

"You said yourself we couldn't trust him, not spikin'."

"We could've called it off."

"I got enough on my head right now, I don't need this bull—"

"Nobody had to die."

"I ain't listenin' to this shit! Now get out of the way, we need to burn this thing and screw."

"Ray-Ray's dead?" Petie asked, his chin trembling and eyes huge. "Why'd you kill Ray, Ally? What the—what the fuck is goin' on?"

Aldo slapped him across the face. "Shut the fuck up and get in the car."

He stood there like a scolded child, his face streamed with tears.

"Ally," I said, "I want my money."

"What?"

"You heard me. I want my cut."

"Now?"

"I'm out. I'm runnin'. I'm not gonna wait around for them to come pick me up. Fuck that."

"Look, man, we need to stick together, we—"

"Dino and Fritz are dead! Hell's wrong with you? *Stick together*? Fuck you, gimme my money."

"Move, we'll talk about this later." He put a hand on my shoulder and tried to push me out of the way.

I slapped his hand away, stood my ground.

Aldo leveled a dead stare at me. "You really want to do this?"

"I want my money."

He tried to move by me, and this time I put a hand on his shoulder, stopping him. We stayed that way, neither of us saying a word.

Then he grabbed me by the throat.

I tried to wrench it free, but he was too strong, so I threw an uppercut.

It caught him clean under the chin, snapped his head back and sent him stumbling away from me.

Petie yelled for us to stop, but it was too late.

Fists clenched, Aldo moved back toward me. "Okay," he said. "This is how you want it? Come on."

I swung again, but he dodged it and countered with a hook that caught me in the mouth. I swung back blindly, missed, and he caught me again, then followed with a kick that he'd meant for my head but slammed my shoulder instead. It was so powerful it dropped me to wet pavement anyway.

He could've beaten me down from there, but didn't. He just stood over me, breathing heavily, and said, "We all set?"

I spat out some blood, wiped my mouth and got back to my feet.

"Don't make me do this, Richie."

Petie stepped between us, patted me on the back. "Easy, bro, easy now."

"I run this motherfucker," Aldo said. "And I do my best, Richie. I do my best by all of you. I never asked for nothin' in return but loyalty and friendship, and I ain't askin' for nothin' more now. I die with you. All of you. No matter what. Understand?"

"I understand Dino and Fritz and Ray are all dead."

"But we're alive."

"If you say so." I pushed Petie away from me, getting some distance from them both.

"We don't get out of here now, and I mean *now*, they're gonna find us."

"Then burn the motherfucker," I told him.

Aldo flipped open a silver Zippo, cupping it against the rain with one hand and firing it up with the other. His face wore a grimace of pain, anger and fear.

Petie staggered over to the Cherokee, bent forward into the backseat, touching Fritz's gloved hand. "Fritzy," he said, softly at first, and then, his body bucking as he cried, he screamed it like a little kid calling for his mother. "Fritzy! Fritzy!"

I moved him away. He didn't put up a fight, he just slumped against me, crying his eyes out and muttering Dino's and Fritz's names over and over again.

Then it got quiet, and no one said anything more. Only the rain was talking. Maybe it was crying too. It had every right.

Aldo threw the lighter into the Cherokee, right on top of Fritz.

The flames kicked up almost immediately.

Still holding Petie by the arm, I led him away.

Aldo stayed where he was, stared into the mounting flames and whispered, "Love you, brother."

With our bag of money, the three of us, moving like

zombies, got into Aldo's car. We pulled out as the flames picked up and giant plumes of black smoke began billowing from the burning Cherokee.

My jaw ached, and I was sure my hands would never stop shaking, that the awful feeling of panic and terror throttling me would never go away. Even then I was replaying what had happened in my mind. Had I really shot someone? *Killed* someone? A cop? I kept seeing Dino flying backwards through the air, the horror in Fritz's beautiful eyes and the strangled cries emanating from his throat as he lay dying.

I wanted to feel more, but I was cold inside, already dead, too, in a way.

Sitting in the backseat, Petie continued muttering incoherently and sobbing at the top of his lungs. I'd never heard a grown man cry that way. Neither Aldo nor myself tried to stop him. No one spoke at all, we just drove back into the city, and when we'd hit a public playground in the South End, Aldo pulled over. I knew exactly what he was doing.

Without a word, he got out and jogged across the street to a payphone.

"Richie, what—what the fuck are we gonna do, man?"

"I don't know. Hold it together best you can."

"Dino, he's—he's fucking dead and Fritzy, he—Jesus—Jesus *Christ*!"

I wanted to tell him it was almost over and everything would be fine, but we both knew that wasn't true. Nothing would ever be the same. For any of us.

After only a few seconds on the phone, Aldo walked back across the street, his hands in his pockets and his head and body slumped into a slouch. He looked like someone had hit him in the stomach and he was trying hard as he could not to double over.

He got into the car, slammed the door closed behind him and just sat there, staring at the dash. "My uncle, he...he can't help us on this one."

I couldn't believe he'd thought anything different. "Nobody's gonna help us. Not with dead cops in the street."

Dejected and in shock, Aldo nodded. "He said we're on our own."

"What do we do then?" Petie asked.

"We got to make our own alibis, we'll…we'll work this out, we—"

"Are you out of your fuckin' mind?" I snapped.

"We got to hang on, guy."

"There's nothin' left to hang on to, *guy*."

He looked at me, eyes saddled with horror and sorrow. "We just…"

"Soon as they ID Dino they're gonna come lookin' for us and once they find out the body in that Cherokee is Fritz, there's gonna be no doubt who the rest of the crew was."

"We can work it out, we—"

"Work out *what*?"

"We can…we-we just have to…"

"It's over."

"Nothin's over. They can't prove shit! What? We were their friends? So what? Don't prove we did that job with them."

"Ally. It's over."

"*Nothin's* over!"

"This isn't some dead junkie whore the cops don't give a shit about, with your uncle's influence workin' behind the scenes. We're fucked, understand? We're fucked. Dino, Fritz and Ray are dead, and we're *fucked*."

"What are we gonna do?" Petie screeched from the backseat.

Aldo held a hand up, like he'd had a thought, but all he said was, "I…"

"Ally, we're done."

He looked like he might cry. I couldn't blame him, but I'd never seen Aldo like that before. Even when we were kids, I'd never seen him so destroyed, so vulnerable. "I didn't mean for this shit to happen, I…I loved those guys too, you know. They were my brothers too."

"I know," I told him, softening my tone. "I know."

The rain kept falling, blurring the windshield. The world outside felt like it was a million miles away.

"Ally, I want my money," I said.

"I fuckin' heard you before."

"Then don't make me take it."

"We gonna do this again?"

"I'm out, Ally, I'm runnin'. I told you I'm not gonna just wait around for them to come pick me up. Fuck that. You got to let me go."

"You askin' me or tellin' me?"

I just stared at him.

"Look," he said, "we're all we got left now, we got to—"

"We're gonna burn for this. What the fuck is it with you? We're done."

"We—"

"It's over, Ally! Jesus Christ, get that through your fuckin' head!" I pulled my cigarettes out, but my hands were shaking so bad I couldn't even get one out of the pack. "We killed cops. That means we got a bounty on our heads and every cocksucker with a badge in this city's gonna be gunnin' for us, comin' after us with everything they got. And if they don't kill us in the street—*if* they don't—they'll make damn sure we're put away for good. I ain't gonna spend the rest of my life up Concord or Walpole, getting the shit beat out of me every fuckin' day and night and tradin' those degenerate cunts smokes and cups of Ramen to keep their dicks out of my ass. Fuck that and fuck you. Gimme me my money."

In that moment, I knew I'd broken whatever was left in him. I couldn't take him physically, we both knew that, but he also knew if I felt I had to, I'd keep trying. He looked at me like I'd betrayed him, abandoned him in the hopes of saving my own ass. He'd lost everything. Even me. But I had no choice. I had to make a run for it, there was no other way. It was my only chance, and the longer it took for me to do it, the lower the odds were that I'd be able to pull it off.

"Where you gonna go?" he asked.

"I got no fuckin' idea."

He went quiet and just sat there staring at the dash again.

"Petie," he finally said, "hand me the bag."

"There's blood all over it," he sobbed.

"Just gimme the fuckin' thing."

Petie threw the bag between the bucket seats then sat back.

"I don't know how much is in there exactly," I said, "some of it fell on the floor, but should be close to two hundred thousand. Since there's only three of us now, and obviously that whole tribute to your uncle thing ain't gonna be happenin', that's around sixty-five thousand a piece. The bills are all hundreds, banded into ten-thousand-dollar stacks. Give me six of them, and we're good. I'll walk with an even sixty. You two split the rest."

"Watch the windows, Petie," Aldo ordered. "Bad neighborhood to be flashin' cash in."

"Windows are fogged over, can't nobody see nothin', Ally."

"Just do what I tell you and keep an eye out."

"Sure, okay. No problem, I'll keep an eye out for you, man."

My God, I thought, *Petie's placating Aldo.* The world had gone crazy.

Ally counted out six stacks of banded cash and handed them to me.

I tucked them into the inside pockets of my leather jacket then stuffed the rest down my pants. As I did so, he noticed the Glock in my belt.

"Told you to burn that with the Tec-9s and the shotgun."

"Yeah, well it didn't work out that way."

Aldo had lost all control of us and he knew it. Because there was no us.

Not anymore.

"Were you planning to use that on me?" he asked.

"Not you I'm worried about."

"That ain't the question, Richie."

"Well, that's the answer. Don't ask me stupid shit."

"I always had your back."

"And I always had yours, motherfucker."

"Yeah," he said softly. "You did."

"This ain't about us," I told him. "Not no more. We got to do what we got to do now, man. All of us."

"I know."

I'd heard him, but I wondered.

"You know," Aldo said a moment later, "from the first time we met when were just kids, and durin' all the shit we been through since, I always figured if we went out, it'd be together, and swingin'. Like Butch and Sundance, yeah?"

"Me too. But there's no other way now."

"I can't believe Ma's gone," Petie sobbed.

"He went out like a fuckin' badass," Aldo said, his voice cracking.

"That's how he would've wanted it," I said.

Maybe it made us feel better to say such things. Maybe we even believed them. Didn't much matter anymore. They were dead, and Ally and I were killers.

Aldo dropped the car into Drive and we headed deeper into the city.

I had him pull over about two blocks from my apartment.

We all got out and stood there looking at each other like morons. There was no one on the street, not even any cars moving. Just us and the rain.

"Maybe we should run together," Aldo said.

"If we split up we got a better chance," I told him.

"Yeah, you...you're right. Besides, I can't just leave Candy. I—Christ—I got to find a way to get her to understand..."

"Take her and go. Run, man, just run. While you still can."

"What about me?" Petie asked. It was impossible to know where his tears ended and the rain began. I don't think I'd ever seen anyone look so pathetic.

"It'll be all right," Aldo said without looking at him, holding my gaze instead.

"Richie?" he asked, looking to me for confirmation.

"Just do what Ally says, Petie, and it'll be all right. Okay?"

"Okay," he said softly. "O-Okay."

"I got to go," I said.

Aldo put his hand out. I shook it.

Then we hugged. Hard. And held it longer than we ever had before.

After a moment, Petie fell into us, hugging us both, and we all stood there in the rain with our arms around each other.

I'm sure there were things we all wanted to say, wish we could've said, maybe even needed to say, but we knew all that already. We loved each other, we had since we were kids, and we always would.

I pulled free. We all stood around awkwardly for several seconds.

"See ya," I finally said, though I knew we'd never see each other again.

Aldo somehow managed one of his shark-like grins. "I'll look for you on the other side."

"I'll be there."

I walked away, hurrying through the rain and headed for home for the last time.

Head down, I walked to the apartment, sure that at any second the whole world would end with the screeching sounds of cop cars closing in all around me.

But nothing happened, so I tried to think about what I was going to tell my mother. I planned to leave her half the money. She could stash it somewhere safe, as the cops would likely end up searching the place anyway, and that way she'd be okay until I got to wherever the hell I was going and could arrange to send for her. And if I never got there, or died trying, at least she'd have some cash to hold her for a while, maybe keep her free from parasites like Bronski and others who'd start circling her once they knew I was no longer around to protect her. I didn't want to leave her behind, but she was too sick to take with me.

There was no other way.

When I got to my block, I crossed the street and approached the building from that side so I could get a better look while still maintaining some distance. Nothing looked out of the ordinary, but I waited a couple minutes anyway, scanning the area best I could.

Satisfied, I hurried across the street, up the steps and into the building.

When I opened the door, I heard the shower running, so I rushed through the apartment to my room, grabbed a large nylon gym bag from my closet and began jamming clothes into it. After a moment of frantic packing, I stopped and looked around my room. The idea that I'd never be here again, in this cramped little room that for so many years had been my sanctuary, didn't seem real. Even with everything that had happened, the world still felt like a dream, like at any moment someone would wake me and all this would fade back into the darkness where it belonged.

A siren a few blocks over snapped me back.

I crouched before my little bookcase. My books were about all I had. I couldn't take them all, so I quickly snatched a few of my favorites from the shelves and jammed them in the bag. I rifled through my record collection, remembering how the guys and I used to switch price tags so we could get them cheaper or just shoplift them if we could get away with it, from places like Zayre and Woolworths. Deciding they were too bulky—and besides, not like I could lug a turntable with me—I grabbed a handful of cassettes and my Walkman instead and threw them in there too.

On a small mirror over my bureau, I'd taped several small

photographs along the border. An old black-and-white photo of my father standing next to my mother, one arm around her and the other holding me as a baby, drew my eyes first. I carefully peeled it free, dropped it into the bag. There was another, a faded color photo of me and the guys all huddled together, holding up beers and laughing. It had been taken at a party when we were in high school. I took that one too, and was about to leave the room when another caught my eye: a narrow strip of pictures from a photo booth at the mall. A series of black-and-white photos of Mariana and me, when we were dating in high school, it was all kissing and mugging for the camera, laughing, sticking our tongues out and crossing our eyes, being kids who thought they were in love. Maybe they were. I'd been meaning to take it down but hadn't yet.

I looked at it a moment, remembering the night we'd gone to the mall on a date and slipped into the photo booth, more as an excuse to have Mariana sit on my lap and make out with me than to take pictures. But now I was glad we'd taken them and glad I hadn't thrown them out.

Still, I left that one there. That's where it belonged. In the past.

After transferring the cash from my jacket pockets and jeans into the gym bag, I hoisted it over my shoulder, gave my room one last long look, then hurried out into the hallway and knocked lightly on the bathroom door.

When my mother didn't answer, I knocked again, harder.

Still no answer. I figured she couldn't hear me over the shower, so I tried the door. It was unlocked. I pushed it open enough to stick my head in. Greeted with a wall of steam, I couldn't see more than a foot or so into the bathroom, but was able to make out that the curtain was pulled closed.

"Mom?"

Nothing.

I called her twice more, and when I got no answer, I feared she might've fallen or passed out in the shower, so I put the bag down and cautiously approached the shower.

"Mom, you all right?" I asked, pushing on the curtain to signal her.

Christ, I thought, *not this bullshit. Not now.*

Trying to avert my eyes while still getting some sort of peripheral view, I pulled the curtain back enough to see inside.

The shower was empty.

With a sigh, I turned the water off.

"Mom?" I called. "Where are you?"

She wasn't in the kitchen or living room, so I checked her room and found her lying in bed. On her back, she had one arm across her face, shielding her eyes. The other was at her side, a used, bloody syringe and the remains of a heroin baggy on the sheets just beyond her open palm and outstretched fingers.

On her nightstand was a cheap bottle of booze still in brown paper, an empty condom wrapper next to it.

Goddamn Bronski, I thought.

I went over and sat on the edge of the bed. "Mom," I said, "you need to wake up and talk to me. I have to go. Something happened and I—I got to go."

When she didn't respond, I touched the arm lying across her face.

It was cold.

I'd never forget how cold.

I can't be saved.

And I knew. Right then, I knew.

It's true, baby. I can't be saved.

I slumped, almost collapsing forward and on top of her, but I caught myself and just sat there staring at her, afraid to touch her again, afraid to look at her.

"Mom. Jesus...Mom?"

I'm tired.

The room blurred through the tears filling my eyes.

I'm so tired, Richie.

Shaking, I took her arm and moved it from her face, placing

it gently next to her. Her eyes were open, but empty, lifeless. Her mouth was open. Bits of white spittle and traces of vomit were caked along her lips and the corners of her mouth.

I had a terrible dream, Richie.

Whatever Bronski had brought her this time had killed her. After he left she'd likely turned the shower on then shot up. Not feeling well, she must've laid down for a bit. Only this time she never woke up. This time she wasn't okay. It had finally happened. My mother had been dying for years, and now it had finally happened. The worst day of my life, the last day of hers.

I dreamed you were dying, Richie.

I placed my head on her chest, put my arms around her and cried like I hadn't cried since I was a little boy.

You were lying on a floor, on your back, in a strange place I didn't recognize. You were in so much pain, bleeding from your stomach and crying out for me.

Flashes of Fritzy writhing in the street flooded my mind.

There was so much blood, and you were lying on this horrible red carpet.

Ray, dead on that bank floor.

Dino dead in the street.

Fritz dead and burning, lost in the flames and black smoke.

Those dead cops.

Joanna Holt beaten to a bloody pulp in that horrible apartment.

It was all death and destruction.

Pain. Blood.

I don't how long I stayed in that room with my mother, longer than made sense, I guess, but when the crying stopped, so did everything else. It was all too much, so I felt nothing. No rage, no sorrow. Nothing.

I finally knew what Dino had meant that day when he'd said he felt nothing. I finally understood.

Run, Richie, run.

Kissing my mother on the forehead, I closed her eyes and

told her one last time that I loved her. Then I covered her with the bedspread and left her there.

Up on the roof, I saw him from the shadows. The rain was still coming down, but it had let up some. I don't know where he'd got it, but he'd taken a big table umbrella and leaned it on the ground in a way that he could sit in his lawn chair beneath it, shielded, mostly, from the rain.

"What it is, young lion?" Woody finally said, smiling at me with his giant white teeth through an exhale of weed smoke. "Come on now, I managed to stay alive in the jungles with Charlie behind every fuckin' leaf, think I can't pick up on somebody hidin' in the shadows ten feet away?"

I stepped out of the darkness, into the rain.

"What you doin' lurking like the VC?"

"Need to talk to you, Woody."

"You all right, man?"

"Not this time."

Woody squinted at me then motioned to an empty lawn chair next to his own. "Cop a squat, talk to me."

I stayed where I was. "I came to say goodbye and to ask for a favor."

"Whole city's popping," he said. "Been hearing nothing but sirens all morning. That got to do with you?"

"Yeah. I'm in trouble, Woody."

"How bad?"

"Bad. People died. Cops are gonna be lookin' for me soon."

He put his joint down in a plastic ashtray next to him and took up his bottle of tequila. "What can I do?"

"I got to run. No other way."

"Your mom know?"

"My mother's dead."

"Oh shit, I..." Woody took a hard pull on the bottle. "I'm so sorry, man. What happened?"

"Looks like she got some bad shit. Bronski gave it to her."

"That dirty cunt."

I moved closer, held out a stack of banded cash.

"What's this?" he asked.

"Ten thousand in cash. Take it."

"Richie, I can't take no—"

"Take it."

Slowly, he reached out and took the money.

"I need you to handle some shit for me," I told him. "I got nobody else, Woody, no family, nobody I can turn to on this, you understand? Clock's tickin', I got to go."

"Okay, man. What do you need?"

"She wanted to be buried next to my old man. He's at Sacred Heart. There's already a headstone, just needs to be engraved with her date of death. Get her a nice coffin, I don't want her in no cheap pine or nothin' like that. And make sure she's buried in a new dress, somethin' nice."

"Done."

"Whatever's left, put in your pocket."

Woody tucked the money into his shirt, then stood up and pushed the bottle of tequila into my hand. "I give you my word, Richie."

"Thanks, man. For everything."

"Gonna miss you, young lion. Sorry shit went down this way."

I took a swig of tequila, handed the bottle back. "Me too."

"I've seen the look you got in your eyes before, my man. Guys back in the jungle had it. Fuckin' void. Nobody's born with it, kind of thing happens to a man when that switch gets thrown and he doesn't care about anybody or anything no more, because it hurts too bad. *Walking Dead*, we used to call those types. Until we were that way too, then it all made sense. But looking back, I can tell you, Richie, if you don't kill it, if you don't let it die, it doesn't stay that way. You never care the way you did before, there's no going back to that, hard as you might try—and if you get the chance you will try, brother, trust me, you *will* try—but it doesn't stay the same. In time, it comes back. Not like you want it to. Shit, not even like you need it to. But enough of you comes back to get you through the goddamn night. Some days even enough to make you want to, dig? Whatever you're facing, it doesn't have to be the end. Only thing out there waitin' on you is the future. That belongs to you. Go get it. Hope you do better with it than I did. There's no do-overs, Richie, remember that."

"I got to go, Woody."

"I know you do. Stay safe, young lion."

"If I ever make it to Falesá, I'll figure out a way to let you know."

"Fuck that, send me an airline ticket."

I wanted to smile but couldn't. We hugged instead.

Then I slipped back into the shadows and out of the rain.

Bronski's apartment was on the first floor at the end of a dimly lit hallway. There were no windows here, and the lone light came from a small fixture on the wall about halfway down the hallway. There was an overhead fixture as well, but it wasn't working. Either the bulb had burned out or the light was broken, and the stupid bastard hadn't yet gotten around to fixing or replacing it.

I moved down the hallway, Woody's description of the *Walking Dead* playing in my head on an endless loop as I stopped outside his apartment. The door was battered and scarred. I knocked twice. Hard.

A moment later came the sound of locks disengaging. I could hear Bronski mumbling irritably from inside even before he'd opened the door.

It swung open to reveal Bronski in a pair of filthy work pants, tattered work boots and a lightweight tank top with numerous stains down the front of it. He was unshaven and looked like he'd been napping.

"Hey, kid," he grumbled, "what are you doin' here, huh? Whattaya want?"

"What did I tell you?" I asked.

He wiped at his nose, like it was itching him. "Huh?"

I remained perfectly still, hands at my side. "What did I tell you?"

Bronski leaned out, looked down the hallway, as if expecting to see someone else with me, then returned his bleary eyes to me. "I'm busy here, kid. Whattaya want?"

"I want you to answer my question."

He laughed, his chest rumbling. "What are you talkin' about?"

"*What* did I tell you?"

"What'd you tell me about what?"

"What did I tell you would happen if you ever went near my mother again?"

"Hey, listen up, kid—"

"I told you I'd kill you wherever I found you. Do you remember that?"

He scratched at a mustard stain on his shirt with sausage fingers. "Stop foolin' around, huh? Your mother sick or somethin'? You need me to call an amb-u-lance or what, huh?"

"My mother's dead," I told him. "And they won't get here in time for you."

As he stared at me, confused, I raised my hand.

By the time Bronski realized I was holding the Glock, it was too late.

I shot him between the eyes.

The discharge was deafening in the small hallway, and as my ears rang and my vision blurred, I saw his head snap back with incredible violence as a mist of bone, blood and brains exploded from the back of his head.

He never made a sound. He just collapsed, convulsed a few times then died at my feet in a slowly growing puddle of blood and urine.

I was at the building doors and almost to the street when the screams from his wife echoed down the hallway after me.

As I stumbled down the stairs and onto the sidewalk, I vomited onto the pavement but kept walking. I wiped my mouth, slipped the Glock into my jacket pocket and hurried across the street, up the block and around the corner.

Three blocks over, I found an unlocked pickup truck, hot-wired it and escaped the city.

It stayed dark the rest of that day. The rain eventually quit, but everything was drenched, and it looked like the sun might never come back, like it'd always be dark from then on, even in the daytime. Eventually the sun returned, of course, but the rain and shadows had finally killed the heat, and that never did come back. Not like before anyway. There were still a few weeks before fall hit, but the brutal heatwaves of that summer of '84 were over.

I didn't find out until much later, but eventually learned that Petie was arrested that same afternoon while the cops were executing a search warrant on Aldo's house. Just like I figured, once they ID'd Dino, they came looking for the rest of us. They found Petie hiding in the cellar crawlspace, where Ally had told the poor bastard to wait for him until he came back and got him. Within minutes the cops broke him, and Petie spilled, told them everything.

An APB went out for Aldo and me, and they immediately began searching the airports, train and bus stations. They picked Aldo up at Logan in Boston later that night with Candy. They were trying to board a plane to Europe. Aldo had all the cash, except for what I'd taken, duct-taped to his body beneath his clothes. Poor Candy knew nothing about what had happened. Aldo told her it was a surprise, spur-of-the-moment vacation to France, and like always, she believed him.

He was arrested and taken into custody, but not before breaking one cop's jaw and knocking another one out with a round-house kick.

Candy never spoke to him again.

She married an accountant a few years later. Had some kids and a life.

The cops knew I was the fifth guy on the job, but Aldo still wouldn't give me up, swearing I had nothing to do with it and that he had no idea where I was, only that I'd moved away days before the robbery. Cops didn't buy it, of course, and they already had Petie's statements, so the search for me continued.

Because he was only the driver and didn't kill anyone, Petie got fifteen years. They sent him up Concord. I don't know how, but he managed to do his time, and after six years, he got paroled. Like most guys, he didn't come home the same person he was when he went in. Petie couldn't make it on his own, not on the streets, and not in prison. Word was, they split him up the back on a regular basis in there, and he wound up owned by some guy who pimped him out as a whore for cigarettes and favors.

When he got home, Tammy had long-since divorced him, married another guy, divorced him, and was living with some dude in Providence. Petie hadn't seen his kid in years, since Tammy never visited him in prison, so by the time he got out, his daughter had no idea who he was. He moved back in with his grandmother and got a job busing tables at a restaurant in Fairhaven. When his grandma died, he got the apartment. Last I heard, he was working for a landscaping company in Acushnet, lived alone and had a serious drinking and prescription drug problem.

Aldo wasn't so lucky. Found guilty on armed robbery and multiple homicides, including the death of a police officer, they gave him so much fucking time he would've had to live and die two lifetimes then come back for a third and do ten more years on top of that before he'd ever get out. They sent him to the maximum-security prison in Walpole, with no possibility of parole. Supposedly at his sentencing, he refused to apologize for anything, bragged he'd have killed more cops given the chance, then told the judge to go fuck herself. They dragged him out in shackles and threw away the fucking key.

Aldo always loved the bad guys, and he stayed one until the very end.

Still, I couldn't imagine Ally locked in a cage for the rest of his life.

Sadly, I didn't have to. Couple months in, he was killed by another inmate, shanked while he was mopping a floor. Rumor was the Black Mambas were behind it, that it was payback for Ray-Ray. Nobody knew for sure, but within weeks of his death, three members of the Mambas, including both of Ray's cousins, were dead too, executed gangland-style on the streets of New Bedford.

Their murders were never solved.

In the end, despite all his schemes and plans, all his bravado and badass confidence, he wound up in the joint just like his old man, and came out the same goddamn way. Feet first.

Aldo was twenty-one years old.

Me, I made my way across the country, stealing cars and changing them up every few days, taking buses when I could, sleeping in cheap motels, paying cash and keeping my head down. I kept waiting to get caught—and almost did a couple times—but it never happened. Eventually, I got to California, then down into Mexico.

Burn it all down, Woody had told me.

Turned out, that's exactly what we did. And all for sixty thousand dollars.

The money's long gone now, of course, but all the blood and death that came with it is still with me, and always will be.

I don't know what happened to Holly, but I like to imagine she got to experience all the things she dreamed about, and then settled down with a nice guy and had the kind of life she deserved, the kind I could never give her.

I hope she thinks about me sometimes. And I hope it makes her smile.

Never did get to that Beach of Falesá, but I came close.

It's not much, but it's a life, and I found someone I care about to share it with. Maybe that's enough. It's probably more than I deserve. I'm older now, and I'd like to think wiser. I'm trying to do it right this time around. I pray a lot more than I used to, ask God for forgiveness for the things I've done. I'm not sure He can hear me, or gives a shit if He can, but what the hell have I got to lose? Either way, I'm still on the clock. Never stops ticking, not for me.

Jesus may forgive. The Law don't.

To this day, I'm still a wanted man.

The nightmares have never left me, and I don't think they ever will, though sometimes I have dreams where we don't do the job at all. I talk Ally out of it and none of this ever happens. But I always wake up in the same place, with those same devils crawling on my skin. I lie there sweating and struggling to catch my breath, torturing myself trying to imagine where we'd all be if that were true.

Ally, Dino and Fritz are alive and doing straight time. Petie's with Tammy and their kid and has a good job. Ray's clean and boxing pro. And I'm married to Holly and living in a nice house somewhere in the middle of fucking nowhere.

But I don't think about those years much anymore. Not on purpose anyway. It hurts too much, so instead, when I do, I try to remember me and the guys when we were happy, together, hanging on the wall, running wild at The Park, cruising The Avenue, chasing girls, brawling, drinking, drugging, causing trouble and having the time of our lives. We thought then we had to steal it all, to fight for it. But we were wrong. The whole world was right there at our fingertips, only we didn't know it. We were just kids, after all, why would we? I try to remember us that way, as a bunch of young guys, crazy and alive in ways none of us ever would or could be again.

Dangerous Boys all.

* * *

That day I left New Bedford for the last time, when the moon rose in the night sky, I found myself hours from home, parked on the side of a lonely highway somewhere in Pennsylvania. I kept thinking about the dream I'd had and the things my mother had said in it.

Did you see how beautiful the moon was?

I looked out through the windshield at the moon hanging full and so menacingly beautiful in the darkness before me.

Run, Richie. Run.

But it wasn't the same moon.

Don't stop until you see that moon again, Richie.

I closed my eyes and tried to picture my mother's face, happy and alive.

Don't stop until you can reach up and pluck it right out of the sky.

When my eyes opened again, I was alone and the moon was gone, lost behind a bank of black clouds.

With the Glock on the seat next to me, I dropped the window and lit a cigarette. I was tired and afraid, but none of that mattered now. As the smoke twisted and circled me like barbed wire, I pulled back out onto the highway and raced into the night.

I had a moon to catch.

Author's Note

As many from the area will realize, I have taken numerous liberties with the city of New Bedford and many of the locales, institutions, hangouts and people described in this novel. Like anywhere, New Bedford is a city of both good and bad. Most of the residents there are hardworking, good people, and the city itself has some wonderful sections and lovely areas and attractions. However, this novel isn't about those aspects of what is otherwise a great and hugely historical city. Set in 1984, many readers today may find some of the dialogue and situations in this novel offensive or off-putting (and they are), but as with any novel, it really came down to a series of choices. In *Dangerous Boys*, the most significant choice facing me was how to accurately and truthfully present and develop these characters, and to what extent I'd be willing to go to effectively do so. I decided it had to be all-in because it seemed to me, that to sanitize the way these young guys talk and behave, would've been a huge disservice to both the novel and the characters. If nothing else, it is true to both, and that is exactly what I intended. The challenge with this kind of novel is to present characters that are not wholly likeable or sympathetic—these guys are criminals after all—but to still find a way to make them interesting, so the reader will want to follow them on their journey. Hopefully I have accomplished this, particularly with the lead character of Richie. My goal was to present all of these characters—these *people*—exactly as they were, with all their flaws and scars and limitations. But also with their wonder, their love, loyalty, passion and dreams of not only a better life, but better selves. All of the main characters are based on compilations of real people I knew and ran with back in the day. While I could play a bit with settings and even peripherals, in terms of the main characters, truth was essential. Offensive as much of it is, without it, the novel would've lost its grit and realism, and all its power along with it. Though many of the characters are not exactly the type of people you'd want in your home (or in many cases, anywhere around you), ultimately, *Dangerous Boys* is a coming-of-age piece about young men who have already faced extreme adversity and hardship in their short lives, and who are more lost than truly bad. If you're inclined to believe such things, in the end, they all pay dearly for their sins anyway. I spent a year of my life with these characters, and I will miss them, as I miss many of the actual people some of them are based on. Like all of us, they're far from perfect, but they are, as the saying goes, what they are. This is their story.

—Greg F. Gifune
12/27/2016
New England. Night.

ACKNOWLEDGMENTS

Thanks to my family and friends, and all of my fans and readers all over the world. Your continued support means a great deal to me, and I am deeply appreciative.

Greg F. Gifune is a bestselling, internationally-published author of several acclaimed novels, novellas and two short story collections. Working predominantly in the crime and horror genres, Greg has been called "The best writer of horror and thrillers at work today" by *New York Times* bestselling author Christopher Rice, "One of the best writers of his generation" by both *The Roswell Literary Review* and horror grandmaster Brian Keene, and "Among the finest dark suspense writers of our time" by legendary bestselling author Ed Gorman. Greg's work has been translated into several languages, received starred reviews from *Publishers Weekly, Library Journal, Kirkus* and others, is consistently praised by readers and critics alike, and has garnered attention from Hollywood. Greg resides in Massachusetts with his wife Carol, a few cats and two dogs, Dozer and Bella.

BOOKS

On the following pages are a few
more great titles from the
Down & Out Books publishing family.

For a complete list of books and to
sign up for our newsletter,
go to DownAndOutBooks.com.

The Devil at Your Door
A Lars and Shaine Crime Novel
Eric Beetner

Down & Out Books
February 2018
978-1-946502-43-8

Lars and Shaine have returned to a quiet life on the islands, but for Lars there is unfinished business. When he gets information that will lead him to exact revenge on behalf of his young protégé, the young woman he's grown to think of as a daughter, he decides to take action in secret.

When he lands in a hospital Shaine is called in from a thousand miles away and she must take the lead in the last job of Lars' storied career of death for hire.

Down on the Street
Alec Cizak

ABC Group Documentation,
an imprint of Down & Out Books
June 2017
978-1-943402-88-5

What price can you put on a human life?

Times are tough. Cabbie Lester Banks can't pay his bills. His gorgeous young neighbor, Chelsea, is also one step from the streets. Lester makes a sordid business deal with her. Things turn out worse than he could ever have imagined.

Cleaning Up Finn
Sarah M. Chen

All Due Respect, an imprint of
Down & Out Books
September 2017
978-1-946502-49-0

Life is a constant party for restaurant manager, Finn Roose. When he seduces an underage woman on one of his booze cruises and loses her—literally, it sets off a massive search involving the police, her parents, and a private investigator. Finn is an expert manipulator but his endless lies only tighten the screws on himself and his unsuspecting best friend. Finn scrambles to make things right which may be too much to ask from a guy who can't resist a hot babe and a stiff drink.

Dead Clown Blues
A Carnegie Fitch Mystery Fiasco
R. Daniel Lester

Shotgun Honey, an imprint of
Down & Out Books
September 2017
978-1-946502-02-5

Carnegie Fitch, once-upon-a-time drifter and now half-assed private eye, has a sharp tongue, a cheap suit and dog-bite marks on his fedora. Yes, that's just how he rolls through the downtown streets of Vancouver, BC, aka Terminal City, circa 1957, a land of neon signs, 24-hour diners and slumming socialites. And on the case of a lifetime, a case of the dead clown blues.

CPSIA information can be obtained
at www.ICGtesting.com
Printed in the USA
LVOW12s1733290318
571634LV00003B/819/P